Finding Peace

A Tale of Resilience

ADELYN ZARA

For 'Aunt' Betty. "Where is your book?" she demanded at my mother's funeral. And then I took off! Thank you for your enthusiasm and encouragement.

Author's Note

Thank you for reading **Finding Peace**, the premier book of Resilience Tales.

Donovan Rue is finally finishing his walk to Lynn Cerami, finding peace for himself and for her. It's been a journey of love.

Since I've been told that I'm resilient, and in writing Finding Peace about a woman who is also resilient, I decided to do a Resilience series featuring some of the characters who are in this book. In **Making Magic** you will read about Dara who is battling the demons of bipolar disorder while her hero Connor fights intensity. **Overcoming Obstacles** will feature Alek Grambler, Lynn's CPO, who has faced an abusive father, the loss of the job he dreamed of since childhood, the loss of a son, and enduring a military career. He meets his true love Heather who also has a hovering parent. They must overcome many obstacles to get their happily ever after (but they do – I promise). In **Caring for You**, we meet Bea, Lynn's best friend who cares *too* much and forgets to focus on herself. Asia Barber – matriarch of all things Resilient – will have her strength tested repeatedly in **Fine, Just Fine.** There are at least two more resilient characters yet to come, one of them Rafa from **Caring for You.**

I promise that they will all have Happily Ever Afters even if they must endure struggles to get there. And throughout these books, Lynn and Donovan will pop up to aid the main characters, continuing to show resiliency.

One cannot be resilient without the support of others. I am

blessed with three extraordinary children (and one amazing daughter-in-law), many good friends who've encouraged me to keep going, and absolutely, hands down, the best husband who was my biggest cheerleader and is a true optimist. He won't let me sink when I am down which only encourages me to keep going On Word & Upward!

Best,

ADELYN

Trigger Warning

This story deals with breast cancer issues and mental illness.

Chapter 1

*N*othing ever changes. I work, I sleep. I go to functions. I deal with artists, more and more of them becoming nasty as soon as they become successful.

Surveying the huge ballroom, looking for a clearer walkway, Donovan Rue strolled toward the beautifully appointed central table, its sparkling silver vases overflowing with light blue and white flowers.

"Hey, Donovan." Larry Knightly from Knight's Music Emporium came toward him.

I didn't even see him. Don't want to see anyone.

"Hey, Larry. You guys did well tonight."

Donovan's own company had done much better at the earlier awards ceremony. Larry tried to whisper his news, which wasn't easy with the clinking of dinnerware, the clashing of china, and the light background music.

"You've heard?" There was a cautionary tone in Larry's greeting.

"Heard? Heard what?"

What the hell should I know now? Isn't this a party? Aren't we supposed to be having fun? Celebrating?

But he kept his smile plastered to his face, bending down so that the shorter man, his breath smelling of gin and tonic, could speak into his ear.

"They're charging Peter Freiler with sexual harassment tomorrow morning."

Donovan's face hardened. Although not a friend of Peter

Freiler, Donovan knew Peter gave opportunities to many artists that other firms – such as Knightly's and Donovan's – would not.

He reared back to look at Knightly. All areas of the entertainment industry had been hit by allocations of sexual harassment; it was not a surprise to hear the charge.

But Peter? I would never have thought ...

"Yeah," Larry said. "Who's next? Seems like everyone is getting accused of doing something."

"If the guy did what he was accused of, then he should go. It's a new era. We don't need casting couches, or starlets marrying directors – or whatever – just to get ahead in the industry." *But Peter ... he had a family, he seemed like a decent guy ...*

"All I'm saying is watch your back, Rue," Larry slapped a hand on Donovan's shoulder. "Could be one of us next. I'm thinking some of these charges are just to get attention. Know what I mean?"

As Donovan was shaking his head, Larry walked away.

Donovan glanced over all the usual Music Extravaganza participants, stopping for a bit longer when he spotted Asia Barber.

Now there's someone who knows what it means to be a celebrity.

Donovan admired the older woman, thinking that although age might have slowed Asia, it did not take away from her decorum and beauty as she sashayed toward her table. He knew what was happening as she stopped at each table. Head held high, white rose clipped behind her ear, Asia would murmur hello to everyone she passed by, her voice always gentle, her cadence as slow and sultry as the music she used to sing. Some held out their hands for her to clasp; others touched her arm softly. Donovan knew that she would be aiding some, praising others, and commiserating with a few. Long past being a shiny new star in the music industry, Asia maintained the respect of everyone in the room.

His father, Paul Rue, had found Asia when he was talent-scouting in the South. Just beginning a business, Paul Rue was looking for talent and he struck gold when he introduced Asia Barber to the world.

Dad sure didn't need a casting couch. I bet he never even thought about it.

Yet even seeing Asia, one of his favorite people, did not elevate his mood. Donovan was out of sorts. His day had started out bad and went to worse. And it wasn't over yet.

Early in the day – before the sun even rose – his accountant had called. Once again, his daughter Dara had used his credit card to purchase three thousand dollars' worth of shoes.

Bipolar or not – this is inexcusable. Champagne taste and beer money, that's what she has. Where do I draw the line? How can I make her see that a person starting out doesn't just buy whatever the hell she wants? And that she should not be using my credit cards if she's as grown up as she claims to be?

At a more reasonable morning hour, he confronted Dara about her spending and before he finished speaking, she was screaming at him, "Dad, Dad, *Dad*! I need these shoes. I need professional clothing. I can't go to meet clients looking like a college student."

Following his call with her, he'd met with his lawyers about a lawsuit over someone who claimed that Rue LA LA had stolen her music. It was going to court, but the lawyers were working on finding someone to analyze each note of the music to find differences.

Then there'd been the human resources meeting, where they were having difficulty finding a new health care program that would benefit all personnel. Donovan was called on to make the final choice.

Nothing good will come out of that. Some people will hate the change; others will benefit.

Following that, meetings with Creative who had new talent that they wanted Donovan's opinion on.

I can only listen to so much ... I can't make an instantaneous choice on talent.

He'd spent a rough day in meetings with lawyers, human resources, new prospects, more lawyers, aggravated stars, managers. He never seemed to get a break from it, bringing work home or going to events like this evening, an extension of his job. The job he once loved was starting to burn him out. When Beatrice Owens requested that he say hello to her friend, he had agreed but only as a favor to Bea.

Go glad-hand someone, make nice, leave.

It wasn't just an easy walk to that center table. Along the way, he was stopped by other employees and people in the industry. Sometimes it was just a handshake; sometimes it was a request for a client; often it was for a photo. And then there were the surprises like being told that a fellow executive was in trouble.

I wish I could come once to this event – one time – and not have people stand in my path just so they can get my time.

"Donovan!" Sara Reilly called out from the table next to his target. "I just need you to meet my sister."

Always polite, Donovan stopped long enough to meet the visiting sibling, and get his picture taken with her. He turned toward the table Bea had indicated. The woman was sitting by herself, her face turned toward the live band, a glass of water by her right. Something told him that he should be careful in his approach so as not to upset her.

I'll just meet this woman, say hello, and head out of here. Go home.

Quietly, stepping as if he barely let his feet touch the carpet, Donovan reached the table.

"Lynn?"

Big blue eyes turned up toward him revealing so much. In their depths, Donovan saw kindness, intelligence, extreme sorrow, exhaustion.

How can someone show all these things at once?

Sleepy blue eyes looked questioningly at him, the last expression seeming to state *"What could you possibly want with me? I'm nobody."*

7

To Donovan, this woman was beautiful, a shocking surprise after his long day. Her pretty, blue gown with its modest neckline and full, full skirt was dazzling. Her short, blond hair was shiny and a bit spiky. Delicate earrings poked out but did not make the dress at all gaudy. Amid a sea of strapless-gowned women, this woman was notable.

"Yes?"

"I'm Donovan Rue."

Lynn nodded politely.

"I'm a friend of Beatrice Owens," he continued, puzzled that she seemed unimpressed.

Lynn did not seem surprised that he knew Bea, but then Donovan realized that most people would know of Beatrice Owens, one of the top Los Angeles fashion designers. He wondered if Lynn would be angry that her friend has set this up but then decided to let curiosity take him where it might. Just as he was trying to find more words, Lynn politely turned in her chair to better greet him.

"I'm sorry. Bea didn't say she was sending anyone over to say hello."

Better and better. This is refreshing! She truly has no idea who I am
...

"May I sit down?"

With a gracious arm movement, Lynn indicated a vacant chair, oblivious to the dress's sparkle. Beatrice Owens' haute couture gowns were sought after by celebrities worldwide, often showcasing or defining a celebrity's style. But this woman was not showy or deliberate in her movements.

"Quite a gathering," Lynn said. "I don't go to things like this. Ever."

"But you know Bea?"

"Yes. She's a long-time friend. And she wanted someone to model this gown. *Needed* someone is what she told me." Lynn chuckled. "Why she didn't get a model, someone who knows how to show off this gorgeous dress, someone sexy, I don't know."

"I think you look lovely," Donovan remarked. And continuing his openness, "Refreshing after all the bared shoulders and big side slits."

"Thank you," Lynn extended her arm toward the ballroom, the fabric again glittering in the room's soft light. "Do you work with some of these people?"

"Yeah ... a few."

Donovan glanced around the ballroom.

More than a few. Like practically everyone in this room.

He rubbed his achy, tired eyes.

"Rough day?" Lynn asked, her voice soft, caring. She reached a hand toward his arm but stopped just short of touching him. "Maybe this party is a way to get your mind off all of it?"

Donovan looked at the soft face, feeling a calmness settle over him. His body relaxed as he realized that in her innocence, she was right; he needed to leave work behind.

Donovan again glanced around the huge ballroom trying to see beyond the glamour and glitz. His eyes closed in on Asia Barber who had stopped to talk with two younger women who were, no doubt, trying to glean wisdom from her. At the same moment, Asia turned to Donovan and nodded, as if encouraging him to have some fun.

I need to focus on something other than work.

He looked again at the woman seated next to him, her foot tapping to the rhythm of the live band's sound. A moment passed before Donovan found his nerve to ask, "Do you dance?"

Surprise flitted across her lovely face, those big blue eyes so easily read.

"Yes, I do. But not to this modern stuff." Another soft smile. "And it's been a long time."

As if cued, the music changed. *Crystal Blue Persuasion.* Perfect for the woman in a glittery blue masterpiece of a gown.

Donovan extended his hand and Lynn took it. Her face registered surprise at the same time Donovan felt the thrill of touching her.

What is this? I've danced with many women. Why this feeling? Why now?

As they stepped onto the dance floor, Donovan felt a carefree mood take over. The day's angst left as he extended his arm, as if the negative feels traveled out of his body, leaving his fingertips. The happiness of his movement encouraged Lynn to enjoy herself as she extended her own arm to its full length. Then Donovan pulled her closer, spun her in a big circle, showing off his partner. Slightly giggly, Lynn obliged, doing a perfect twirl, then exaggerated her own arm's extension when the twirl ended, her bell-like sleeve creating a lovely arch of glitter.

For Donovan, the room brightened with Lynn it – the glamour of the dress, her obvious skill in dancing, her ease of movement, and the look of bliss in her eyes. He pulled her into him, softly, respectfully, afraid that he might be too personal with someone he did not know.

"I haven't danced in a long time," she admitted with a soft, almost nervous chuckle.

"I'm happy to lead you," he replied, offering a kind smile, his first of the evening.

After a slight nod from Lynn, Donovan took them again around the dance floor. His confident movements helped her find the way. She kept the sweeping movements up, adding some graceful leg moves and twirls when he indicated.

They did not notice the appreciative glances of their fellow dancers or the cameras directed their way. They did not hear others' laughter, the tinkle of silverware, the swish of dresses in movement. Although they heard the music to which they danced, they did not really notice the band. They did not notice anyone or anything aside from one another.

As the song ended, they stepped apart and politely clapped.

Donovan retrieved Lynn's hand when she dropped it to her side. Once again, her face was expressive.

Shock? Surprise?

"One more?" Donovan asked, reaching for her other hand, praying it would not be a fast song. Lynn opened her mouth to speak but was interrupted by a man more casually dressed than anyone there.

"Hey. Donovan! We need to talk."

He did not wear jeans, but the low-slung black pants, untucked shirt, and casual stance told everyone that he thought himself a star who followed no fashion rules. He sauntered up to Donovan and Lynn, elbowing himself between the couple.

"We gotta talk, man."

Continuing to hold Lynn's hand, Donovan repositioned himself to make Lynn comfortable before looking at the scruffy, younger man.

"It's a party, Roy. Let's take a break."

"Look, you own the company, so you gotta do something!"

As he spoke, Roy became agitated, getting louder, shifting his feet. Donovan remained calm and quiet.

"Tomorrow," he said again.

The beginning of slower dance music interrupted the diatribe. This time Donovan had Lynn twirl away from the angry man, a wide enough step to get them into the center of the dance floor. Then he pulled Lynn close as if protecting her, or maybe himself. She placed her hand gently on his back, making soft, calming circles. Donovan found himself relaxing yet again.

She's very soothing.

"Sorry." Donovan gave Lynn a soft grin while slightly shaking his head. He looked into clearer eyes. "Artists!"

"Who is he? Seems like he's very upset."

Donovan sighed. "He's a rapper. They all get that way when they aren't doing well."

Now Lynn's eyes got bigger. Donovan could almost see the "ah-ha" moment as she figured out who he was. Her dance steps fumbled.

"You're Donovan Rue." It came out as a breathless whisper. When he didn't answer, she continued. "*The* Donovan Rue of Rue LA LA. The Donovan Rue who owns a huge music company. The Donovan Rue who is always featured in social media, on TV, at award shows … like this one … oh my God."

Lynn stopped her monologue, her eyes now betraying something akin to horror. Donovan tried to strengthen his hold around her slim body, then said, "Yeah, that's me. No big deal."

Lynn's reaction – her stiffening body, slight stumbling of steps, eyes growing impossibly larger – told Donovan that for her, it was a big deal.

As the song ended, Donovan placed a hand on her lower back, steering Lynn away from the dance floor. Like a cat waiting to pounce, Roy jumped into their path, this time demanding Donovan's attention.

"Look! I want to talk now! It's bullshit to make me wait. We're here. Now."

"You are out of line!"

Pushed beyond his limits of patience, Donovan straightened up, his demeanor becoming commanding.

"Excuse me," Lynn said and headed toward the restroom sign. Donovan tracked her bright blue dress as she wandered out the door, hearing only a fraction of Roy Alloy's complaints.

After he finally placated Roy Alloy by agreeing to a meeting the following Monday, Donovan walked around the ballroom once again, looking for the beautiful woman. Although there were lots of women in blinged-out dresses, none were his Lynn.

My Lynn?

While looking, he was stopped frequently again: beautiful women who flirted; others who wanted career help, more picture taking. Some stopped him for advice. Managers also wanted him to meet someone. Legitimate stars stopped him to thank him, other artists angry that things weren't going as well as they had hoped and wanted him to know about it. No one respected his time. He did a lot of networking at a soiree like Music Extravaganza and usually stopped to accommodate all those who wanted him or wanted a photo opp. Tonight, however, he had met someone he felt peace around. He wanted that tranquility back. The tranquil angel had flown away when she'd realized his identity and heard the harshness of Roy's demands. Peace was elusive this evening as he completed a circuit around the room.

Desperate, he saw Bea Owens standing off to the side, a tall, gorgeous woman in her own right, observing the world before her.

She'll be checking every gown here, comparing it to whatever she designed for tonight, including that gown Lynn wore.

Bea dressed simply in a long, black, column dress, deliberately not taking away the glamour of any of the people in the room. Her gaze was aloof, cold, daring people to approach her. Donovan had no such qualms. She turned her deep brown eyes to his as he neared.

"Donovan Rue, how can I help?" Her tone was businesslike; he'd purchased many of her gowns for his clients and knew her well from all these events.

"Hello again, Bea," he said and then gently kissed her cheek. "I just met Lynn."

A big smile lit up Bea's face. "Isn't she great?"

Donovan nodded.

"Yes, I'm very intrigued by her. Much lovelier than you described. And it wasn't just because of your beautiful creation," he said.

When Bea raised both her eyebrows at his comment, he smiled again.

Yeah, yeah, yeah ... I can be manipulative if need be.

"But I can't seem to find her right now," he continued. "Do you know where she is?"

A smirk came to Bea's face. Donovan misread it.

"Powder room?" he asked hopefully.

"No." Bea's answer was terse. Then she added, "She went home. Probably couldn't stand the vultures and sharks."

Donovan felt his hopes drain with her announcement. Bea pounced on his upset look.

"Too busy to miss her for sixty minutes?"

I could squirm now, but I'll be damned before I let this woman think that I'm a stalker.

"No, you are not at all like the players I know," she was saying, and Donovan knew that she was referring to her former playboy husband.

Beatrice was on a roll. Her look was very proprietary as she adjusted her height to its full six feet and stared at probably the most influential businessman in the room.

"Can't handle the fact that she didn't stand by and wait for you while you did business?"

"It wasn't like that," Donovan replied. "Actually, I've been trying to find her for the last sixty minutes or so. We got waylaid by one angry Roy Alloy."

"Oh, God." Bea rolled her eyes.

"Yeah. She left for the restroom, I thought," Donovan continued, "but she didn't come back."

"Come on, Bea! Give me a break!" he begged.

"What do you want to know?" Bea's voice was haughty, teasing him. "She left. Evening over, for her anyway." Crossing her arms, Bea looked back at the room.

Donovan shifted nervously. Only a self-confident woman like Bea – who held answers to his questions and knew she did – could rattle him. *What do I do now?*

"Look," Bea took a deep breath. "Maybe I should take pity on you. I'm just very protective of Lynn."

Even more intriguing.

"Why?"

Bea took another deep breath. "Okay. I probably shouldn't tell you this, but Lynn is my best friend. She's always been there for me – since college. She is my relief from my crazy world."

"Yeah. She's pleasant, soothing. I understand why you feel that way," Donovan said.

Hell, Bea's days are probably as hard as mine.

Bea started again. "She's been through hell these past few years. Three years ago, Lynn was diagnosed with aggressive breast cancer. She underwent horrendous chemo, radiation, and two surgeries. She still isn't fully recovered, so I imagine she went home to bed."

Now Donovan understood the exhaustion he saw in those pretty blue eyes. Although their dancing had an energy to it, he had sensed that Lynn could not have endured anything livelier.

"Husband?" he asked. "Where was he tonight?"

"Dead."

Bea's answer was short, as clipped as Donovan's question had been. Then she lost patience.

"Look, Donovan, I sent you over to her table because I know you are kind, and easy on the eyes. But Lynn is fragile right now, and although I dragged her here to get her mind off her troubles, I don't think I should give you any more information. It's Lynn's business."

A considerate friend.

Donovan frowned, slammed his hands into pants pockets.

This is not going the way I want.

Then Bea relented a little.

"You big shots can trace anybody, right? Find out anything you want? Right?"

Donovan did not want to pursue this woman that way.

"Bea," he resorted to begging. "Give me something to work with here."

Chapter 2

*L*ynn punched the snooze button on her bedside clock.

Ten more minutes. Please, only ten more. Maybe I'll feel rested for once.

She drew the third blanket up over her shoulders to fight the constant cold that made her shiver. Sleep eluded her as she thought over the previous evening.

It had been fun to dance again. Fun to be with the most handsome man in the room. Fun to wear that beautiful gown that caught the light so well. Fun to have outrageously expensive jewels and shoes picked out for her as if she were a princess. Okay, maybe not a princess, since at fifty she was more the age of a queen.

Flinging back her covers, Lynn found the scarce energy needed to get out of her king-sized bed.

Gotta put the jewels in a safe spot and hang up that beautiful dress. No maids for this royal.

She needed to wash off her makeup, a task that she'd purposely ignored last night.

She passed by a picture of Michael on her way to the master bathroom. In it, he wore her favorite of his shirts, a Christmas red with a blue jacket over it. His hands were at his thin hips. The Pacific Ocean waves crashed on the shoreline that was well beneath the mountain ledge Michael stood on.

Lynn ran a soft finger over his framed face. As frequently happened, she remembered the knock at the front door, the two cops who came to give her the worst news imaginable. A cancer diagnosis was rough, but it was nothing like hearing her husband had been killed in a terrible car accident.

"I'm sorry to tell you, ma'am, but Michael Cerami was involved in a fatal vehicular accident today."

She and Michael had been so hopeful then. Her cancer treatments were over, and she was working to get energy back just as her hair was beginning to grow in. He understood her exhaustion, her timidity in showing off her now deformed body, and her low energy. But it all ended when a drunk idiot ran a red light and t-boned his car. The only thing she could find good in the entire situation was that his death had been instantaneous. Michael had not suffered.

She sighed and made her way to the big heap of blue fabric, the prettiest cloth she'd ever seen. Memories of dancing in a glittery whirl momentarily warmed her. Dark, gentle eyes smiling encouragement. A tall, lean yet muscled man taking her around the dance floor with ease. So graceful. Moving perfectly with him despite being so fatigued that she should have dropped the floor from the exertion.

Sadness, guilt took over the previous evening's memories.

It's too soon ... it's not right! No! I shouldn't feel this way so soon. I had a great marriage. And I love Michael still. How could I betray him with this Donovan? And I'm not even part of that world.

But as she hung up the lovely blue garment, all Lynn could think about were crystals of blue and the persuasion of Donovan Rue as he danced with her.

Donovan wasn't surprised when the phone rang the day after Extraordinaire.

"Donovan," the sultry voice purred. "That young woman you were talking to last night was beautiful."

Trained to be polite to his elders, Donovan did not roll his eyes at his Other Mother's comment which he knew was mild interference in his love life. Asia Barber had been part of his family for as long as he could remember. She was his mother's best friend, often helping Phyllis figure out how to handle his volatile father and chastising her when Phyllis was too lenient.

Donovan leaned back in his home office desk chair, looked out at the ocean.

"Hello, Miss Asia. I didn't get a chance to visit with you last night."

"No, you did not." It was said without judgment, but Donovan still felt guilty.

It always took a minute to acclimate to the slow, slightly Southern drawl of Asia Barber's speech. He'd grown up hearing her – laughing with his mother, arguing with his father, and then listening to her instructions concerning raising Dara and running Rue LA LA after his father's death – but he had not spoken to her in months.

Way too long. I should have called sooner.

"And how are you, Miss Asia?"

A huge sigh came over the phone before Asia answered, "Fine, just fine. Tired today since last night's doings lasted so long. But I've got nothing to do today except visit with folks like you."

"You're good to go to those events," Donovan told her.

Celebrities half her age would not attend unless they were being honored or getting their own award. But Asia Barber almost always attended and so far, the press and social media continued to revere her for beauty, her voice, her authoritative mentoring of those younger than her.

"Somebody's got to show these youngsters how to behave."

"You've read my mind."

"Is it bad, son?"

Donovan raked a hand through his hair. "It's just getting harder and harder to deal with some," he admitted. "Maybe I need a vacation. Or a break."

"I saw you with Roy Emerson."

It took Donovan a moment to remember Roy Alloy's real name.

"You saw that, huh?"

"I saw him come up to you twice last night," she said with a hard edge to her tone. "Why can't he leave you alone? Especially at a party! Especially when you're wooing such a nice young woman."

Okay, I better get this over with.

"How do you know she's nice?"

Asia laughed. "Well, Bea Owens told me that her former college roommate was coming. Now I didn't know what she'd look like, although Bea did say she was white, but I figured she'd send you over to meet her. She wanted this woman to have a good time, 'meet someone nice looking'. Am I right? Was she Bea's roommate? Is she nice?"

"Yes, you are right," Donovan said. "But how are you feeling, Miss Asia? And isn't it great that Exeter got recognized? You know that guy could go –"

"Quit trying to change the subject, Donovan Rue," Asia interrupted, steel still in her tone. "Your mother would want me to watch out for you. I am doing that. That woman seems like she might be just what you need."

"And what is it I need?

"Exactly what you said before," Asia answered slowly. "Either a vacation or a break. Or maybe someone to take your mind off Rue LA LA!"

Donovan shook his head, smiled, glad that Asia couldn't see him.

"You really are reading my mind," he admitted, then added, "She was pretty special, I admit."

"So, go get her, son. What are you waiting for?" Asia paused for just a minute. "Or do you already have something lined up for today?"

"Goodness! Give a guy a minute, please."

"Life is too quick, Donovan. Over in a second. And you've been alone a long time," Asia paused as if she needed to take a breath. "Now. When will you see her again?"

Donovan allowed himself to laugh out loud. "You really never give up, do you? Okay, I'm going to try and catch her at a coffee shop that Bea says she goes to all the time."

"Good! Go for it!"

"Could I take it slowly? I mean, she seems great, but I barely spoke to her last night."

But as he said that Donovan remembered a glittery dress, expressive eyes that lit up as they danced, and consoling words from someone who radiated kindness. Digging into his ability to read people well, Donovan thought that maybe Lynn Cerami could be someone special.

Asia continued, "Can't hurt to see her again. So, you're sure she'll be there? At this coffee shop?"

"Well," Donovan ran a hand through his curly hair, "Bea told me that Lynn's a creature of habit. She likes to go hang out at this one shop. So, I'll try there."

"Hmmm. If she's not there, get Bea to give you a phone number."

"Yes, ma'am," Donovan agreed, then re-asked, "So, Exeter's winning was good, right?"

"It was excellent," Asia's declaration came out in extended syllables, like she was enjoying saying the words. "He deserves to win. He works hard."

"That he does."

"Nothing like Roy Emerson. And that Dymettra!" Asia made a few sounds that Donovan knew to be negative tones. "That woman just doesn't know how to be gracious."

Not going there. Start talking about one artist, I'll talk about more, and we'll be here all day long.

"Miss Asia? How about we meet for lunch soon?"

"Musso's?" she asked. "I've wanted to go there for a while; it's like a craving."

"Alrighty then," Donovan said and then glanced at the clock in his office. "I'll look at my calendar at work, call you. But now I have to go courting."

Asia whooped with laughter.

"Courting? Boy, how old are you? Who courts anyone anymore?"

Donovan stretched then found determination.

"I do. See you soon, Miss Asia."

DONOVAN MADE HIS WAY TO THE GRIND. THE COFFEE SHOP WAS almost empty when he entered. Today he wore dark jeans, a forest green Henley, boat shoes without socks, and sunglasses to try to avoid being noticed. Sometimes it worked. The shop was in a remote Los Angeles suburb, so he had hopes of not being recognized.

Glancing around the small shop, Donovan found Lynn. She, too, was dressed casually in navy leggings and a denim shirt over a bright blue tank. Her head was bent over an e-reader, a large coffee nearby. Seeing her do something as simple as reading created feelings in Donovan that he thought no longer possible.

Peace. That's it! I feel peace where I see her.

"Hello," he said quietly. Lynn gave him a startled though tired look.

"Hello back to you," she said with a slowly growing smile. "Let me guess. Bea told you that I come here."

He placed his hands on the back of the chair across from her and chuckled.

"It was tough negotiating to get this information," he said. "I almost had to promise to buy the entire Bea Owens spring line!"

This time they both laughed.

"Well, in that case, I'd better allow you at least some coffee and conversation," Lynn said and indicated that he should sit down. A young man came to get Donovan's order, then darted away.

"You like tea," Lynn stated.

"More than coffee. You?"

"Coffee. Too much coffee! Especially with anything chocolate."

A few quiet moments passed as Donovan searched for words. After the drink arrived, Donovan placed the tea bag in his cup, dunking it around, looking for the right thing to say. He took a breath.

"Why did you leave so early?"

Lynn smiled again, toyed with her coffee spoon.

"Are we playing Twenty Questions?" she asked.

He glanced up, then down, a little embarrassed.

Not used to dating games, he thought, but answered, "Okay. Let's play that game a bit. Do you come here every Sunday?"

"Just about," Lynn answered looking around the tiny shop with its worn tables and chairs, newspapers tossed around, bookshelves holding dogeared best-sellers from years ago.

"Your turn," Donovan said when she failed to ask him anything.

"Oh!" Lynn sipped her drink. "Do you live near here?"

"No. I live in Malibu." Without waiting he asked, "Do you have a family?"

A dark shadow crossed Lynn's face before a deep inhalation.

"I have two sons. One is beginning a career as a professional photographer; the other works in computers."

"They live here? In California?" Donovan went to get his teacup, stopped, and said, "Oops! I should've said 'follow up question.'"

"No worries," Lynn's kind eyes held a twinkle when she answered, "Connor lives here. Owen lives with his new wife in Colorado."

She paused, toying with a dangling earring, her eyes casting downward as the smile left her face.

"My husband died a few months ago."

"I'm sorry," Donovan murmured.

Lynn took a deep breath and then exhaled sharply as if pushing the tragic memory away. "And you? Married?"

"Divorced. Years ago. And I have a twenty-four-year-old daughter."

"Oh! Same age as Connor, my oldest."

Nodding, Donovan hoped his face remained passive.

Please don't ask me about Dara ... yet.

Instead, Lynn said, "I've lost track, but I believe it's your turn."

Thank you.

"Work?" he asked.

"I work for Brandstone University with international students." She smiled again, then said, "I guess I already know what you do!"

Another chuckle between them and then Donovan asked, "And you don't like that?"

Lynn worried her other earring now.

"I don't know your world at all, Donovan, so I'm not sure what to think. I don't fit in, that much I know for sure."

Now Donovan scoffed. "How could you not fit in? You were – are – so beautiful, pleasant ..."

"And *not* in the music industry." Lynn sounded determined. "And more than twenty years older than almost anyone in that room. Plus, look at me!" She motioned to her body, pointing a finger up and down. Donovan had not stopped looking at her, but he inclined his head a bit to indicate that he was paying attention.

Lynn continued, "If I could wear leggings or jeans and a t-shirt every day, I'd be happy. Not obscenely rich gowns."

"You *were* gorgeous in that gown, *are* pretty in everyday wear; I imagine you'd look beautiful in burlap."

When Lynn started shaking her head in disagreement, Donovan changed course.

"But you enjoyed wearing that dress? That jewelry? You enjoyed the music? The dancing?" he asked and then more quietly, "The company?"

"Yes," came an answer after a slight pause. "The dancing was fun. I enjoyed it! I haven't danced in years."

Donovan settled differently in his chair and finished his tea.

"Is it me then?"

"You?" Lynn acted surprised. "Not at all! I just don't know you all that well, and the evening was a bit overwhelming, and Bea had expectations for that dress, and ..."

Donovan took over, clasping the hand on the table across from him.

"Then get to know me," he said. "I really want to know you."

SEVERAL HOURS LATER, BEA WAS WAITING FOR LYNN TO COME TO her townhouse to return the dress and accessories. As she sat there, she reread the report again. Bea felt triumphant. Thirty-five orders for the Lynn Dress – so dubbed by the media – in one day.

I knew it. Knew if I could get one person in a gown that wasn't bare shoulders and long slits, I'd score.

Strapless gowns had been popular for years, but not all women could wear them. She had asked Lynn to the event because she wanted her friend to have fun. Then it dawned on her that Lynn could wear the crystal blue dress that Bea had drawn a few weeks before. She had kept the drawing in a special place in her home so that no one on her staff would have access to it.

Never know about spies who could leak it to the world.

Not that sleeves were a brand-new idea. Nor was an overlay. The trick was to make a full dress look slimming. And to have the under-dress that could be sold separately or used as a second dress later that evening.

Finding the blue glittery fabric had taken time, too, but once purchased Bea also put that into hiding. When stars began ordering for Music Extravaganza, and Lynn agreed to go as a model, Bea went to work. She engaged a freelance seamstress whom she used for special gowns, someone she knew would not leak any information about the dress. Once it was almost completed, she allowed her staff in on the secret. They became engaged when they met Lynn.

Who wouldn't want to help Lynn? Kindest woman on the planet, with the worst luck.

The staff appreciated the effort it took Lynn to come to fittings and worked hard at making the cancer survivor shine like the gem Beatrice knew and loved. And it worked. The orders Beatrice Owens LLC received in less than twenty-four hours proved that her idea had merit.

Just as Bea finished reading the latest report, the doorbell rang.

"Lynn!"

Bea gave the other woman a strong hug, then pulled her into the sleekly appointed townhouse. Lynn handed her a garment bag and a small bag that held the shoes and jewelry.

"Figured you'd come here today. Do you like him?"

"Was the whole plan for me to meet Donovan Rue?"

Lynn acted perturbed, but Bea could tell that she was happy for his overtures.

"Not at all!" Bea scoffed at Lynn's suggestion, hung the bags in her hallway closet, then stretched the truth. "But when he asked me if I knew the beautiful woman wearing my new design, I told him who you were."

Now Lynn scoffed. "Liar! How can he tell a Beatrice Owens creation? Most men don't know anything about fashion ... well, straight men anyway."

Bea smiled kindly. "I've known Donovan Rue for years," she said. "He was the first big professional to ask me to clothe one of his stars. And he keeps coming back to me with other Hungries."

When Lynn look at her questioningly, Bea explained, "That's what I call the newbies at events like last night: Hungries."

Bea led the way into her very modern kitchen. She poured herself juice and waved the carton at Lynn with a questioning look. Lynn shook her head and sat on a silver stool near the kitchen island while Bea leaned against the counter.

Bea continued. "He is straight. Probably one of the nicest executives in the biz. So, I gave him your name and asked him to walk over to you, say hello." She eyed Lynn carefully. "Do you like him?"

Lynn smiled, then responded. "He's nice ... so gorgeous. And I haven't danced in a long, long time. That was fun, I guess ..."

"But?"

Lynn shrugged, a sad movement. Then she tipped her head down to her chest.

"Michael?" Bea guessed. "Or cancer?"

"Both," Lynn whispered.

"The docs have said that cancer treatment is over. And Michael would not want you to be in perpetual mourning, Lynn," Bea said sharply.

"I feel guilty none the less," Lynn admitted. Shifting in her chair, Lynn changed the topic. "I just saw him at The Grind. You set that up too, didn't you?"

Bea smiled again. "I don't see how one dance or having a cup of coffee with someone should make you feel guilty. Take it easy. Have some fun!"

Chapter 3

Their first official date was at the beach. A slightly cool day, the waves lapped up to the shore in a consistent rhythm that lured Donovan and Lynn to relax as they sprawled on the green and white striped blanket. Their discussion led to the Twenty Questions game they both enjoyed.

"Where were you born?"

"Los Angeles." Donovan smiled and lean back, balancing on canted arms. "Been here my entire life. You?"

"I was born in Chicago, but I've lived a lot of places." Lynn's tone told him that she was lost in memories. Then it was her turn to ask, "Define 'entire life'?"

"Can't just ask 'how old are you?' Huh?" Donovan teased.

"Nope," Lynn answered. "So?"

"I'm fifty," he answered. "And you?"

"Forty-nine." When he started to laugh, she continued. "Really. I'll be fifty in a few months." Lynn shifted on the blanket, then asked, "Did you start your company?"

Before he answered, Donovan recalled his father screaming at him about becoming responsible, learning enough to take over the company.

"It's time for you to come work at Rue. You need to learn the ropes ... I started this company thinking that I'd turn it over to a child someday."

"Not my choice."

Paul's hand slapped Donovan's face before he saw it coming.

"You will come to Rue. Learn the business. You can't work at some men's clothing store in a mall forever!"

"No," he answered. "My dad started Rue; I took it over when he died. I didn't know what I wanted to do when I was young. I kinda fooled around after I finished college. Then I got a little wiser, started listening to him, learning a bit. He dropped dead of a heart attack before I learned enough."

He drew a line in the sand next to the blanket.

"Fortunately, I had Len who worked for Dad. Len has always been there for me. He's my right-hand man. I could not run Rue LA LA without him."

"The name changed?"

"Only to keep up with the times and inject some life into it," Donovan said. "Plus, I added music genres like hip hop that my father never would have. It was a kind of 'do this or die' moment and I stepped up." He smiled, then changed the subject. "My turn."

For an hour they quizzed one another about music interests and found out that neither one liked country music. They went on to discuss sports, education, and their hobbies, which included hiking and swimming for Donovan.

"Your favorite color?"

"Favorite color! Really?" Lynn teased, then answered, "Blue."

Even the goofy questions stirred something long dead in Donovan.

When was the last I talked about ordinary things with a woman? Pets, minor politics, books, movies, and yeah, even colors.

She liked to read – anything. Hated violent movies, didn't pay much attention to local politics, did not want any more pets, and yes, she liked blue. She could discuss modern and ancient literature and reviewed movies like an expert. Enthralled with her, Donovan listened to softly told, confident answers.

She knows who she is.

In turn, he told her about the dog he'd had for years who'd just died, how he had to keep up with politics for his business. They skirted around the topic of his business, coming close when discussing the latest couple in trouble with drug charges.

"Do you deal with that kind of situation often?" Lynn asked.

Donovan was drawing in the sand. He paused, looked at her, and smirked.

"Bad behavior comes with the territory, I'm afraid." Standing up, he dusted off the sand from his clothing. "But I usually don't deal with those things. I pay people to handle artists. And they used to have their own handlers. That night when Roy approached us used to be a rarity." He sighed, wiping at unseen sand on his pants. "But it's becoming more commonplace. Young artists have no respect."

"Is your day full of stress?" Lynn asked.

"Yes, it is."

Donovan nodded and then looked down at the woman sprawled on the blanket. "But I think I've found something peaceful."

Chapter 4

*H*is peace was short-lived. The following morning, Donovan walked into his downtown office where fires were erupting everywhere.

Roy Alloy was in Donovan's office, pacing back and forth across the room, highly visible through the large glass windows that made up the hallway wall. Despite the closed door, everyone could hear Roy talking angrily to his manager who sat there, waiting for Donovan to come in.

Without even a greeting, Donovan's second-in-charge, Len Matthews, grabbed his arm and steered him toward another office.

"Roy Alloy is here. Maybe you should wait here until he calms down."

Donovan sighed. "He was all over me at Extravaganza. Would not leave me alone."

Len smiled at Donovan's news. "I heard that you were pre-occupied with a stunning blond!"

"Pre-occupied?" Donovan grinned, too. "More like captivated, I'd say."

" 'Bout time, man," Len cried out. "Glad to hear that something – or someone – is taking you away from the business once in a while."

Not surprised that Len knew so much without even asking, Donovan nodded, remembering the blue eyes that held so many emotions. As he sat down on a sofa, he thought about mocha coffees and beach strolls.

What is happening to me?

Then he shook his head as if to stop the constant distraction of thoughts of Lynn Cerami.

"Back to Roy," he stated, becoming the boss. "Is this about his latest flop?"

Len nodded. "That and he feels Rue LA LA isn't paying him enough attention. He's claiming we're not fulfilling our side of the contract."

When Donovan shook his head again, Len let out a long sigh. "That ain't the only person who's here to see you and is angry as hell."

Donovan knew he was not going to like this at all. He also knew who it probably was.

"Dymettra, right?"

Suddenly, Len's door flew open and a tall, leggy woman with a long wavy weave of hair stormed in. Her trendy clothes were tight on her curvy body, screaming for attention, warning any voyeurs to watch out.

"Donovan Rue! You will listen to me!" she said loudly while tossing her purse and light coat on the sofa nearest him.

Ever respectful, Donovan stood with easy grace. Dymettra did not give him time to open his mouth in greeting.

"They didn't give me my orange juice. No fresh strawberries! No bright-colored napkins like I usually get!" She sunk into a chair nearby, then added, "They can't treat me like this, Donovan. I got riders in my contract that tells them what to put in my dressing room and I didn't get it."

Donovan eyed the beautiful young woman and remembered a girl who was giddy with excitement when she'd first come to Rue LA LA. She was beyond talented, with a singing voice that could make you cry or laugh as you listened to it sweetly soar with happiness or plumb tearful depths of emotion. She showed all the promise to be successful. Within two years she was winning numerous awards, appearing on celebrity shows, and was all over social media. But now, five years after her success, Dymettra was

31

demanding and snotty, like a sullen teenager whose parents never said no.

"Why didn't you tell your manager about this?" Donovan asked.

"Al?" Dymettra shrieked his name. "He doesn't care at all. He never comes to shows anymore, and he barely talks to me on the phone." She re-crossed her legs and sniffed. "You'd think he was mad at me or something."

You think?

Suddenly Dymettra spoke more softly.

"Donovan – honey – what can you do for me?"

This again.

One evening early in her career, Donovan gave in to the infatuation with Dymettra. Since that time, he had sworn to never get involved with anyone from his company, star, co-worker, or staff.

And now there's Lynn ...

"First," he said as he eyed Dymettra, "I am not your honey. I never will be your honey."

Seeing a little fear in Dymettra's eyes, Donovan continued, "Second, I am not the person who handles these complaints. I don't create riders or contracts with facilities. You either talk with Al about it or find another manager."

As she looked down at the floor, Donovan moved to leave. Doorknob in hand, he nodded at Len who shrugged his shoulders back in exasperation. Donovan walked toward his office, taking in a deep breath, his mind still on that beautiful California beach.

Wonder how Lynn's doing?

Drawing closer to his office, he almost collided with Roy Alloy who was leaving it along with his manager Pete.

"There you are! You aren't too busy for me today are you?"

Roy glanced at the reception area. "What? No brown-haired piece to dance with?"

"Roy! Damn!" Pete was turning red.

Donovan felt his usual calm temperament vanish. It was a struggle not to scream at the young man.

"She's blond," he stated. "But, of course, you are too wrapped up in yourself to take the time to notice. You also were determined to ruin my evening."

"It was my night, too!" Roy's eyes bulged with anger, looking as if he would erupt. "Where's your support for a bro who needs it right now?"

Donovan turned to his administrative assistant Ana who was trying to keep busy, pretending not to hear every word.

"Ana," he called. When she looked up, red-faced with embarrassment, Donovan said, "Please schedule an appointment with Roy, his manager, and the PR department."

Then he looked at Roy and said, "There. I've made you an appointment. You can make your demands and concerns known at that time. You cannot just come in here and vent. Now go calm down."

Roy was not done. Although much shorter than Donovan, Roy stepped inside Donovan's personal space and stretched up as far as he could go, not quite reaching Donovan's nose.

"I made you a lot of money! Aren't you afraid you could lose me?"

"You haven't made me enough money to make me want to kiss your ass," Donovan said as he skirted around Roy and entered his office.

Chapter 5

orth of Los Angeles, Lynn's day was irritating, too. She was working on getting things together for commencement, soliciting students to carry in their countries' flags at the start of the ceremony. The hard part was convincing students of the honor it was to do this.

Finally, weeks after working on it, Lynn thought that she had a complete list. At least for five minutes.

As she set the list off to the side, a student entered her office. Lynn looked up to see one of her favorite students, Jesper, from Sweden.

"Can I meet with you about an internship?"

"You need to make an appointment with Dr. Manders," Lynn told the tall blond student.

"But I want to meet with you!" he said. "I don't like her. She's not as nice to students as you are."

Lynn sighed, having heard that sentiment all too many times.

"Sorry, dude, I can't help you. Cassie handles this; I don't."

Jesper muttered something in Swedish and walked to the office next to Lynn's. The walls were so thin that Lynn heard Jesper ask for an appointment, heard Cassie respond that he needed to make an appointment through Sally, the administrative assistant.

"What's his name? Eric?" Cassie called out after he left. She never remembered any of the students' names; Lynn excelled at that.

"Jesper," she called back, then settled into formatting the flag list for the printer. She kept placing the wrong name beside the wrong flag.

Why did I put Kaia Ahmanson with the Chinese flag? She's Danish! And look! I've got Zhao Wei carrying Taiwan's flag and he's Chinese. Must be my computer; the spacing isn't working again.

Something was going on; Lynn couldn't figure it out and kept redoing it until she finally brought it into Cassie.

"Lyyynnnnnn?"

Four times she went into Cassie's office with a list and four times she went back to her desk to try to re-do the damn thing.

And she was exhausted. Now that all the breast cancer treatment was done, she was supposed to be gaining energy. This was what all the medical people told her. Instead, Lynn felt her energy draining away.

After Cassie called her in to re-do the list yet again, Lynn put it aside and decided to do her expense report. When the numbers started spinning in her head, she put that down, too, and walked into the reception area of the office. Two low club chairs were available for students waiting to speak to a counselor, or to just sit and fill out paperwork. Currently, they were empty. Lynn needed to sit. She leaned back in her chair and stretched her legs out in front of her.

"Lyyynnnnnn?"

CASSIE WAS, AS ALWAYS, LOUD. HER HUSBAND'S REFUSAL TO WEAR hearing aids at home meant Cassie's amplification carried over to the office.

As Lynn straightened up, Cassie wandered into the reception area, eyeing Lynn with anger. She was a large woman of medium height with long, curly hair that she barely combed, and clothing that reminded Lynn of hippies. But she was an expert in immigration laws and policies. People from other institutions called to ask her advice on their tough student questions. Brandstone administration knew this and ignored the callous attitude, the sloppy outfits, and the loud voice.

As she stood over Lynn, Cassie shook a finger in anger.

"You can't slouch like that! What if a student comes in? It's unprofessional looking! What's wrong with you?" she screamed.

Lynn sat up but didn't move from the chair.

"The Cergan hall event is all set to go," she said, hoping it would redirect Cassie's mind.

Cassie's eyes narrowed as she grunted. "Have a tech there; you know that room's sound is seriously damaged." Then she flicked a hand in the air. "You know I'll be there; I always am."

When? She never goes to evening events she can avoid.

"You must get over this," Cassie continued, changing the subject. "Your treatments are over, right?" When Lynn nodded, she continued, "You know, professional athletes push themselves to get back in shape. They get hurt, and they want to get back into the game right away, so they work out harder."

Right. Like I could ever, ever, ever be a professional athlete.

Lynn almost laughed out loud at the idea of pushing herself when she felt so bad. When she didn't respond to Cassie, the director took a new stance.

"Don't you like your job?"

"Of course, I do!" Lynn said, straightening up in her chair. "I love my job!"

"Well, you sure can't tell it today!"

Unbelievably, Cassie was getting louder. "You're always exhausted. Don't you sleep at night? You can't make a simple list, something a fifth-grader could do. And now you're lounging around during the workday!"

Lynn did not know how to respond, so she said nothing. Embarrassed that Cassie was once again harassing her in front of Tom, and Sally who was smiling smugly, Lynn struggled to stand from the plush chair. If they noticed her having difficulty, no one offered to help. If anything, they looked embarrassed at her distress.

"You better get your act together, Lynn," Cassie said and flounced into her office.

Chapter 6

*A*t the end of the difficult week, Donovan and Lynn walked along the Ventura Promenade. Lynn wore a brightly colored sundress with a white shrug and big black sunglasses. Simple, strappy sandals allowed the ocean sand to slide easily against her feet. Donovan wore his large sunglasses again, making Lynn wonder who recognized him despite his wish to be left alone.

"Do you come here a lot?" Donovan asked while reaching for her hand. A thrill shot up Lynn's arm.

Stop it! You're too old for this.

Finding her voice, she said, "I used to come here all the time."

"What happened? Bad weather kept you away?" he teased.

Lynn did not laugh.

"Cancer happened, Donovan." His look was encouraging, his hand felt supportive. She glanced at him, asking, "Are you sure you want to hear this story?"

His nod gave her courage.

"It was supposed to be my routine, yearly mammogram," Lynn began. "I'd been called back before when mammograms were suspicious, but this time when the nurse called to say that something was off, and they also wanted to do an ultrasound, I knew it was anything but routine."

The ultrasound technician pushed and prodded and said, "So far, I don't see anything but healthy tissue." Then the woman got quiet while she pushed around her wand. Finally, she said, "Excuse me a minute."

"I laid there debating about bargaining with God..."

"You've done that before?" Donovan asked, his look one of concern.

"Oh, yeah," Lynn said. "Anyway, she came back, resumed her pushing, but this time she concentrated on one area. And she was pushing so hard. After she was done, and I'd redressed, she took me back to the radiologist on call. He was standing in front of two big monitors. One had a simple color image – my mammogram from the previous year – and the other had what looked like fireworks all over it – the recent image." Lynn focused on the ocean as she told more.

"So, from there I was sent to a breast surgeon. The following week I had a lumpectomy," Lynn bit down on her lower lip as she recalled that time. "I wasn't supposed to feel any pain – at least that was what I was told." She shrugged. "Not true. It was very painful, and I like to think that I have a high pain tolerance level. But you know what? That pain was nothing compared to the phone call I got the following Monday saying that the surgeon wanted to see me. Right then. As soon as I could get there."

Lynn's words had speeded up with her story. "I called my husband at work and told him, 'I have breast cancer. I know it.' He argued with me; said I hadn't yet heard a doctor say those words. But I just knew."

Lynn pulled the brim down on her hat. Although her eyes were trained on the brilliant blue of the ocean waves as they crashed along the shoreline, she was not seeing them; they were filling with tears at the memory. Taking a deep breath, she launched back into the story.

"So! The surgeon gave me a list of oncologists' names, two of them circled. One doc was in a medical complex right next door to our neighborhood, so I picked that name. I didn't know who to ask … didn't know anyone personally in California who'd had cancer."

She glanced again at Donovan who still looked engaged and concerned.

"I was lucky. Dr. Meyer is compassionate, firm, and funny! At our first meeting she said that she hoped to have me feeling better in one year. She told me my cancer was 'ugly' and that her treatment would be aggressive. I told her, 'I'll do whatever you tell me to do. I want to get well!' First thing she had me do was get a damn port."

"A what?"

Lynn motioned to the area above her left breast. "Port. It's a thing they put in to give you chemo right into a vein, and to take blood out for testing."

"So, more surgery?

"Yeah," Lynn scrunched up her face. "More twilight sleep. And this time the doc putting in the port and the other people in the room were making jokes, laughing, and so, so loud."

When Lynn shook head after telling him that, Donovan said, "I guess the surgical team didn't think about the impact that might have on a patient."

"No, they didn't. Probably because they thought I was 'out' enough that I wouldn't hear them." Lynn moved her body slightly as if to find a new focal point.

"Anyway, the following week I began six months of chemo-therapy."

"Six months ..." Donovan's voice trailed off. "I'm sorry, but I don't know if that's a lot or normal, or maybe just a little?"

"It's a lot." Lynn paused for a second, then said, "It was aggressive. I'd sit in a chair for three and a half hours while I got anti-nausea meds, then steroids, then two different drips of chemo-therapy meds, and then another final drip of anti-nausea medication. Dr. Meyer would come into the chemo room not just to go over your meds with you, but to see how we all were. She'd ask about our families, our jobs, and even the books we were reading!"

"I'm glad you had a compassionate doctor."

"Yes. She's the best." Lynn grabbed her purse straps as she continued. "They told me my hair would fall out by the second week, but I had hair until week five. At week three I began to think

I might be one of the lucky ones who wouldn't go bald, but it was just a tease. It fell out at a staff meeting as I ran my hand through it."

Donovan watched as Lynn raised her hands to her head, running her fingers through her short locks. She turned her head toward him and said, "It's really hard to lose your hair, you know."

He nodded, thinking how courageous it was to tell someone about any of this experience, including losing hair. Aloud he said, "I don't know what that's like, but I do know men who've gone bald – not by choice. And they're not happy."

Lynn placed a hand in Donovan's curly full hair.

"No, I bet you don't know," she said as she massaged his curly hair. "Trust me; baldness is not feminine."

As she pulled her hand away, Donovan caught it and then asked, "So, six months of the same drugs?"

"No," Lynn said, "I got stronger drugs in the second course, or round, about four months into it. One drug is nicknamed 'the Red Beast.' It went in red and came out red."

"Red?"

"*Bright* red. One of the nurses said some women can never wear that color afterwards, but I just visualized things like 'seeing red' or being angry or fighting. I didn't mind the color."

"You made it work for you," Donovan said.

"Yeah," Lynn said. "I did. But I still threw up on the second day after every treatment. Even though they increased the anti-nausea medications."

Donovan ran his fingers gently down her arm.

"With all the medical breakthroughs in the world, you'd think research could find an easier way to treat cancer," he said.

Lynn nodded, then glanced at yet another spot in the ocean, seemingly fascinated by another roiling wave of white foam.

"Finally, chemo ended. Then I had another larger lumpectomy where they pulled out lymph nodes."

"Twilight sleep again?"

Lynn shook her head. "No, that time they did knock me out. Afterwards the surgeon declared me cancer-free. But the oncologist said, "Maybe she sees it that way …" and sent me off for thirty-seven radiation treatments."

"My God, Lynn! You've been through hell."

Lynn's nose scrunched up and she tilted her head to the side.

"Radiation was okay, not as hard as chemo," Lynn said. "They warned me that my skin might burn because I'm so fair, but it didn't. I did get more exhausted, though."

Lynn sighed, then watched as a noisy wave crashed nearby.

"So now I keep telling them that I'm not getting any energy back. And they keep saying that it takes time, usually a year. And I want the damn port out, but Dr. Meyer wants it to stay in even though it doesn't really work. She calls it a talisman."

"Why does she want to keep it in?"

"She thinks it wards off any chance of the cancer returning … and there is always a chance. You never really are completely free of it." Lynn turned her attention to Donovan's face, her first complete look in thirty minutes of storytelling.

"So, the reason I haven't come here is because as treatments went on, I lost so much energy that it was hard to do anything extra. But my treatments are all over – almost a year now – and they say I should start feeling better." Again, her hand went to the short blond, curly locks that snuck out past her sun hat. "And my hair is growing back which makes me feel a little better." As her hand went down again, she sighed, "But I'm still exhausted."

Donovan's look did not change. He was listening intently, absolute concern and attention in the deep brown eyes. He grabbed her hand and they began walking again, quietly, Lynn thinking of all she'd just shared. Donovan, she knew, taking it all in.

"Were people there for you?" he asked as they stopped at one point, so Lynn could take a breather.

"Sure," she said. She broke eye contact, staring back out at the Pacific. "Bea. She came with me to chemo sometimes. When I complained about surgeries – like the laughing surgical staff – she wanted to call the doctors! When the damn port didn't work, she wanted to call the manufacturer!"

They both laughed about Bea Owens' quirkiness and absolute friendship.

"My work colleagues were understanding during treatment," she acknowledged, "but my boss wants me to 'get over it' and be normal." Lynn shrugged again. "Her words. Not mine," she added softly. "And my sons were supportive. One cooked for us throughout this thing. Still does occasionally."

Donovan was serious now.

"And your husband?"

Lynn took a sudden deep breath, took her hand out of Donovan's, wrapping her arms around herself. Donovan felt the instant break.

"He was wonderful …" her voice began to quiver. "Kind … very supportive …"

And then she lost it. Facing the ocean, huge gulps of sobs came as she tightened her hold on her body. Not saying a word, Donovan went slowly behind her, wrapping his arms around this tired, tortured woman, her back to his front.

"Take me home, please," Lynn whispered.

Wordless, Donovan drove her home. Soothing music played in the background as they drove toward her Thousand Oaks home.

"No need to get out," she whispered as the car came to a halt. "I can get inside." Then, after she opened her car door, Lynn looked at him, sheepishly. "Sorry I lost it."

"Don't be!" Donovan's voice was clear, commanding. He softened to say, "I'm glad you shared it with me."

She opened the door further as he reached out to grab her left hand.

"Later. Okay?"

Driving back to his Malibu home, Donovan kept the music off. His mind ran through the story his gorgeous Peace had told him. It explained her exhaustion and sadness. It also spoke of modern-day torture. *I don't know anything about breast cancer.* He had never heard a first-person account like Lynn's. He didn't personally know anyone who had suffered from the disease.

Lynn's words played over and over and over in his head. His heart ached for her. This afternoon it was all he could do to turn off Lynn's story. He wandered aimlessly through his house. Normally he found relief – escape – in the big mansion which had six wings spreading out like a huge spider on the mountainside. Donovan's favorite room – his master bedroom suite – also had floor to ceiling windows that faced the ocean. Decorated in muted grays, Donovan found himself wondering what it might look like in blues.

Yep, blue the color of Lynn's eyes. He ran a hand over his own eyes. *What the hell is happening to me?*

Donovan Rue was not a man who avoided women. Sometimes his companionship lasted for a good length of time, sometimes for one night. But this woman was different. And it was not just the sad story he heard this morning that made him yearn for her presence. It was her confidence in herself. Her soft presence and sweet smile which calmed him down. He had not planned on anything other than saying a quick hello when he strode over during Extravaganza. But the moment he saw Lynn, he was overtaken. Now he was caught up in a spell that he did not want to break.

What do I do now?

He had the rest of the day ahead of him, but no plans. He had sensed that Lynn needed to rest, all he could do was drop her off at her home. He had said that he would see her later, but now wished that he had not left her alone.

Should I call? No.

She was resting, hopefully. Donovan knew that he did not want to do any work. His decisions concerning new artists or the deals requiring his approval were tumultuous, needed his complete attention.

It's a Sunday, not a day of work. I'm going for a swim.

LYNN WOKE FROM A NAP, NOT SURPRISED TO FIND HERSELF STILL tired.

Nothing new. I guess this is what my life will be like now: constant fatigue.

Stretching, she found herself thinking of Donovan again. For several weeks they'd seen each other at beaches, or promenades, or coffee shops. It was hard to find places that granted him anonymity, he'd told her during Twenty Questions. Lots of talking and laughter consumed their time together. She was grateful for this and glad that he had recognized that she was physically and emotionally overwrought after sharing her cancer story.

Now what do I do?

She went out into her hallway that overlooked the cathedral-ceilinged living room. Her home was not big, but she loved it for its open floor plan and hominess. It was comfortable, and hers. Michael had seen to that.

Michael.

As she went out into the backyard, Lynn acknowledged that she had not thought much about him for the last few weeks. The more time she spent with Donovan, the less time she thought about Michael. It scared her. She didn't want to lose any of her memories of Michael. But Donovan was here and now, and he made her happy. She almost couldn't believe that she had told him about her cancer. He had listened so intently, encouraging her to tell everything. And she had loved those muscular arms cocooning her.

No passionate moments, yet. Donovan was very respectful of Lynn's unspoken need to take things slowly. They'd held hands, and he'd pecked her on the cheek coming and going from her. Lynn wasn't sure if she wanted any more than that yet.

But she wondered.

Shaking her head, she glanced at her dead flower garden. Neglected for the last two years, it was a pitiful sight.

That's what I'll do! I'll get some flowers; do some gardening.

Her favorite store was in a suburb closer to Los Angeles. She looked at her watch and knew she had to hurry.

Chapter 7

$\mathcal{L}$ ambert's was a one-stop-shop to buy planting flowers, seeds, the ticky-tacky stuff sold with flowers, and even cut flowers to put in vases or to give as bouquets. Situated on the second floor of a two-story outdoor mall, the store's entrance faced inward toward a courtyard. Numerous social activities were scheduled on the weekends to draw people to the area. This Sunday was no exception. A team of men dressed in black was erecting a dance floor. Large speakers were already set up, waiting for action.

Donovan entered the store, looking for something to give Peace. Instead, he found her. He stood admiring Lynn's quiet, purposeful nature as she turned flowers around, changing out colors.

"Peace."

She heard Donovan's voice, which was as quiet as the word.

"Searching for some?" she teased while trying to gracefully stand. Donovan reached down, took her elbow and helped her upright.

"Or did Bea send you here, too?"

"I've found her," Donovan said, "And, no, Bea has no knowledge of where I buy flowers ... I hope!"

"Don't be too sure," Lynn warned. She put her plants into a cart and started toward the cashier.

She grinned knowingly at Donovan, hoping he saw that she was glad he was there.

"How about some dinner?" Donovan asked.

"That would be nice! Let me just pay for these."

Lynn paid for her things, then asked a few questions about re-working soil. Turning to find Donovan, she rammed into his chest, nearly crushing the bouquet he held out to her.

"For me? Thank you!" She inhaled the bouquet's sweet scents, then said, "I love flowers."

They stepped out of the shop, hearing bright, lively music. Finding an empty spot for two by the railing, they placed Lynn's purchases at their feet. Because they were on the second floor, Donovan and Lynn had the best view of an event that was meant to promote an adult dance school. Looking down, they saw young people swing dancing. Dressed in vintage clothes, each of the five couples took turns going onto the main floor. Most were very good dancers, twirling around each other. Giggles, war whoops, and infectious smiles lit up the scene which made Donovan, Lynn, and the other observers grin and bop along with them. One song blended into another. This time all the couples were on the floor, some exchanging partners. The music ended to great applause.

"I love that!" Lynn exclaimed. "I can't imagine that many people dance to swing music anymore."

"Do you?"

"I did when I was young. Tons of dance lessons."

"Swing?" Donovan didn't seem surprised, just excited. When Lynn nodded, he took her arm and headed toward the exit.

"C'mon. I know a place to dance."

They entered Rue LA LA's main lobby half an hour later. It was sleek and modern with exposed pipes and concrete floors in the lobby. Donovan opened a hallway door, leading her further and further into the office.

"We have a dance studio," he said as he led Lynn down a winding hallway. "Sometimes we use it for practice before filming videos."

They entered a quieter room. No exposed beams here, just a long bar that took up the entire length of the wall in front of a ceiling to floor mirror. The big room could accommodate many dancers. Donovan opened the door to a tall cabinet that housed soundboards and other electronic music equipment. As he punched in commands, Donovan's cell phone beeped. Glancing briefly at it, grimacing at whatever it told him, turned it off.

"Do you dance?"

"It's been a long time." Lynn echoed the words from the first time that they'd danced, anticipating the fun of being in Donovan's arms, under his control.

Seconds later they were swing dancing to *Little Brown Jug*, laughing as they both made mistakes from years of inactivity and lack of practice. Having programmed the impressive machinery to play slower music for two more dances before morphing back to swing, Donovan led her from swing to two-step, back to swing. Lynn was laughing as the last dance ended.

"Where did you learn to dance like this?" she asked as she sought to get back her breath.

Donovan, not at all winded, grinned.

"I've always been interested in anything to do with dance," he admitted almost shyly. "When Michael Jackson songs came out, I was imitating him. When I went to family gatherings where there was dancing, I was dragging my mom onto the dance floor." He shook his head again, the memory making his eyes shine. "I even took lessons for a few years."

When Justin Timberlake's *Can't Stop The Feeling* began, Lynn glanced at Donovan, her huge eyes betraying nerves.

"I don't know if I can dance to this type of music."

"Sure, you can!" Donovan grasped her hand while Lynn placed her left hand on his shoulder. "I have a theory that you can do any dance move to some songs. Like this one. Let's test the theory."

Effortlessly, he started to move her around the studio. Waltzing. Swing Dancing. Jitterbugging. Other moves that she would never have associated with this song. Sometimes it worked; other times it was a definite flop. Lynn played along, crying out, "Let's twist!" and then laughing with Donovan when that dance most definitely did not work. As the song ended, both Lynn and Donovan were half bent over from laughter.

The music that started after that was quiet, and not swing.

"We should quit," Lynn said, as Donovan pulled her into his arms, placing her hand against his chest. Lynn curled her other arm around his neck.

"One more," he urged, beginning to move his body, feeling hers following. Lynn felt his supportive hold and pressed into him as a beautiful rendition of *Lean On Me* began. Lynn turned her face up to see a wonderful man smiling softly down at her. And then his soft, reverent lips met hers. A sweeping feeling, intense, needy, even lustful, passed through Lynn's body, things she had not felt in a long, long time.

"I'll help you carry on, 'Peace,'" Donovan whispered as he stopped dancing once the music ended. He did not break his hold of her, continuing the kisses.

His stomach rumbled after a few more minutes. He grinned while Lynn took that moment to gain control.

"Guess we need to eat?" she asked, allowing a nervous giggle to escape after the noise repeated.

Donovan nodded. "I hope this isn't too forward, but would you mind going to my house to eat? It's nearby, and I have to be there to accept a client's package."

After figuring out how to get her car back home and locking up the music room, Donovan led her down the hallway toward his car. But not without one final dance twirl.

Chapter 8

*D*onovan had people who took care of everything – his houses, his cars, his yard, his clothing, even a body-guard. It wasn't time to explain to her that being a celebrity meant acquiring fancy things and required people like bodyguards. It also didn't seem to be the time to let the staff – or world – know that he was interested in Lynn.

When he drove, he used a car that he felt was more mainstream. But even the Lexus he drove tonight was top of the line. Lynn remarked on all the bells and whistles. His other cars were far more luxurious, including the limousine that he frequently used for events like Music Extravaganza.

What is she going to think of my house?

As they drove up the Pacific Highway side of the mountain that secured his privacy and then down the Pacific Ocean side toward the mansion, Lynn exclaimed, "Look at all the azaleas lining this driveway! Are they bright colors? It's hard to tell by car light."

She would notice the flowers first, Donovan thought as he eyed his bouquet Lynn held in her lap.

Aloud, he said, "They're pinks, and a few whites." He reached for her hand. "I haven't thought about the color of those flowers in years."

Lynn's sudden gasp told him that she spotted the enormous, private house as he turned toward it. Donovan felt his heart racing as he drove the car around the circular driveway, nervous about her reaction to his wealth.

"Wow!" she said with a slight shriek. "A hidden home! And look at the flowers right by your front door!"

While Lynn continued to be distracted by his home's gardens, Donovan got out of the car and opened her door.

"Chivalry is not dead," Lynn announced as she took his hand and swung her legs out of the car. Donovan noted that it took Lynn great effort to stand, that she grimaced with pain as she held his hand tightly for balance.

Opening the double doors into the home brought another shriek.

"You can see the ocean from your house!"

Donovan watched a delighted Lynn float over to the full-length great room windows.

"Yeah, and I can even swim in it once in a while," he added. "When there's time."

As Lynn wandered around the room, checking everything over, Donovan began to relax. Lynn remarked about everything – the view of the Pacific Ocean, the window height, the mixture of gray and white colors, the furniture – while Donovan found a small package on the coffee table.

"Oh. It must've come earlier."

Lynn raised an eyebrow in question.

"The demo CD. Must've come and Mariel, my housekeeper, took it in. She's here sometimes on the weekends. Look around!" Donovan called as he wandered into the kitchen. "I have to poke around in the refrigerator and see what there is to eat. Sometimes Mariel leaves me something. I'm not home much for food."

Glancing into his huge refrigerator, Donovan made a frustrated noise. Lynn ignored it, wandering over to an entertainment unit that held family pictures.

"This must be your daughter," she called as she set the silver frame back into place and then picked up another one of an older couple.

Donovan walked back into the room.

"Yes, that's Dara, taken a few years ago. And those are my parents," he added as he motioned to the frame Lynn was holding.

There weren't any other photos. Plenty of books, mostly about the music entertainment industry, and a few best-sellers.

"Hey, Peace," Donovan said, "I'm sorry, but there isn't a lot to eat here. I didn't think before I asked you up here. But there's a Chinese place right down the road. How about I get something? Shouldn't take too long."

"Okay. I am hungry."

"You can look around the house, or just relax until I get back."

"Did you just call me 'Peace'?" Lynn looked a little shocked. "Is that a nickname or something? I mean, you've been mentioning peace on and off, but I didn't even think – didn't associate it with me!"

"Yeah, it is," Donovan said, smiling. Grabbing his keys, he headed out the door.

LYNN WAS STARTING TO FEEL THE OLD FAMILIAR EXHAUSTION AS Donovan closed his door. She took her shoes off and snuggled into his couch.

It seemed like hours later when she heard voices – one soft and masculine, the other female, angry, and high-pitched – coming from another room. She didn't mean to eavesdrop, but she couldn't help hearing.

"So, who the hell is she?" the angry voice demanded.

"Lynn," Donovan answered softly. "Keep your voice down, Dara."

"Who the hell is this Lynn?"

A hard knock indicated that someone had set something down hard on a countertop. "I came here to see YOU, walk into YOUR house, and find this white woman sleeping on YOUR couch. I almost called the cops!"

Donovan's voice kept its steady, patient tone.

"I told you that I was seeing a very lovely woman – Lynn. She just happens to be here tonight." He paused before adding, "I wasn't expecting you."

"Oh! So now I can't even drop by to see my own father?" The voice was growing louder, if that was possible. "This white woman matters more to you than your own daughter!" she accused.

Lynn swung her legs off the couch as she heard Donovan's reply to that accusation.

"This *person* means a lot to me, Dara." He was almost whispering. "More than anyone else has meant to me in a long time." Donovan paused before adding, "Of course you matter a ton to me. You're my daughter."

Lynn stood in the doorway of a magnificent kitchen, the beauty of it lost to her as she regarded Donovan and Dara. Dara was lovelier than her picture. Very tall, thin, with hair cascading down her back in a thick, black wave. Although tense and very much focused on her father, Dara was the first to glimpse Lynn in the doorway.

Acknowledging her, Lynn said, "Hello. I'm the white woman named Lynn who your father is seeing."

Donovan laughed, a hard, full-throated laugh that Lynn had not heard before.

Lynn, not sure what to say, was grateful for his laugh. Continuing to be angry, Dara stood there, giving Lynn a thorough once over.

Taking Lynn's hand, Donovan made the introduction.

"Dara, this is Lynn Cerami. Lynn, this is my daughter, Dara Rue."

Snorting a garbled hello, Dara grabbed her purse and mumbled something about needing to be somewhere else. Lynn noted that Dara had not given her father a kiss or look goodbye; she just raced out a side door.

"I'm sorry for falling asleep," Lynn said with a slight grimace after the door slammed behind Dara. "I didn't even hear a door opening. I'm sure she's not happy finding me here."

Donovan began taking the food out of brown bags, pulling out plates and silverware.

"Dara is angry all the time," he explained, weariness in his tone. "She was in rare form tonight, however."

Lynn helped set up for dinner by finding placemats and setting them on the kitchen counter. It was then that she really woke up to see the kitchen, noting state of art appliances and very sleek, modern décor. But it was the size of the room that threw Lynn.

This is enormous ... two or three times the size of my kitchen!

"I'm sorry for her rude behavior," Donovan said as he finished moving the food to the center island.

"Don't be. I'm sure it was a surprise to her." Lynn sat on a tall stool and helped herself to some cashew chicken and fried rice. "I imagine it's hard to have your father's attention drawn away from you – especially if you're an only child."

"Maybe." Donovan took a mouthful of broccoli beef then asked, "Would either of your sons react in that manner?"

"I'm not sure," Lynn replied and then looked directly at Donovan. "I haven't invited any dates to my house ... I wonder." To change the subject she asked, "You said you've been divorced for a while. Hasn't Dara met other women that you've dated?"

"Of course, but –"

"They've always been black?"

"No!"

Donovan ran a hand through his hair, looking at his plate.

"Total truth time," he said, seemingly to himself. Then he turned toward Lynn. "Dara is bipolar, Lynn."

Lynn nodded, but her face didn't change. She'd worked with college students, and knew a great deal about mental illness. Placing her fork down, she stopped eating and leaned toward Donovan. He read the movement as encouragement to continue the conversation about his daughter.

"I'm not sure that's an excuse ... but it is what it is. I never know if she'll come here and be friendly and great company, or if

I'm in for a diatribe! Tonight, was a diatribe. It started when she was in college. Her friends couldn't find her one night; one of them called me. An hour later I finally found one who did know, but it took all my persuasion to talk her into telling me that Dara was at a hospital, checked in by police."

"Police? Did someone call to complain about her?" Lynn asked.

Donovan placed more food on his plate and passed the carton to Lynn.

"No," he said, "One of her roommates called the police when she threatened to hurt herself. They took her to be held in the psych ward at the area hospital. Took me forever to find her."

Lynn reached out and grabbed his hand.

"Did you know," Donovan started, pointing his fork at her, "that kids of age can tell doctors they can't talk to you? Dara made that very clear the minute she entered the hospital."

"I'm sorry," Lynn said. "That must have been rough."

Donovan nodded. "Awful. And then she was so angry at the friend who ratted her out so I could find her. Then she was afraid that the school would throw her out."

Lynn took another bite before she looked up. "Most schools have policies. The private school I work for tries very hard to help these students, not judge them. But I know every school has a different policy."

"The hospital told her that if she was compliant, they wouldn't need to tell her school anything," Donovan said as he stirred his chopsticks around in the last of the broccoli beef. "So, she did as they suggested, at least the first time. But it was hell trying to find a decent psychiatrist."

He placed his fork neatly to the side. "Quacks! There are a lot of quacks out there. Most just gave her drugs, said 'see you next time'. They made her a zombie. She slept almost day and night with some of them. She refused to let me know what was going on. And if I asked too often, I got a night like tonight! Or worse. She's just really angry."

"You said there was another time?" Lynn asked, her voice almost a whisper.

"Yeah ... the second time was worse." Donovan's dark eyes looked straight at Lynn. "Second time she tried to kill herself. Took a whole bottle of mixed meds, stuff she'd been hoarding. Her friend Ce'Lia got her to a hospital that time. The hospital called me after Dara got scared." He stood up from the steel stool. "But at least that time I met a compassionate doctor, an older man. He saw right through Dara, made her realize that I was only trying to help. And he had a list of doctors, one of whom is perfect for Dara." Donovan rolled his eyes. "As far as I know, she still sees her."

Donovan sighed, then glanced into compassionate big blue eyes.

"I mean, Dara's a great kid. She works hard; she even started her own business," Donovan told Lynn. "But she still has her moments ... like tonight."

Donovan rubbed his hands together, looking down at his empty plate as he finished his discussion about his daughter.

"And have you found some care for yourself?" Lynn asked as she pushed her plate away.

Donovan smiled.

A true counselor. Lots of listening and caring.

"A family support group helped," he said, "and I did see a family therapist for a short time. It's a vicious cycle for Dara, and I am her only concerned parent."

Donovan took their plates to the kitchen window looking down toward the sand, remembering when Dara would run around the private beach laughing and singing.

Not anymore.

"Have I scared you?" he asked Lynn, mesmerized by the moon's shadow across the calmer ocean.

Lynn's laugh was light, commiserative. "Not at all," she answered. "If you only knew how many students I see each year with something like this. Doesn't make me an expert, even though I have a counseling background."

Donovan sighed the breath of someone who'd been through a lot. Lynn went behind him, placing her arms around his torso, hugging him gently from behind, comforting him just as he had done with her earlier in the day.

"We've had a day full of truth-telling, haven't we?" Lynn whispered.

With no warning, he turned around and crashed his lips against hers. Lynn responded by moving her arms up to his shoulders and around his neck, kissing him as she'd never kissed anyone before. Donovan turned them both so that Lynn's hips rested against the counter. She could feel his arousal as he pushed her harder against the granite ledge, his lips demanding *more, more, more.* His hands went to her hair, gently pushing through the short strands, pulling her even closer. She responded by kissing his neck, inhaling his scent, wishing the moment could last forever.

A tentative hand moved down her neck toward her chest. Lynn grabbed it, held it tightly for a second, then gave it another gentler squeeze. As the moment broke, Donovan moved his hand back to her neck.

"You give me such comfort," he whispered, "such peace. I haven't felt this way in a long time."

The softly spoken words made Lynn smile, but her face became more determined as she said, "I need to get home. Work tomorrow, you know."

Donovan could see that she was tired again, exhaustion evident in her eyes.

"Donovan?" Lynn looked away, shy for an instant, but still caught in his embrace. When she looked back, she saw full attention. "It's not that I don't want you. It's just that … well … I don't want you to be put off by me. By what I look like."

When his look turned quizzical, she said, "I'm not one of those pretty young girls who went to Music Extravaganza the other evening. I'm an adult who's been through a lot physically." She sighed now. "And emotionally."

Donovan stood ramrod straight but continued holding Lynn tightly against him.

"I can wait," he said.

Lynn couldn't decide if the gleam in his eye was his own determination or the result of the moon's shining through the kitchen window.

"I thought I'd never find peace," Donovan continued. "But I have. With you." Another soft kiss, then Donovan released her. "I can wait."

When Lynn opened her door the next day and found Dara Rue standing at its threshold, she was surprised.

"Dara!" she called out. "Hello!"

Dara lifted her head regally, then said, "I'm here to apologize." She thrust a huge bouquet of flowers into Lynn's arms. "Here! Dad says you like flowers." As Lynn gathered them up, Dara gave her a side-eyed look. "I was terrible to you last night. I'm sorry."

She motioned Dara into the house. "No worries, Dara," Lynn said as she walked through her living room into her kitchen. "I do like flowers. Thank you."

As she grabbed a vase from a shelf, Lynn searched for a way to start a conversation with someone who'd been so inhospitable the previous evening. The only thing they seemed to have in common was Donovan.

"So, your dad is going on a big hike this weekend, I hear?"

Dara placed her purse on Lynn's counter, then looked around the kitchen.

"Yeah, he likes to go to the more difficult trails. Takes his mind off work."

Glancing out the backyard window, Dara saw the flowers Lynn had purchased the evening before at Lambert's.

"Are you going to plant those?"

"Yeah, eventually," Lynn said while arranging Dara's gift. "I was going to plant them when I got home from work earlier but got kind of tired. I took a nap instead."

Dara looked first at the flowers, then back at Lynn.

"Want some help?" she asked. "Not that I know much about planting, but I figure all you do is put it in some dirt, right?"

"Well, basically that, but there are a few rules," Lynn chuckled as she answered. "I would love some help."

DARA DIDN'T KNOW ANYTHING ABOUT FLOWERS, BUT AS THEY worked in the dirt, she seemed to relax and appeared eager to learn. She asked lots of questions about the type of gardening Lynn had done. Lynn was happy to tell her stories about her various gardens and her family's reaction to them.

After they planted the Lamberts flowers, Dara said, "Looks like there are some other parts of the yard that could use some work."

Lynn took the criticism well.

"Yeah, I really let it go these last few years. I just wish I had more energy." Lynn said.

Serious dark brown eyes looked at Lynn, piercing in nature.

God, she looks at people like she's an arrow aiming to get in.

"I can help," Dara offered. "That is, if you want help."

"I would love your help!" Lynn said quickly, wanting to better know this young woman and fix her garden to its glory days. "My sons could care less about the yard."

"I'll do some research about it all," Dara said, typing rapidly on her phone as they walked back into Lynn's house. Lynn took Dara to the family room where she pulled a dusty book off a shelf.

"Sorry about the dust. I'm letting everything get away from me," Lynn said, "but this is a pretty basic how-to-garden book."

"Can we go to a flower store ... maybe the one where you got those flowers?" Dara pointed to the back yard. "Maybe it'd be good to get information from experts?"

With a beginning gardening book in hand and an appointment to meet Lynn at Lambert's later, Dara left Lynn alone with the hope of perhaps revitalizing her yard.

Chapter 10

They were sitting on the floor in his living room, backs against the couch. The only light in the room other than the laptops came from the fireplace.

Quiet, soothing music surrounded them. Donovan was going over spreadsheets that were laid out on the coffee table in front of them; Lynn was reading from her tablet.

Lynn put her book down and glanced at Donovan.

Such a good-looking man.

He'd stretched his long, jean-clad legs out in front of him. His red t-shirt had an indie band's name on it; another one Lynn didn't know. Lynn, her feet flat on the floor while she braced against the couch, wore white embroidered jeans, an off-white tank covered by an unbuttoned green blouse. They were both barefoot.

He was working away at studying the numbers, pausing to analyze them, a pencil behind one ear, tortoiseshell reading glasses perched on his nose. She smiled when she realized that they both needed readers.

He looked up at her when he heard the giggle.

"What?"

Pushing the laptop off to the side, he reached for her. Their lips met in a soft kiss, influenced by the gentle fire and soft music. As the kiss went on, it became urgent. Lynn's hands wandered all over Donovan's back as her kisses deepened, becoming needy. His hold brought her impossibly close. Breaking for air, he stood up, then held out his hand to her. It took her a few seconds, then Lynn nodded as he pulled her up.

Donovan walked her to his bedroom. He didn't turn on any

62

lights, threw the bedspread to the floor, and gently pulled Lynn on the bed. She responded to his kisses as he pressed into her body, his arousal evident.

Lynn was grateful for the dark. She wasn't ready yet for him to see her damaged breast; she thought it would turn him off. And she was forty-nine, had given birth to two children who had left her body war-weary. She was not a pretty, young thing.

Lynn sensed that Donovan understood that she was leery about certain parts of her body as he avoided touching her breasts. Shoving her shirt off, Donovan then wrestled with her tank top, avoiding touching anywhere near her bra. Lynn, however, pushed him back, then took off the tank and her bra.

"What about you?" she whispered. "Time for you to take some clothes off, too, Donovan."

Permission granted, he pulled off almost all his clothes. Lynn slowly removed her jeans and panties. When she heard his sharp intake of breath, she decided to touch him through his briefs, then removed them and grabbed him, stroking him with gentle hands, up and down, up and down. Donovan groaned, then touched her as well, overwhelmed by the pleasure he felt from her caresses.

"You'll make me come, Peace."

Her face tightened with bliss while he rubbed. She stopped touching him, her own body moving as her body built with expectation. Suddenly she was coming – hard – crying out with a startled *"Donovan!"* as the orgasm moved through her. When the thrashing subsided, and Lynn quieted, Donovan moved over her body, looking at her face intently despite the dark.

Is he asking permission?

"Please," she whispered. She concentrated on Donovan – his large body, his soft hands which were everywhere on her when they weren't finding balance at her sides. She closed her eyes to concentrate and felt a build-up again that she wasn't expecting. Opening her eyes, she met his, and the two of them exploded together.

DONOVAN USUALLY WOKE EARLY, SO WHEN A SHAFT OF SUNSHINE first hit his bed, he stirred. Glancing to his side, he noted that Lynn was not there, and for a moment panicked.

Where is she? Did she leave?

Getting up, he pulled on shorts and a t-shirt, then wandered into the great room. No Lynn. A look into the kitchen told him the same: she wasn't there. Glancing out the window by the kitchen sink, he saw a pretty woman sitting in the sand below, glancing out at the crashing waves.

It wasn't a long walk, but the crooked uneven steps were steep in spots. As he approached Lynn, Donovan wondered how she managed to navigate the rickety stairs to the beach.

Time to get these fixed.

Crouching down next to her, Donovan wrapped his arms around Lynn, settling her back against his chest, his legs surrounding hers. He felt her stiffen and knew that they needed to talk.

"Morning," he said after a rough wave ended well beyond their feet.

Lynn smiled as he kissed her cheek.

"Good morning to you, too."

"Sleep well?"

"I never sleep well anymore," she said as he nuzzled her neck, "and last night I didn't get a lot of time *to* sleep."

He nodded, kissing the spot beneath her ear.

"Sorry 'bout that. But I loved every non-sleeping moment," he said, running his fingers through her short hair. Lynn shivered as he began to knead her scalp.

"In fact," Donovan continued, "I'll be honest with you – I'm a little amazed at myself for being able to keep you awake as much as I did. I'm not a young man with raging hormones."

They both chuckled. Lynn reached up to touch Donovan's cheek with the back of her hand.

"This exhaustion I feel all the time reminds me that I am not young." She paused, running her fingertips down his face again and again. "But who says you have to be young to enjoy sex? Not that we have the stamina of steamy romance characters …"

"I wish!"

"… but it's nice to know that we can still enjoy ourselves," Lynn finished, then grabbing his chin she forced him to look at her so that she could give him a kiss.

"Well, that's good to hear," Donovan said as he finished massaging her head.

Lynn had her eyes closed; her head tilted back as if to catch the early morning rays. Donovan watched her for a while, listening to the sound of water lapping against sand, waiting until it was becoming uncomfortable to be silent.

"How about we play Twenty Questions again?" he asked.

Lynn opened her eyes and straightened her head, then nodded.

"Okay, I'll go first," she said. "Do you bring a lot of women home to fuck?"

Startled by the harsh word, Donovan winced.

"No, I do not," he answered. "Yes, there've been other women, Lynn. But not a ton of women, never without their consent, and certainly no one like you." He paused to give her another kiss on her head. "And last night was not fucking. At least in my eyes."

She nodded, considering what he'd said.

Finally, he asked, "Why didn't you sleep well last night? Other than because I kept you awake a bit."

"A bit?" Lynn sighed and turned on the blanket to face him. "I felt guilty … a little. And then, later, I felt guilty for *not* feeling guilty." She ran her hand through the sand, scrunched her nose, and said, "Did that make sense?"

Donovan stroked her jaw.

"Follow up question: what do you feel guilty about?"

65

"Michael."

The answer was automatic, said through a thickened voice. Lynn fought hard at keeping tears out of her eyes, a battle she won.

Donovan noted that Lynn was really struggling. "Can I take my turn again?" When she nodded, he asked, "What was Michael like?"

Lynn knew it was time to tell him.

"We met in college," Lynn said looking out at the sand. "He was raised by his Italian grandparents after his parents died. I was always amazed that he was interested in me."

"Why?" Donovan ran his hand through her hair again. He knew it felt good to her and hoped it was encouraging.

"Well, he was handsome, charming, very intelligent, and I was just …" she paused for a moment "… just me. I don't know. Nothing special."

"Peace …"

"I know," Lynn threw a handful of sand in front of her. "I'm much more self-confident than I was at eighteen or nineteen."

She gave Donovan a mischievous look. "I wanted to be his. We were married twenty-five years, moved around a great deal because he was always chasing a better job in the banking industry. We were always relocating because of mergers, acquisitions, or job improvements. And I was okay with that."

"So, he ended up at Ownership, right?" Donovan referred to the California banking company that was once at the top of its industry.

Lynn nodded. "Yep, we came here when Connor was going into high school," she said. "And once we got settled, he encouraged me to get my master's degree – something I'd always wanted. So I did, and that led to my current job at Brandstone."

Now Lynn scooped up the sand with both hands and let it sieve through the funnel she created as she said, "It was a dreamlike marriage in a paradise setting, until the year the bottom fell out of the mortgage industry and I got cancer."

She dug deeper into the sand, making a pile, making more sand funnel through her hands.

"But even though the industry collapsed, Michael kept his job. The boys graduated high school, went to college, and I even managed to continue working."

Donovan shifted, feeling Lynn stiffen as she stopped scooping sand.

"He was always there for me," Lynn said, a tear trickling down her cheek. "He went with me to doctors' visits, chemo sessions, surgeries, stuff like that. He held my hand when I was waiting for news about test results, and he asked questions that I never thought to ask. He kept spreadsheets of all the appointments, the medicines, the costs." Lynn remembered. "He was very protective of me – of us." As she paused a pained feeling came to her face which along with the distance already in her eyes made Lynn look sad.

Donovan waited a minute before he asked, "How did he die?"

"A car crash." Lynn said it quickly, then took a deep breath before continuing. "Some asshole came out of nowhere and plowed into Michael's car." Lynn shook her head as if trying to shake the memories away. "The cops said he was dead the minute the car smashed into him."

"That must've been awful," Donovan acknowledged.

"Yup," Lynn said, a quick, clipped word as she ran her fingers under her eyes. "It still is."

They readjusted themselves on the ground, moving legs to get some feeling back in them while Lynn fought back the strong emotions. She took several deeper breaths to help her gain control. After a third breath, looking directly at Donovan, she said, "And now it's my turn."

He started to object, but she interrupted. "No! We take turns during Twenty Questions, right?"

He smiled. "Fire away."

"What happened to your marriage?"

"It just ended. She was fooling around; I was tired of that. We fought a lot towards the end." Donovan shrugged. "She and I married when we were young because she got pregnant and I wanted to do the right thing."

Donovan started imitating Lynn's earlier activity, scooping up sand but instead of throwing it, he turned it over. Then he took another scoop. And another. And another, until he had a large pile.

"I was just getting into the groove of working for the company, and I was inundated with stars, paperwork, budgets, meetings …"

As if it acknowledged the tremendous workload, the hill became too large. Soft grains started falling down the sides in an avalanche. Donovan took his hand and began to pat the existing hill.

"At first, she thought it was cool to be married to someone who was on the rise. Good money, fancy clothes, being popular, going to awards shows. But she didn't like the fact that I had to work late nights often, or weekends. The baby started taking all her time. I admit it; I was no help to her. She was angry, spent a lot of time yelling, threatening to leave me. I wanted to save the marriage for Dara's sake, but my ex-wife did not want that. Finally, I heard that she and a star managed by another company got together at one of the events." Donovan took one last scoop of sand. With the last comment, "And I mean together, together," he threw it hard. "So, we divorced," he stated almost matter-of-factly. He looked hard out at the ocean. "She was mean to Dara, rough. I didn't want her around my baby. Then Dad died suddenly, and I became head of the company." He grimaced. "I was too busy with the business and Dara; I forgot about Mandy."

Lynn took his hand. "Follow up question: where is she now?"

"Don't know. Don't care," Donovan answered with clipped words. "My turn," he said, looking at her. "Why are you feeling so guilty?'

He thought he knew. Her descriptions of Michael spoke of true love.

"Well …" Lynn pushed her sunglasses down from her head's crown as the sun started to blare brightly, then adjusted her seat in the soft sand. "I feel like by sleeping with you, I've betrayed Michael."

I knew it.

"I know the vow is 'til death do us part, that Michael is gone," Lynn continued, "but I hadn't thought I would meet someone so quickly and feel like I do about you. I feel unfaithful to Michael."

"But …"

"Nope, my turn, buddy," Lynn squeezed Donovan's hand. "Why haven't you married again? Or lived with someone? You were so young when you and your wife split."

Donovan turned gentle eyes on Lynn.

"Because up until now," he said as he leaned toward Lynn, "all I've ever found in women was stress: people who wanted my money, or my status." He lightly kissed Lynn's lips. "You are the first person to make me feel great just to be Donovan! It makes me feel peaceful." He kissed her again. "Thus, your nickname."

Another kiss met with Lynn's more active participation, causing her to remove the intrusive sunglasses.

"My turn again, Peace," he said. "Would Michael want you to be happy?"

Lynn's eyes filled up.

"Yes! He would want that. We even discussed 'what ifs' once. I know he'd want me to be happy." She sniffled. "I'm just having a hard time accepting everything."

Donovan's demeanor had gone very serious.

"Maybe it would help if I told you this: I believe in fidelity, Lynn," he said fierceness in his tone. "You won't have to worry about me. From last night on, I am yours."

Lynn smiled, then kissed him again.

"Actually, that does help," she said. "Ditto for me. But then who would want me?"

"You gotta work on that attitude, Lynn. You are not in any way ugly."

"Oh, come on, Donovan –"

"But you will start shrinking away if I don't get some breakfast in you," he said.

He helped her up and then turned toward the damaged stairs.

"How did you make it down here?"

Lynn shrugged. "I just took my time."

"Before I forget," Donovan took Lynn's hand as they started up the stairs. "I have another event to attend soon, and I'd like you to come with me."

When he sensed Lynn's reluctance, he knew it was going to take a lot of skilled negotiating.

"We'll talk while we eat," he decreed, then, pausing on one of the wider stairs, said, "Let's enjoy our happiness, Lynn."

Chapter 11

Donovan delayed telling Lynn about the next big social event for a week.

"I have another event coming up," he began, pausing to sip his tea. "It's not quite as formal as Music Extravaganza," Donovan went on. "We need to dress well, but nothing like long dresses and tuxes."

Lynn took a sip of her drink, her eyes shining over the cup's lid.

"But I like you in tuxes," she teased, then added, "I am not so keen on constantly wearing a new gown to these events. It seems wasteful."

"Dresses can be donated. Or resold," Donovan said, almost absentmindedly. "Bea can make you a dress. It's good publicity for her. That last dress you wore made a huge impact on her name in the industry."

"Bea was well known before I wore that dress." Lynn objected, placing her mug down a tad too hard on the table. "And I am not a young starlet that everyone wants to see!"

Donovan nodded. "No, you are not, thank God. That kind of thing gets men my age in trouble." He thought of the latest actor who'd been accused of sexual harassment. "But what you wear hits a whole new market for Bea. Women your age need nice clothing. Especially stars of a certain age."

"Stars of a certain age?" Lynn couldn't resist objecting. "Not sure I like the sound of that."

"It's more than just about showing off Beatrice Owens' designs," Donovan continued. "I want you there, Peace. I want you to be with me. I can use the support."

"Support?" Lynn scoffed. "You hardly need any support from me. Everyone knows who you are, with or without a date." She gave a short laugh. "Well, everyone except me until about two months ago!"

"But that's just it!" Donovan's eyes grew large with disgust. "They see me coming! The new stars, the managers, the media. It's hard to fight them off sometimes. But with you there, they might leave me alone, let me relax."

"So, you see me as a shield."

"Lynn …" Donovan's voice held a pleading sound. Lynn looked at the slumped shoulders, the pitifully fake look of angst on his face, and almost laughed.

"Okay," she agreed.

"Yes!"

"I'll go with you," Lynn said. "But you buy the dress."

"WE'VE GOT A DRESS TO MAKE!" BEA ANNOUNCED WHEN LYNN showed up at their next coffee date.

Lynn half-listened to Bea's discussion about styles, fashion, and accessories. She didn't understand this world at all, but she knew it made her best friend happy and successful. She understood that Donovan could hardly show up with a frumpy middle-aged woman as his plus-one.

Besides, who knows that the dresses are Bea's? Lynn smiled smugly. *Who even knows or cares about me?*

"So, I think you should wear this dress," Bea said she pulled up a design on her tablet. Lynn looked at the sketch, then put her readers on to get a better view.

"It's got ruffles."

The words were dry, toneless. Not wanting to insult Bea, Lynn tried to keep judgment out of her tone.

"No, ma'am," Bea was insistent. "Those are layers. Layers of gray and black fabric, an ombre effect. And it's waisted – which suits you – and it's longer in the back, but not long enough to be formal. And as you are so fond of pointing out, it is age-appropriate."

ON THE DAY APPOINTED FOR THE EVENT, LYNN SLIPPED ON THE short, gray and black layered dress and felt wonderful despite being so tired that she should have been in bed.

Donovan knocked on the door as Lynn finished running a comb through her hair. Smiling, he looked her up and down then nodded with approval.

"Wow! Maybe you don't need these," he said as he handed her a red box.

Lynn took the box slowly, saying, "What is this? A gift?"

She opened it up to find a slim gold rope necklace with a diamond pendant hanging at the end. She'd already placed her diamond studs in her ears. The two pieces of jewelry were gorgeous together.

Lynn waited until Donovan clasped the necklace around her neck and then walked over to the large mirror in her living room. As she ran her fingers over the necklace, she asked, "It's lovely. Thank you. But a bit much, don't you think?"

"Not for you, Peace," he replied as he took the empty Cartier box, placing it on a side table. "C'mon. Let's get going."

"You'll tell me all about this event, right? On the way there?" Lynn's nervous hands went to her throat, groping the pendant.

Donovan nodded. "Of course," he said, "It's not that big a deal."

"Not that big a deal? But I have to wear all this jewelry and this expensive dress?" Lynn locked her front door, then followed Donovan to the curb where a very shiny Mercedes limousine waited.

"A limo?" she shrieked. "Now I am intimidated. Did you rent this for tonight?"

"No, I own this limo. We can't exactly park the car and walk from a parking lot that's miles away," Donovan said. "Am I right?"

"Yes," Lynn agreed and then slipped into the car, slowly scooting over to allow Donovan some room. "I wouldn't be able to walk for very long in these shoes when I was 'normal.' I can't imagine doing any serious walking in them now."

As the car pulled away from the curb, Lynn's noisy neighbors stared at it, gap-mouthed. As they turned out of the neighborhood, she decided to focus on the upcoming event.

"Okay, dude. Spill," Lynn said.

Donovan handed her a water and grabbed himself a brandy from the car's liquor chest.

"Okay." He gulped as if to find confidence in the amber liquid. "This is an event for artists from the past," Donovan started. "Older stars in the music world. Dad started this event; I've continued the tradition. It's showing respect, Lynn."

Donovan tossed back the brandy. Lynn noted that he didn't seem as calm as usual.

"You're nervous …"

"I am not nervous," he countered, but Lynn saw the lie in his eyes. "I just don't want to say anything insulting. These people are from an era when people were respectful to one another, not just artists out to get a following of groupies based on their manufactured image. These people paid their dues; they deserve all the accolades they get, respect included."

Lynn took his hand into her own.

"No worries there, Mr. Rue. You couldn't be rude to your elders if you wanted to."

As Donovan raised his eyebrows in disbelief, Lynn continued. "I admire all you do for your employees, even when some of them don't respect you."

"Would you believe I was once a very rebellious child?" he asked. "The stories my father could have told you …"

"So!" Lynn sought to change the topic. "Is there a red carpet? Paparazzi? More Roy types?" She giggled at the last question, hoping that it would make Donovan laughed. It worked.

"None of the above," he said. "Maybe a few reporters who need some photos for a last-minute story, but not like the bigger events. No carpet. No anchors from television shows. If there are fashionistas here, they won't bother us. We just have to walk inside, shake some hands, and look pretty."

"And be respectful."

"Yes."

As the car slowed to a stop, a privacy window separating the back from the front of the car rolled down.

"Oh!" Lynn had not even noticed it.

A large man in a sharp black suit looked back at them.

"Mr. Rue?" he interrupted. "We're here, sir."

"Thank you. Desmond, meet Lynn Cerami," Donovan said, then turned toward his date. "Desmond Davis is my driver, my bodyguard."

Donovan put two fingers softly over Lynn's open mouth.

"Please don't shriek. I haven't told you about the body-guard/driver and the limo because I didn't want to scare you away."

Lynn took the fingers away from her mouth but held them as she nodded at Desmond and said, "Nice to meet you."

"Ma'am." He nodded and then quickly got out of the car.

"I've heard of this place," Lynn said as she gazed at the elegant placard above the door that read *Elegance*.

"Elegance is as good as its publicity."

The restaurant's beautiful ambiance was what Lynn took in as Donovan placed his hand at the small of her back, guiding her toward the restaurant's luxurious banquet room. Dark, paneled walls with light sconces of gold, dark red carpeting, and black wrought-iron chandeliers with gold shades appointed the room.

True old-fashioned elegance, just like the name says.

As Lynn took it all in, another tall African American man approached them and held his hand out to Donovan.

"Good evening!" Len said as he clasped Donovan's hand and then dragged him in for a man-hug.

Donovan replaced his hand at Lynn's back and said, "Don't give me that, man! You just want to meet Lynn." He moved Lynn forward and said, "Lynn Cerami, this is Len Matthews."

Len took Lynn's hand. "I keep him in line," he whispered with a wink, then said, "I am so glad to meet the woman who's stolen his attention these past few weeks."

Lynn nodded at Len, taking in the relaxed man. A bald man with a short beard, he was as tall as Donovan, but had nothing of Donovan's presence.

"Well, I hope that hasn't affected his work," she said with a friendly smile.

"No, no," Len admitted. "Nothing can keep Donovan away from the business. He's completely committed to it. But personally, I'm glad to meet the lovely woman who's taken some of the stress out of his life."

"That's enough!" Donovan began prodding Lynn toward their table. "We don't need your approval, Len." As he backed away from Len, Donovan bumped into a woman who was also on the way to her table.

"Oooh!" The startled female voice was musical.

Horrified, Donovan lightly grabbed the arm of the older woman, righting her before she completely lost her balance. Lynn instinctively reached her hands out to help, then noticed Asia Barber.

Is this ...? Oh my God.

Asia met the demographic for the evening: older artists from another time. A little stooped with age, but otherwise bright with positive energy as Donovan continued to hold her arm. Asia's dress was a classic, expensive, straight cut, the fabric holding a slight sparkle. A fresh flower, tucked into her hair, reminded one of the 1940s or 50s. Large brown eyes looked to hold the world's wisdom yet shown with mirth.

"You two! Look at you trying to save me!" Those magnificent eyes sparkled with laughter.

"Oh, Miss Asia! I am so, so sorry."

Donovan's horror at almost knocking down the elderly woman was evident as his hand continued gripping Asia's arm, staying there until she was secure on her feet. Lynn, too, had clasped Asia's hands to support her. Asia straightened herself out, smoothing her hands over her dress.

"For what? I'm fine, just fine."

Simultaneously, Donovan took his hand away from Asia's arm as Lynn lowered her hands to her side. All the time the woman surveyed them, eyes darting from Donovan to Lynn, then back and forth again, finally resting on Donovan, her eyes still shining with humor.

"Donovan Rue," she stated in an elegant, refined voice, her cadence slow and measured, "I have not seen you lately. We must be missing each other at these get-togethers." Glancing at Lynn, then again at Donovan, she asked, "Or have you just been busy?"

Donovan smiled back at her. "Miss Asia, you know I would never miss an opportunity to see you. Where have *you* been?"

"Oh, I've been around," Asia answered, those glittering eyes now looking around the room before they landed back on Donovan. "But introduce me to your lovely companion, please."

Donovan placed an arm around Lynn and then became quite formal.

"Lynn, this is Miss Asia Barber. Miss Asia, this is Lynn Cerami."

"I'm thrilled to meet you," Lynn said. "My mother adored all your music. I'm sure she had every record you ever made!"

Asia chuckled. "Those things still around? Kids don't like that sound anymore."

"Well, they lack taste," Donovan stated. "Seriously, Miss Asia, how are you doing?"

"Fine, I'm fine," she repeated, an almost stern emphasis to her words. "Glad to still be walking around on God's good Earth. Still singing at church and helping a few folks out occasionally."

"They can sure use your wisdom, Miss Asia."

Asia started to walk off, a soft sway to her step.

"Well, maybe," she said, "but everyone has an expiration date, you know. I can't be too far from mine. Nice to meet you, Lynn. Donovan, you hang on to this lovely woman. She's good for you."

She gave them a slow wave as she turned toward her table.

Lynn continued to watch Asia as she slowly strolled away from them, stopping at each table, greeting others with warmth and humor.

"Wow. Asia Barber!" Lynn felt star struck.

"You recognize her?" Donovan couldn't help teasing her. When she made as if to hit his arm, he continued, "You told me you didn't keep up with celebrities."

"Yeah, but she's Asia Barber." Then, remembering their discussion on the way to Elegance, Lynn added, "Now there's an entertainer who deserves respect."

Lynn began meandering with Donovan toward their table. She knew Donovan was teasing her, but he was right: she didn't keep up with who was popular. To continue her defense, Lynn said, "I mean, if they're a hip-hop artist, I probably don't know them. But everyone knows who Asia Barber is."

"Well you're in luck tonight because this crowd is most definitely not into the hip-hop genre."

Lynn's eyes followed Asia as she made her way from table to table. At one, she was hugging an older man, the two of them laughing while the rest of the table guests cast eyes on the two.

"Did you know her other than as an entertainer? She seemed very interested in you. In us."

"Well, that's how it started. My dad signed her before I was born," Donovan said. "One of his first great signings. He was very proud of that accomplishment. She became Mom's best friend, was often at our home."

Although the only entertainment was quiet dinner music, Donovan's table was filled with Rue LA LA employees and guests who were pleasant and interested in hearing about Lynn's job, something very different from the music industry. As they ate the sumptuous meal, everyone relaxed and listened to Lynn describe her students, her eccentric boss, and a few challenging students.

Sensing an end to the conversation, Donovan stood up. "I've got some hellos to make. Can you handle sitting here with these legal types?"

Lynn smiled as she looked up at him. She wasn't as tired as she usually was by this time of night. She was enjoying being out.

Chapter 12

*L*ambert's? Lunchtime?

Dara's text came in very early in the morning on a quiet day.

Can't go there today, but somewhere local?

I'll pick you up. I'll text once I get there.

With little going on, and Cassie out of the office again, Lynn could afford to take a longer lunch, go flower shopping with Dara.

As Lynn was about to turn off her computer, there was a knock on her door.

"Mrs. Cerami?"

She looked up to see a couple, both sad and tired looking.

Parents. Who else could they be?

Lynn stood up, held her hand out to them.

"Yes, I'm Lynn Cerami," she answered. "How can I help you?"

They look familiar.

She knew it was not going to be good when the man closed her office door. They settled into chairs, the woman looking up, twisting a tissue in her hands.

"We're Zeke Olsen's parents, Marta and Louis," the man said. "The receptionist said we could come back here. Can we talk with you?"

"Ah …" Lynn smiled as she shook their hands. "Now I can see the resemblance." After they were all seated, she said, "You must be here to visit! I haven't seen Zeke in a while. How is he?"

Lynn's stomach knotted as she remembered Zeke's difficulty in getting decent grades, his struggle with mental health issues. He'd arrived at Brandstone as an elegant European who'd dressed in fashionable, brightly colored pants with a clean t-shirt, his thick blond hair well cut. Less than a year later he was dirty, his hair oily and plastered to his head, unclean clothes and shoes that needed replacing. Professors and other students emailed her with requests for help for Zeke. After time with a counselor, he seemed to be better, even applying to work in the United States.

Several months later another student came in telling her that Zeke was once again lashing out at friends and even writing on social media about ending his life. When Lynn reached out that time, she got an angry response.

Leave me the hell alone. Who do you think you are?

After consulting with the counseling team, Lynn left him alone. His parents' arrival meant things weren't going well.

"Give me one second," Lynn said as she quickly texted Dara to say she running late. She turned the cell phone over on her desk, after she'd turned the sound down.

"So how can I help you?" Lynn asked, knowing that there was very little she could offer them. "How's Zeke doing?"

Marta blotted her eyes with a tissue as Louis said, "We don't think he's good. But he won't let us see him." He ran a consoling hand over Marta's, then said, "We'd hoped he talked with you?"

"You were always his favorite person here," Marta added, almost a plea for help in her tone.

When Lynn shook her head, the mother wiped away more tears. "He won't talk with us," she said softly. "We went to his apartment and he was inside, but he wouldn't let us in. Told us to go away."

"I'm so sorry."

"He never finished his degree, you know," Louis said.

"I didn't know that, no," Lynn admitted. "Last I heard from him, he said he'd finished, had a job. He seemed excited."

"He was until the grades came out. He cannot seem to pass that one math class he needs to graduate."

AS SHE PULLED INTO THE BRANDSTONE PARKING LOT, DARA GOT A text from Lynn.

Running late. Come in, have a seat and I'll be there as soon as I can.

"Can I help you?" asked the goth-looking woman behind the reception desk. Her nameplate said her name was Sally. She shot her dark, kohl-lined eyes at Dara, her tone and hard exterior showing none of the welcoming interest that her words tried to portray.

"No, thank you."

Dara sat in one of two reception chairs. The woman stood, revealing a super short black skirt and low-cut red top.

"Are you an international student? Do you have an appointment with Dr. Manders or Lynn?"

Dara placed her bag beside the chair and said, "No. And no."

"Well, what do you want then?"

Oh, real welcoming, this one.

"I'm waiting," Dara said, drawing out her last word, "to see Lynn Cerami. For lunch."

"But you don't have an appointment."

"She knows I'm here," Dara said. "She asked me to wait." *You bitch.*

Goth chick sat down with a plop, returning to her desktop computer. Dara saw a gambling game pop up.

Now that really shouldn't be allowed, I'm sure.

As Dara considered this, a shaggy, blond kid, dirty, smelly, in disheveled clothing, burst in the door.

"Where's Lynn?" he demanded, forcing the chick behind the desk to minimize her game and give him a modicum of attention.

"She's got someone in her office. If you'll take a seat, I'll let her know that you're here." Sally pointed at Dara. "But she's ahead of you."

He turned hazy blue eyes toward Dara as he threw a backpack down on the floor.

"I'm pretty sure she'll want to see me NOW!" he thundered.

Dara stared back for a few seconds, then picked up the phone on her lap.

Hmmm. Schizophrenic? Depressed? Whatever this guy is, he ain't well.

"Look! I want to see Lynn. Tell her it's Zeke. I never have to wait. Why are you making me wait?"

He pounded two fists on the counter in front of Sally, then began yelling again.

"I need her! Now!"

Dara watched Sally flinch, then push her rolling chair back toward the wall. She had nowhere to go from there, trapped into a corner.

"I told you," Sally snarled back. "She's got people in there. It's private. Do you understand private? It means –"

"I know what it means, you bitch!"

Holy Jesus, he's unglued.

Zeke began rounding the counter, caging Sally in further, halfway into Sally's escape path. He didn't notice Dara calling up her messaging app, telling Lynn, *You better get out here. This guy Zeke is going to explode.*

No responding text.

C'mon, Lynn. Pick up your phone. Come into the twenty-first century.

Dara texted Lynn again.

Urgent! Get out here!

Zeke now completely blocked Sally's exit route. The young woman was wide-eyed as she stared up at him.

"Just take a seat, dude. I'm sure she'll be done soon."

He took another step, now right next to her.

"I want Lynn to see me now! She's with my parents, I'll bet, and I need to see her *now!*"

83

His voice was so loud that people walking outside the large, vibrating windows turned their heads. Dara's hands flew over her phone.

Lynn! Even I'm getting a little worried here. Pick up your stupid phone.

As Zeke picked up a foot to take one more step forward, Lynn's door opened, and she emerged.

"What's going on out …? Oh, Zeke!"

He turned around and started walking toward his student advisor.

"Are my parents in there?"

As Zeke slammed down each heavy foot in his march toward Lynn's door, the floor vibrated. Lynn stood there calmly, her feet planted squarely on the ground, her arms at her sides, her usual peaceful countenance in place.

How does she do this?

Dara watched Sally grab her bag, then skate out the main door.

What?! She's leaving us alone with this guy. No way!

"Your parents just came to see me," Lynn was telling Zeke. "They'll be so glad to see you."

"I don't want to see them!" Impossibly, Zeke's voice got louder, his hands fisting again as if he was going to hurt something.

Or someone. Shit, what do I do now?

Dara quickly pulled up the Brandstone website on her phone.

Where's an emergency number? How do I find it? Jesus, what if he blows!

"They're right here," Lynn was saying, her voice never rising, her tone soothing … at least to Dara. "I'm sure they'd love to have a few minutes with you. Just a few, Zeke."

"*I don't want to see them!*" he yelled and shook those fists. "Why can't you fuckers understand that I want to be left alone? I don't need them. I don't need you. Leave me alone!"

Zeke took another step toward Lynn, placing Dara behind him.

That's it.

84

Dara finally found a department called Campus Security. Right on its front page was the number to call in emergencies. As quiet as she could be, Dara stood and snuck outside to the hallway where she called the emergency number.

"There's a student In Lynn Cerami's office having a major meltdown ..."

Dara paused, growing more frantic as the person droned monotonous questions into her ear with no sense of urgency at Dara's answers.

Look! Can you get down here because I really think he's going to lose it and hurt somebody."

"What makes you think that, miss?"

"Why? I gotta tell you a reason?" Dara looked back through the windows. "Just get here. He's going to blow up! Please!"

As she hung up, Dara considered calling 911. Just as she got her phone up again, two men dressed in white shirts with *Campus Security* embroidered above a pocket ran by her. Simultaneously, Lynn exited her building, Zeke with her.

"Officers," Lynn said in a mild tone.

They eyed her and then Zeke.

"Everything okay, Mrs. Cerami?"

Lynn smiled, her hand on Zeke's arm. Her face was calm, almost serene, and Zeke, standing next to her, appeared to be calming down, too.

"Everything is fine, Steve. I'm just walking a student over to Dina's office. You know? The counseling center?" The officers – and Dara – relaxed a little. Lynn nodded at Dara.

"I'll be with you in a few."

HALF AN HOUR LATER, DARA AND LYNN WERE EATING AT A SMALL pizzeria near Brandstone.

"You sure you're okay, Lynn?"

Lynn took a bite of her pepperoni slice and nodded before saying, "Yeah, I'm fine."

"I could never do what you do," Dara admitted.

"What's that?"

"Work with crazy guys like that kid. Do you have many of them? Is it a daily occurrence?"

Lynn chuckled. "No, if it happens once a year that's a lot."

"Has a student ever tried to hurt you? Or threatened you?"

Lynn paused to swallow her pizza before saying, "Today is as serious as it's ever gotten in our office."

Dara pushed her plate away.

"Wow. Are you sure you don't want to be a shrink? I don't think my shrink could handle that."

Lynn winked at Dara. "She'd handle it better, Dara."

Chapter 13

*D*onovan pulled up in front of the small home in a nicely manicured neighborhood, recalling all the times he had dropped Lynn off, but had never been past the foyer.

A handsome, traditionally Italian-looking young man answered the door. His striped polo shirt and neatly pressed khaki slacks screamed conservative.

Donovan extended his hand. "Hi. I'm Donovan Rue."

"Connor Cerami." The intense individual held out his hand, too. "I'm Lynn's oldest son." Connor gestured toward the foyer. "Please come in."

Donovan entered a very different environment from his mansion: a living room, a quarter the size of his great room. Beyond it was a dining room with an older oak table and chairs and china hutch. Large windows wrapped around the two rooms letting in brilliant California sunshine.

The traditional décor included family photographs that adorned every available tabletop. Donovan noted pictures of two boys in various sporting pursuits, some with a man who mirrored Connor's dark looks. The other boy was very blond and, judging by the funny poses in most pictures, quite wild compared to his big brother. A few had Lynn in the pictures, her hair long and thick, her eyes brighter than he'd ever seen and unencumbered by any pain or sorrow. Donovan picked one up to look a little longer.

"Hey! You made it!" Lynn called as she entered from a side door. The older version of the blond kid in the pictures came in behind her.

Donovan put the frame down and went to her. He gave her a

quick kiss on the cheek, aware that the boys might be watching his every move. Again, he stuck out an open hand to Lynn's younger son.

"Donovan Rue."

"Owen. It's great to meet you."

Owen also extended a hand, then laughed as he realized it was covered with an oven mitten. Removing it, he again stretched out his hand, adding, "But I recognize you from the pics I've seen all over social media."

Owen shook hands heartily, then turned to the opening door.

"This is my wife, Maribelle," he said. She smiled, then asked, "Lynn, can I help in the kitchen?"

"Any help I can get would be wonderful! Owen, Connor, why don't you guys take Donovan out back? I'll help get Maribelle started." Lynn led her daughter-in-law into the small kitchen.

As Connor and Donovan chose their seats, Owen investigated the cooler.

"Out of beer." He said. "Let me go get some more."

With that, he left Donovan and Connor in an uncomfortable silence.

FLIPPING ON THE GARAGE LIGHTS, OWEN NOTICED HIS FATHER'S FUN Car in one of the three stalls. Unable to help himself, he went to it, running one hand lovingly over the sleek convertible.

It's starting to get dusty. Probably the longest it's ever sat still.

Owen's eyes filled with tears as he remembered Michael taking him on long, fast drives late at night.

No matter where we lived Dad always found some deserted streets where he could drive his favorite car.

He turned his head to the car in the next stall, a practical and safe Hyundai Sonata that his father purchased for Lynn when she got her master's degree. Unlike Michael, Lynn just wanted something to get her to work and back.

Nothing fancy for the Momster.

Owen started toward the third stall which was used as storage. An extra refrigerator, used mostly during the holidays, stored extra soda and beer. As he went to reach for the handle, Owen noticed the driver's side mirror on the Sonata dangling by its wires.

What the hell?

Further inspection showed it needed to be taken to the shop for repair.

Better ask Con about this. Why isn't Mom taking care of her car?

Grabbing a six-pack, he headed toward the kitchen to see his wife.

As Lynn left the kitchen to rejoin her guests Maribelle looked around in concern. She felt like she'd truly walked into hell.

One of the smaller counters was loaded with spices; there wasn't an inch of space to put anything down there. The other two counters, also cluttered, gave her little working space.

When Maribelle opened the refrigerator, she gasped. None of the salads that Lynn had talked about were prepared.

How could she do that?

Then she remembered that Lynn was so tired all the time.

Maybe she just didn't have the energy to do these ahead of time.

Maribelle pulled out the ingredients for a green salad. She also found the corn – still in husks – that was to go on the grill with the burgers.

"Everything under control?" Owen asked as he came into the room. First, he gave his wife a big kiss.

Maribelle thought about complaining about all the work ahead of her, but instead she said, "Yeah. It's all fine." Then she noticed that Owen was red-eyed and more agitated than normal.

"What's going on, Owen?" When he shook his head at her, Maribelle said, "C'mon. Tell me what's got you going."

"Mom's car has a broken mirror," he replied. "I need to tell Connor about it – get it fixed."

"No biggie," Maribelle said. "Maybe it happened today, and she was putting off calling the dealer until tomorrow?"

"Could be …"

"What?" Maribelle wasn't used to a contemplative Owen. "What's the matter?"

"Dad's car," he answered. "It's out there. Just stirred up lots of memories." He set the six-pack on the counter, asking, "Did I ever tell you about it?"

"That your dad's only outlandish purchase was when he first got promoted? Yeah, you told me." Maribelle started to husk the corn for their meal. "And that he had a more practical car –"

"Yeah, *had* being the operative word," Owen interrupted. "It died when he died." He shook his head, then announced, "I'll be okay. It just threw me."

"Wonder what she'll do with it?"

"Guess that's something she hasn't considered," Owen said as he grabbed the beers again. "So, wait 'til you say something before I grill, right?"

"Yes," Maribelle began to wash the corn. "Just don't start the hamburgers until I bring out the corn."

"No problem, baby."

I CAN HANDLE SILENCE, DONOVAN THOUGHT. *LET'S* SEE IF *Connor can.*

Donovan studied the little backyard, noting that Lynn had planted the flowers she'd purchased at Lambert's.

Lynn returned and with the glance she gave them, Donovan could tell that she was concerned that they were sitting in silence.

"Everything okay?" she asked. "I'm sorry Dara couldn't be here to meet the boys."

He saw the strain in her eyes. He knew she was anxious about bringing him here to meet her sons, wanted them to accept their mother's new relationship.

"It's all good, Peace," he said. "Dara is trying to land a new customer, was meeting him for coffee this evening."

He could not help but feel Connor stiffen in the chair next to his. Along with the silent treatment, Connor had not even glanced at Donovan.

Coming back with the six-pack, Owen handed a beer to his brother with a very direct look that gave Donovan pause.

What's that about?

Then after giving a cold one to Donovan, Owen asked, "Can I get you anything, Mom?"

"I have my water," she said, as she held up her plastic cup.

"Good! Good." Owen turned toward Donovan. "Mom's not much of a drinker."

There was an awkward silence. Donovan was not sure what to say. He remembered asking Lynn after her horrid first encounter with Dara how she thought her sons might react to a man being in her life. While they weren't being mean or horrible, one was sullen, the other trying too hard. Lynn wasn't helping. In fact, it was like she was not even aware of how quiet it had gotten. Owen finally succumbed to the silence in the backyard.

"So, Donovan … it's okay to call you that?" Owen went on once he got an affirming nod. "Mom said that you met at Music Extravaganza in Los Angeles?"

Donovan appreciated his attempt to be friendly.

"Yes," he said, smiling at the younger man. "Bea Owens asked if I'd make sure your mom was okay. She said your mom wasn't used to being around ... what did she call them? Oh yeah – *vultures and sharks.*"

Owen laughed, saying, "That sounds like Aunt Bea!"

Connor cracked a slight smile as he stood and went to a more shaded part of the patio. "Yeah, Mom hasn't been going out much lately," he said. "She gets pretty tired, has to save her energy for work."

"Gotta have fun, too, Con," Owen said shooting Connor another glare.

What is with the silent conversation between these guys?

Connor didn't appear at all unruffled by his brother's comments or behavior.

"How is work lately, Mom?" Owen asked. "Cassie treating you okay?"

Lynn crossed her legs and answered, "Oh, you know ... she can be a bit rough sometimes."

"Now what's she doing?" Connor asked, his tone brusque.

Lynn sighed. "She just expects me to 'get over it.' She doesn't understand why I can't regain my energy magically. Says I should be 'normal'. Turns out one of her friends had breast cancer the same time as me and that woman is back to normal. But she only had radiation – no surgeries, no chemo."

"So, because the treatment has ended, you have to be well?"

"She doesn't realize that yelling at me in front of anyone, making 'Let it Go' my ringtone, or telling me that I should lift weights are insults." She shrugged. "What can I do?"

Connor muttered something under his breath that sounded like "damn hippy" and then took a swig from his bottle. Owen was shaking his head.

"Anything we can do to help, Mom?"

"Not unless you can cure this damn chemo-brain I'm experiencing," Lynn said. "They told me it would take a year after treatment ended to get over it. That was fourteen months ago." She sighed. "But it just doesn't seem to be going away." Lynn's sad eyes studied her patio floor. "And, honestly, I do make mistakes at work that I never would have done before. Things are harder when your brain is in a fog."

Donovan was listening intently as he always did to Lynn. Leaning forward, he asked, "Can you take some time off?"

"Not right now," she answered. "I'm trying to get ready for the start of the next academic year. It's brutal. No one gets time off."

Owen changed the subject.

"What about your work, Donovan? Is there a hard time for you?" he asked.

I like this kid. He's kind, he's energetic, he seems in tune with the feelings around him.

"Every day! Some days are harder than others."

Like dealing with Roy Alloy and his manager. Another meeting tomorrow. Again.

Connor let out a rude grunt causing everyone to look at him.

"Not like getting over a physical ailment is it? Or working throughout cancer treatment," he snarled.

Lynn's face displayed clear alarm at hearing her oldest son's nasty tone. Connor stood, one rigid arm at his side, the other clutching the beer bottle like it might give him more support for his vitriol.

"Ease up, Con," Owen said. "Everyone has rough days, whether they're because of cancer or from running a business. Hell, my day is a disaster if I get a rude model at a photo shoot!" He eyed his older brother before prodding, "Don't you have bad days?"

Connor swigged the last of his beer, then said, "I'd better start grilling those hamburgers. Maribelle should be done by now."

"Um ... let's give her a few more minutes. She said she'd call out when she's nearing being done."

Connor walked toward the door.

"I'm off for another one."

He didn't ask if anyone wanted anything as he sauntered toward the kitchen.

After the meal, Owen and Connor were cleaning up while the ladies and Donovan relaxed back out in the family room. Wanting to refill his water glass, Donovan headed toward the kitchen, stopping in the doorway when he overheard Connor and Owen talking about their mother.

"I think it's getting worse."

Connor's deep voice was impossibly lower, as if he was trying to keep the information private.

"Yeah," Owen's voice was also quiet and low as he handed his brother a dish to dry. "Did you know that the driver's side mirror on Mom's car is hanging on by a thread?

"On the Sonata?"

"Yeah! She must've hit something recently – hasn't had it fixed. Did she mention it to you?"

"No. I'll check into it," Connor said. "How'd you find that out?"

"When I went to the garage refrigerator to get more beer."

"She's probably too busy with this –"

"And Maribelle said *nothing*, absolutely *nothing* was ready for dinner tonight. She had to prepare everything."

There was a moment of quiet as Donovan heard one plate being placed atop another. Then Owen added, "Not that Mar minds helping Mom out. But Mom told her it was all set to go. And it wasn't."

Another plate was placed on top of the stack as Connor said, "She's probably too busy with this Donovan character."

"You don't like him?" Owen's voice got a little louder. "I think he's great for Mom."

"Too soon," came Connor's judgment. "Dad's not gone long and she's already –"

"Geez, Con," Owen set another plate down, this time with a lot more force. "Why are you so harsh, man? Can't Mom enjoy herself? She's been through hell!"

There was a moment of silence between the two brothers. All Donovan heard was splashing water, or the sound of the faucet being turned on and off.

"Dad's car is still out there."

Owen's voice was softer again, melancholy in sound.

Connor didn't respond for a beat, then, "It's probably hard for her to get rid of it. Dad babied the hell out of the 'Fun Car.'" He laughed, a tight, low noise. "'The Fun Car.' How the hell did we come up with that name?"

Connor was chuckling softly as he said, "Well, you know he loved to brag about it."

"Oh, yeah. Dad and his stories."

"And his practicality! A 'Fun Car' he held on to for his entire adult life. And a 'Practical Car' that took him everywhere else!"

"Well, that's gone."

More silence as the two brothers were hushed with sorrow, lost in their grim memories. Just as Donovan was all set to head back to the women without his drink renewed, Connor said, "You think I'm wrong about Donovan and Mom? You don't think it's too early for her to be dating?"

"Lighten up, big brother!" came Owen's immediate reply. Following another quick laugh, he added, "Get laid, dude."

Donovan heard the water splashing before he heard Connor respond, "Fuck off, Owen. I don't even want to *think* about that kind of stuff and our mother."

Donovan was tiptoeing away when he heard, "Hey! You didn't need to flash that wet towel at me!"

"What makes you think I'm not?" Connor asked. "Getting laid, I mean."

This I don't need to hear.

Chapter 14

*L*ater the next week, Donovan snuck into Cergan Hall, hoping to surprise Lynn at one of her international student events. As he looked around the space for her, a horrible high-pitched noise began, forcing him to cover his ears.

What is that noise?

The screeching mic was causing everyone in the crowded space to put their hands over their ears for protection. The speaker's words were first muffled, then concealed, then overly loud.

"Typical Brandstone function," a student was saying to his friends. "They always have bad sound here." After a sigh, he said, "Let's go. Anywhere is better than listening to this."

Just then Donovan saw Lynn and a young Asian man at the podium. Both wearing khaki pants with blue polo shirts, the words *Brandstone College* and *International Student Services* embroidered above a breast pocket, they looked confused and were fiddling with something that Donovan couldn't quite see. A student in similar clothes with *Media Services* stitched to his shirt ran up on the platform and took over from Lynn and her colleague.

Nothing changed. As the sound continued to be awful, more people left the room, clearly disappointed in the evening. Lynn looked up at one point, exhaustion clear in her big blue eyes. When she saw Donovan, the look softened. He smiled back at her and made his way to the podium.

"Donovan."

He glanced at the controls. Even with his significant knowledge of control boards, Donovan could not have helped the ancient mechanism. It was damned before Donovan even arrived.

"I don't think this is fixable, Lynn," he said. "It needs to be replaced."

"Tom," Lynn addressed the Asian man, "give it up. We've been trying this all night. It isn't going to get any better."

Tom shrugged and walked away, telling the students with *Volunteer* on their red shirts to let the participants know that the event was over and clean up.

Lynn was placing things in a box when the president of Brandstone University came to the platform.

"Good evening," he greeted her. "I'm sorry I'm late, Lynn. I had another event to attend." He looked around, "Is Cassie here?"

Lynn straightened up from the box she'd been filling.

"Oh! Dr. Rawlings!"

Lynn glanced at Brandstone's president.

"I guess we weren't sure you were coming. I know how busy you are. Um, Cassie isn't here tonight. Tom and I are running the show."

"Looks like you're having difficulty with the sound again, huh?"

Donovan stepped forward.

"Dr. Rawlings, I'm Donovan Rue," he said, holding out his hand.

Chris Rawlings was surprised. "Donovan Rue from Rue LA LA?" His own hand was out a minute later, pumping Donovan's hand. "I recognize you from media, of course, and I think we may even have been to a few events together? Maybe for charity?"

Donovan just smiled. *Nod whenever someone acts like we're acquaintances. I've never met this guy.* Tonight, for Lynn's sake, Donovan was willing to play along. "I think I can help with the sound issue," Donovan said.

Chris looked more surprised than Lynn, both staring at Donovan. Before either Brandstone employee could comment, Donovan continued.

"Our company makes contributions to colleges all the time,

offering musicians' services for fundraising events, things like that," he explained. "We've also fixed a few sound systems in my time."

Chris shook his head. "I'm told that this thing is beyond repair."

Donovan smiled, nodding. "Yes, sir, you can say that. This system is very old. Please let Rue LA LA donate a new sound system for this room."

"Wow!" Unable to control herself, the words escaped Lynn's mouth. Her eyes sparkled with delight, looking from man to man.

"I'm sorry if this seems blunt, Mr. Rue, but why are you here at our university tonight?" Chris was eyeing Lynn now. "It's not like we get music executives to our student events very often."

Donovan put a hand on Lynn's shoulder and said, "I came to be supportive of Lynn." He smiled down at her, then looked earnestly at Chris Rawlings. "How about I have our lawyers contact whoever it is that handles donations here on Monday?"

LATER DONOVAN WALKED LYNN OUT TO HER CAR.

"Well, I think you saved my night ... sort of," Lynn said as they loaded a box in the trunk of her car.

"Sort of? I know I saved everyone else from having their hearing destroyed." Purposely shuddering, Donovan shut the lid. "Seriously, how long has it been like that?"

"As long as I've worked here," Lynn admitted. "But I think your donation will make Cassie forget that we had to end the event early. She'll probably figure out a way to blame it all on me. Or Tom."

"But, how can she do that?" Donovan was exasperated. "It's not your fault that the school hasn't done something about the sound in that room. You can't be expected to know that it was going to be that bad tonight."

Lynn sported a wan little half-smile as she looked at Donovan.

"Cassie can find a way, believe me. Plus, she wasn't here, and Rawlings will take note of that and not come to the next event."

"So, politics involved, too?"

Donovan wrapped his arms around Lynn's waist. She snuggled up against him and sighed, then closed her eyes.

"Okay, time for you to go home," Donovan said, kissing her head. "Don't want Connor to accuse me of keeping you out all hours!"

He led Lynn to the driver's door, opened it, and watched as she slowly got into the seat.

When is this exhaustion ever going to end?

"Goodnight, Peace. Don't forget about Saturday," he said as he closed her door. Rolling down her window, Lynn asked, "Saturday?"

"Yeah. The walk. Remember?"

WALKING INTO THE OFFICE THE NEXT MORNING, LYNN WAS HOPING for a few quiet minutes before the boss thundered in. As she set her purse down on her desk, Lynn heard the loud demand, "I need to talk to you two when you're both settled."

A few minutes later both Tom and Lynn sat before the Queen of International Student Services, getting the usual grim look.

"I heard it ended early," Cassie stated, too loud for the little room to bear. "Why?"

Lynn took the lead while Tom seemed to shrink in his seat.

"Bad sound – again. They were all leaving before we even announced it was over."

"Did you have a tech there?"

Tom shifted in his chair. "Eventually. We didn't order one before the event started, so we had to call one in when things weren't going well."

Cassie shuffled some papers and then gave Tom a hard look.

"You won't forget to set that up again, will you?" she asked, her volume increasing.

Tom nodded. Then Cassie shifted her attention to Lynn.

"And I heard President Rawlings was there, too."

"Yes."

"So why didn't I know that he was coming?"

"Cassie," Lynn tried to keep her tone even, calm. "We had no idea he was coming."

"Did you invite him?"

"We always do," Lynn looked directly into Cassie's eyes. "You have made it clear that we always invite him to everything, Cassie, and we do that."

Cassie was not amused.

"Fine thing … I decide to stay home one time – just one time – and he shows up, the sound is bad, and I'm not there!"

She always tells me at the last minute that she's not coming. This isn't something new or unusual.

Tom suddenly burst out, "One really good thing happened, Cassie! Donovan Rue showed up and is donating a new sound system for that room."

Uh oh...

This was not news that Lynn wanted to reveal.

Cassie's mood brightened.

"Donovan Rue? *The* Donovan Rue? The music guy? Why'd he come?" She eyed both of her colleagues. "Well? It isn't a hard question. Guys like him don't just show up at little gatherings like last night!"

Lynn twisted the cap to her pen, debating how to tell Cassie about Donovan.

"I've been dating him," she said to two shocked faces. "He wanted to see me in my work environment, so I invited him to come last night."

Lynn saw that Cassie was impressed.

"So, you talked him into a new sound system. Good for you, Lynn! It's a nice reflection on our office."

Losing her patience, Lynn stood up.

"I have another meeting," she said, turning to leave. "And Donovan Rue was not talked into anything. He walked in, heard the horrible screeches, and made the offer directly to the president of Brandstone. I had nothing to do with it."

Cassie sat back on her throne, a pen near her mouth.

"Hmm ... well, at least we'll have a nice system now for our events," she said as she reached toward her stationery drawer. "Still, I think I'll write him a thank you note. Maybe he'll meet me for lunch sometime."

Chapter 15

Connor drove Lynn to the cancer walk on Saturday morning. As they pulled into the Dodger Stadium parking lot, Lynn began to feel tendrils of fear along her spine.

How am I ever going to complete this? Five K? I can barely manage five feet!

"I'm glad you're feeling up to this," Connor said as he opened his car door. "It's good that Donovan and Dara can join us, too."

"You're cool with that?" Lynn couldn't resist teasing Connor. "Please treat him better than you did the other day," Lynn told her oldest son. "I was embarrassed by your behavior."

"Mom ..."

"No 'Momming', please. You're old enough to know that you should treat people respectfully. All people, Connor."

"Yes, ma'am."

"No ma'aming me! You know I hate that," Lynn said as she swung her legs out of the CRV that Connor drove.

When Lynn mentioned having participated in the walk the year before, Donovan brightened before her. Although his company was one of the corporate sponsors, he had never attended. To walk with Lynn, someone he loved being with, meant that he could go, represent, and enjoy it, too. Even Dara had agreed to come with him, another surprise. Connor, who had always accompanied his mother, seemed especially eager to walk this year.

Connor was peering inside his darkened car windows while his mother watched.

No doubt he's checking to be sure that there's nothing to lure criminals to break into his car.

"You covered my purse with my coat, a sweatshirt, your coat, and your hockey bag," she reminded him. "No one can tell that my bag with its paltry twenty dollars is at the bottom of the pile."

"Can never be too careful," he mumbled, then caught sight of the Rues. "There they are!"

Down the hill and across the massive parking lot stood Donovan and Dara. As Connor and Lynn approached them, the cancer walk area came into view. A pink and white balloon archway indicated the lineup area for participants. People were already standing there.

On one side of the lineup area stood little booths – a first aid station, places to check in and pick up a race t-shirt. The fun side had food tents, corporate sponsor tents, booths selling all kinds of items, places for children to get their faces painted, plenty of chairs. Bright pink balloons were everywhere, some of them making their escape as children could not hold on.

A comedian was warming everyone up, introducing dignitaries and singers between skits, and finally bringing an athletic trainer up to the stage to get everyone stretched out before the event began. During the brief quiet times, live music blasted from a sound system courtesy of Rue LA LA.

As they drew nearer, Dara waved with both arms raised over her head, moving in a frantic rhythm in time to the music. Lynn smiled back and made her way to Donovan who was wearing the bright pink shirt with his company emblem next to the walk organization's logo. Dara, wearing the same shirt, threw one to Connor.

"Oh! Connor, this is Dara, Donovan's daughter," Lynn said as she watched the shirt exchange. "Dara, this is Connor."

"Um, yeah. Hello. Connor," Dara seemed a bit stilted as she said hello before asking, "Did you get your shirt yet, Lynn?"

As Lynn started to answer, Donovan said, "Lynn gets a Survivor's Shirt. You go over there, Peace." He pointed to a large tent, the word SURVIVORS in bold letters above.

This is what I hate about cancer – maybe more than even getting it. You get seriously ill, then get all this swag and attention that you don't really want.

"Can't I just wear a shirt like you guys?"

The three were all shaking their heads no, pushing her toward the tent with the garish sign, exclaiming that she needed the special recognition. Stumbling up to the check-in table, Lynn attempted to smile at the young woman who greeted her.

"Here's your shirt!"

She handed Lynn a white shirt with the same markings as the pink ones but with the word SURVIVOR scrawled across the back – in pink.

"Just follow this little hallway behind me; there's room to change your clothes and some special treats just for you. Congratulations on fighting this awful disease!"

Lynn took her shirt, trying to find something gracious to say to the over-bright receptionist.

"Um, thanks."

Beating. fight. Warrior. Courageous. Survivor! As if I had any choice

...

"My friends ..." Lynn remembered that Donovan, Dara, and Connor were waiting for her. "Where do they go?" She motioned toward them noting that they all had their cell phones out.

"We'll show them where to meet you. Your supporters can walk into the Survivor area and wait for you; even eat with you. It's cool. Oh! And here's a bag to put your other clothes in."

The word SURVIVOR screamed out from the cream-colored plastic bag.

Minutes later, her new shirt on, Lynn walked down the rest of the gauntlet toward a breakfast area. Only a few people stood waiting for breakfast. Small booths lined either side, all giving away items that all shouted SURVIVOR on them. A woman at the end of the runway greeted each survivor before allowing entrance to the eating area. Eyeing Lynn, the woman placed unwelcome hands on Lynn's arm, saying, "Are you okay? Do you need to sit down for a while? Rest?"

Lynn felt herself shrinking away from the unwanted grasp, yet she tried to be kind.

She means well.

"I'm fine. I just need to find my group," Lynn answered.

"How about I get you a plate of food? Bring it to you? Would you like a bacon and egg muffin sandwich? Or there's a veggie option. Would you rather have that?" The woman, dressed in a purple Staff t-shirt, kept her hand in place on Lynn's arm, turning them toward the buffet table.

Her heart's in the right place. But ...

"No, I can get it."

Lynn tried to sidestep the too-compassionate volunteer.

One more step and I'll be away from her.

The woman repositioned her hand on Lynn's lower arm, then said, "But I'm sure you'd like some help. Just let me –"

"No!"

Lynn stopped, jerking her arm away.

"What part of the word Survivor don't you understand? I'm well right now; I can do this."

As she wandered away from the hurt-looking woman, Lynn felt a moment of shame.

All she was doing was trying to help. I didn't need to be that cruel.

"Quite a spread, Peace!"

Donovan's deep, pleasant voice momentarily broke through Lynn's resentment of the woman, the situation, her cancer. Still, she scowled and said, "Yeah, all you have to do is get cancer, endure treatment, wear a shirt that singles you out, and run the gauntlet of over-concerned people in *that* line."

Lynn turned and pointed two sharp fingers behind her, noting that the concerned volunteer was holding another Survivor's plate.

Donovan stepped back from her sharp retort, then took her arm to lead her to the buffet. Lynn calmed down during their light breakfast, listening to Connor's tale of the previous year's walk which included Owen, Maribelle, and, of course, Michael.

Her large sunglasses kept Lynn's misty eyes hidden from the group, but her set mouth and complete silence during and following Connor's tale expressed her thoughts.

Why am I even here? Why didn't I just try to sleep? Let the others do this ... No! I promised Donovan that I'd be with him.

Before anyone had a chance to remark, a loud announcement asked runners to take their positions.

"Ten minutes until we gather the walkers! Could I have Mr. Donovan Rue to the microphone, please?"

Donovan stood, then leaned down to kiss Lynn who noted that the Survivors' volunteers were all ogling her date.

"I'll catch up with you after I finish this gig," he whispered.

Lynn tried to smile back. "You don't need to hurry. I don't think I'll be bypassing anyone today."

Minutes later the walkers including Dara, Connor, and Lynn, were ready to go as Donovan was introduced.

"I want to thank everyone who's come out for such a great cause. This disease needs a cure. Am I right?"

Lynn noted women nodding, calling back their responses.

"Yes, sir!"

"Yeah, 'bout time!"

"Donovan Rue, you tell it, honey!"

"Just by participating, most of your fee is going towards research at some of the great hospitals right here in Los Angeles. My company – Rue LA LA – is throwing our support behind this great effort."

Applause and cheers came from the waiting runners. Donovan ran a hand through his curls and pinched his nose before saying, "And I want to let one beautiful woman in this crowd know that I am with her all the way!"

As the crowd's cheers worked up to a frenzy, Donovan counted down. His loud "*Go!*" and the foghorn blast let the walkers know that they could start.

Lynn took one tentative step.

Okay. Let's do this thing. I need to push myself to show him that I am fighting, damn it. I want to live.

Leaving the stadium's dusty parking lot behind, the crowd entered Echo Park. The scenery went from the brown, open space of the parking lot to a lush green. Old trees shaded the curving roadway that wound through it. Picnic benches sat near swing sets, while fields for softball and soccer, and large restroom areas made it a complete recreation area.

Soon, Lynn noticed that Connor and Dara were walking too slowly as if Lynn was tugging a leash to keep them back with her. Connor looked like he was counting the beats between each step. Dara would pause, then take a couple of quick paces.

This has got to stop.

"Look," Lynn said, "why don't you guys walk at your own pace? I'll catch up with you at the end."

"What? And not stay with you?" Dara asked. "That doesn't seem right."

Connor was nodding. "Mom, we're here for you."

"That's great. And I appreciate that." Lynn paused, already winded and they had not gone even a football field's length. "But it doesn't say anywhere in the rules that you have to walk with me. Just go at your own pace. Get to know one another!"

When Connor looked like he couldn't decide, Lynn said, "Donovan will be here with me soon. I won't walk alone."

"Well ... if you're okay with that ..."

Lynn gently pushed him.

"Go!" Then she turned toward Dara who was watching her with enormous brown eyes filled with indecision. "You, too, Dara. Get to know my son. Watch out that he doesn't want to create spreadsheets for you."

Grinning, Dara skipped to catch up with Connor. Lynn

watched them both walk away at a quick pace. When she could no longer see Connor's dark hair or the long braid that cascaded down Dara's back, she walked to the curb. It seemed like a long drop down to sit, but she knew she already needed rest.

This is my life now. I must accept the fact that I won't be able to walk quickly with anyone. That I will always feel exhausted. That others will treat me like an invalid.

Tears built up in Lynn's eyes as she considered the life that lay before her. Once again, she was grateful for large sunglasses.

God, I hate this.

"Hello, Peace."

Dark, dark eyes zeroed in on hers, the look one of concern, care, and something else that Lynn could not yet name. Exceptionally agile, Donovan plopped down next to her on the tiny curb. He allowed the silence to linger as they both watched the other walkers. Groups in pink tutus sauntered past, one of the women wearing a Survivor shirt, but also sporting fabric wings. Another group wore purple shirts with their family name on the back. The front proclaimed JUANITA'S TEAM for some; others said JESSIE'S TEAM.

"Multiple victims," Lynn murmured. Donovan just nodded and reached for her hand.

"Shall we walk?"

He pulled Lynn up to a standing position, kissed her lightly, and then let her take the first step up the hill. Lynn moved almost in slow motion, dragging her left foot so that it scraped along the roadway.

No ... my leg is not dragging. It's just my imagination.

Her balance was that of a person coming home after a long night of drinking – ragged, not straight. Occasionally, she shot out a hand as if trying to keep herself from falling. As she stumbled, Donovan shot his arms out as if to catch her.

"You okay?" he asked, concern coloring and quietening his voice.

"Fine, fine," Lynn answered, then looked up to say, "I sound like Asia Barber, don't I? And I'm probably young enough to be her daughter."

They made it up the hill. Lynn was about to sit down again when she noticed a group of protestors on the corner. Handmade signs were lifted high in the air while men and women taunted the passing walkers.

"Big Pharma is controlling your health!"

"Only holistic medicine will work!"

"God decides who lives, who does not! Make your peace with God!"

One defiant woman wearing a Survivor shirt strutted toward the group and began screaming, "What do you know about medication? Chemotherapy? Radiation?"

"You could've beat this if you tried something other than pharmaceutical companies' poisons," the big pharma protestor answered, lifting her handmade poster – a pill bottle with a slash line through it – higher.

Walking around them, Lynn could not avoid the exchanges.

Another Survivor yelled out, "Do you know what it's like to hear that if you don't do something *immediately*, you could die?"

"Doctors don't know everything!" came the response from another protestor.

Another Survivor came up behind the first two who had spoken.

"I pray every day. I'm a Catholic sister, a BVM. I still got cancer."

"You didn't pray well enough, sister," answered the man who'd been calling out about God's choice over cancer victims' deaths. He was staring at the nun with cold eyes. "You need to ask God for mercy now."

"And you do?" The older woman was defiant, forcing her way through the gawking walkers to face her accuser head-on. "Who are you to judge me? Last time I looked, only God passes down judgment."

The protestor, a tall, thin man wearing construction boots and jeans, with a bandana wrapped around his neck, was not backing down either.

"Maybe God has judged you. Maybe that's why you got cancer."

Lynn's heart began to beat faster, a knot growing in her throat.

What did I do to get this? Was I not careful enough? Should I have investigated alternative health care? I didn't have time! I trusted the doctors would know what to do.

As she continued her mental self-harassment, a gentle hand settled at her lower back, Donovan comforting her without knowing it. He urged her away from the crowd.

Another protestor began calling, "Eat only organic foods! No processed foods! No chemically altered substances!"

"Donovan!" Lynn had had enough. "Please. Help me get around this group."

She struggled to get far away, around the corner, her foot dragging, causing her to stumble.

Donovan took her arm and swung them well out and away from the growing group of angry walkers and loud protestors. When they were decently away, he continued to guide Lynn over to an empty bench.

"What was that shit?" he asked. He offered Lynn a water bottle. "People come out to do something decent – raise money to help research – and those idiots are making it into a protest gathering. How'd they even get into this event?"

Lynn took a sip of water, eyeing Donovan's hand grazing his hair roughly.

"Hey, my big savior," she said, "it takes all kinds." Then after sighing, she added, "When I was diagnosed, all I wanted was to get well and do whatever I had to do to get better. You don't have a lot of time to choose what to do."

They sat a brief time before Lynn decided to continue. As they started on the course again, she spied a tall, big, African American man wearing the pink shirt with Rue LA LA's logo. Desmond Davis, Donovan's bodyguard, was surveying everyone walking by.

"Desmond is here!"

"Yep," Donovan saluted him surreptitiously. "We can't get away from him. I told him to take the day off, but Len had other ideas. Insisted that Desmond come along. There are others here, too. We make it a big volunteer project for the entire company."

Lynn forced her concentration away from Desmond, trying to make sure that she put one foot firmly down before picking the other up. At the very top of the hill, she paused, looking around at the thinning group of participants. A woman with a walker strolled past. Lynn felt herself giving in to a pity party.

I can't even keep up with a walker.

Minutes later she stopped again, wondering if she could finish.

"Donovan, why don't you run ahead? I know I'm holding you back."

"I'm not going anywhere, Peace," he answered immediately. "I only came to this because you said you were going. I meant what I told the crowd earlier; I'm here for you all the way."

"And I appreciate that, I really do. But why? You could have your choice of women! Many of whom are far prettier, have more hair, and can keep up with you. And enjoy your lifestyle, too! And haven't been sick!" Lynn whipped her glasses off to wipe away the freely falling tears. "Why me?"

Donovan was not deterred.

"Peace ... I've told you before. You make my life calm. I enjoy being with you. I want to be with you! I wouldn't come to this thing just because the company is sponsoring it. I could go on a walk like this probably every month to represent Rue LA LA."

He grabbed both her hands, perhaps a bit too roughly.

"I'm here for you. What do I have to do to make you realize that?"

Lynn sighed, then leaned her head on his shoulder.

"I'm sorry, Donovan," she said. "I'm feeling sorry for myself today. I see all these energetic people and I'm not one of them. I just feel so tired all the time ..."

Donovan put his hand under her chin, lifting her face to look into ocean-blue eyes.

"I know you're trying ... and I know you like your doctor ... but what if you were to get a second opinion? Maybe there's something else that the doc you have hasn't thought of?"

Instead of answering, Lynn stood up, dusted off her bottom, and began the walk down the hill. As the road flattened out, she paused yet again. There was only one other set of walkers, laughing and teasing one another about being one of the last groups to make it past the finish line. Lynn paused again, placing both hands on her thighs, bending over to catch her breath.

"Lynn." Donovan was now entirely businesslike, "Do you want me to have Desmond bring the car here?"

Lifting her head to look up at Donovan, Lynn saw the worry that covered his face.

How will I even make it a few more feet let alone to the end?

She caught sight of the race officials, their shirts saying *Security*, eyeing her with concern, talking into their walkie-talkies.

"Lynn?" Donovan's tone insisted that she answer him. "Tell me what you want to do here."

"Call Desmond, please. I don't think I can make it any farther."

"Hang on. I'll ask these guys if he can drive up here."

As he walked over to the officials, Lynn took off her hat, running her hand through the sweaty, short blond strands, wondering if she'd be able to sleep once Desmond brought the car. She watched Donovan nod at the officials, then raise his phone to his ear.

I am such a wimp.

Ending his call, Donovan was all smiles as he walked back to the curb where she'd seated herself.

"Sorry about that," Lynn said.

I'm just relieved it's over.

"I suppose I'm the last one, right?"

Before he could answer, Donovan's phone rang. Lynn noticed Dara's name on the Caller ID.

"Dara? Oh, Connor; sorry," Donovan said. "Yeah, she's fine; just exhausted. Desmond is bringing the car from the lot. Yeah, do you want to talk to her?"

He handed the phone to Lynn.

"Hi, Connor," Lynn said. After a pause, she continued, "Yeah sure seems like it. Ok. Later. Love you."

Donovan couldn't resist asking, "Seems like what?"

Lynn played with the brim of her hat before she answered. "Seems like I'm never going to be like I was."

Chapter 16

A month later Lynn thought that perhaps her stamina was better. A little. She was still tired, but there were brief flashes of time where she had more energy. For once she was eager to attend a music awards show with Donovan. After Bea's beauty crew left her home, Lynn felt the soft folds of the fabric as it slid over her legs, then once again admired the intricate beading and coloring.

Now, this dress I really like!

At first, she wasn't too sure that someone her age could get away with this bateau neckline, but Bea made it work. Even though the dress was sleeveless – something Lynn teased Bea about – the neckline banded around the top of her arms while the body of the dress flared down to an almost bell-like long hemline with a short train. The color cascaded from a light blue at her neck to a navy blue at her feet.

Donovan had insisted on purchasing this gown, saying that she needed to be *really* dressed up at this event as it was one of the biggest music awards programs of the year, and there was to be a red carpet. Lynn didn't think much about it until Bea came for one last fitting.

"Now, when you're on that red carpet, you'll want to twirl around to show off the ombre," Bea instructed. "And we have to make sure that Max goes all out on makeup."

"All out?" Lynn was surprised. "I don't do much makeup, Bea."

"This is different," Bea instructed. "This is a bigger show; fancier. They take a ton of pictures. You will be with Donovan Rue

– his arm candy, so to speak. And you'll be wearing my design. You need to look especially beautiful."

When the doorbell rang, she jumped as if she'd been caught doing something immature.

Donovan was just as dressed up; his tux was the one he wore for Music Extravaganza. It was conservative yet fit him well and showed off a body that he kept fit.

"Hello, Peace."

He gave her an admiring glance. Lynn obliged him with another twirl.

"You seem very upbeat tonight," He said as Lynn settled into place, facing him. "Are you ready, Cinderella?"

Lynn took his offered arm.

"You're very handsome, too," she said as she exited the house and walked toward the limo. Desmond was standing at the open door, greeting her with a "Hello, Miss Lynn."

Lynn slid all the way over on the seat, allowing Donovan some room.

I'm feeling amazing tonight!

Aloud she teased Donovan, "Finally over trying to hide your wealth from me?"

"Oh!" His sudden outburst caught Lynn off guard. "Thanks for reminding me," Donovan said as he pushed his hand into one of the tux's hidden pockets. "Almost forgot!"

Lynn gasped as he handed her a red box with Cartier scrawled across the top. She glanced at the box, then at Donovan, then back at the box.

After I told him that all this stuff was too ostentatious, he gives me something this nice.

"Open it."

It would be rude to say that I didn't want it. Lying, too.

She flipped open the lid to reveal a beautiful diamond cuff.

"Donovan…"

"I know you don't have one of these. A little birdy told me."

"Someone whose name begins with a B and ends with an A?"

"I'm not giving up anyone's name!"

Donovan held his hands up in guilt, then reached for the box.

"Let me help you adjust it."

They held hands as they traveled to LA for the event, Lynn glancing down at the three-inch cuff on her wrist, moving to catch the occasional streetlamp's light. As they neared the Staples Center, and the streets became more congested, Lynn settled into a tight bundle of nerves, holding on to Donovan's hand for strength.

"Don't worry," Donovan said. "We'll leave as soon as we can."

Desmond followed more limousines as they lined up to release their patrons. When it was their turn to be let loose, Desmond threw the car into park, then rounded to the passenger's side to open the door for the couple.

"Ready?" Donovan asked.

He stepped out, smiling warmly at the crowd, then extended his hand to Lynn. Smiling back, Lynn glanced at the throng of people waiting for them, unsure of what to do. There was not a lot of clapping or noise on their behalf and she was glad of it. Then a person approached them

"Mr. Rue? I'm Nicole. I'm here to help you this evening," she said. "And this must be Lynn Cerami? Am I saying that correctly?"

She looked at a clipboard. Lynn, overwhelmed by the crowd, simply nodded at Nicole who motioned to a spot on the red carpet. Donovan placed his hand gently on Lynn's waist and steered her toward the spot.

If he's noticed my heartbeat is racing, he isn't acknowledging it.

They stood together, cameras flashing from all sides. At the last minute, Lynn remembered Bea's instructions about twirling her skirt, so at the next spot Nicole pointed them to, Lynn did a short, flirty twirl.

Almost a dance move!

Cameras flashed away as she moved gracefully back to a smiling Donovan.

"Well done," he purred as he escorted her to the next spot. "You're a natural at this."

"Mr. Rue?" Nicole was at their sides again. "NBC wants a short interview. Are you ready?"

Again, that strong hand was at her waist, guiding Lynn to a slightly raised small platform where an elegantly dressed, popular television anchor stood. The blonde's façade was impeccable, done for the cameras. Lynn was glad that Bea had insisted on getting the makeup done a little heavier this evening although the heat of the cameras made it feel as if the makeup was melting off.

"And who are you wearing this evening?" the anchor asked as the interview with Donovan was winding down. Lynn startled a bit when she realized that the woman was addressing her, not Donovan.

"Beatrice Owens," came the ready and proud answer.

"Oh!" As she exclaimed, the anchor turned toward the camera with a surprised look, then back at Lynn. "Are you the infamous Lynn that the Lynn Dress is named for?" she asked.

Lynn was surprised.

A dress has my name on it? When did that happen?

When she stalled with her answer, Donovan came to the rescue.

"She is," he said firmly, then guided Lynn away as the anchor was stating her thanks for the interview.

They continued into a beautifully decorated ballroom.

"Hard to believe a Sports Center could ever look this nice, isn't it?" Donovan said as he watched her take it all in.

Lynn took a second away from all the auditory and visual intake of the event to look at Donovan. Large almost-black eyes shone with happiness as he moved them throughout the stylized arena.

Lynn knew that the set was all constructed to make the Staples Center look nothing like a sports venue. It was bold blues and shiny chromes, with special fabric stretched taut behind the stage.

Projections of the nominated musicians, their names and categories, scrolled on two huge jumbotrons on either side of the stage.

The tables were also decorated with blue and silver, the chairs and silverware a beautiful, highly polished chrome.

Bea knew what the color scheme was going to be – again. Explains why I match.

Unlike Music Extravaganza, this event had numerous film cameras and crew stationed all over. Lynn could never tell when they were directly focused on Donovan and herself, but she noticed that some people were making faces at the cameras, some showing off their clothing.

He pointed at Asia Barber's white-flowered head bopping from table to table.

"Can't remember the last time Miss Asia won anything," he added, "but here she is. She's here to support Exeter."

Certain that Lynn had no idea who Exeter was, Donovan glanced down at his date before stating, "Exeter. We hope he wins the best male entertainer tonight."

Lynn's head went back as Exeter stood to greet Asia Barber. Asia placed her hand on the young man's arm before wrapping her arm around him and accepting a kiss on her cheek.

"They seem close," Lynn murmured as she watched Exeter pull out a chair for the older woman.

"They are. He's like a son to her," Donovan said, then grinned while remembering his own description of his relationship with Asia Barber. "Another son! Asia's helped him tremendously. She couldn't have found anyone more grateful to her for all her care."

Lynn now turned back to her own tall, handsome date who motioned toward their chairs.

FOLLOWING A SCRUMPTIOUS MEAL, THE AWARDS STARTED. DONOVAN was there to support his stars, standing, fiercely clapping when Exeter was announced as recipient of the expected award. Another Rue LA LA female star won an award in the gospel music category. That woman paid the production company high compliments and mentioned Donovan by name.

I need to ask Donovan who she is. I really am bad at knowing celebrities.

After the awards, curtains were drawn back to showcase two more rooms created specifically for dancing - one for modern dancing, one for more of a mixture. Donovan steered his date toward the latter, saying, "C'mon, Peace. Let's dance a bit." As he directed her toward the middle of the floor, he asked, "Do you dance?"

Lynn played along. "I do, but it's been a while."

The music began quietly. All around them couples were slow dancing, relaxing into one another, relieved that the cameras were not allowed to enter their private celebration. Donovan pulled Lynn in close. She reached her arm around his back, then placed the other hand over his heart. Lynn marveled at the handsome, strong man who held her so securely in his arms. No one else existed for either of them at that moment. No music, no people, no spectacular decorations. They looked into one another's eyes and swayed. They were only Lynn and Donovan; nothing else mattered.

I don't even think about how to dance. My body is just following his so perfectly. Like we were made to dance together.

"Donovan," Lynn's eyes sparkled in the beautifully created low lighting. "I feel so wonderful when I'm with you." She turned her head down as if shy. His fingers went beneath her chin, tilting her face to look up at him.

"I love looking at these blue eyes," he whispered.

"I'm crazy about you," Lynn whispered back. "It's almost scary ..."

He bent his head down to lightly kiss her, then surprised her by pushing her gently back into the crowd and pivoting her around. Not deliberate, yet the twirl showed off the dress as Bea intended with Lynn's unconsciously graceful movements making it highly noticeable.

The music finished as Lynn ended up back in Donovan's arms. After three dances, Lynn began to drag, her newfound energy depleting as the night deepened. Fighting the rising exhaustion, she continued to dance, but her steps were less confident, her feet lagging behind Donovan's.

It's like I'm Cinderella. I have a timer that says, "only three dances, then rest."

Donovan noticed right away that she was having difficulty keeping up.

"Let's go home," he whispered in her ear. She did not take much convincing. As they walked toward the exit, people nodded to Donovan and called out to Lynn, "Love your dress!"

"I NEED SOME WATER," LYNN SAID ONCE THEY REACHED DONOVAN'S home. She kicked off her heels, heading for the kitchen. Even in the soft glow of the pendulum lights that Marisol had left on for them, her dress sparkled and swished with each step. Following Lynn, Donovan paused in the doorway to watch his beautiful date tilt her head back as she drank water at the kitchen sink. She was gazing out the window where the light of the moon reflected off the ocean, the waves subdued for the moment.

Suddenly, Donovan was overwhelmed with feeling, struggling to hold back.

I want her all the time. I don't want to worry about details like whose house will we be in tonight? What will the kids think? What if the media finds out? Who the hell should care?

Then he couldn't help himself. He crossed the kitchen quickly, silently. When he reached the sink, Donovan wrapped his arms around Lynn, snuggling into her neck, inhaling the fragrance that was Lynn, spice, sweetness.

Peace. She's peace. This is what I've been missing.

Gasping, Lynn placed her hands atop his. Tilting her head back again, she felt his lips on her neck, gently kissing her behind her ears.

"God, that feels so good," she whispered.

When he stopped, she slowly turned around, then placed her mouth gently against his.

"Lynn," he whispered once they stopped to breathe, "Lynn, I love you."

She met his mouth in another fervent kiss. The kiss grew in urgency with Donovan becoming more demanding in his quest for the feeling, intimacy, and peace he wanted. He placed his hands around her upper arms, lifted her, then twirled the two of them around, setting her on the larger center island countertop. Lynn moaned as she felt his need but was unable to do anything other than ride through the moment.

Donovan's hands went to her skirt, pushing it up to her waist, then pulling her panties down and off. Donovan was frantically pushing away the full skirt, pulling her legs apart. Not protesting, Lynn ran her hands through the curly head in front of her, watching as Donovan bent his head toward counter level settling his tongue on her, circling her sensitive center.

Donovan could not have stopped if he wanted to. His pants were uncomfortable, tight with his own arousal, but he didn't stop. He wanted this moment with Lynn, wanted her to know that he would always put her needs first – before his own. He briefly reached up to Lynn's shoulder, gently pushing her back so that he had more control over his own motions. Lynn obliged, closing her eyes as she canted her arms back on the granite. If she saw his hand moving toward her breast, she didn't stop him. Pushing the sparkly band off her shoulder, he tugged the top of the dress downward until he could cup her left breast, the one she considered damaged.

Reverently, Donovan caressed this breast, not knowing what he would find. At first, it was just a breast, the same soft tissue that all women have, the same areola that tightened when aroused. Then he felt an indentation in the middle. He resisted the urge to finger it so that Lynn would not feel self-conscious. Succeeding, he continued the gentle kneading as he continued soft licks.

Bracing herself on the cool countertop, Lynn could do little other than let the sensations build and build. The ferocity of her orgasm almost caused her to lose purchase on the hard stone, and she grabbed Donovan's hair as she let go, screaming his name in delight.

A few seconds later, he had her wrapped in his arms, carrying her to his bedroom. After placing her on the bed, he began to undress. The only light continued to come from the kitchen, normal when Lynn was over. He could hear her unzip her dress, then stand and pull it over her head which took some doing since he had pulled the front aside forcefully enough that part of her was already outside the garment. Once naked, she laid flat on the bed. Before Donovan could finish undressing, she leaned over to the lamp and turned it on. It was not a high-powered bulb but certainly bright enough that Donovan could see the body he had been making love to in the dark for the several weeks.

Hesitating momentarily, he looked into Lynn's lust-filled eyes and whispered, "You are gorgeous."

Lynn smiled back, answering, "Thank you."

He sat down next to her and began to caress her arms in a fluid motion from shoulder to hand, slow in movement. As she shivered in response, Lynn watched him gaze at her with obvious delight. She was enjoying her view too. When he wore the indie band t-shirts he loved so much, Donovan's muscles rippled when he walked. Now those muscles were in full sight. There wasn't any extraneous skin; he was in perfect, fit shape. His eyes were shiny, full of expectation, as she took his hands and pulled him to her.

The night would last a long time.

WANDERING DOWN HIS BACKYARD STONE STEPS THE NEXT MORNING, Donovan knew that he'd find Lynn facing the ocean. She loved water, loved gazing at the lapping ocean waves. He had caught her contemplating the ocean more than once, sometimes with a slight smile, sometimes with misty eyes if unhidden by her sunglasses. Today her increasing smile urged him to come nearer.

I've won!

He almost felt jubilant, glad that the specter of Michael Cerami's ghost was dissipating.

"Morning, Peace," he called.

"And to you," she replied. After settling on the beach towel, Donovan leaned in for a kiss, then prepared for another round of Twenty Questions, knowing that Lynn might have a few questions about last night.

"So, Exeter won."

"Yup," Donovan smiled at the thought. "He deserved that win."

"And now I know who he is," Lynn said. "But who is the winner of that gospel music award?"

"Melissa August?"

"Yeah," Lynn smiled back as Donovan shook her head. "I know, I know; I don't know many artists' names. But I haven't listened to much gospel music."

"One trip to a black church should cure that," he replied. He started to scoop sand.

"And who's Larry Knightly?"

Donovan stiffened at the name. His Lynn may not know the names of celebrities, but she was quite astute at keeping track of industry gossip. Last night's event was filled with conversations that were about more than just congratulating winners.

After making a face, he replied, "He owns Aristotle, another music entertainment group. Similar, but not quite as good as Rue LA LA."

Donovan hoped that would end the conversation. It did not.

"Of course, it's not as good," Lynn smiled at his arrogance. "So, what's going on with him?"

Her sunglasses hid her eyes, the one part of her face that gave everything away.

"C'mon," she urged. "I know you probably know. Something to do with 'morality clauses' is what I heard last night. Lots of whispers about that, contracts, and I even heard someone say, 'I wonder who's next?' Is there more than one guy that this is happening to? Whatever this is?"

Donovan sighed, threw a fistful of sand toward the shoreline, then eyed Lynn.

"We can't just let this one go?"

"No," she said succinctly. "It's Twenty Questions. And I really want to know what it's about."

Donovan placed both hands in the sand and pushed it forward, forming a little hill. Just as quickly, he smashed the hill and dragged the sand back toward his body. After he'd made and destroyed the hill two or three times, he finally looked up at Lynn.

"You've heard about all the executives, stars, anchors who've been accused of sexual harassment, right?"

"The *Me Too* movement? Yeah. Can't miss hearing about it; it's all over the news, social media ..."

"Larry Knightly just got accused by five women who've worked for him. The news was released right before last night's show started. That's why he didn't show."

Lynn pulled her glasses off, her eyes wide with what appeared to be horror.

"Another one?"

"Yeah," Donovan said. "Another exec. Right before I met you someone else was charged. Anyone in the entertainment world is subject to scrutiny."

"Scary stuff?"

Donovan shrugged. "It can be if you're accused wrongly. It can ruin a person's reputation. Remember that TV anchor who got accused?"

"Lionel Markeson? I do remember him because my parents watched him every night," Lynn readjusted her glasses. "I couldn't believe that he did what the woman was accusing him of. What happened to him?"

"Nothing that I know of," Donovan replied while making yet another hill. "He made very strong statements against the woman's accusations, demanded proof, and then things just went quiet."

He looked up at Lynn as he pulled another hill down.

"I'd like to think that he was wronged. He seemed like such a decent guy," Lynn said.

"Me, too!" Donovan said. "I hate to think that people can get away with ruining a good man's name."

He stood suddenly, held his hands out to Lynn to assist her in joining him. It took her a while to move from sitting to getting on her side, to finally grabbing his hands. Then, he practically pulled her body off the ground.

"You, okay?" he asked with concern.

Lynn smirked. "So far, today has felt like one of the energy-less days of the last few months. I'm more tired today than I was all last week." Lynn glanced at a loud ocean wave, then said, "But I did have a big night, or morning. Makes sense to be tired."

"And this balance thing?"

"Just part of getting old, I think." Lynn was dusting her own clothes. "One more of my Twenty Questions?"

"I'm really hungry, Peace –"

"One more!" She held up one finger and waited until Donovan

looked at her expectantly. "Is there any possibility that some woman could accuse you?"

The million-dollar question ... literally.

As he raked his hand through his hair, Donovan snorted and then answered, "No! But if there's someone out there who wants to destroy me ..." He shook his head.

Lynn placed her hand on his chest. "I have no reason to ask this, but ..."

"You want to know if I have anything in my past that could come back to haunt me?"

Lynn rubbed her fingers on his chest and although he couldn't see her eyes, Donovan knew that she was embarrassed and maybe afraid to ask the question. But she had.

"Look, Lynn," he paused for a moment then took both of her hands in his, pulling them to his chest. "I have never forced a woman to sleep with me. I don't believe in hitting women – or anyone for that matter! I have never told a new singer that if she fucked me, she would get further in the industry. I have tried most of my life – since Dara's mother left us – to be careful about who I was with."

He stopped for a breath and Lynn wrapped her arms around his shoulders.

"I'm sorry; I should know better."

"Well, we're still learning about each other," he said, then mumbled, "I guess I thought you'd trust me by now."

"I do!" Lynn gave Donovan a big hug. "All that talk last night, you know, I'm not used to it. I just ... I just ..." Her eyes went out to the ocean. "I guess I just need to know."

"Lynn." Placing his own sunglasses atop his head, Donovan took her chin, gently forcing her to look at him. Before he spoke, he removed her glasses and placed them in the short blond curls. "Since I started working for Rue, I have tried to maintain good character. I wanted my father to be proud of me. I *still* want my father to see that I'm more than that wild-ass young man I was before he forced me to straighten up."

Lynn's eyes were starting to tear as he neared the end of the short speech.

"Can you trust me on this?"

He knew his own eyes were showing fear. Fear that one person could accuse him of something that could ruin his company, his family, and his relationship with Lynn. As he continued to stare into her concerned eyes, Lynn raised up on tippy toes and kissed him.

"I can do that," she replied. "But you've got to feed me first."

Chapter 17

*A*fter such a nice weekend Lynn knew her office would be the opposite. Exhaustion returned with Lynn hitting the alarm clock repeatedly for more sleep time. She knew that she'd be closing her office door to catch a quick nap.

One of Lynn's main responsibilities during Cassie's month-long hiatus was to coordinate orientation. Each summer she coordinated with other campus offices that sent representatives to orientation.

Sitting down to look the agenda over, Cassie immediately got angry.

"Did you wait until the last minute to do this?" Her screams were loud enough for the entire office to hear. "You had a month to do this."

Then with an angry stroke of a red pen, she went through the agenda line by line, taking out what she didn't like and restructuring the agenda to suit her own needs. Lynn stood up wearily, ready to go back to the drawing board. Again.

"Are the binders done for Peer Mentor training?" Cassie asked as Lynn got to the doorway.

"Yes. They were done before you left."

"Well, at least that's done," came the brusque retort. "Now go re-do those agendas."

Back and forth went the agendas, all day long. When it was finally ready to print, Lynn acknowledged that Cassie had indeed straightened it out.

Why am I having so much trouble with these agendas this year?

Relieved that one iteration remained red ink-free, Lynn went to print it out at her desk. A ping from her computer told her that she had an incoming message from Dylan, a student assistant in Student Life.

Olsen Hall is not available for you next Friday.

Lynn stood, leaving the agenda behind, going immediately to the student planning center. Inside that office, six students were planning various aspects of the domestic students' orientation program alongside three of Lynn's much younger colleagues. Lynn entered, calling out, "Dylan! You better be joking about me not being able to have Olsen Hall for orientation. I have that hall every year!"

Dylan, a slight, nerdy-looking student, peered up at her.

"Angela has that room booked," he said.

Lynn barely waited for him to finish speaking.

"Angela books every room on campus for orientation!" Lynn was fuming, her pent-up anger over the impossible agendas scratched out in Cassie's bold red ink becoming hot as dragon fire toward this poor student. "I always get her okay to use Olsen. I got it last May!"

Dylan's confidence was beginning to crumble.

"Well, I'll check again, but …"

"Good! You check."

Lynn left the room, hearing a door slam behind her, not even aware that her rough attempts at closure caused the noise.

"DID YOU YELL AT A STUDENT?"

Cassie came into her office an hour later, a rare visit from someone who thought her own office a throne room.

"What?"

Lynn looked up from inserting the dreaded agenda into new student welcome folders.

"Of course not. You know I would never do that, Cassie."

Cassie looked a little relieved.

"Good. Last thing I want on my first day back is drama!" She paused to straighten her peasant top. "The big boss called; said he got several complaints about you yelling at students. I told them that wasn't like you at all, that they must be wrong."

Lynn, troubled by the accusation, tried to smile. She managed to say, "Thank you for standing up for me."

LYNN DIDN'T EVEN HAVE HER THINGS PUT AWAY THE NEXT MORNING when Cassie called out, "LLLLYYYYNNNNN? We're going to Grounds. We need to talk."

When they reached the campus coffee shop, Cassie declined any coffee while Lynn ordered a lemonade. Sitting down in a booth, Cassie sighed.

"Tell me what to do with you, Lynn!" she said loudly, people around her taking steps to the side to avoid the thunderbolts aimed at Lynn. Lynn remained quiet, not sure what to say.

"You don't seem to care anymore about your job," Cassie went on. "Is it grief – still? You have to be over all the effects of cancer treatment; it's been a year since it ended. You really need to just let it all go."

She plopped a manila folder on the booth top, then cried out, "God, I hate drama, especially just coming back from my vacation!" She let out another loud sigh, then said, "So what do I do with you, Lynn?"

A wave of exhaustion and despair rolled over Lynn. Her already sleep-deprived body ached with physical pain, her mind acknowledging that now it, too, was falling apart.

Gotta save this. I can't end my career at Brandstone this way. Fight! Fight, damn it.

"I love my job," Lynn said. "I'm not sure what happened yesterday. I'm sorry."

"You have a funny way of showing it," Cassie said, again loud enough for those around them to cast not-quite-surreptitious glances at their booth. "Look, if you keep making mistakes at work, I'm going to have to start documenting them. I can't keep doing your job and my job. I have too much to do now that I'm back. I depended on you to have that agenda done and I spent most of yesterday fixing it. I didn't hire you to have to constantly monitor you."

LEN WALKED INTO DONOVAN'S OFFICE AND SLAMMED SOME paperwork on his desk, an action so unlike him that Donovan was startled.

"What's this?" he asked, pointing at the skewed pile.

"This," said Len as he waved his hand toward the stack, "is a lawsuit from Roy Alloy. He's alleging that we didn't publicize his last album enough, that we aren't supporting him per his contract."

Donovan looked from the paperwork up to an angry Len. He'd never seen him so angry, his dark face bright. He looked like he could either murder someone or die of a heart attack.

Flattening his hands on Donovan's desk, Len locked eyes with Donovan before saying, "This guy is shit, man."

"Okay, okay," Donovan went into soothing mode, worried that his friend would drop dead in front of him.

Not another one. No way could I handle that.

"Let's get our expensive legal team on this. If necessary, we counter-sue."

Len settled down, nodded his agreement with the course of action, then removed his hands from Donovan's desk. Still looking directly at his younger boss, Len asked, "You still seeing that Lynn?"

Donovan smiled, relieved that Len's skin tone was receding to its normal shade.

"As often as possible," he answered.

"Bringing her to that charity thing next week?"

"Yeah," Donovan answered then saw that Len's eyes were full of worry. "So?"

"So, I'm worried about a scene Roy might make there, worried that your Lynn might be an object for him to terrorize. He likes to single people out. You know that; he's done it with you."

"I can handle it."

"I know *you* can," Len said, "but can Lynn? You told me she's not used to this."

Donovan felt his own anger rising at the idea of anyone – *anyone* – upsetting his Peace.

"Just let him try," he said with ice in his voice.

Chapter 18

The column-style gown that Bea designed for the charity event was not Lynn's favorite. A gown of bright red with an embroidered cape that fell gently over her shoulders and down to the floor, Lynn found the color garish, the material old. Removing the cape revealed a cap-sleeved, Queen Anne-neckline with a bodice that gathered under the bust and then falling severe and straight to the floor. Lynn felt obligated to wear the piece to the charity event for disabled and retired performers. Unofficially, she was the representative for The Lynn Line of Beatrice Owens' clothing.

How did this happen? I wore two, three pieces, and now it's a Line?

Agitation about the dress and another awful workday, didn't help Lynn's mood. Connor didn't help when he called to see if he could cook her dinner, found out Lynn had a date, and went ballistic.

"Again? You see him too much, Mom."

After throwing back three painkillers in yet another bid to get rid of now constant headaches, Lynn knew she needed to take Connor to task about his views on her dating life.

"What is it you have against him, Connor?" she demanded. "Or do you just not want me to date at all? Or are you certain that no one will ever measure up to your father?"

When there was pronounced silence on the other side of the phone call, Lynn went further.

"Look, I'm a big girl. I know good guys and bad guys. Donovan Rue is a good guy."

"Maybe …"

More silence. Lynn imagined Michael's clone sitting in his dull apartment, nothing to do but work on computers and wait for hockey to start up again. No brother in town to hang out with; no father to talk about his future. Grim. Intense. That was Connor.

Calming down, Lynn said, "You know that your father is irreplaceable, don't you? I'm not looking for his replacement. I'm not looking for anyone."

Lynn rubbed her forehead, right above her right eye.

"I'm not dating to be disloyal to him, or to hurt you and Owen. I'm trying to find some happiness – some peace – for myself. My life was pretty shitty before Donovan came into it."

A growl came from the other end of the line. Lynn knew this meant that Connor had heard but didn't necessarily agree.

"And I'm not old, Connor," Lynn took a deep breath, her tone still soft, motherly. "I'm enjoying Donovan's company and for the most part, enjoying being with him even at these events. So," her tone turned pleading, "can you just be glad for me?"

When he didn't answer, Lynn asked, "And pray that I have enough energy to make it through tonight's event."

"You're tired again?" Connor sounded contrite mixed with worried. "I thought you had some energy last week – that it was finally coming back."

"No. Yes. I don't know," Lynn reached up to run a hand through her hair, then stopped when she remembered that it had been styled for the evening. "Yes, I'm tired all the time, work is awful, and my balance is worse than it's ever been."

She knew she was whining, but she couldn't stop.

"And I have this awful red dress that Bea designed. I hate it. But I figure I gotta wear it … and another awful, formal night with people falling all over Donovan while I stand off to the side trying to stay awake while I'm dead on my feet!"

There was another moment of silence. Lynn knew that she'd stunned Connor.

Used to moan to Michael, never Connor.

"Geez, mom," came the deep voice on the phone. "Maybe you ought to stay home tonight. He can go by himself, I'm sure."

LATER THAT EVENING DONOVAN ESCORTED LYNN TO THE CAR, slowly. Extremely slowly. He was alarmed at how tired she'd appeared, more than he'd ever witnessed. When she almost tripped walking toward the limo, his concern ratcheted.

The balance thing isn't new or unusual. But is her right foot dragging? No, that's my imagination, I'm sure ...

"You're beat tonight, aren't you?"

Concerned as he looked to those blue eyes that lately seemed to be losing all brilliance, Donovan wondered what he could do to help, what he should say.

"I'll be fine," she snapped at him.

Donovan was trying to justify all the alarming things he was seeing in Lynn. Even at her healthiest, Lynn couldn't walk a straight line. But the crabby mannerisms were something new for him. And the walking seemed worse tonight. Something was very, very off.

He watched, worried, as she focused on making it to the car. Getting inside, she leaned her head against the backrest, flashed the first fake smile Donovan had ever seen from her, and said hello politely to Desmond before lapsing into complete silence.

After an entirely silent ride to downtown Los Angeles, Desmond dropped the couple at a grand hotel's entrance. No red carpet here, but still they had a long walk into the event, the carpet cordoned off by red velvet ropes. Paparazzi were held behind the line, snatching pictures of celebrities as they made their way inside. Donovan was shaking everyone's hand but holding onto Lynn's waist as well, afraid to let her go. He could sense her irritation as her body stiffened, then tried to pull away from him. As

Lynn finally escaped his grasp, a gorgeous, very recognizable woman approached them.

"Dymettra," Donovan acknowledged as she approached, trying to maintain his calmness as Lynn stood off to the side.

Donovan watched Dymettra's seduction of the press. Dymettra stood, her best side facing the photogs, giving Donovan her cheek for a kiss. He gave the briefest buzz possible, but only so the media didn't write photo captions to imply that he was seeing her again, or that could imply Rue LA LA was upset with another one of its stars. As she pulled herself away from Donovan's face, Dymettra looked at Lynn, running her eyes top to bottom before motioning a well-manicured finger up and down Lynn's frame.

"Who's this?" she asked.

"Dymettra," Donovan said, "this is my friend Lynn."

"Oh!" Dymettra paused to smile at one of the photographers. Then she looked at Lynn directly. "The Lynn of the Lynn line, right? Another Beatrice Owens number?"

Unsure of how to handle this megawatt personality, Lynn answered simply, "Yes."

"Her things are old hat," Dymettra shot out, flicking her hand in a casual, dismissive manner. "No one wears that grand bitch's clothes anymore."

Lynn's face was becoming as red as her dress.

"Well, I do," she shot back.

As Dymettra began to laugh, Donovan started moving Lynn away from her.

"Time for drinks!" he announced.

They escaped into the ballroom, free of Dymettra's grasp. As soon as Donovan got himself a scotch and Lynn a sparkling water, Roy Alloy marched over to them. Again, he was dressed shabbily, as if to snub the event, the industry, even the charity itself.

"Well if it ain't Donovan Rue and his lady."

Donovan watched as the second pair of dark eyes seemed to undress his date.

First Dymettra's assessing look, now Roy's carnal overview.

"That's enough!" Donovan became the dominant force. "Apologize."

Roy laughed.

"Hardly 'enough', bro. You owe me for that last record deal and until we get that straightened out, it ain't enough."

Roy gulped his drink, then started walking away. At the last moment, he turned to Lynn, leaned down, and said, "I don't ever apologize for nothin', lady."

Lynn grabbed Donovan's hand. Donovan was grateful for her grasp, realizing that it prevented him from throwing a punch. Another sense told him that Lynn was being supportive. A third idea was that she was simply upset by the rudeness.

Roy sauntered away, his grin fueled by one too many drinks and an encounter he seemed to think he'd won.

"Sorry," Donovan placed his glass down and put his other hand over Lynn's shoulder. "I wish we could leave now, but I have a speech to give, you know."

"Yes," Lynn looked grim. "I know."

They sat through another uncomfortable dinner. Their table partners included a new star named Denise, her boyfriend Terryl, Len and Cassandra, and an older artist called Ernest Lahoy. The conversation was contentious with neither musician understanding the other's genre or generation. It didn't seem to matter to the artists that the head of their music production company and his second were seated with them. They groused and groaned throughout the meal.

Lynn sat there, mute. Try as he would to bring up a neutral topic that Lynn might help feed along, Donovan could not pull Lynn out of her sullenness. She played with her food and when he did ask her questions concerning a topic, it was as if Lynn wasn't there. She threw one-word answers at him. She seemed unable to follow along.

And she appeared tired. So tired. Her fatigue overwhelmed

everything about her – the beautiful dress, the precious jewels, the stylized hair – everything looked drawn, drained, lifeless.

Donovan knew that her mind had grown more clouded with extreme exhaustion. He saw the melancholy take hold each time she withered from lack of energy. He recalled that after the cancer walk, she'd said, *"No one told me that this is what happens to cancer patients. All you hear about are the huge success stories, or about those who died young. Not stories of how those who do survive can't function like they used to."*

Despite his growing concern over Lynn's uncharacteristically rude behavior, Donovan gave a wonderful speech. He spoke of the contributions retiring musicians made to the industry, relating some of the stories of his father promoting these great men and women. After a huge round of applause, he headed back to the table. Lynn had wilted even further.

We gotta get out of here.

"Ready to go?" he asked trying to keep the rising alarm out of his voice and off his face.

"Let me visit the bathroom," Lynn said. She picked up her clutch and slowly wandered away. It was all Donovan could do not to follow her and make sure she didn't fall.

"DID YOU SEE THE GET-UP SHE HAD ON?" CAME THE NOW-FAMILIAR voice of Dymettra.

An unfamiliar laugh, then someone answered, "Well, everyone knows that some women got no style."

"Some white women you mean."

"Girl! You did not just say that."

Cackling laughter echoed all over the room.

"Yeah, but Bea Owens dressed her," a voice said. "You'd think Bea would want her clothes to look good no matter who wore them."

"And this woman, ain't she Bea's best friend or somethin'?"

"Well, ain't no way that bitch could look good," a third voice contributed. "She's skinny, has no sparkle, and that hair!"

"Oooh! That hair is not good on her!"

"And what's a man as fine as Donovan Rue doing with a skinny white woman anyway? Can't he find a beautiful black woman to take to this? Gotta settle for Bea Owens' friends?"

Dymettra's voice registered louder than the other women. "He can't find a woman as good as me!"

More cackling. Lynn had had enough. She came out of her stall. Several women looked chagrinned and hastened out of the room. Dymettra stood there, proud, triumphant, beautiful. They stared at each other, Dymettra appearing strong, proud while Lynn felt drained, weak.

"What?" Dymettra snapped when she couldn't stand the silence any longer. "You know it's all true! You are no match for a man like Donovan Rue."

She turned away from Lynn's gaze, looking into the mirror while patting her hair. Then digging her knife deeper, Dymettra added, "It was good when he and I were together."

Lynn struggled to swallow back sudden tears.

Donovan was with this woman?

Just the thought of Donovan with this she-bitch was more than she could handle.

"What is it you don't like about me?" she asked, finally finding some words. "The fact that I'm white?"

Dymettra turned away from the mirror, facing her opponent.

"That, and the fact that you don't belong in this world. Face it: you are ignorant of what goes on in Donovan Rue's world – all of it."

Lynn glanced down at the ground. Afraid to say anything more, she clutched her purse close to her chest and started toward the door.

Dymettra grabbed her arm.

"Admit it! You don't belong here!"

With what little strength she had left, Lynn pulled herself out of Dymettra's grasp and ran out the bathroom door.

As the restroom door slammed shut, Asia Barber exited her stall and made her way to the sink area where Dymettra was once again patting her hair. Their eyes met in the mirror, Dymettra's smug with success, Asia's angry, cool.

"You think you did good calling that woman out?" Asia asked, keeping her voice even and calm.

Dymettra broke her eyes away, snorted before answering, "Doesn't matter one way or another. Just spoke my truth is all."

"Your truth?" Finished with drying her hands, Asia turned toward the younger woman. "Do you think speaking the truth, breaking someone's heart, is the right thing to do?'

"In this case, yes." Dymettra picked up her small black bag. "And what's it to you anyway? You don't know that woman."

Asia shook her head but continued to stare at Dymettra, then finally turned away from it.

"I know that Donovan Rue loves her. That she's been through some horrible medical treatment and is still recovering from it. That her husband died about a year ago."

"How? How do you know all that?"

Dymettra started walking toward the door which Asia partially blocked with her body.

"Because Donovan Rue told me." Asia said with force, then added, "Now you should go out there and apologize to her, Dymettra." Asia paused to let her heart settle, her breathing calm. "If word got out that you were treating other women this way, it wouldn't do your career any good." Asia threw the paper towel in the garbage before asking, "Or don't you care about your reputation?"

Dymettra's eyes turned into daggers as Asia's words hit home.

"Out of my way," she said as she curved herself around Asia and managed to open the door.

Asia, usually relaxed during confrontations with younger, temperamental artists, was not giving up. Walking at a speed she thought long gone, she followed Dymettra to the ballroom's entrance, near a small seating section just outside of the door. When Dymettra slowed to move around it, Asia grabbed her arm.

"Let me go!" Dymettra flailed around, trying to get the older woman to release her.

"Like you let Lynn go?"

Asia caught her breath when Dymettra stopped moving. Gasping, she asked, "What's the matter? Does unwanted touching brother you, Dymettra?"

Dymettra tried once again to remove Asia's grip but it was useless. The woman had an iron clutch of her arm.

"Oh!" Asia continued. "It's okay for you to hold others like this. But not for me to grab you?"

"Let me go!"

Dymettra finally freed herself of Asia's grasp.

"Who do you think you are anyway?" Dymettra called out. "You're a used-up has-been that no one listens to anymore."

"Dymettra! What the hell are you doing?" Roy Alloy walked up to them. "No one talks to Miss Asia like that."

Asia turned her punishing gaze on Roy.

"And you, Roy Emerson," Asia stated, addressing him with his real name, "What's gotten into you that you would strike out at the hand that feeds you?"

Roy shuffled slightly, his toothpick set to the side of his mouth, his cap on backward, his shirttail hanging beneath a rumpled tuxedo that he'd probably picked up off his bedroom floor. Shrugging his narrow shoulders, he said, "They ain't paying me any attention, Miss Asia. My contract says –"

"Your contract says that you work for Rue LA LA. They pay you for your work. If your work isn't to the standards the public expects, people won't buy it."

"But I gotta have backing! Support!"

He turned his attention back to a still, silent Dymettra.

"Don't I, Dymettra? Don't I need support?"

Dymettra shook her head and hands, saying, "I'm not part of your grievance, Roy. I just did you a favor and kicked Donovan's bitch to the curb. Not that I did it for you, but it's done. Now you got your own work to do."

Amazed at Dymettra's insolence, Asia gasped and watched the young diva saunter away. Then she turned to Roy.

"If you want a lasting legacy, you must earn it," Asia told the young man, drawing out each syllable. "It means working hard, doing what Rue and your manager suggest is necessary to do, and keeping your voice in shape. Now, I don't know anything about hip-hop –"

"No! You don't –"

"– but I do know that times change, styles change, and the public right now wants respectability and talent in their artists."

Roy laughed. "The public likes it when artists are bad boys. They look for us. Why do you think I keep this up?" He moved his hands up and down the length of his body. "I sell because this sells." He made a quick jabbing motion toward his chest.

Asia shook her head.

"Sooner or later the public won't like 'this.'" She copied Roy by gesturing at his appearance. "They'll want good music, a gentle person, someone who has been good to the industry and the people in it. You have to work on both your talent and your respectability."

Roy stood there, finally pulling the toothpick out of his mouth. Asia continued, "And if you think the public will respect you when you're going after the head of Rue – and his beautiful woman – you are mistaken! You will only damage yourself, even if you hurt Donovan Rue."

As she finished her words a sharp pain forced her to double over. Asia took a deep breath, then sat in one of the nearby chairs. Roy quickly came to her side, bending over to touch her arm.

"Need some water, Miss Asia?"

"Water isn't going to fix me," Asia admitted. "What might help me is if I see you give up that lawsuit and leave the Rues alone."

Asia watched as Roy stood again, becoming again the bad boy. His face got darker, his stance straighter and the toothpick went back into his mouth.

"I'm not sure you'll ever see that happen," he said. "I want justice."

"I'm sorry to hear that."

Asia Barber got to her feet and glanced around the lobby outside the grand ballroom, hoping to offer comfort to Donovan or Lynn. Not seeing them, she straightened and began to walk inside the ballroom.

"Let me help you, Miss Asia," Roy's nicer self said as he offered her his arm.

"Who are you, Roy Emerson?" she glared at him. "One minute you want to help an old lady; the next you're a gangster-wannabe." Asia placed her arms firmly at her sides. "No, sir! I've been helping others my whole life and I can handle myself just fine. You, however, will not be attending many more of these functions if you continue on this self-destructive path." Opening the ballroom door, Asia turned to give him one last chance. "When you're ready to talk about being a better person, or working on being a better musician, I'll meet with you. I will help you then."

Blinded by tears, trying to leave quickly, Lynn wasn't sure where she was heading as she left the restroom. She ran right into Donovan's outstretched arms.

"Peace!"

"Get me out of here!" Lynn wailed. "*Now!*"

He took her elbow and guided her through a huge throng of people, all looking at the couple with concern. Grabbing his cell phone with his free hand, Donovan blared, "Bring the car around to the front. Now!" By the time they reached the hotel's entrance, Desmond had the limo at the curb and was opening the back door.

They had barely pulled away when Donovan started his inquisition.

"What happened?" he demanded as he took Lynn's hand.

She pulled it back, withdrew a tissue from her clutch.

"Nothing."

"Nothing?" Angling his body toward her, Donovan looked for an injury or some physical reason that could explain how upset his Peace was. Seeing that she was fine, he tried again.

"Lynn! Tell me what happened!"

Lynn looked at him, her blue eyes fierce with hurt, determination, and fatigue.

"I just need to go home," she stated, paused, then took a deep breath before stating, "And I need you to leave me alone from now on."

Surprised, Donovan shrank back into the limo door.

No! No! No! How can she want that?

"You can't mean it," he said in a softer tone, trying to take her hand in his again.

Getting more agitated, Lynn glared at him.

"Yes, I can. And, yes, I do. I don't belong in your world," she told him, echoing Dymettra, yanking her hand away from his reach.

"What 'world'?" Annoyed by the entire evening, Donovan began to lose his patience. "The music world? You love music! As much as I do!" He paused, searching her eyes for what it was that was bothering her enough to push him away. "Or the stupid dressed-up-to-impress world that I have to endure?"

When Lynn didn't answer he knew he'd hit on half the truth.

"You think I like this?" he asked, his voice going impossibly low.

"Yes," Lynn was quieter, too.

Donovan ran a hand roughly through his hair.

144

"Well, you're wrong! I hate this part of my job," he said, his hands fisting into tight balls. "But like all jobs, there are things that you have to do. Part of my job is to schmooze these fools, be there for them when they do well; endure their idiocy when they don't succeed and get vocal and angry about it. And go to charitable things like tonight to show the world that I have a heart – that I'm not just the son who runs the old man's company."

Donovan adjusted his body, so it was no longer leaning against the uncomfortable car door.

"Please, Lynn," he began again, a plea in every word, "My days are so much better because I have you in my life. You've made me very happy. I haven't had someone make me happy in a long time."

"Ha!" Lynn's reaction was loud. "I doubt that. I'm maybe the first white woman."

"You know that has never mattered to me," Donovan stated, anger, defense changing his tone.

"The first white woman who's made acquaintance with you in a while, but from what I heard in the restroom –"

"What did you hear?"

Donovan's voice was a boom in the back of the car.

Lynn resettled in her seat, not sure that she wanted to go any further. She glanced at her hands, worrying them together.

"No!" Donovan finally caught hold of one hand, and said, "You will tell me what was said! I need to know."

Lynn stared into angry brown eyes. She allowed him to hold her hand and said, "You told me – that first morning after we were together – that there had not been many women in your life since your divorce."

"Yes, that's the truth."

"Not according to Dymettra!"

"Dymettra." The word came out sounding disgusted, irritable. Donovan looked out the car window, huffing through a cone-shaped hand before turning back to Lynn.

"Dymettra? You believe that bitch? Dymettra and I had a two-minute relationship. Very short and not very sweet. I didn't want anything to do with her after our one night together which was a long time ago, and she's still pissed," he stated. "She still wants something. But it is not ever going to happen."

When Lynn began shaking her head, Donovan got louder and pleaded, "Don't let that bitch ruin what we have here!"

"I have to be realistic," Lynn yelled back. "I'm a middle-aged woman. Pretty simple in most ways. A mother. A widow. A cancer victim. A –"

"A cancer *survivor!*" Donovan said, speaking over her.

Lynn eyed him, saying, "Whatever." When she saw that he wasn't going to allow her to end it, and held the same intense look whenever Lynn poured out her anguish, Lynn decided to continue.

"I am not as into music as you are, although we do both love dance music," she admitted. "I don't have the ability to go to all these fancy parties, wear the clothes that Bea Owens gets thousands of dollars for, and make nice to people I don't even know!"

"Sure, you do! You're kind to everyone, you're –"

"I'm not black either." Lynn cut him off deliberately.

"What? Why do you keep saying that? That has never mattered to me and you know it!"

"I do; I know," Lynn said. "And it doesn't matter to me. But it obviously does matter to the music world, your daughter, and even my son."

After making an exasperated noise, Donovan said, "You are an independent woman, Lynn. You can make your own choices." He threw his arms up in the air, saying loudly, "To hell with what everyone else thinks."

Donovan stared at his Peace, noting how the night lights made halos behind her head. She was an angel for him, the moments of sanity in a day and an industry where people were too concerned with being famous, making money, and taking advantage of others. Lynn was not into any of those things. She brought happiness to others, strove to help people. As the car turned slightly, the halo behind Lynn's head moved, too, becoming larger. She turned wet eyes in an exhausted, sad face toward him before bringing her face down to her hands. Shaking her head, Lynn cried out, "No, no, no, I can't do this anymore. I may seem independent to you, but I'm not strong enough for this. It's too soon."

"You know it's our decision to see one another! Not our kids', not social media's, not the paparazzi, and certainly not some used-up star who only wanted to be with me for the fame and my money."

Lynn started to weep into her hands, the sound of her crying tearing Donovan's heart and soul.

What can I do? I have to save this somehow.

"I wanted this to work," Lynn said between sobs. "But I should have waited until I felt better to get involved with someone."

She paused a moment. Wiping her eyes with her fingers, she said, "I'm still missing Michael."

Donovan stiffened at the mention of the other man. He'd thought the ghost of Michael Cerami had been put to rest months before, but apparently not. Slowly he moved his hand away from Lynn's, cast his own eyes downward in case she noticed the tears that were becoming increasingly difficult to hold at bay. The whisper that came from Lynn only added to his torment.

"It would be better to just let me go."

As if it knew this was the end of their argument, the car stopped in front of Lynn's house. Before Desmond or Donovan could get out, Lynn opened her door and was wobbling as quickly as her heels would permit toward the front door. One of her shoes caught in a sidewalk groove, causing her to lose her balance and lurch forward. Donovan, following closely behind, caught her to prevent a complete fall.

"Lynn ... please."

Lynn was twisting away from him. Angrily, she pulled out of his hands, tears blinding her eyes as she finished the walk to the door. Fumbling with her keys, she finally found the right one.

Donovan kept pleading with her.

"Lynn! Peace, please!"

"Goodbye, Donovan," she called from the threshold as the huge door finally opened. "I love you."

WHEN HE GOT HOME, DONOVAN SLAMMED THE LIMO'S DOOR so hard it screeched back at him. Always discreet, Desmond nodded, then pulled away. Standing in his driveway, Donovan called Lynn's number, knowing that she would not answer, determined to leave a message.

"Peace ..." he started, feeling his throat constricting on the word. "Lynn ... I'm sorry. I should've told you about Dymettra ... shit ..." He pulled the phone away briefly, took a deep breath, then swung it back up to his ear. "Please just text me and let me know you're okay. Please ... I love you."

He entered his home, going straight to the music center, playing a metal band's latest song. Grateful that his home was so secluded, not concerned that Desmond could hear it in the security wing, he turned the volume up as high as it could go. Then he tore off his tux, shirt, tie, shoes, and socks on the way to his bedroom where he retrieved his swim trunks. He headed to his pool, the one place in his house that he had not yet taken Lynn. The entire time he changed and walked, a symphony of screams ran through his head.

Why? Why did this happen? Why didn't I tell her about Dymettra? Why didn't I warn her about the heartless bitches that would come after her to get to me?

He dove into the pool's deepest end. Surfacing, he started doing laps. Back and forth and back and forth and back and forth.

Why? Why? Why? Why?

He had never seen Lynn look so upset. He couldn't blame her; the public thought the industry was sexy, fun. All those popular people in one spot, all dressed up, luring others into thinking that entertainers hung out together dressed to the maximum. No one knew the real drama that went on behind the scenes – like the restroom. A kind innocent woman like Lynn never stood a chance with Dymettra and her friends.

And I didn't even explain it to her, or ease that awful pain.

Back and forth and back and forth and back and forth.

Donovan's body wasn't even tiring. His thoughts continued to review the end of the evening, failing to come up with suggestions on how to fix things.

What do I do?

Ideas were eluding him.

THE NEXT DAY LYNN GATHERED UP THE HATED RED DRESS, SHOES, clutch, and jewelry and threw them in her car, to bring them back to Bea. Lynn knew that her best friend would be expecting her.

Gathering the dreaded dress from the car, Lynn felt guilt at having to tell Bea that she didn't like it. It was as if all the bad memories were woven into its fabric.

No. I don't like it; I don't want to even see it again. Lynn knocked on the door with determination. *I will get through this. It was too soon. I will ...*

A very bright Bea answered the bell.

"Hello, Peace!"

"Don't call me that!"

Lynn trounced in, dragging the garment bag and a box with her. "Don't ever call me that again."

Surprised at her friend's demeanor, Bea studied Lynn for a moment, then took the garment bag over to a coat closet.

"Okay ... Trouble in paradise?"

Lynn sputtered. "Paradise? It's an illusion," she replied, forcing back threatening tears. "I wanted it to be paradise, but it is not."

Lynn slumped onto the arm of a plush chair in Bea's living room. "And I was very rudely told that by Dymettra."

It was Bea's turn to snort.

"That bitch? Wouldn't listen to anything that woman ever says," she declared. She threw her arms up in the air, then said, "Once I designed a gown for her. She had ideas —we fought so much over that dress design! I should've quit. I tried to please her, told her that what she was asking for was going to accentuate all the wrong parts of her body."

Bea shook her head, sputtering, "Sure enough, the day after that event, all the fashionistas had a field day with that gown. And what did she do? She blamed it all on me! Said I picked the color! I picked the fabric, the strapless low-cut front, the horrible slit!"

Bea was shaking her head.

"No way in hell I'll ever let another star tell me what she looks good in."

Lynn moved to sit at Bea's center island after pouring a cup of coffee. She took a sip, then said, "She told me that I have no business being in Donovan's world."

Bea's head continued shaking as she said, "Well, who the hell gets to tell you or Donovan that?"

"She said that he should be with a black woman."

"That fact that you're white, Lynn, does not seem to bother Donovan. He doesn't seem to care! Am I right?"

"You are," Lynn agreed. "It wasn't something that interfered with our relationship."

Bea took a sip of her coffee. "See. Told you."

"But –" Lynn examined her cup, as if trying to read the grounds for insight "– what if I am preventing him from finding someone who'll fit in better with his lifestyle? What if someone else would like all these events, dressing up –"

"Shut up!" Beatrice was on her feet. "Shut up! He is asking you to be with him because he enjoys being with *you*! He's not looking for someone who enjoys the galas, or is in the business and therefore understands, or even someone who likes music! You are makin' a lot out of nothin'."

Silence ensued as the two took another sip from their mugs, Bea acting like a fire-breathing dragon, Lynn lost in painful memories of the night before.

"What about Michael?" A bare whisper of a question.

Bea blew out a long breath, reining in her annoyance

"I love you more than my own sister," Bea said. "I will stand by you no matter what." Bea paused to straighten the placemat. "I liked Michael Cerami well enough, Lynn. But Michael is dead. I know it's hard for you, that you're sad ... that the hurt won't just go away. But he is gone. Are you going to hibernate? Spend the rest of your life in mourning?"

Chagrinned, Lynn stood to leave, washing out her mug first.

"I can't do it anymore, Bea. I'm constantly tired; I can't seem to get healthy. This stuff with Donovan doesn't help."

"Maybe you need another doctor?"

Lynn planted both hands on either side of the kitchen sink, trying to hold her temper at bay.

"That's what Donovan said the other day," she said. "That's what Cassie says every time I fuck something up at work. Now you're saying it."

Lynn grabbed her purse and headed toward the front door.

"I still think all this stuff is taking its toll. It isn't easy to have someone tell you that you don't fit in – not matter what your age is, or your color. It's all too much."

She turned the knob and said, "Bye Bea." One second later, she stepped back inside the house and said, "Oh. I meant to tell you: I hated that dress. Red is not my color. Please don't make it another Lynn dress."

Chapter 19

*L*ynn's hope that Monday morning might bring normality to her life was short-lived. The day started off when Lynn could not locate the off-campus building for her division's professional development meeting. By the time she got there, the others were irritated by the caterer not showing up and the echoes of a room with exposed ceilings and concrete floors.

By the time Carol Omson, the head of marketing, came to show off a new logo for the college, everyone in the room was in a foul mood.

After a whole group presentation on creating brand uniformity throughout the college, Carol gave instructions for everyone before splitting into their department groups.

"Okay, people, here's what I want each department to do: write down the top ten things your department does. Whittle those down to the five most necessary things you must do. Then use nineteen words – only nineteen! Not twenty or eighteen! – to describe your mission. Do not use any form of the Be verb. Exclude these words …"

She handed out a list.

As Cassie, Tom, Sally, and Lynn moved to their assigned space to begin the activity, Lynn couldn't believe what she was hearing.

Why is Cassie going along with this nonsense? Why isn't someone questioning this Carol's authority? Who the hell is she anyway?

While the others were trying to participate in the activity, Lynn sat there, mute. Brad Petrona, the division vice president, wandered in and listened for fifteen minutes before calling out to Lynn.

"Lynn! You're too quiet. I know you have an opinion," he said while smiling at her. "Tell us what you think."

All eyes swiveled to Lynn, who read each person's different expectation.

Brad is eager; Tom looks worried; Sally hates everything (why the hell does she continue to work for us?). Cassie's look says she wants to be the boss, wants total respect. And this Carol chick – the smug look of the head cheerleader who thinks she has all the damn moves down pat.

"I think this is wrong," Lynn said without any preamble, not thinking of the ramifications of her answer. She got louder as she said, "It's a mistake to limit our use of words to nineteen or less. And to tell us to eliminate words that are important to under-standing immigration issues? How can someone in marketing who's never done our work know what words to use? And to tell us not to use the "to be" verb is insane!"

After a slight pause, Lynn finished, "What does the marketing department know about international student needs? Are they suddenly experts in that, too?"

Everyone's facial expressions changed to horror as if they couldn't believe what they were hearing. Lynn blinked in surprise at their reaction, wondering what they were each thinking.

What? He asked me to say what I thought. Did I swear or something?

BACK ON CAMPUS, LYNN FINISHED THE FINAL PREPARATIONS FOR THE orientation agenda. Right and left, those who had committed to presentations were backing out. Cassie didn't care.

"Figure it out. Make it work. This is what I want!"

When she wasn't planning orientation, Lynn was working on upgrading all the currently enrolled students' immigration paper-work. Cassie had decided this should happen immediately, despite the time crunch. It required a signature from a school official.

Lynn began signing away, the five hundred signatures so rote and routine that she couldn't escape drifting off into the memory of the night she had broken things off with Donovan. His crushed face entered her mind first, his brown eyes misty with tears. Whenever she thought about him a knot tightened in her stomach.

Why? Why did this have to happen? Why couldn't he just be a nice guy with an ordinary nine-to-five job without the baggage of these people with oversized egos?

As she signed another form, forcing Donovan from her mind, Dymettra entered her mind.

Lynn picked up another student's paperwork and began to sign away.

Am I that wrong? Is Dymettra right? No one should care, right? It's just between Donovan and me. But what if she's right?

Echoes of Dymettra's verbal assault played in her mind (*"You don't belong in this world!"*) along with memories of the singer's strong hand clutching her arm as she told Lynn that she was not right for Donovan.

"Lyyyynnnnnnn!"

The call came from Cassie's office.

"Were you supposed to do a presentation in Humanities for new Peer Advisors last Thursday?"

Pulled from her nightmares, Lynn stopped signing and pulled up her computer's calendar, but saw nothing about a meeting on that day.

Why does this sound familiar?

Cassie stormed into Lynn's office.

"I just got a call from Brad. He said you were supposed to speak to the PAs about international students."

She grew redder as she spoke, louder, too.

"He said this was scheduled three months ago!"

Lynn started to shake with the increase in voice volume. Grasping at anything she could, she said, "I remember being asked, but it was never confirmed."

Cassie continued to turn red with anger, running her hand along the edge of her scalloped-edged smock top.

A few minutes later a piece of paper was placed on Lynn's desk by Sally, a self-satisfied grin on her face. Cassie had signed the note which said, *"Since you seem not to care about your job, I have no choice but to document this mistake in your HR record."*

Chapter 20

*D*ara's first clue that something was up was when she heard the mournful lyrics of an old song, *She's Gone,* blaring from the house. Entering the front door, she saw her father sitting in the dark, slouched on the great room's couch, head tilted back and a glass of some dark liquid in his hand.

What the hell happened?

She waited until the song ended to make herself known.

"So, what's up with you, Dad?"

Donovan took a deep drink of the bourbon.

"Lynn broke it off with me."

Another sad, soulful song began. Dara watched her father take a deep breath, then another gulp of booze. Alarmed, she threw her keys next to Donovan, moved the half-empty bottle to the entertainment center, then took the remote with the other hand, forcing the sound down to a more bearable level. Donovan didn't move, staring out the big windows, his look unfocused, sad.

Poor Dad. Shit. I liked her.

Sitting next to Donovan, she said, "Sorry, Dad. She was cool."

"*Is* cool," Donovan countered. Finally moving forward, Donovan placed the empty glass on the table, then ran both hands through his messy hair. When he spoke again, he turned toward his daughter, his eyes glassy and red.

"She was everything to me. I love that woman. I want to be with her forever." His head went down briefly, then rose again. "Damn Dymettra."

Dara's face was somber.

Figures. Dad always said she was trouble.

"Dymettra always ruins things for you," she sympathized. After releasing a sigh, Dara said, "I'll miss Lynn. She was one person that I could talk to, lean on, you know? Someone who understood me."

"You know Lynn?" Donovan looked surprised. "Last thing I knew you were treating her like some kind of intruder."

Dara nodded, cocked her head to one side, and said, "I went there the next day to apologize, you know? After you called and were upset about me. She and I, we got talking, and she was going to do some planting, so I helped her."

Dara laughed, a rare thing for her father to hear. His eyes brightened slightly and there was a small smile as he faced her.

"You plant?" he asked, nudging her.

"Yeah ... I'm addicted to it. I go there to help out," Dara admitted, then added, "Dr. Allerbee says working with plants is therapeutic for some people."

They sat quietly listening to yet another mournful tune until Dara asked, "How long ago did this happen?"

"Two weeks – about."

"Have you tried calling her? Or texting?"

Donovan nodded slowly, reaching for the empty glass and glancing at the bottle across the room.

"Yeah. She texted back that she was fine." He snorted and darted angry eyes at his daughter. "Fine! I'm supposed to leave it at that?"

"So, try again!" Dara blurted out.

"I don't like pushing her," Donovan admitted. "She's so fragile at times, even if she doesn't want to admit it. And that night she was a mess. Her balance was off, she was crabby, she hated her dress ..."

The music changed again. Another sad one about being dumped. Dara grabbed the remote, turning it off. Alarmed at her father's uncharacteristic depression Dara said, "Dad! This music is not helping you!"

Donovan gulped, glanced at the empty glass.

"And liquor won't bring Lynn back either!"

Donovan slouched back into the couch again. Dara stood up, uncertain about what to do, but knowing that she couldn't let her father wallow in his misery.

She pointed her finger at him, then said, "You know when I get down, you always say to make a plan."

Donovan looked up at her, his eyes glistening again.

"So, I'm telling you," Dara said, "Make a plan."

Chapter 21

*L*ynn was sitting in her office, stamping and signing the new forms that Cassie had insisted they finish by the end of the week.

I can't seem to do this. Lynn noticed that the stamps weren't quite on the line, that her signature was always skewed upward. *It's stupid that I'm having so much trouble with this.*

Concentrating hard, Lynn was startled when Cassie bounced into her office.

"Wang Xu needs his new paperwork," Cassie said. "Do you have it?"

Cassie looked over the mounds of paperwork on Lynn's desk, then at the side shelf where more paperwork was waiting, then at the top of the filing cabinet where a box labeled TO BE FILED was overflowing. She began rifling through a stack, uninvited.

"How can you find anything in here?"

Cassie's volume increased as she spoke.

"Really! You must clean this up. Everything about this room is unprofessional!"

Sally, the ambitious admin, waltzed into the office, grabbed another pile of papers and began looking for the student's paperwork. Lynn was coming to the end of a third pile, praying that she'd find the paperwork before Cassie or Sally, when she pulled the paper out.

"Wang Xu. Here it is."

Cassie grabbed it and checked the name on the paper. She flipped to the second page, checking Lynn's signature on the form.

Lynn held her breath, knowing that a lot of the stamps were off-kilter, expecting the wrath of Cassie over that at any moment.

"You used black ink!"

All three women stopped any movement. Sally gasped. The government only allowed the use of blue ink.

Cassie finally asked, "Did you use black ink on ALL these new forms?"

"It was blue!" Lynn blurted out as Sally went through the pile again, turning each page over, looking for the damning black ink. Lynn saw heartlessness in the younger woman's eyes. No one found another black-inked signature.

It was a fluke! Thank God.

After she returned from lunch, Lynn found another note from Cassie indicating a notation in Lynn's personnel file.

AS LYNN ENTERED THE OFFICE SUITE THE FOLLOWING DAY, SHE noticed that Cassie was in earlier than normal. Lynn saw her supervisor seated at her desk, red pen in hand. As Lynn settled into her office Cassie flounced in.

"Lynn," she stated, her voice quieter than normal. "Come into my office."

Lynn's stomach started knotting up.

Whatever this is about, it isn't good.

Lynn followed Cassie in and closed the door, then sank into the office chair directly in front of Cassie's desk. Cassie fidgeted for a few minutes, shuffling some papers, glancing at her Caller ID, running her computer cursor up and down a list of emails. Finally, she turned her attention to Lynn.

"Look, I hate to do this," Cassie started, "but HR insists."

She pushed over performance-review paperwork. With that awful red pen serving as a pointer, she started reviewing each section.

The review was devastating. There was absolutely nothing written that was good or complimentary. Some of it, Lynn thought, was Cassie's jealousy over Lynn's ability to remember students' names, or her outgoing, pleasant personality and good rapport with colleagues. But Cassie's comments on the administrative and clerical parts of Lynn's job were right on; Lynn forgot things; she made mistakes in student files; her office was a mess. The incident where she had yelled at the student over the orientation space did not help her. Missing the RA presentation left a big gap in their education.

It was painful to sit there and listen to Cassie going over it line by line. Between each section, Cassie would say, "They're making me do this." Lynn, sick to her stomach and mind clouded by fog, didn't respond.

"You need to sign this," Cassie said, handing Lynn a pen. Lynn, momentarily awake, noticed a separate section for the Employee to comment.

"I'd like to fill this part out. And get a copy."

Cassie was now back to acting like the queen who ruled overall.

"Of course. You have a right to do so," she said. "But I want it back this morning."

Stunned by the entire event, Lynn went back to her office. Cassie had not gone over the section where she had written suggestions for change. But she had written suggestions.

Get psychiatric help. Eat more healthily. Exercise!

Lynn wondered if some of those suggestions were even legal. Sighing, she scribbled her response to Cassie's reviews, almost pleading.

I've never been documented until recently. I'm recovering from cancer. I love, love, love my job.

There was limited space in which to write; Lynn's handwriting was shaky with her anxiety, her words going outside the lines.

"Done?"

Cassie's booming demand came ten minutes later. Standing in the doorway, hands on her ample hips, she said, "I need to turn it in this morning."

Without waiting for Lynn's response, Cassie took the paperwork from Lynn's desk. Then she eyed Lynn as if deciding what more to say.

"Brad wants you to take some time off; a medical leave," Cassie announced. "I don't know the details of how that works, but you have no choice. He was upset at the way you acted during the division meeting with that woman from marketing. What's her name?"

Lynn's words came out slowly, sadly. "Her name is Carol."

Cassie nodded, placed the red pen behind her ear. "Yeah, that's the one. He's upset about that. Also, he didn't like to hear that you yelled at that student. David? Was that his name? He asked about the quality of your recent work."

Lynn almost groaned. She knew that Cassie's answer could not have been good.

"So," Cassie was going on, "go see the HR people; find out what you need to do for that leave."

"Now?"

"Right now!" Cassie's volume went to its loudest level.

During the brief meeting with an HR benefits lady named Roseanne, Lynn learned that she was entitled to a twelve-week medical leave. Roseanne handed Lynn forms that needed to be signed by a doctor before her leave could start.

Fortunately, Dr. Meyer had an immediate appointment, so Lynn decided to get it over with. She had filled out most of the paperwork, but there was a portion that only a doctor could fill out.

"So how much time do you think you'll need?" the doctor asked as she looked over the forms. Lynn sat across the desk, numbed in a trance.

Is this really happening to me? A nightmare? even though I'm not sleeping well.

"Lynn?"

"I'm not sure," Lynn answered, then thought, *What the hell; go for broke.* "Six months? A year?"

"A year?" Dr. Meyer's head rose from the document, surprised. "Do you feel that bad?"

"I'm exhausted!"

How often have I complained about this in the last year? Doesn't anyone care?

"I've been feeling this way for over a year. I'm not getting any better even though everyone tells me that I will. And I'm screwing things up at work. It's like this chemo-brain is taking over my mind."

Dr. Meyer wrote something down on the form. She tapped her pen on the paper, reading over instructions, filling what she could.

Lynn sat there, her feet glued to the floor, hands clasped in her lap.

Dr. Meyer looked the form over again, scribbled on it, and then said, "Okay. Time for you to see a neurologist. You've been complaining about this chemo-brain for a long time. Let's get you checked out."

She handed Lynn the HR paperwork along with a card for a local neurologist.

Lynn immediately took her paperwork to the falsely cheerful Roseanne who offered no privacy despite the reception area being full. Roseanne took the papers, set her inappropriate smile on super wide, and said, "Okay! Leave!"

"What? Now?" Lynn couldn't believe that it was all happening so quickly.

Don't I have to pack up my things? Say goodbye to my students?

The others waiting in the office glanced at Lynn, then glanced at the floor, trying to ignore what should have been private. Being a small school, everyone knew each other.

And by the end of the day, everyone will know that I'm on leave. And talk about what could possibly have happened to Lynn Cerami? Did her cancer come back? Is she worse? Is she dying?

Roseanne continued with her insincere smile, her lack of discretion continuing when she said, "Your doctor indicated that you can't work, so you have to leave!"

She escorted Lynn to the door, still smiling.

DAZED, LYNN BEGAN WALKING BACK TO HER OFFICE, STOPPING FROM time to time to rest.

Leave. Now? But I need to get things out of my office.

She paused at a bench, trying to gather emotional and physical strength to continue the awful day. As she stood, a campus golf cart swung to a stop just in front of her.

"Need a ride, Lynn?"

Bryan Dennis managed the campus' events team. Older than Lynn, riddled with all kinds of ailments that weren't publicly known but still gossiped about, the university gave him something to ride in so that he did not have to trek the eighty miles that made up Brandstone College. Lynn couldn't manage a smile for the man even though he was one of her favorite people.

"Get in," he called. "I don't got all day."

"You'll get in trouble –"

"With who?" Bryan motioned to the spare seat. "C'mon, get in. Are you going back to your office?"

I can't walk much farther. To hell with it.

Lynn got into the cart, noting that it was easier sliding into it than getting into her own car.

"Thanks, Bryan."

"Eh," he said. He was a gruff man, used few words. "Why don't you park closer?"

"No spaces, usually. But I had to go to HR, thought I could manage the walk."

"Don't you got one of those handicapped things that people hang in their cars?"

Lynn wondered at that. "I never thought to get one ..."

"Well, I'm sure you are eligible," he snorted, then looking her way, said, "Sorry if that's personal."

Lynn noted eyeglasses that were so old they were held together by wire at the temple, a stained plaid shirt, pants that were held up by suspenders.

Whatever they pay Bryan Dennis, it's not enough if he can't replace things.

"Where do you park?"

"The big lot on the other side of our building."

"That far?" His agitation was evident.

Lynn nodded.

"Y'know," Bryan was on a roll, "I keep telling 'em that they need to provide a shuttle service for employees who need it. You know – people on crutches, pregnant women, people who have ... you know ... have ..."

His pause told Lynn that he was as embarrassed to know about her cancer – news he probably got from the campus gossip – as she was to know anything about his personal illnesses.

"Cancer."

"Yeah! Cancer." He was driving the cart as slowly as possible, deliberately taking the longest trek back to her building. "I mean, wouldn't that have been helpful today?"

Lynn again nodded, grateful that her sunglasses prevented Bryan from seeing the tears in her eyes.

He doesn't need to know that I'm leaving today.

"How're they treating you?"

"Who?"

"Cassie? That silly girl she hired as your admin?"

Lynn raised her eyebrows wondering what anyone knew about her office, her morale.

"Everyone on campus knows that Cassie Manders is hard to

work for," Bryan went on. "Some of us are just amazed that you've been with her for as long as you have."

"I love my job!"

It came out on the tail end of a sob.

Bryan pulled the cart over.

"No doubt," he said. "The kids love you, too. Any international student who's worked for me in the last ten years has raved about you. But Cassie – she's difficult. We all know it."

"Well, she's going to get a break from me."

"A break?"

"Yeah," Lynn reached into her pocket for a tissue, wiped her eyes under the glasses, then said, "I'm taking a twelve-week medical leave."

Now Bryan's eyebrows rose. He pushed the aging frames up, then turned the cart back on.

"I had one of those once," he said. "It'll be good for you to rest."

"Think so?"

"Know so."

He pulled the cart to the front door of her building, stopping again. As Lynn went to get out of the cart, Bryan said, "Now don't be telling anyone I gave you a ride. I could lose my cart privileges."

Lynn nodded, then placed her hand on Bryan's arm.

"Thank you, Bryan."

"I'm serious!"

"Oh! Don't worry," Lynn said. "I won't tell a soul."

"No, I'm serious about getting some rest."

DETERMINED TO GET HER PERSONAL THINGS, LYNN ENTERED HER office suite without greeting anyone. She found a couple of storage boxes had already been placed atop her desk. She filled them with her belongings, being careful to leave anything that was Brandstone's behind. As she was pulling picture frames off a shelf, Cassie poked her head in.

"So?"

Lynn looked at Cassie, sad, mentally detaching from the horrible things that were happening to her.

It's like this is happening to someone else ...

"I have to leave," Lynn said. "Roseanne said to go now."

"Well then, you'd better leave!" Cassie announced, taking the picture frame from Lynn's hand and placing it inside the closest box.

Determined to protect her things, Lynn took the frame out and wrapped it in the bubble wrap someone had put on her desk.

"I just want to bring home my personal things," she protested.

"Better hurry," Cassie said, her tone razor sharp. "You probably aren't covered by insurance anymore."

"No, Cassie, insurance stays with me throughout leave. I'm still considered an employee."

A headache bloomed as Lynn started to pack more quickly. Cassie became more insistent.

"You can come back later to get things. Rafa will help you carry this stuff to your car."

Rafa grabbed a box and followed Lynn out the door. On the walk back to where Lynn had parked, the student looked scared, concerned, and overwhelmed by what was happening to his supervisor. He said nothing until they reached the car.

"Lynn! I cannot work for Sally!"

Rafa's strong accent, his obvious confusion about the situation, and the fear in his voice jarred Lynn. She looked up from unlocking her car door, dragged out of her own misery by seeing her distraught student worker who was struggling not to cry.

Rafa continued, "She told me that I work for her now. She's mean, Lynn; I hate her. She hates any students, but me because I'm Hispanic. I'm going to quit!"

Lynn plopped the box in her car, waited until Rafa had done the same, and then embraced the tall young man.

"You cannot quit, Rafa," Lynn said softly. "You need the money. You are a good student – a hard worker. Promise me you won't quit!"

Rafa had tears in his eyes as he hugged Lynn, pulling away suddenly.

"Come back soon, Lynn," he pleaded, his accent thickening with broiling emotion. "Don't you give up either! We all need you."

As she drove away from the college, Lynn wondered if she'd ever come back to the job that she loved very much.

Chapter 22

*A*fter taking time off to wallow in misery, Donovan returned to his office.

Dara said, "make a plan." I gotta start doing something. But what?

He'd reached out in text messages to Lynn, who at first responded with one-word answers. She wasn't even doing that now, crushing him even further. Finally, Donovan's sense of duty to his father's company won over his depression.

While sifting through the hundreds of emails that had accumulated during his absence, Donovan was startled when Len burst into his office, accompanied by Donovan's personal attorney Martin Lawson.

This can't be good. Martin doesn't come here unless it's something serious. And Len looks like he could kill someone.

Despite concern over the lawyer's sudden appearance, Donovan stood, smiled, and held his hand out in greeting.

"Hey, Martin!"

Martin's lips formed a thin line across his large face. Len was tense, his eyes appearing as if he wanted to apologize, but couldn't find the right words. As Donovan watched the two men approach, his heart began beating, his palms sweating. Neither Len nor Martin smiled back, although Martin did shake Donovan's hand.

"Please," Donovan motioned at the club chairs in front of his desk. "Have a seat." He waited until they were all in chairs, then said, "Tell me what wonderful news has brought you to my office, Martin."

Martin shook his head and pulled a briefcase onto his lap. After he removed paperwork from it, he looked directly at Donovan.

"I wish I had good news, but I'm afraid this is far from it," he began. When Donovan didn't answer, he said, "Mandisa is accusing you of harassment."

Donovan's smile vanished.

"Mandisa?"

Donovan looked around his desktop as if that might give him a clue.

"As in Mandisa, my former wife?"

Martin held out some paperwork. Donovan took it, glanced at the first few lines, and then ran a hand roughly through his hair.

Shit.

"She goes by Mandisa Phillips now," Martin continued, "and she's alleging that, while she was dating you, you physically abused her."

"*What?*"

Donovan stood up quickly, upsetting his coffee cup as he did so.

"That you also abused her physically and mentally while you were married –"

"*Bullshit!*"

"—that she left you because of that."

"Martin! You know me! You know that I did no such thing!" Donovan thundered. He began stuttering in fear. "S-she hated being home – but loved all the parties and shit that go with my job. S-she wanted all of that! You-you know that!"

Len jumped in. "Of course, we know you wouldn't do this, Donovan. Your ex is climbing on the current bandwagon with all the other females that are accusing men of not being able to control themselves."

"Doesn't matter what we think," Martin stated, his large eyes staying on Donovan. "She's put it out there."

"Is it public yet?"

"Yes," Martin answered, cocked his head to the side, then glanced at Len. "You were right," he said to Donovan's assistant.

"He's totally out of it." Then to Donovan, he asked, "Haven't you been listening or watching any news, man?"

Donovan shook his head, knowing that he'd been having what Lynn would call a pity party. He had not read anything, even work emails. When he wasn't moping or trying to drain his sorrows away with a liquor bottle, he was hiking or swimming alone. His only company had been Desmond who had remained quiet, stoic.

"No. I - I haven't been paying much attention to anything," he admitted, catching Len's sympathetic look.

"It's all over the news," Martin said. "She's holding a press conference this morning. Well, she called it, but her lawyer – that Alison Berg – will probably do the talking. I know a lawyer in her firm. He says that Alison is going to say that you hit Mandisa all the time, that she kept quiet about it to save the Rue name."

Martin paused as disbelief filled Donovan's eyes, one hand repeatedly raking his curly hair. When Donovan calmed a little, Martin added, "She even implied that your father was abusive."

"*What?*" Donovan knew his blood pressure was rising to an alarming level. "Everyone knows that my father was the most decent man alive."

"He was hard on you," Len countered, "but Paul Rue was a true gentleman."

"Hard on me. True," Donovan acknowledged. "But he never hit me or hurt my mother. And from what Asia Barber tells me, my mother was his only girlfriend!"

For one moment Donovan wished he could cry out his anguish, let big fat tears roll down his cheek, and find a comforting hug. The one person that could possibly be there for him had made herself completely unavailable.

This one I'll have to face totally alone.

Donovan centered himself and sat back down. He cast his eyes on the end of the room, thinking over what had just happened, remembering his father's warning, made long ago, about Mandisa only being a gold digger.

"And lose the girl ... she's nothing but trouble. You will only have heartache with a girl like that."

Donovan wondered what his father would say if he knew that the girl was stomping all over Paul Rue's name as well.

"Can she go after my dad after all this time? For God's sake, he's dead!"

"Let's focus on *you*, Donovan," Martin advised. "Your father has passed; she can't get very far with him except to ruin his good name," Martin said grimly. "But she can try to get more from you *as* she ruins your name."

"Just like that, she can just come back into my life like this?" Donovan asked. "I gave her a big chunk of money in that divorce."

"She can, and she is, coming back into your life."

Donovan ranted, "She didn't want custody – *any* custody. She wouldn't see Dara except when it suited her."

Martin cast a suspicious eye at Donovan. "I always thought there was something you weren't telling me about Mandisa's behavior."

Donovan was quick to answer, "Nah ... she was just a bad mother. She never really wanted anything to do with her."

Donovan noted the anger in Len's eyes, recognizing the man's concern.

"The last time I spoke to her was almost twenty years ago."

"Did you ever hit her?" Martin asked. "Man, I hate asking you this, but –"

"*No!* I've never hit anyone in my life!"

"Before you were married?"

"No. No, sir!"

"Did you harass her?" Martin continued his questioning. "I know when you first came to me for the divorce, you said she was cheating on you. Did you do anything to get back at her?"

"Nothing!" Donovan stood up again. "Sure, I yelled at her; we had these huge screaming matches. Dara was even in the room for one of them ... she was three ..."

He paused to remember the final confrontation in his marriage. They began yelling at one another, unaware that Dara had snuck into the kitchen.

"I want to know if it's true."

"Demetrius is a nice guy."

"Is that a yes?" Donovan's voice exploded with anger.

A whimper from the other side of the island announced Dara's presence.

Donovan ran a hand along his chin, then shivered with the memory of an evening long ago.

"But I did nothing wrong! You know all this, Martin! I took our daughter because she hated her. I gave Mandy the house, a car ... shit! I think I was probably *too* good to her! And now this?"

He began pacing along the wall behind his desk. One hand gripped his chin, his index finger running over his lips, his other hand ran through his curly hair repeatedly as he walked the length of the wall and then back.

Shit, now what do I do? First, this Roy thing that won't go away. Then damn Dymettra says all that shit to Lynn and ruins that. And all around me guys are getting accused of being assholes! And now me. And I've done nothing wrong! Nothing.

He stopped in front of his desk, tilting his head back, closing his eyes. His actions spurred a memory of Lynn. Beautiful, peaceful Lynn with the huge ocean-blue eyes and the short curly hair, speaking about what sounded like medieval medical torture, tilting her head back as if fighting away the emotions and turmoil associated with that memory. Beautiful, anguished, sick Lynn.

Fuck ... I can't even talk to her, can't even get her view, can't even get the peace I need to get through this.

It took great effort, but finally Donovan straightened his head, opened his eyes, and placed his hands firmly on his desk.

But ... I need to get through this. I need to keep the company going and keep my good name. And my dad's.

He took a deep breath, knowing the two men were waiting for

him to decide what to do, to act in a rational, calm way, without anger, with his usual laser-edged focus on problem-solving. Donovan knew that he needed to take control.

C'mon, Donovan; get it together. What did Dara tell me ... that I always tell her to "make a plan" and that I'd better make one. Damn straight.

"Okay, Martin," he started to say, the CEO voice coming alive after a two-week absence. "What do we do? I need to fight this."

"Yes, you do," Len said, raising his head from studying his shoes, almost gleeful as he smiled at the younger man.

"I've not done one damn thing wrong in all my years here at Rue," Donovan stated.

Len called back, "Yes, sir!"

"And even though I was a partier when I was younger, I still was a decent man with women."

"Yes!" Len continued to act like he was in a church, answering the pastor on the chancel. Donovan briefly paused before he ended the entire discussion by saying, "My mother and Asia Barber wouldn't have let me live if I'd been any other way. They raised me to appreciate, admire, and be respectful to women."

Len was practically bouncing in his seat while Donovan turned to Martin.

"So, lawyer, what do I do?"

"Well," Martin gave a small smile, "I'm glad to represent a decent man – something I've always thought you were, Donovan."

Donovan smiled back, an equally small smile.

Glad he knows I'm honest. But I think the fight is just beginning ...

"First, we need to have a statement from you that says you're not guilty of anything your ex-wife is implying," Martin said, looking directly at Donovan. "I imagine you have a PR department who can help you with that?"

"Yes, we do."

"Ask them to read what Matthew Albinson just put out."

"Matthew Albinson? That television anchor who's retired?"

"Matt Albinson was accused, by some woman he worked with in the seventies, of fondling her while they were on assignment in Europe somewhere," Martin explained. "He wrote a terrific reply to her accusation and it appears to have done the trick because the lawsuit has gone no further."

Len smirked. "He didn't pay her off, did he?"

"No," Martin was succinct. "A good man wouldn't do that. To pay someone for their silence – especially since this is such a huge issue in our industry with women now – would only make things worse."

He took his papers and placed them back in his briefcase, saying, "Next, we wait and see if Mandisa turns this into a civil lawsuit."

After Donovan nodded, Martin continued, "Your ex-wife will have to prove these accusations. That's if she wants to go forward. So," Martin placed a hand on the man's arm, "We need you to stay strong. Be direct. State the facts as you remember them. If there's no dirt, she won't get very far. She has not listed specific times or dates, or police reports – nothing."

Martin walked to the door, opening it slightly.

"And one more thing," Martin said, turning to face Donovan. "Keep up with the news. This harassment thing is touching a lot of people. Some innocent men could be ruined by it. My goal is to keep you from being one of those guys."

As Martin exited, Donovan turned his attention to Len.

"Call Maddie Rollins in Public Relations. Have her come in here."

"On it!"

Donovan told Len. "Let's get my statement written."

He glanced at his computer calendar.

Shit. Not a good day to be out in public, but I must do this.

"I have lunch with Asia Barber. I can't put it off."

Len smiled at him as he reached for the doorknob.

175

"It'll take PR some time to write your statement. Go see Miss Asia."

DONOVAN HAD NEVER SEEN HIS LIMOUSINE SHINE AS MUCH AS IT DID. Despite his worry over Mandisa's allegation, and the continuing pall of agony whenever he thought of not seeing Lynn anymore, Donovan couldn't resist teasing his protective officer.

"Trying to impress Asia Barber, Desmond?"

Desmond pulled the rear door open and waited for Donovan to get inside. Before he lowered himself to sit, Donovan crouched and glanced over the clean leather, the shiny chrome touches, the dustless surfaces. Whistling appreciation, he glanced back at Desmond, before entering the car.

"It's Asia Barber, sir," Desmond said before closing the door, as if that explained everything.

Donovan nodded, knowing full well what he meant. When they got to Asia's modest Hollywood Hills home, Desmond threw the car into park, saying, "I'll get her, sir."

Donovan didn't argue. He knew Asia's effect on others, had witnessed it with his daughter and his parents throughout their lives. Although he might not ever hear how Desmond had met Asia, or what had transpired between the two of them, he knew that Asia had offered a kind word, some advice, or even reassurance to the young military veteran. As he sat there trying to envision it, Donovan watched Desmond escort Asia from her home, her hand wound around his arm, his other hand gently over hers, guiding her toward the vehicle. When they reached the small step just past the door, Donovan heard Desmond say, "Mind that, Miss Asia. Don't want to be taking you to any hospitals today!"

He's under her spell, too.

Donovan glided out of the back seat, extending the door so that it was fully opened for Asia.

"Good afternoon, Donovan."

Donovan bent down to kiss the much shorter woman, taking in her neat appearance. A red brooch was pinned to her coat, a gift from his mother years ago. A dressy, wide-brimmed hat black with white stripes held a large white flower in its center, fronds shooting off from inside the petals. After a quick kiss, Asia placed one hand on the top of her hat, another on the car door to balance herself while getting inside. Donovan waited until she was in, then climbed in himself, taking the bench seat that faced Asia.

Thirty minutes later they were seated in a well-used leather booth at Musso's and Frank's. Although lunchtime, the restaurant was not crowded, a victim of time and age. The waiters still wore red tuxedo jackets, white linen still covered all the tables, and the menu still included the remarkable martinis for which they were famous.

"Did my dad bring you here?" Donovan looked around, imaging Paul Rue sitting at the mahogany bar.

"Your father would not be caught dead here," Asia remarked. "He didn't think it right that I went here. There were few things that I refused to cater to him about – this was one of them."

"Can't imagine you doing anything that would make him angry," Donovan said, knowing that it was often Asia who got angry with Paul.

"Well, it wasn't like this place was disreputable," Asia said, her hand running down the fancy menu. "He just felt I should go to places that catered more to us."

Donovan nodded, knowing his father supported other black businesses. Paul Rue tried to be a pillar in the community, had mellowed only to marry Phyllis his wife who was half white.

"Say, Miss Asia," Donovan asked, grabbing his own menu. "Did my father ever cheat on my mother?"

Large brown eyes shot to his.

"How could you ever think that! Your father was totally devoted to your mother," Asia declared. "Phyllis was his only girl-

177

friend, only wife. And she never looked at anyone else after she met Paul Rue."

Asia flattened the menu with her hands. Then, as if she remembered something, she said, "It's all that talk about men who aren't gentlemen! It's that nasty Mandisa trying to get back at you after all these years! Am I right?"

"I hope you know that I would never –"

"Of course, you would not!" As another red-coated server approached the table, Asia held her hand out as a stop sign. "Not yet! Give us some more time, would you please?"

The waiter disappeared as Asia said, "Your father warned you about that girl, Donovan."

"Yes, ma'am, he did."

"And now she's making all these accusations ... looking to be popular again." Asia ran her hand over the embossed menu. "Not that I disagree with your divorce. Best thing that ever happened to you – and Dara!"

"Dara has never wanted to see her," Donovan admitted.

Another waiter approached the table with drinks, a martini for Asia and a scotch for Donovan who drained his glass immediately, Asia looking on in surprise.

"What else has you shook up?"

Donovan set the glass on the table, hard.

"I wish it was just Mandisa."

"That question about your father ... is that because of Mandisa?"

"I guess she made allegations against him, too," Donovan said, running a finger along the rim of the glass.

Donovan felt a glitch in his throat as he remembered his parents. His mother had always been soft, loving, only wanting to please the child that it took so long to conceive. Totally devoted to her family, a typical 1950s wife of a man who wanted that kind of respect and adoration.

"Your father was very kind to your mother. I'm sure you're the same way with Lynn."

"You remember her name?"

Asia leveled her eyes at Donovan, then took the olive-speared toothpick from her drink.

"I'm *not* senile, Donovan." She popped the olive into her mouth. "I can remember names."

"Of course, you can. I apologize."

Asia waved it off.

"Accepted. But tell me," she leaned toward Donovan, "where is she? I thought for sure you'd bring her with you to lunch."

Donovan resettled in his seat. "We've run into a glitch."

"Let me guess," Asia brought the glass to her lip, took a sip, set it down. "Dymettra."

Now Donovan's eyes widened.

"You know?"

"I was there," Asia said, her voice almost a whisper. "I was in the restroom when Dymettra and her few friends made those horrible comments."

"What?"

"Yes … About her dress, her hair –" Asia was nodding "– and the fact that she's white."

"That's not an issue!"

"Of course not," Asia took another drink. "I know it would not be. It was very jarring to hear Dymettra say those things to Lynn. And when she grabbed her arm –"

"She grabbed Lynn's arm?"

Donovan's voice was so loud that the few other patrons glanced toward their table. Asia reached out, patted Donovan's hand. She hushed Donovan before continuing, her voice lower yet.

"I tried to make Dymettra see how she was wrong, but that woman is just nasty." Two more pats, then she added, "She's another bullet you dodged, Donovan."

Donovan was nodding as he said, "You told me that when I dated her."

"Thank God, that didn't last long."

"I knew right away what she wanted was not what I was looking for," Donovan admitted. He picked the empty tumbler up, wishing that he'd left just a little in the glass for a second drink. "Not anything like Lynn. But Dymettra, Roy, the press, the fakeness of some of those award shows – they just all got to Lynn that night."

Asia was nodding, encouraging Donovan to vent.

"Plus, she just isn't feeling well. At all! Like she is not getting over her cancer treatments."

"Cancer?" Now Asia's voice was below a whisper. "She has cancer?"

"Breast cancer. She finished treatment over a year ago, but she can't seem to regain any strength. She's tired all the time," Donovan said. "That night – the one that you're talking about – she was exhausted. Crabby."

"Cancer will do that to a person."

"You know, Miss Asia?" Donovan looked off into the restaurant, willing himself to keep it together. "I didn't know anyone who had cancer before."

Asia placed her menu to the side. "Now you know two," she said.

"You? When?" Donovan's shocked eyes went to Asia's.

"Long time ago, I had breast cancer," Asia told him. "It was grueling treatment. Your dad kept it under wraps, didn't want my privacy breached. At the time, the press respected privacy. Now …" Asia tossed one hand up in a helpless motion.

Donovan motioned a waiter who indicated he'd be there as soon as he could.

"How did she handle the Dymettra thing?" Asia asked. "I mean, I tried to catch up with her – and you – but you left while I was speaking to Dymettra. And Roy."

"She broke up with me," Donovan said. The waiter came by and Donovan handed him the empty glass. "Another one, please. Miss Asia?"

Asia shook her head, said to the waiter, "We'll order when you return," and then turned inquiring eyes back to Donovan.

"She broke everything off with me," Donovan told her. "She said she couldn't handle it anymore."

He looked at Asia, shrugged his shoulders.

"I've only come back to work today," he added. "I was miserable at home. Dara told me that I need to make a plan to get her back."

Asia smiled at Dara's name, then shook one finger toward Donovan.

"That girl is magic! If she's telling you that, then you better do as she says. Go after what you want, Donovan."

Donovan placed his elbows on the table, then ran both hands through his hair.

"I wish it was that easy, Miss Asia. All this shi... I mean stuff coming at me: Roy Alloy suing the company, Lynn leaving, Mandisa's allegations."

"Donovan Rue." Asia sat up straighter in her chair. "You come from strong stock. You need to go after what you want. Be firm about it. Don't wallow in what's going on."

Donovan sat there, wordless.

"You know, I always say that life is peaks and valleys," Asia continued. "You are in a valley right now. But you'll figure out what to do when the moment comes to climb back out."

The waiter placed a new glass in front of Donovan, then took out his order pad.

DYMETTRA STOOD OUTSIDE OF DONOVAN'S OFFICE, TRYING TO THINK of a reason to see the boss. As she was contemplating what to complain about, the door flew open and Len Matthews exited. He nodded at her but flew down the hallway toward the elevator. Dymettra caught the office door before it closed, sliding in.

Donovan stood with his back to the room, gazing out the window, lost in his own thoughts. He turned from the window just in time to see Dymettra throw her coat on one of his club chairs.

"Donovan."

"What are you doing here?" He rounded the desk in three long strides, came right up to Dymettra's face, and almost grabbed her arms. But if he'd learned anything in the hour with his lawyer, it was that having kept his hands – and other body parts – to himself would save him and his company. Asia's confidence in him also influenced him, although he really wanted to lash out at the person who was ruining his chance of happiness. Donovan fisted his hands in frustration.

"How can you even come into my office?" he thundered.

"What?" Dymettra put on an air of innocence. "Are you upset that not many of us won last week?"

"You know what I'm upset about."

"I do?" Dymettra picked up her coat and slid into the couch, crossing her legs. "What?"

"You and your friends bullied Lynn Cerami."

"Who says?"

"*She said!*" Donovan ran a hand through his hair, then took several deep breaths to steady himself. "I thought you were an adult, Dymettra."

"I am," she said while she changed positions. "Adult enough to know that she's not right for you."

As he watched her contort on his office couch, Donovan brought his fisted hands up to his chest and erupted, a feral sound coming from his chest.

"Who the hell are you to think you know what's right for me?

"I was once with you –"

"Once!" Donovan said. "We went out to an award show where

you hung all over me until we weren't in front of cameras. That's not what I want. Or what I need!"

"You liked that once!"

Donovan cocked his head, then said, "I need more than just sex, Dymettra."

"But it was good!"

"It wasn't enough. And you weren't interested in anything other than how much I'm worth."

Dymettra looked at her long, red nails, buffed them against her shirt, and then said, "You don't need some sickly white woman either."

Donovan dropped his hands to his sides.

This is going nowhere. This woman is delirious if she thinks I'm taking her back.

Donovan's intercom sounded with Anna's pleasant voice. "PR has that statement for you now, Donovan. Should I send them in?"

"Give me a minute, Anna," Donovan called. Anyone could see into his glass-walled office. Two members of his PR team stood with their laptops in hand, ready to help him with his counter-statement against Mandisa. He wanted to get it finalized, fight for his good name, and then work on figuring out how to get Lynn back. He didn't have time for the trash that was taking up space on his office couch.

"What is it you want, Dymettra? I have a busy day."

"Just wanted to stop in … see if the boss could find some time for his best talent," she purred.

"Best talent … is that what you think you are?" Donovan said the words in a low, slow roll. "My best talent wasn't even nominated for any awards."

"That's because I haven't gotten anything good to do," Dymettra screamed out. "All the good ones are going to the youngsters now. Like that Bri girl."

"She's easy to work with – hungry like you once were."

Dymettra stood, then sauntered toward him. Reaching one

long, red-polished nail toward Donovan, she said, "Maybe I just need a little one-on-one with the boss. C'mon. Let's go out. Like old times, maybe?"

"No. No lunch. No dinner. Nothing. You've managed to make Lynn angry enough to leave me, but that doesn't mean that I would ever take you back." He watched Dymettra sway back to the couch, then put on her coat. "And I'm firm about this."

"You're firm, huh?" Laughing, Dymettra stood tall, proud, angry with her boss. "Let's see how firm you are when another woman adds to Mandisa Phillips' allegations!"

"Are you threatening me, Dymettra?"

"You don't want to lose two of Rue LA LA's big names now, do you?" she said as she picked up her oversized bag. "Two big names and the allegations against you are nothing but trouble for you, Donovan. Dating that white woman was a big issue for you."

"Big issue?"

"Don't you wonder what being publicly romantic with a white woman when the majority of your talent are people of color would do to influence upcoming talent?"

"That's none of your damn business." Donovan's hands were fisting again as he watched Dymettra walk to the door. "No one's business but mine."

"You think so? I probably saved your ass," Dymettra said, pulling the door open.

SHE SLAMMED HIS OFFICE DOOR, THEN WAITED WHILE TWO OTHER employees went inside Donovan's office. A large television screen near Donovan's office kept replaying the press conference where Mandisa's lawyer read the former wife's statement.

Mandisa Phillips ain't nobody. Who cares who hit her? Now if it were someone popular like me ...

A new idea entered Dymettra's mind like a dark fog.

Yeah, me. I'm a somebody. If I accuse him, it'll take him down a notch or two.

"Anna?"

Donovan's administrative assistant looked up from her desk.

"Yes, Miss Dymettra?"

"Have you been watching all this media coverage about Donovan's ex-wife?"

Anna looked cautiously up and down the hallway between her desk and Donovan's office.

"A little," she admitted. "It's kind of the only thing on television. Even here!"

"Well, it's something, isn't it? I wonder how she got that lawyer to help her out? Can't remember her name, but I know she's popular ..."

"Alison Berg?" Anna suggested. "Seems like that woman attracts all the women who are part of this Me Too thing. They all want her." Anna was ensnared in the gossip, unable to help herself. She leaned over the ledge of her desk and lowered her voice. "Someone told me –"

"Oops! Gotta run," Dymettra was pulling her phone out of her bag as she walked away from Anna. "Nice speaking with you."

By the time her driver pulled the car in front of the Rue LA LA building, Dymettra had secured an immediate meeting with Alison Berg to discuss the harassment she'd experienced while dating Donovan Rue.

ALISON BERG WAS WELL KNOWN AMONG CELEBRITIES FOR GETTING them what they wanted, especially if it had anything to do with men treating women badly. When Dymettra called insinuating that she was sexually harassed by Donovan Rue, Alison was happy to fit her into an already busy day. Mandisa Phillips needed support for her allegations.

"So, what can I do for you, Miss Dymettra?"

Dymettra threw her bag down on a chair, followed by her coat. She slumped into the seat next to her things and said, "I heard that Donovan Rue's wife is accusing him of harassment. I want to do that, too."

Alison took out a leather binder, opened it to a blank page and said, "Tell me what happened when you were with him."

"Well, we didn't date for long, but ..."

One thing about not working ... I can watch as much television as I want, read as much as I want ... sleep whenever I want ... cry whenever I want ...

Lynn had just finished making her breakfast and decided to turn on her favorite morning show. As she settled back with her bowl of cereal, Donovan Rue's image flashed up on the screen.

No, no, no, no no! I'm not up for seeing him, hearing about him. I don't want to see any pictures ... he's probably already got new 'eye candy', as Bea put it. No! Where'd I put the remote?

Spying it on the edge of the television stand, Lynn reluctantly put down her bowl and struggled to a standing position from the cushy couch. It seemed to take forever to get up and walk to where the remote sat, but it was enough time for the breathless anchors to read the latest news about women making accusations against prominent celebrities. By the time Lynn reached for the remote, she forgot about switching the machine off; she turned the volume up.

"Donovan Rue, owner and chief operating officer of Rue LA LA, has been accused by his former wife of physical and mental harassment. Within hours of her statement, Rue LA LA performer Dymettra came forward to also accuse the CEO. This comes in the wake of other music celebrities and executives who've been accused."

What? Donovan? No, he wouldn't do something like that.

Lynn plopped down on an ottoman nearest the black box.

The other anchor took over the announcement as the screen filled with Donovan's response to their accusations.

"Mr. Rue released a statement this morning to combat these allegations, saying, quote:

I wish to state unequivocally that I did not verbally or physically assault Mandisa Phillips Rue either before or during our marriage, nor have I ever laid a hand on any person ... We live in a country with a free press who should not convict a man simply on someone's accusations.

"Mr. Rue took over the company from his father. Paul Rue, who started the music empire, is also accused of harassment. Donovan Rue ..."

As the anchor droned on with the accomplishments of Donovan, the history of the business, and video of Donovan at various events, Lynn found herself remembering tender dark eyes, open honesty during their silly game of Twenty Questions.

There's no way ...

Her cell phone began ringing. When she saw her oldest son's name on the Caller ID, she knew it wasn't going to be an easy talk.

"Mom," Connor's intense voice radiated anger down the line. "Are you watching the Today show?"

"Yes ..."

"That asshole! Aren't you glad it's over? Aren't you glad that you won't be seen with someone who's violent!"

"Connor!" Lynn angrily switched her television off, fought with herself for control before she went into mother mode. "Look ... these are accusations. They must be proven. In this country –"

"Yeah, I know. Innocent until proven guilty," Connor's voice sounded sharp as he cut his mother off. "But you know that a lot of these accusations are true. A lot of these accused guys themselves are saying that they did stuff they're not proud of."

"It's a new era, Connor."

"Doesn't matter. Women don't and didn't deserve this. Then and now."

Trying to maintain her patience with Connor, Lynn said, "What I'm saying is that many of these guys came into power when it was considered normal to do what they did." *Oh, God. Listen to me. I'm trying to make the situation good and it just isn't. Connor is right.* "Connor," Lynn felt herself getting more tired as the discussion went on, "of course it's wrong – then and now. Your father never would have treated me like those men, and he certainly did not belittle women in the workplace."

"Like Donovan Rue!"

"No!" Lynn blinked back sudden tears. "I don't believe he'd do that kind of thing. I know he had a tumultuous marriage, that his first wife was out for all she could get –"

"He told you that?"

"A long time ago," Lynn answered.

The silence at the other end of the line spoke volumes about Connor's disapproval of the entire situation.

No. He does not get a say in who I date. He doesn't get to judge a man that he's choosing not to know.

"Look, I need to finish my breakfast, lay down for a while."

It was enough to change the subject.

"Already?" Connor asked. "When did you get up?"

"About an hour or so ago," Lynn lied, knowing that she hadn't even been up for half an hour.

"Okay," Connor's voice relaxed. "You sure you're okay in getting to that test by yourself?"

"Yes," Lynn answered. "It's just another stupid test."

Chapter 23

*A*nother test.

Reluctant to leave the warm covers, Lynn turned to look at her alarm clock. Eight in the morning. Her appointment was at ten. She could try to sleep some more, but sleep was elusive with her racing mind.

Yes, more tests. But listen to yourself. You wanted this. You're screwing everything up! You've been forced to take a medical leave because you screwed up at work, yelled at some student. Granted, you don't remember doing that, but four people witnessed it, and Brad said to take a leave and get better.

Or quit. No one told me to do that, but I could ...

But I love my job! Well, not my boss. But I love my international students! I'm not old! I'm just ...

Turning the other way, Lynn dragged the covers up under her chin and began rehashing the evening everything with Donovan had gone wrong.

You're the one who messed things up with Donovan. He didn't seem to mind your quirks, and even though Dymettra made all those ugly comments, he didn't care. You shouldn't care. But you ran away. You ended it.

Moving from her side to her back, Lynn smelled her sheets.

They need to be changed. Everything in this house needs to be cleaned. I can't find my cleaning stuff – I can't find anything – unless it's in plain sight.

Fisting her bedsheets, Lynn yearned to fall back to sleep.

Five more minutes ... just five. Who am I kidding? That won't help. Half the time I sleep, but I wake up exhausted. I'm so, so tired.

The alarm clock buzzed. Lynn hit it again, then pushed the blankets aside.

Something must be wrong. Right? That chemo nurse can't be right, can she? "It can take some chemo patients three to four years to get back to normal."

Lynn struggled to sit up.

Damn. Ridiculous. It shouldn't be hard to get out of bed. No way I can survive another three years feeling like this – coming up with all these tricks to function.

After momentarily dangling her legs over the side of the bed, Lynn stood and turned the alarm clock off just as it began sounding again. She recalled the visit to the neurologist, a Dr. Chang, who had politely listened to her cancer story but seemed distant, as if he'd had a million women complain of chemo-brain. It had taken his equally disinterested staff two weeks to set up the MRI.

But it's just another test.

INSIDE THE OLD MEDICAL BUILDING, THINGS WERE DARK AND OLD, nothing like the bright and cheery atmosphere of her oncologist's office. Lynn could barely see to write out the admittance paperwork.

A cheery nurse, her smile a direct contrast to the drab surroundings, called Lynn back to the exam room and then instructed her to lie on a very narrow bed, her neck cradled, earplugs inserted, and a final support pulled over her face.

"Here's something to hold," the bright nurse said. "If you need anything, just squeeze it."

The nurse pushed a side button which moved Lynn's gurney back into the MRI machine.

Hmmm ... now I know why people get claustrophobic.

She knew that some people likened the experience to being

inside a coffin. All Lynn could do was lie in a narrow tunnel-like machine, unable to see anything. After a few pops and crackles, the machine made loud, angry noises like the fire alarm sounds in her office. Lynn felt her heart start kicking into overdrive, her breath coming in fearful bursts.

Good God, what kind of test is this?

The ongoing fire alarm sounds ended. A short, staccato noise started up, a new, pulsating sound. Without thought, Lynn began counting each pulse of the awful noise. It stopped abruptly, after one hundred and sixty-one beats.

"How are you doing?" a voice asked. Lynn realized that although it was impossible to move her head, she had closed her eyes. Her breathing had evened out, her heartbeat was normal.

"I'm good," she replied, knowing that she was indeed handling it better. She settled in for the remainder of a test that the nurse had said would take thirty to forty minutes.

Suddenly that nurse was back.

"I'm pulling you out," she called out.

Oh, good. I'm done. That went quickly.

As the gurney rolled out of the machine, Lynn was greeted by the same woman whose face now appeared upset, tears threatening to spill out of brown eyes.

"The doctor wants to inject you with a drug that will show images better," the nurse said. "It's not in Dr. Chang's original order, but Dr. Rubenstein – the radiologist observing this test – feels it's necessary. But before we proceed, I need you to sign these forms."

Why?

"But Dr. Chang didn't order any drugs, right?"

"No." The nurse seemed to sound pleading as she said, "But the radiologist thinks it's warranted. I'll give you an injection then we'll complete the scan."

What do I do?

Lynn allowed herself a minute to consider, wondering what

had happened to this poor nurse who was beseeching Lynn to sign the forms.

Well, I'm here now. Don't want to do this again. Might as well sign it, get it all done at once.

"Okay, let's do it." Lynn signed more shabby forms and settled back into her uncomfortable bed. The nurse left the room with the signed documents, then returned with a syringe of something cold that she injected into Lynn's vein. Finishing the injection, she pushed the button sending Lynn back into the horrible noise. Twenty minutes later, the somber nurse returned, pulled Lynn out, and instructed her to dress and go to the waiting room until she got a copy of the doctor's findings.

Findings? It's just another stupid test ...

Ten minutes later, a tall, portly man came out.

"Mrs. Cerami?"

Lynn stood, nodded, and he indicated that she should follow him back into the testing area.

"Well, I have good news and bad news," the white-coated man said. Lynn glanced at the embroidery of *Dr. Sam Rubenstein* on his jacket. He barely drew a breath before he continued. "The bad news is that there is a four-centimeter mass on your brain. The good news is that is that it's not *in* your brain."

Lynn's chemo fog shrouded her understanding as she listened to the dire words.

A mass. Four-something meters. Is that large? What drugs do they use to fix this? Oh, shit ... is this a tumor? Surgery? Oh, my God ...

The doctor was continuing. "You need to go immediately to the hospital. I've already spoken with Dr. Chang. He and a neurosurgeon will meet you there."

Lynn was grabbing her keys from an outside pocket of her purse, turning to leave, mumbling, "I need to go home first ..."

"Don't wait too long," Dr. Rubenstein was saying. Lynn forced herself to shove the chemo fog aside, to hear what he was saying. "I can't emphasize how important it is for you to get to the hospital," he said. "That tumor is quite large, and they will need to do emergency surgery."

"Yes, I heard you," Lynn acknowledged.

In the parking lot, she stopped, wondering who to call, what to do.

Michael! Michael will know.

Then she realized that the old comfort that she'd relied on for twenty-five years was no longer available. Briefly, she allowed the sadness to overwhelm her. Getting in her car, she grabbed her steering wheel, bent her head down to it, trying to figure out what to do.

She kept reviewing the morning's test, the awful noise, the nurse who at first was so cheerful and then so sad looking, the doctor saying, *"I've got good news and bad news."*

Not sure who to ask for help, Lynn was dialing her eldest son's number before she even realized what she was doing.

IN DOWNTOWN LOS ANGELES, DONOVAN LOUNGED BACK IN HIS office chair and closed his eyes briefly. His defensive statement had been issued. In it, he answered all his former wife's harassment allegations. Now all he could do was wait to see what returning volley Mandy might launch back. *Maybe she needs money? I gave her so much back then. How can she even do this?* He'd thought that speaking to Dara, his daughter, would be difficult.

"Guess she hates you as much as she hates me," had been Dara's first reaction. Then after considering the damage Mandisa's claim could do to both Donovan and the company that was her grandfather's legacy, Dara got angry, spewing words that contained vitriol Donovan didn't know she possessed.

One bright moment in the last two days had been a text from Lynn.

Sorry you're going through this. Hang in there.

But when he texted back with a question as to how she was doing, there was silence.

The sound of a quick knock and his door quickly opening forced Donovan to open his eyes. Len was coming in, his face betraying concern.

"Donovan," he said, "I have some news I think you need to hear."

Donovan gave him a questioning look, held his breath in case it was more allegations. Len was shaking his head, as if reading Donovan's mind.

"Not work-related," the older man said then took a deep breath before rushing out the words. "It's about Lynn."

"Lynn?"

Donovan's entire frame stiffened with alertness, his words bursting.

"What about Lynn?"

"Donovan, I –"

The sudden ringing of Donovan's cell stopped Len from speaking.

"Donovan Rue."

A long pause while Donovan listened to the voice at the other end. Finally, he replied, "I'll go there right now. When are you coming in?"

Another silence, then he said, "I'll have my admin make arrangements for you. Is this the right number? Good. She'll call you. You need to be here."

Ending the call, he stood gracefully, pulling his charcoal gray suit coat back on. Then he jotted down the number from his last call and handed it to Len.

"I don't want to know how you found all this out, Len," he said, "but I could kiss you for bringing me this information."

He started toward the door, saying, "I will be at Simi Valley Hospital. Have Ana make arrangements to get Owen Cerami out here as soon as possible."

As he entered the Emergency Room waiting area, Donovan hoped Lynn would not tell him to leave. An aide directed him back down a hallway where Lynn, dressed in a blue hospital gown, was sitting on a bed behind a gray privacy curtain, an IV inserted into her hand. Connor sat next to her in a dumpy beige chair.

Neither Cerami noticed his approach. Connor, dressed in his work clothes, appeared both angry and anxious as he sat there focusing on his mother. Lynn was talking on Connor's cell phone. She did not look any different than she had a few weeks before when she had sent Donovan away.

"No, Owen. I'm fine. Really. You don't need to come here. Connor is with me, and I'm sure Bea will help if I need it."

Bea. Gotta tell Bea. Maybe Connor already called her.

Listening for a few more minutes, Lynn ran her hands over her short blond curls, then said, "It's too expensive for you to come out here again! I'll talk to you when I have more details. I love you, too."

Call ended, she began to hand the cell phone back to Connor and finally saw Donovan standing at the door.

"Donovan!"

Throwing the phone at Connor, Lynn slid off the bed and walked directly into Donovan's arms, stretching the IV tubing to its limits.

God, I have missed these arms. Missed her perfume, missed her hair tickling me under my chin.

Lynn was saying, "I'm sorry, so, so sorry –"

"There's nothing to be sorry for," Donovan soothed her, running his hands up and down her back as he silently thanked God for this reunion. The couple stood there holding one another for long minutes. As they disconnected, Donovan said, "But let's talk about that stuff later. Tell me what's going on."

Helped back onto her bed, Lynn went through the entire saga

of the day, then backtracked to tell him that Dr. Meyer had finally agreed she should have an MRI.

"Oh, wait!" she said as she held on to his hand. "I didn't even tell you that I was forced to take a medical leave."

As usual, Donovan was attentive as he listened to her story, cussing about the forced leave. When Lynn finished, he asked, "Should we find a different hospital? Not that this is a bad hospital; but there are other hospitals in LA that are more respected for brain surgeries."

Connor, who had been texting on his cell phone, glanced up. Donovan could sense the young man's dislike, his anger at someone interfering and suggesting a change for his mother. As for Lynn, she seemed so out of touch that he doubted she was even quite aware that they were talking about cutting into her head. On top of that, Donovan wondered if there was even time to change hospitals or doctors. On his way to the hospital he'd grilled the protective officer that Len had hired. The man made it sound like surgery was going to happen immediately.

Before anyone could discuss the possible relocation, a nurse called, "Mrs. Cerami?" and pulled the curtain aside. "We're going up to your room now."

A male nurse greeted them at the ICU room. Without pulling a privacy curtain around Lynn's bed, he helped her change, took the standard vitals, and then had her get into bed, tying her arm to the bed's side-rail by using the blood pressure cuff. Trying to keep things light, Lynn asked, "I can't get out of bed?"

"We don't want you to get out of bed," the man answered as he finished the adjustment and then pressed a button on the machine nearest her head. Instantly, the machine started the noise associated with the blood pressure cuff filling with air. At the same time a monitor over Lynn's head spewed instant results, including heart rates and oxygen levels. The nurse faced Connor and Donovan.

"Should have introduced myself first," he said. "I'm Dan. I'll be her nurse until seven tomorrow morning. And you are?"

Connor said his name, adding, "I'm her eldest son."

Donovan puffed himself up to full height and said, "I'm Lynn's fiancée, Donovan."

Dan smiled indicating that he'd been played before.

"There'll be some papers for Lynn to sign that will allow you to be here, Mr. Rue. But I don't imagine that will be a problem."

Donovan smiled as the nurse left the room.

Good. Or I'll buy this hospital and then let's see if they throw me out.

"Just bring me the forms," Lynn was telling Dan.

Connor glanced at his mother. "Mom, are you sure?"

Lynn smiled. "Sure? Sure of what? Donovan is welcome to stay, Connor."

Her tone made no allowances for disgruntled sons.

Another man entered the room. Tall, wearing small wire-framed glasses, he appeared cold, stoic. He approached the bed and introduced himself.

"I am Dr. Urambu, the neurosurgeon."

He was so serious looking, sounded so foreign with his African accent, that Donovan was uncomfortable with him. While the man asked some routine neural questions, Donovan studied the dark-eyed, ebony-skinned man who stood at the end of Lynn's bed.

Is this guy good enough to work on Lynn?

Astonished at his own unexpected racism, Donovan realized that he was judging this man simply by looks.

Me. Of all the people in this room, how can I let this person's looks turn me off so quickly?

Yet he still wondered if some Los Angeles hospital might be better suited for Lynn's problems – UCLA, USC, or Cedars Sinai.

Really. We really should consider going to a better, bigger hospital. But who am I to force this family – Connor or Lynn – to make a different choice? Connor would probably ask Lynn to stay here just out of spite for me.

"First we need a few more tests. And we need to schedule an

OR for the six or seven hours the surgery will take," Dr. Urambu said to them.

Connor, finally putting his cell phone in a pocket, became silent.

Lynn did not ask for more details. It was Donovan who decided that this doctor needed some vetting.

"How many of these surgeries have you done?" Donovan asked, worried that perhaps Dr. Urambu was a rookie.

A rookie, a new doc, ain't touching my Lynn's head.

Dr. Urambu looked Donovan directly in the eyes.

"Sir," he said firmly. "This is what I do for a living."

The surgeon's quiet confidence relaxed Donovan, and he thought he could read the same relief on Connor's face. Lynn continued to be quite out of it, as if she was so stupefied at what was happening to her that she tuned it all out.

Dr. Urambu turned his steady gaze to Lynn.

"Do you have any questions for me?"

Lynn shook her head.

The rest of that day and all the next were full of tests and doctors' visits. All the medical people wore somber faces, telling Donovan that what was going on was pretty damn serious.

Dr. Chang, the neurologist, let go of his serious composure only once, to ask Lynn, "How did you even manage to walk across a room?"

Donovan recalled the walks they had taken, including the horrid cancer walk, when Lynn seemed to lose her balance, drag her foot, and required frequent rest breaks. Now that they knew the cause, Donovan could see why Lynn hadn't been able to finish it. And it explained how she almost fell during the last angry walk away from the limo on the night Lynn broke it all off.

AFTER THEY WHEELED LYNN TO THE OR THE FOLLOWING MORNING, Donovan sat in a waiting room with Connor. They were the only two waiting, alone in their worry.

Connor could barely contain himself.

"I can't do this, man," he said suddenly.

Connor's eyes darkened with anger. Donovan couldn't help but be fascinated while watching the dark brown eyes blaze to black as the younger man's anger flared out at him.

"I can't sit here with you and not know why the hell you think you can just walk back into my mother's life after you left her just a few weeks ago." He slammed the top of his ever-present laptop closed. "Tell me!"

Donovan, worried about Lynn, wanted to ignore the younger man's negative vibe, to focus on Lynn. Sitting there, calm on the surface, hands in his lap, he had not expected the volcano of emotion that was Connor to erupt that morning. After a moment of consideration, he looked into Connor's eyes.

"I did not leave your mother," he said, forcing his tone to stay quiet. "Your mother left me."

"No way!" Connor moved his laptop to a side table. "My mother is crazy about you!"

"As I am about her," Donovan stated with resolve. "But unfortunately, when you're in the public eye like I am, and you bring someone into it like I did, people can make things difficult. They become predators, wanting to take the weaker person down."

"But they're not just out for people like my mother," Connor said. "Your ex-wife is out for you, right? Accusing you of harassment? That doesn't affect my mother."

Donovan winced as if Connor had punched him in the gut.

This kid can really throw shade.

Donovan cocked his head to the side, trying to decide how to best address that situation. Before he had a chance, Connor was firing again.

"And your old man, too! She's accusing him as well," Connor blasted. "Two peas in a pod and all that."

Donovan's eyes iced with anger.

"My father was a fine, upstanding man – a gentleman. He loved my mother more than any man I've known loves his wife. She was his only girlfriend, his only wife," Donovan stated. "Was he difficult? Yes. Hard to work for? Yes. He was very hard on me, but he loved my mother and me with all he had."

A brief pause and then Donovan sent a volley back to Connor.

"Probably as much as your father loved your mother."

Now Connor caught his breath. They both reached for coffee cups, Donovan hoping that Connor would calm down. When he thought he saw a bit of it, Donovan continued.

"Here's what happened. Your mother and I went to big event on a Friday. It was like everything came to a head – the paparazzi with their constant picture taking, screaming her name, yelling out my name. Media people were dragging her into interviews, and even a few people harassing her in the restroom."

Connor shifted in his chair, taking in all the information. "She did say that she hated all the stuff that went with your events. I can't say I blame her – sounds like hell."

Donovan nodded. "It is, and I'm used to it."

"So … what?" Connor turned toward Donovan. "Did she tell you that she was done? What happened?"

Donovan's tried and failed to keep the pain from his face.

"We argued the entire ride home," he said. "She was devastated by the entire evening." He shook his head, then added, "She was upset and agitated from the moment I picked her up." He sipped the watered-down coffee, his eyes unfocused as he remembered their last encounter. "And she hated her dress!" Donovan chuckled at that part of the memory.

"I'm sorry, Donovan," Connor said, contrition in his words as he shook his dark head. "I knew Mom was suffering. This chemo-brain – or at least what we thought was chemo-brain – made her so exhausted. It made her crabby sometimes, too. She was irritated with me the last time we spoke which, I think, was that night."

They both paused, looking at their shoes, trying not to think that the woman they both loved might not make it through the grueling surgery. Just as they started to come around, the door to the surgical waiting room banged open and Owen bounced into the room.

"Owen!"

Connor stood up and hugged his brother with all his strength. Owen returned the hug, slapping Connor on the back before letting go.

As the affection ended, Connor said, "I thought Mom told you to stay put."

"She did! But when have I ever listened to her?" he asked becoming the naughty blond boy in all the family photos. "Actually," Owen motioned to a now standing Donovan, "this guy funded the trip. I couldn't do it on my own."

Owen turned to Donovan and gave him a big hug, too.

"Thanks, man. It means a lot to me," a quieter Owen told him.

They settled into the waiting room chairs just as the computer board changed, listing Lynn as officially in the operating room. Tendrils of worry climbed up Donovan's back.

Shit. This is really happening.

IN DOWNTOWN LOS ANGELES, ALISON BERG WAS TRYING TO HANDLE a last-minute meeting with a very disgruntled client. It was not going well.

"So, I'm not understanding you," Mandisa Phillips said to her lawyer. "You said that we'd have another press conference, say something more about Donovan Rue. I bust my ass to get you information to release today, and now you want to wait? Why?"

Alison Berg closed her door, certain that everyone on her floor could hear Mandisa's loud voice.

"Lynn Cerami is having a craniotomy this morning."

"Too bad for her."

"One of my friends works at the hospital she's at, told me that she'd seen Donovan Rue at the hospital; that's how I found out."

Alison eyed Mandisa, recognizing the tiger facing her.

Does she care how I found out? Does she care about anything?

"I know you want to get this done."

"I want that asshole ended!" Mandisa thundered.

Alison felt a knot of queasiness in her stomach. This push to get Donovan Rue destroyed did not feel justified to her. Mandy Phillips, Donovan's ex-wife, could not give concrete dates or evidence to her claim that she had been hit or verbally abused.

"We will go forward," Alison hedged, hoping to calm Mandisa down. "But not during this time. How do you think the public will react to you going forward on the day your ex-husband's girl-friend, a breast cancer survivor, is undergoing serious surgery?"

After letting loose a curse, Mandisa left.

"So," Owen said as he put his backpack down next to a chair in the waiting room, "what's going on? I got part of the story from you, Con, when you called me to say you were taking her here, and probably a lot of fluff from Mom, and nothing at all other than a 'here's your ticket; get your ass out here' from Donovan."

Connor told the story with Donovan adding some things about various doctors and their comments.

"Well, I knew something was up when we were home for that cookout," Owen said. "First, the side mirror on her car … you got that fixed, didn't you, Con?" When Connor nodded, Owen continued, "Maribelle said that the kitchen was a disaster! Nothing was prepared, the counters were all clogged up, the dishes all dirty – not at all the mother-in-law she knows."

"Yeah! I noticed she wasn't cleaning up as much, that very little was getting done inside the house anymore, *and* she doesn't walk like she used to," Connor said. "Mom was a big walker. She and Dad would walk everywhere, sometimes even in the mountains."

"Really?" Now it was Donovan's turn to be surprised. He assumed that Lynn had not walked much even before the cancer treatment slowed her down. "She was getting wobblier – is that a word? – lately. Claimed that she had bad balance even before she got sick."

Both young men chuckled. Owen began telling a story involving Lynn walking to get the morning newspaper and spraining her angle. Connor's phone buzzed as Owen continued his story, "It always struck me as weird that a woman who could dance the night away, could not walk a straight line if she wanted to."

They were just discussing who would be with Lynn when she left the hospital, wondering what kind of care she might need, when the waiting room door opened slowly, Dara Rue's head looking around it.

All three men stood.

Dara entered, scanning the room to check out the occupants. Seeing Owen, she looked confused. Then her eyes locked with Connor and she smiled with sparkle in her eyes. Donovan was blown away.

What's up with this?

He called out, "Dara! How did you know where I was?"

Dara crossed the room to hug her father, whispering, "Sorry, Dad."

She took the last of the four chairs while Donovan introduced her to Owen.

"So how did you know about my mom?" he asked.

"Len." Dara crossed her long legs, glanced at Connor, and arranged a burgundy tunic over her leggings before she answered, "Len gave me a call." Dara ignored their quizzical looks and asked, "But tell me; how's Lynn doing?"

All the male eyes in the room glanced at the high-tech board that listed Lynn as being in surgery.

"This is really happening …" Dara said in wonder.

Connor nodded and replied, "Yup."

Dara reached for her father's hand.

"I'm glad that you're here, Dad."

Donovan scoffed, then said, "I can't stay away anymore."

He eyed Lynn's two sons and said in earnest, "I am never leaving your mother alone again. These past few weeks have been torture for me. I wanted so badly to come out here, talk to her … but I felt like she needed space. Well not any longer. She's stuck with me. I love Lynn." Donovan continued, "I know that I cannot replace your father. That's not my goal. And you are both old enough to know that. I want to make Lynn happy, just like she makes me happy – and peaceful. I want to give her back some of the fun that life has taken away these last few years. And I am firm about this."

Dara raised her eyebrows, then war-whooped.

"When he says, 'And I am firm about this,' you better not mess with the man."

Once more the door slammed open, this time with as much energy as when Owen entered. From the doorway, Bea Owens looked the little group over and tried to smile. When that failed, she walked in.

"Figured you'd be here," she said as she hastened toward them, hugging each Cerami. "What happened? How is she? What can I do?"

As she looked around for a chair, a waiting room attendee came over to the group.

"You're here for Lynn Cerami?"

When they nodded, she said, "The word from the operating room is that it is underway, she's doing well, and that they anticipate her being there for another six hours."

Although they all seemed to relax in their chairs, the tension was still high. The volunteer said, "Why don't all of you go get a late breakfast? Or early lunch? This will be a long day for all of you."

As they wandered out of the hospital into the California bright sunshine, Connor's cell phone rang. Thinking it might be a hospital call concerning his mother, he answered without looking at the caller identification.

"Connor Cerami."

The voice on the sending side of the phone call was loud enough for all of them to catch the basics. Cassie Manders was making her presence known.

"Hello, Ms. Manders. I mean, *Doctor* Manders. Sorry 'bout that," he said politely while both Owen, Bea, and Donovan grimaced at his hello. Cassie's reputation preceded her.

"We're just leaving for lunch," he continued. A pause, then Connor was saying, "My brother, two friends of my mom's, and a daughter of one of those friends." He rolled his eyes at Dara after he finished that introduction.

There were a few more exchanges with Connor simply saying yes or no. Suddenly, Connor was forcefully saying, "That's really not necessary. We can handle this."

Although the others could not make out distinct words, Cassie's voice suddenly sounded insistent. Then there was a loud click as she ended the call without getting Connor's approval for something.

"Damn bitch," Connor cursed. "Can't even leave Mom alone when she's having surgery."

Bea's eyes were filled with daggers waiting to dart out if she encountered Cassie.

"*Serious* surgery! That woman doesn't have a clue."

Only Donovan was calm about the possibility of coming face to face with Cassie Manders.

"Did I hear her say something about taking us to lunch?" Donovan asked Connor. When he nodded, Donovan said, "I'd like to meet the 'damn bitch'. Where did she say to go?" He motioned toward the black limo that sat in the parking lot. "Desmond can take all of us."

FIFTEEN MINUTES LATER THEY PULLED INTO A PANERA'S PARKING lot. Cassie was there to greet them.

"You poor dears," she said as she gave first Connor and then Owen a hug. Both men stiffened as they submitted to the forced intimacy. Cassie was looking over Owen's shoulder during that hug, eyeing Donovan.

"You must be Donovan Rue!" she squealed. "Lynn has told me so much about you!"

I bet not!

Donovan stepped forward and extended his hand, saying, "Hello, Ms. Manders."

"It's *Doctor* Manders," Cassie emphasized, "but you can call me Cassie. Such an honor to meet you!"

With unwanted familiarity, she slipped her arm through his and led the group into the sandwich shop, completely ignoring Dara's confused, questioning glance toward her father, and Bea's look of utter loathing.

Donovan endured lunch. When Cassie started in again about all the details Lynn had given her concerning their relationship, he decided to be honest.

"I doubt Lynn has told you very much at all. She respects my privacy."

"Oh, well," Cassie did not seem to get the hint. "She told me that you are an amazing man and I can certainly see why."

Because I can eat a sandwich? Because I can listen to this woman go on and on? What makes me amazing?

Cassie giggled, failing to see the worry, nor noticing their side-eyed looks of disdain, or that the food was barely being touched.

The only one who ate much of anything or spoke was Cassie Manders.

Lynn described her perfectly: hippie clothing, sandals, unkempt hair, loud voice.

Just as Donovan was trying to figure out an exit strategy, Owen stood up, saying, "We need to go!" He grabbed his empty tray and turned toward the garbage can. "I'm kinda anxious to hear what's going on."

As they began opening the doors to Donovan's limo, Cassie walked briskly ahead of them toward her Jetta.

"Wait!" she called out. "I want you to take these flowers to Lynn."

She pulled out a huge bouquet of Stargazer lilies from the back seat of her car, the flowers droopy from sitting inside a closed, hot vehicle. She giggled again, handing the flowers to Donovan.

I'm getting super annoyed with this "damn bitch." How does Lynn endure this?

She flounced back to her car, got in, and yelled out, "Byyyyeeeee!"

She's clueless about her effect on others.

"That woman!" Bea was the first to become un-tongue-tied. "I hate that woman! She never even asked how Lynn was!"

"She was more interested in meeting Donovan Rue!" Connor said as he gritted his teeth together.

Dara grabbed the flowers from her father's arms.

"Well, I happen to know that Lynn hates Stargazer lilies. Can't stand the smell of them!"

"Anyone else notice that the hospital has signs all over that say, 'No Flowers'?" Owen added.

Dara strode over to the nearest garbage can and dumped them in. As she turned back to the small group, she said, "Let's go see how Lynn is doing!"

Chapter 24

*D*onovan couldn't sit, his anxiety ratcheting up once they were back in the tiny waiting room. He watched Connor take out his laptop again, pulling up what looked like a corporate email account.

"Might as well try to work," Connor muttered as he booted up.

Dara had placed her laptop on her lap. In the few minutes they'd had alone at lunch, Dara told Donovan that she was working on a client's social media page that she was contracted to improve.

Turning his head, Donovan observed Bea: resolute, determined, looking more than a little worried. She sat in the waiting room, pretending to read emails on her phone. Donovan knew that Bea would always be there for Lynn; it was why Donovan had called Bea when Lynn was taken for one of the MRIs the day before surgery.

A true friend, Donovan thought as he wandered out of the waiting room. He couldn't sit and wait, but he could not leave either.

What can I do?

As he walked toward the hospital's exit, he neared a small courtyard nook.

"You doin' okay?"

Unable to avoid eavesdropping, Donovan slowed his pace.

"Yeah, I know, being apart sucks, but you'll be all right. You're strong." A pause. "Thanks for understanding that I need to be with my mom right now."

"She's still in surgery," Owen was saying. "You know my mom's

208

awful boss? She basically made us meet her for lunch and never even asked how Mom was. The damn bitch."

There was a slight sniffle before Owen continued, "We've only had one update from the operating room. No one has come out of there, but they've got this super high-tech board that tells us what's going on. It says she's doing well."

Then there was a choking noise. Donovan almost walked to Owen, but stopped when he heard, "What if I lose my mom, too? Two parents in such a short time! I can't imagine it. I'm not ready for this, babe."

Now feeling like a voyeur, Donovan left Owen, knowing that Maribelle would comfort her husband. He began to walk the hospital grounds. They weren't large, but they were the typically well-maintained landscaping of southern California. Large bushes of birds of paradise flowers grew in pots everywhere. At one large windowed wall, a tree was filled with small, chirping birds who were feeding from nets that the groundskeepers had to be filling constantly. Donovan found the scene peaceful, serene, thought that it was perhaps the intention of whoever had put that tree there.

Not as peaceful as Lynn, though.

White Nancy Reagan roses also lined walkways plus the usual palm tree or two. There were benches to sit down and wait, but Donovan wanted to move. Activity helped relieve his agitation for other stressful situations; he hoped it would help here.

I should have made her see a brain specialist about this chemo-brain stuff, was his first analytical thought, but then, *Shit, she wouldn't have wanted to change doctors anyway. She likes this Dr. Meyer.*

Then his mind wandered to Cassie Manders and the inappropriate comments made at lunch. *"Damn bitch" is the right nickname for that woman. When Lynn gets better, I want her to get another job.* He slowed down at that thought. Lynn was independent, liked working with international students.

Then he focused on the time since she'd left him after the last event. He wondered again if he should have explained the whole Dymettra thing before that night.

And now I have this Mandy thing hanging over my head, too!

Donovan wandered around the grounds, and then up and down Sycamore Street without thinking about who he was, or whether people recognized him. Occasionally, he thought he saw Desmond in the limo tailing him, but his thoughts quickly went back to the lovely blonde woman in the middle of crucial surgery, the woman he loved.

WHAT WAS SUPPOSED TO BE A SIX OR SEVEN-HOUR OPERATION turned into eight. They were all back in the waiting room, sitting in the club chairs, one added for Bea. It got to the point where no one was talking. Finally, the board announced that Lynn Cerami was in Recovery. Dara noticed it first.

"She's out of surgery!" she cried out. Loud releases of breath came from both sons. Donovan, closing his eyes, was thanking God.

Thank you. Thank you, thank you!

Bea was realistic.

"We haven't heard from a real person yet," she said. "I want a doctor or a nurse to talk to us before I'm relieved."

A few minutes later, Dr. Urambu came in the room, his countenance more relaxed than Donovan and Connor had ever seen him.

"She is out of surgery, doing well," he said. "She won't be back in her room for an hour or so yet, but she's doing fine."

He pulled out a cell phone and pulled up a picture of a reddish blob on a white cloth, a ruler next to it.

"This is the tumor," he said as the others crowded around. "It was quite large, and a bit of it was too close to a sensitive area to remove during this surgery. So, we'll need to do Gamma Knife surgery to get the rest."

"Gamma what?" Bea muttered. "What a horrible name."

Donovan was already planning to do research on that strange name; Dara was googling it on her phone.

"But the tumor – was it ...?" Owen interrupted, then paused when Dr. Urambu looked at him. "Sorry. I'm Lynn's youngest son. Owen Cerami."

The doctor nodded as if he'd anticipated this one question.

"Our initial test said it was not cancer," he said.

Every person surrounding him let out a gasp of relief.

"But I am careful," he interrupted, "and Dr. Meyer and I decided that we should have it further tested. We'll know the results in a few days."

Connor pressed the point.

"But the initial test said it was okay?"

"Yes," Dr. Urambu smiled. "The first test indicated that it was benign. But we need the other tests to be certain. Your mother's original cancer was quite aggressive. I want to be sure."

They all nodded, then thanked the doctor as he walked out the door.

Startled by a hissing noise, Lynn became aware of her surroundings.

What time is it? Did they even do the surgery? How come I'm not in any pain? Where is everyone?

Aware that nature was calling, Lynn looked for help, then noticed a young woman standing quite near her bed. She asked her to call the nurse for a bedpan.

"Lynn, you don't need the nurse. You've got a catheter."

Lynn searched for and felt the unwelcome device and nodded that she understood. Reaching up with the arm that was not tethered by the blood cuff, she tentatively placed her hand on her head's bandage.

211

It's big. Crunchy! Like plaster of Paris around my head. Wish I could see it.

Glancing back again to the young woman, a light suddenly brightened inside Lynn's mind as she realized who was standing by her bed.

Dara!

"What are you doing here, sweetie?" she asked.

Dara was straightening the sheet, repetitively running her hand along the white fabric as if she was trying to iron away the wrinkles. After she glanced at the door, Dara looked Lynn over, her eyes glistening with tears.

"I'm waiting for the others to get back," she said. "They all went for food."

"What time is it?"

"It's around eight o'clock – at night," she answered as she checked her cell phone.

"The surgery was long?" Lynn asked.

"It was eight hours from the time you left pre-op until they got you to the recovery room. Then another two hours there, and then they brought you back here," Dara told her. "Everyone was hungry. I said I'd go later."

Dara pulled out her cell phone again, turned it off just as quickly, then glanced back at the door again.

Something's up with Dara.

A nurse came in and gave Lynn two injections into her IV.

"Can I have some water?" she asked.

"Small sips," the nurse said and then, noticing that the pitcher was empty, said, "I'll go get some."

Lynn was cold – an ongoing effect of chemotherapy – and asked Dara if her socks were nearby. When Dara went to put them on, she could only cover one foot.

"Hard, huh?" Lynn giggled. "The only time I've had to put socks on other people was when the boys were little – and they were wiggly! Thanks, Dara."

The nurse came in while Dara was trying to figure out what to do. A tube of some kind was inserted into Lynn's left foot, preventing anything from being placed there.

"Oh, that's an arterial line they put in during surgery. We have to keep that uncovered for a while," she said. "Would you like a warm blanket?"

Lynn's cell phone rang just as the nurse started covering her with the fresh blanket. Dara took the call, frowned, and covered the mouthpiece.

"It's Cassie," Dara said, shifting back and forth on her feet. "She's insisting on talking to you."

Dara seems anxious. Something is stressing her out, I hope the others come relieve her soon.

Lynn took the phone and immediately heard, "Lyyynnnnn!"

"Hi, Cassie."

"It was so good to see your family today. And that Donovan Rue is more handsome than in his pictures!"

"Oh," Lynn was surprised. "You saw them?"

"At lunch," Cassie sounded annoyed. "Didn't they tell you?"

"I haven't spoken to anyone other than Dara yet."

"Oh." Cassie's voice was disappointed. "Well, I wanted to tell you that I'll stop by the hospital on Monday. Later!"

The line went cold.

She never asked me how I was doing.

As she placed her phone aside, Bea entered the room, approached the bed. From her semi-reclined position in the bed, Lynn melted into her best friend's arms. After they broke apart, Bea started in on how awful Lynn's headdress was. Lynn realized that Bea had reached her limit; she needed to leave now that she knew Lynn was okay.

"Gotta get going. Seeing two Hungries tonight; gotta design some more strapless, slits-up-to-the-hoo-ha trash for another event that's coming up. Be glad you don't gotta go to this one!"

"Bea ... thanks for being here. You know how much I love you."

As Bea left her bedside, two strong Cerami young men took either side. Both leaned down at once, almost knocking their heads. Lynn wrapped her untethered arm around Owen, whispering, "I thought I told you not to come!" and raised her other hand as far as possible to touch Connor. He leaned further down, so she had easier access.

Looking over Connor's shoulder, Lynn saw Dara and Donovan conferring. She caught Donovan's eyes and smiled. As he grinned back at her, she could see that he was exhausted. His usually neat appearance was replaced by wrinkles and a skewed tie. His eyes were shadowed, and his hair needed to be combed. Still, Lynn was glad that he was there; she had missed him the last few weeks and she knew she needed additional strength to get through this new medical crisis. But presently, her sons were demanding her attention.

"Mom, I'm glad this day is over!" Connor said, then kissed her cheek again. "Jesus, you scared us."

"Again!" Owen added.

"Are you staying at home?"

"Yeah," Owen said. "So's Connor."

"Both of you?" Lynn was secretly thrilled, then asked, "Did Maribelle come with you?"

"Hey, excuse me, you two," Connor said as he started walking away. "I need to talk to Dara."

Lynn watched as Connor walked to Dara, saw the look Dara gave her son.

Didn't they just meet?

As she watched her oldest son's interaction with Dara, Owen was answering her question about Maribelle.

"She couldn't come – teaching, you know. But I spoke with her a couple times today and she told me to tell you that she's prayin' for you."

"That's nice," Lynn said as she yawned.

When was the last time I yawned? I can't remember. And this tired feels normal, not like it's unbearable.

A nurse had quietly entered the room, was checking out the monitors, and noticed Lynn's big yawn.

"Mr. Cerami," she addressed Owen, "it might be a good idea for everyone to let Lynn rest. You should *all* probably get some sleep."

"Yeah. Good idea," Owen said. "We'll get going."

He leaned down to kiss his mother who placed her hands in his blond hair.

"I'm glad you disobeyed me and came here," she whispered.

Owen's voice was thick as he replied, "I love you too, Mom. I'll be here tomorrow."

He had barely reached Connor and Dara when Donovan came to her side.

"Peace ..." Donovan leaned down to nuzzle Lynn's nose, then kissed her cheek. "I was so worried about you."

Lynn put her hand on Donovan's arm, closed her eyes in bliss as he kissed her cheek again. One hand was making small, gentle, circular movements on her arm; the other was holding the hand with the IV.

"I'm glad you're here. Thank you."

"No thanks ever necessary," he replied, his voice rough with emotion. "I'm never leaving you alone ever again."

Lynn smiled, ocean-blue eyes looking up into deep brown eyes that were glistening with –

What? Joy? Love? How can I be in this romantic moment while lying in a hospital bed?

"I must look terrible," she whispered to him.

Donovan nuzzled her nose again, releasing a whisper of a laugh.

"You are a sight for sore eyes, just like the saying goes."

"Even with a big white headdress?" Lynn teased. "Maybe I'll wear this forever."

"Mmmm … I might like your hair a little longer." He ran his hand along the very edge of her hairline.

"I love your curly hair," Lynn said as she reached up and ran her fingers through Donovan's silky hair.

"Night, Momster!" called Owen from the door. Both Donovan and Lynn looked over to see her boys leave the room. Dara was leaning against the doorjamb, staring at them with wonder.

"I should go. Let you sleep," Donovan said. His mouth found hers and took a brief kiss.

Lynn made a soft mewling sound, indicating that she wanted more. He met her need, then stood up.

"Seriously. Try to rest. I'll be back tomorrow, early."

Chapter 25

*L*ess than twenty-four hours later, Lynn was released from hospital care. It had been a long day with frequent doctor visits including one by Dr. Urambu who, with the nurse's assistance, removed the bandage from Lynn's head, the last step before release.

"Would you like to see your head?" the nurse asked. Lynn's answer was a quick yes, but she noticed that Dr. Urambu gave a forbidding glance at the nurse who ignored him and brought in an old hand mirror. Lynn looked at her head.

Staples. God, how many are there? And I'm bald. Again. Time to make a joke.

"I look like Robocop."

A headband of large steel staples ran from ear to ear, but the back of her head still had hair which had grown at least an inch with all the steroids she'd received in the last four days. She returned the mirror to the nurse, again seeing a scowl across Dr. Urambu's face.

"Don't wash your head from the staples forward. Keep that area dry. And don't cover it." Dr. Urambu was determined as he again asked her, "Do you have any questions for me?" When Lynn said no, he smiled widely, then stated, "No restrictions. Go home."

"None?" Lynn was incredulous.

"None."

Dr. Urambu's eyes even smiled.

Maybe he gets nervous before doing surgery. I'd be nervous if I had to cut into someone's skull.

Owen and Connor both came, according to Owen, "to spring

you free." Once settled in her own car's passenger seat, Lynn felt like the world looked different. Brighter. Clearer.

Maybe because it's Sunday?

Owen was busy giving a humorous running monologue about all the nurses she'd had. Lynn only half-listened. Connor drove, his hands gripping the steering wheel, driving under the speed limit and taking corners far too slowly.

Nervous? Anxious to get me home before I fall apart again?

Once Owen finished his story, the sons argued about which way she should enter her home. When she entered – using the garage entrance – a walker was waiting for her, Donovan behind it.

"Do I really need this thing?" she moaned.

"The hospital suggested you have it until you are sure-footed," Donovan said gently. Sighing, Lynn grabbed the front bar and wheeled into her family room. Launching for her old green recliner, she flopped into the familiar comfort, curled up, and hoped to pass out. Sleepless for the most part in the hospital, she was now beyond tired.

This feels real. I'm tired, not sleepy like I felt all the time last year.

When she woke a couple of hours later, the men were around her kitchen table eating sandwiches. She heard Owen talking presumably to Maribelle, telling her the same long nurse story. Connor was on his laptop, a box full of medications by his side, taking a bottle one at a time and typing onto a spreadsheet.

Just like Michael used to do.

Donovan was the first to notice that she was awake.

"Hey, there, Peace!" he said with a huge smile on his face. "Good to see you awake."

"Believe me; you get no sleep in a hospital," Lynn said as she stretched her legs out in front of the chair. She placed her hand tentatively on her staples.

"Do they hurt?"

"No." Lynn fingered the entire line going from right to left and then back again. "No, not at all. Isn't that weird? How many of these things are there?"

Donovan came over to look, taking a seat on the ottoman in front of her. He looked her head over, then shook his own.

"Too many to count," he answered. "Now what about something to eat?"

Owen brought over a plate with a full sandwich and some chips. Lynn wrinkled her nose in disgust.

"I'm not hungry," she said. "Hospital food is the worst - very bland."

"You gotta eat something, Mom!"

Connor looked up from his computer screen. "Some of these meds need to be taken on a full stomach."

"How about a shake?" Donovan suggested. "I'll text Dara; see if she can get one. She's on the way here."

Lynn nodded, numb to the idea. She swung her legs down and stood up. Immediately, three men were standing and reaching for her. She avoided them by grabbing the walker.

"I can go to the bathroom by myself," she said to them. "It's nice not to have to use a bedpan *or* to be tied to a bed."

She drove her walker toward the hallway half-bathroom. After finishing, she glanced at the room's large mirror, noting the staples, the bald front part of her head, the dirty hair in back, and the smelly clothes that she desperately wanted to change.

Dara greeted her with a chocolate shake. After two or three sips, Lynn put it down.

"I need to go upstairs, shower, and change."

Connor became the rule master of the group.

"You can't get your head wet."

"Yeah, I know. But I can't stand these clothes anymore. I'm sure I can shower if I find something to cover my head."

He whipped out a shower cap.

"Got one of these when I picked up the meds," he said, smiling at his mother.

"But," Donovan intervened, "you can't go up the stairs by yourself." He was smiling, too. "You need an escort."

Nope, no way. I want some privacy!

As she mulled over what to do, Bea walked in. She'd heard the exchange, took one look at Lynn, and said, "I can take you up there, Lynn."

Bea stood in front, Donovan in back, while Lynn slowly climbed the two short flights of steps.

"I think maybe at least tonight you should sleep in that downstairs bedroom," he said, pointing to the guest room. Lynn nodded, then went into her bedroom. She was stunned.

This room is a mess!

Clothes everywhere, the bedcovers a blue blob mess, and the bedside table full of books, bottles, cups, and the alarm clock with the trusty snooze alarm button. As she gazed at the pit that was her bedroom, Bea located underwear, pajamas, socks, and a robe.

"Now about that hair …" She started becoming the authoritative Bea that Lynn loved. She took the shower cap out of its wrapping and placed it on Lynn's head, covering the staples.

"Can you wash the back of my head?" Lynn asked.

Bea nodded. "Happy to. I'll even shave it for you."

Lynn shook her head. "No … just wash what's there. I'll be Robocop for a while."

"Robocop? Odd name …"

Bea surveyed the skin that was twisted and pulled together under each staple.

"Seventy-two."

"What?"

"The number of staples you have," Bea told her. "There are seventy-two."

"Thanks. I wonder if Urambu will take them out when I see him in two weeks?"

Lynn sat along the bathtub edge while Bea washed the filthy hair that just barely touched the back of her neck. Lynn's eyes went to the two countertops in her large bathroom. Every inch of space was filled with items she'd used and had left on the counter, afraid of losing things. Brushes and combs were scattered among makeup and bathroom cleansers as were necklaces and earrings.

"Oh, my God!" she cried out. "I've become a hoarder."

Bea laughed. "Hardly."

"No! Look at the countertop! There's no space for anything."

Lynn was embarrassed. She was always proud of the way she kept her home. Walking into the bathroom tonight was like entering an alternate world where a stranger lived.

"I knew I was keeping things in plain sight, so I could easily find everything, but this is ridiculous."

Bea finished combing out Lynn's hair and was going to leave her to navigate the shower when she paused.

"Lynn, should I stay in here? Just to be sure you're okay?"

Her dark eyes were sympathetic, caring.

Lynn sighed again. She knew she'd better go along with it since the others would worry if she was left alone in a shower stall.

They'll probably break down the door if I drop the soap and they hear a clunk.

"Can't hurt to be careful, I suppose," Lynn said.

Bea sat on the bathtub edge while Lynn showered, reading aloud celebrity gossip.

"You gotta keep up with this, girl! Especially if you're seeing Donovan."

Four days of crisis washed away – the MRI, the crying nurse, the Emergency Room, the surgery. Down the drain went the hospital's scents, medications, and dirt.

"You *are* still seeing him, right?" Bea asked as the water stopped. "I mean, what with all the gossip about him and his ex-wife ..."

"Innocent until proven guilty," Lynn stated, just as she had done with Connor.

"Don't you ever wonder if it's at all true?" Bea asked.

"Beatrice! You of all people saying that!" Lynn accepted the large towel Bea held out to her.

"Me sayin' it is because I've been one of these women!" She grunted. "Me Too could be my mantra."

"Yes, I know," Lynn said, "and I'm sorry he was so awful to you."

"You don't have to say it," Bea said as she put the wet towel over a bar. "You told me so. I know."

"Wasn't going to say it," Lynn pulled a clean t-shirt over her head. "But I can't believe that Donovan did what Mandisa Phillips is accusing him of. Or that his father did anything like that."

"His father was difficult with a capital D from what I hear," Bea said.

Lynn finished tying her robe and wanting to stop the conversation, asked, "Should we go back down?"

Bea walked in front of her again, going down backward. Glancing to the side of the stairs, Lynn saw her living room and nearly cried. Dust covered everything. Pillows that were normally precisely in place on the sofa were catawampus all over the room. One chair, usually slipcovered to hide severe damage done by an old cat, was bare. Stuffing fell out where the upholstery was shredded.

"Bea, look at my living room," Lynn whispered. Bea nodded and placed an arm around her friend as they both observed the mess. "How could I have let this go?"

"Darling, don't worry about it," Bea urged her. "We all thought you were just too tired and sick to do any housework. This is cleanable. Fixable."

Lynn shook her head as she came down the last step, entering the room.

"But didn't anyone wonder? I mean, it's not like I was a slob before I got cancer."

Her musings were interrupted by Owen.

"Mom! Let's go for a walk!"

When Donovan appeared with her light coat, Lynn decided that it might be good to get some fresh air.

I'm not about to give in. So, I'm walking.

After the short walk, truly exhausted. Lynn crawled into bed. Placing her head on the pillow, she instantly felt the pressure of the staples. No matter how she moved her head, a staple pressed into her scalp.

How will I ever sleep?

Donovan came in to check on her.

"Goodnight, Peace."

"How?"

The word came out as a gulp, quickly followed by tears. The horror of the last few days clicked into place in Lynn's fixed brain, overwhelmed by lack of sleep, new medications, and the worry she felt the others carrying.

"Hey ..." Donovan ran his hand down her cheek. "It's okay. You're home. The tumor is gone! Everything is going to be good now. You'll see."

"There's no way I can sleep with these things pressing into my head," Lynn moaned and then added, "And I'm so tired. I mean, *really* tired."

Donovan kicked off his shoes, laid down next to her, and cuddled up.

"You're probably just overtired, Peace. Just relax," he suggested as he placed his arm around her. "I'll stay here a bit."

LYNN WOKE WITH A STARTLE TWO HOURS LATER. THE HOUSE WAS quiet. Donovan was not there. She hoped that he had gone home to rest, knowing that the last few days had been hard on him.

Hard on all of them.

Creeping into her family room, the house a comforting dark quiet, Lynn hoped everyone was asleep. Puffing up a couple of stray pillows left on the couch, she hoped to find comfort there when Connor came in and flicked on the overhead light.

"Oh!" Lynn said, her eyes adjusting. Her son jumped at hearing her voice.

"Mom!" he called out, placing his hand over his heart. "Geez, I'm sorry; I thought you were asleep."

"For a brief time," Lynn said, then asked, "Why are you up?"

"It's time for your medication." Connor smiled at his mission. "It's good that I don't have to wake you up now, but I might have to at four when there are more meds ... and then again at six ..."

Lynn followed him into the kitchen, saying, "Of course, the meds couldn't be timed for the patient's benefit." Posted on the fridge was Connor's spreadsheet of when Lynn needed to take seven different medications.

"You gradually wean off some of these," he said, using a pen to point out some of the medications while Lynn read the list over. "And some you take until you see the docs again."

He handed her a capful of something. "This one is the steroid," he said, "You took it in the hospital the entire time you were there. It's supposed to help with your swelling."

He explained the rest of the medications with the efficiency of a pharmacist. Lynn knew that he had probably researched every pill and plotted out the exact time she needed to take them. Now he would make sure that she took the doses at the right time. Lynn smiled up from the rim of her water glass.

So much like Michael.

A tear threatened to form, but she took a deep breath then slammed back the pills.

"You okay, Mom?" Connor asked.

She touched his arm, running a hand up and down. "Yeah, I'm good. I was thinking that your dad would've done the same kind of spreadsheet, woken me up like this ..."

Connor scratched his head, then nodded. "Yeah, I guess so."

He turned to place the meds back in a cabinet. His mother asked, "Do you miss him, Connor?"

His eyes moved down to level with hers.

"Yes. A ton." The answer was firm, but not emotional. "There were so many times this week when I wanted to get advice from him. And it occurred to me that I'm the oldest Cerami now; I have to fill in for him."

Oh, boy. How do I change this thinking?

"Connor ..." Lynn rubbed his arm again. "I know I haven't been well for a long time and I appreciate all you've done for me. But you've got to go to work tomorrow. I can handle being home."

"Oh, I am! Tomorrow. I missed four days and I need to get in. Oh!"

His sudden outburst had Lynn looking around to see if something had suddenly poked him, or if he'd stepped on something sharp.

"I forgot to tell you!" Connor's eyes were fully awake, sparkling with joy when he said, "I got a big promotion! I'm getting my own team."

"Wow. Congratulations! When did this happen?"

"The day of the first MRI," he said as he closed the cabinet. "I just put it out of my mind with all that was going on."

"Sorry 'bout that."

"Don't be sorry, Mom. I'm glad I was here, and work was very understanding, but tomorrow after I drop Owen off at LAX, I have to go in."

"Good." Lynn tried stifling a yawn, but it was too late to hide it from her son.

"Bedtime, Mom," Connor instructed. "Remember you used to say that even if you just lay there, you were resting? Go rest."

Chapter 26

Connor's deep voice was the first thing Lynn heard when she woke two hours later. Glancing at the side table's digital clock, she noted the time: five forty-five.

I never wake up this early.

She knew that it would be impossible to sleep any longer; she didn't feel the need to punch a snooze button.

Entering her kitchen, she encountered startled faces, imagined hers was just as surprised looking at seeing Connor, Owen, and Donovan sitting at the kitchen table, drinking coffee so very early in the day.

"You're up early!" Owen called out.

Connor was on his laptop again, checking the flight's scheduled take-off time.

"Plane is on time," he told the group. "We better leave. Who knows how bad the traffic might be?" Then he acknowledged his mother. "Hey, Mom. Did you sleep after four?"

Connor got up and kissed his mother then handed her another capful of pills. Owen walked over and threw his arms around his mother, kissing her, too. Lynn hugged back hard.

"I'm glad you came," she whispered.

"Me, too." Owen's voice was clogged with tears. "Love you, Mom."

He turned to Donovan who was standing and observing the family. Thrusting his hand toward Donovan, Owen said, "Thanks for making this happen. It means a lot to me."

Donovan smiled, slapped Owen's back.

"No problem, Owen."

So that's how he got here, Lynn thought, then smiled her thanks to Donovan, who moved a hand to her face, running his knuckles down the right side.

Lynn chased her boys out the garage door, lingering at it while she watched Connor's car back out of the doorway. Tears filled her eyes as she realized what great kids she had. *Oh, Michael ...*

"Hey, Peace," Donovan's voice interrupted her thoughts. "You've got to be hungry! You barely ate anything yesterday."

She walked back into the room and flopped into the green chair again.

"I'm not hungry."

"Gotta eat, Peace."

When she didn't answer him, Donovan suggested, "I'm not much of a cook, but I can make oatmeal."

He didn't give her an out, making oatmeal which had bananas, raisins, almonds, brown sugar, and a little milk. Lynn took a couple of mouthfuls before putting the bowl aside.

"Not good?" Donovan asked. "Try this instead."

He handed her coffee.

"Everything tastes funny," Lynn said, wrinkling her nose again after taking a sip. "I guess it's a way to lose weight."

She noticed that Donovan had his laptop open on her kitchen table. He was dressed casually in sweats and another band t-shirt.

"Aren't you going to work?" she asked.

"Not at the office," he said. "I'm not leaving you alone – at least for today. I rarely work off site, but the docs said we should hang out with you, at least for this week."

She smiled at him, liking the idea of spending a normal business day with him, especially after all she'd just been through.

"An entire week off work?" She was surprised. "Can *the* Donovan Rue take a whole week away from work?"

Donovan looked back at his computer, picked up his phone, and then shifted in embarrassment.

"Honestly? No," he admitted. "But Bea and Dara are taking time to be here when I can't."

"I really think I could be alone …"

Donovan put his ever-present cell phone down and came to crouch in front of the green chair. Gently, he took her hands, saying, "I know you do, and I respect your independence. But you are just home from the hospital. We were told to not leave you alone for a couple of weeks, so that's what we are going to do. Take advantage of me being around."

His eyes gleamed.

"Hey," she said and stroked her fingers gently down his face. "I'm not ready for *that* yet. Crazy man."

And she truly was not interested. Not in food. Not in television. Or in sex. Looking at how relaxed Donovan appeared was not even tempting. He was sexy. He was handsome. She didn't care.

Is that weird or what?

Donovan took her answer with ease.

"Can't imagine you would be – yet," he purred, then stood up. "What morning talk show should I turn on?"

Later while Donovan was on his phone, Lynn called Cassie.

"I appreciate your offer of coming over, but I'm home and just not up for visitors."

"Home? Already?"

Lynn was trying to count to ten.

Ok, not interested in food, or sex, or putting up with Cassie Manders.

LIFE SETTLED INTO A RECOVERY ROUTINE. NAPS, PILLS, MORE NAPS, television shows, naps, pills, reading, and a daily walk.

On the fourth day home, Donovan drove Lynn to Dr. Meyer's Office, determined to make sure that Lynn was getting good care.

After waiting in the reception area forever, Lynn and Donovan were escorted back to an exam room where they waited an equally long time. Finally, Meyer came in, sighing loudly, and saying, "Sorry. Last week everyone had an emergency!"

"Including me," Lynn said. Donovan couldn't wait any longer.

"Did the test results come back on Lynn's tumor?"

Meyer eyed them both with steely resolve.

"Dr. Urambu and I decided to have further tests done," she said.

Lynn just nodded, but Donovan grew very still.

Shit. Do they suspect something?

"But it was found negative when it was tested during surgery, right?"

Meyer nodded. "Both Urambu and I want to make sure that it is truly negative. Lynn had a very serious, ugly cancer. We'll know in a couple of weeks."

A couple of weeks!

"No way to rush the results?"

"No, there's not. We must be careful," Meyer said, and then added, "Come back in a month, Lynn."

When he saw Lynn was taking it well, Donovan answered the doctor with a soft, "Okay. You'll let us know, right?"

"I can wait for the results," Lynn told Donovan when she sensed his impatience.

Connor, Dara, and Bea were waiting for the results, too. Crowded in her kitchen, each cursed when Lynn told them that it might be a while.

"Why in the hell did they tell you that they would know one way or the other during the surgery?" Bea demanded. "Maybe I should call this Dr. Urambu and tell him he's torturing us."

"Bea –" Lynn began, but Connor interrupted his mother.

"Well, I'm not cooking tonight," he announced, then threw the potholder on the counter and left the room.

Only Dara seemed calm with Lynn's announcement.

The one person I expected to have zero patience with this and she's as cool as can be.

Lynn recognized the anxiety in the room. The group wanted to know that Lynn was well, that this was only a blip in life's radar. They wanted to get on with normal. And normal included having Lynn in it.

Why aren't I concerned? Why am I so patient? For God's sake, let them run their tests. They'll let me know soon enough.

She repositioned herself in her green chair and closing her eyes, found refuge from the whirlwind of emotions around her.

THE NEXT DAY'S APPOINTMENT – WHICH DONOVAN ALSO TOOK HER to – was to see Lynn's internist. Standard procedure, the hospitalist had told her, when you leave a hospital, but just another irritation for Lynn.

"Shall we run some blood sugar tests?"

God, like I want to find out if I have diabetes right now? No thank you.

Lynn declined.

"How about an EKG?"

Doesn't she know that it's all I can do to handle the head stuff, and wait for the cancer testing to come back? I don't need any more tests!

As they headed back to her home, Lynn asked, "Is it crazy that I want some say in my treatment? To tell a doc that you don't want a test that could tell you something *more* is wrong with you?"

Donovan reached across the car's console to take Lynn's hand.

"I think you have a right," he said. "You need a break right now and it seems choosing to not have a test is one minor way to take charge of your life and your health."

Chapter 27

*F*inally in her own bed, Lynn woke at five, marveling at the shadow play on her bedroom walls as the sun filtered through windows, brightening the space. Noting the patterns and prisms on her angled walls, she felt a peaceful presence. Seeing a sleeping Donovan next to her, Lynn was startled. Dressed in yet another black band t-shirt and gray sweats, he was out cold, slightly snoring.

A first. Donovan Rue in this bed. Probably snuck in once I passed out.

At first, she felt guilty that he was in her room, her bed. Then she wondered if his presence was what was making her so calm and had maybe helped her sleep better. After several weeks of crashing hard and then sleeping only a couple of hours, she had finally slept most of one night.

She glanced again at the early dawn light, growing in intensity by the minute. It was strangely soothing. While Donovan enjoyed his deep sleep, Lynn was analyzing all that had happened to that point, wondering why she felt as if Donovan's presence was not the only one.

Wow. All those doctors. All these meds. No wonder Cathy hated it so much.

Lynn recognized that her sister's spirit was with her. She wasn't one to believe in much spiritual mumbo-jumbo, but she was certain she felt Cathy's strong persona as she lay there, remembering her sister's smell, voice, and stubbornness.

Okay, Cathy. I get it. I understand why you wouldn't take the meds you were supposed to take; why you refused to see all the docs; why you were so stubborn. All this stuff is overwhelming. I get it.

231

As the light finally came full inside the bedroom, Lynn renewed her determination to try to get well. She was not Cathy. She did what her doctors told her to do, had done so throughout her chemo and radiation treatments. She knew she'd follow the neurosurgeon's instructions so that she could be as healthy as possible. She could easily remember which medication was prescribed by which doctor and when to take it.

I could put together that Peer Mentor training agenda now. Or the orientation agenda. It wouldn't need any editing either!

Her musings were interrupted when Donovan inhaled loudly and stretched.

"Good morning, beautiful," he said in a sleepy, sexy voice.

Lynn smiled down from her semi-seated position against double pillows, responding, "Hardly. I have staples in my head, partially covered by congealed blood. Half my head is shaved; the rest is greasy and long." She ran her fingers through the longer hair. "And I'm sure my head is swollen."

She touched her face, stroking her fingers over it, stopping when she reached her right eye.

"Is my eye swollen?"

Donovan sat up and ran his fingers gently over the right side of her face.

"A little," he admitted. "You're still beautiful, Peace."

Then he moved his hands away and gave her his usual intense stare, his eyes wandering over her entire head, then back to the eye.

"I'm so glad that you're here."

Lynn smiled widely.

"Me, too," she said. "Although it's weird, isn't it? In the hospital, I was never worried, never afraid that I wouldn't be here."

Donovan stretched again.

"We need to talk, Lynn," he said. "I need to clear up something."

"Not now." Knowing that Donovan wanted to talk about

Dymettra and Mandisa, Lynn's answer was firm. "Not in this bed and not now."

She gave Donovan a half-smile.

"I should be mad at you for being in my bedroom, uninvited."

"So ..." he reached over and made to tickle her, but quickly stopped as if realizing that it was perhaps too soon for that. "Should we call Mandisa and ask her if you can get added to her lawsuit?"

"Donovan!" Lynn swatted his arm.

"With your eye looking like it does, you could say I punched you."

"Don't even joke about that."

"Well, it needs to be talked about! If I have to joke to get you to listen –"

"Look, I want us to talk, too, but I'm not ready for it," she said, folding her hands in her lap. "Also, this isn't the place where I want to talk about that woman and that evening, or your ex, for that matter." She sighed. "My emotions are all over the place. Can you be patient with me?"

"Not an issue."

As Lynn neared the last step after Donovan cleared her for independent walking, she inhaled several combined fragrances of the flowers people had sent her.

Thank God there aren't any Stargazer lilies.

As she sat in her green chair, Dara brought over cereal and toast. Lynn wrinkled her nose.

"Gotta eat!" Dara instructed. "Just try." Dara noticed Lynn's swollen eyes. "Wow! That eye is a mess!" Opening her laptop, Dara said, "Let's see what Mr. Google says to do about swollen eyes."

Lynn set her cereal aside, one spoonful taken. Next the toast was added to the bowl. A bowl of grapes had been left near her. She tried one and gracefully spit it out on a napkin.

It all tastes terrible. Now I understand what loss of appetite means, why Cathy wouldn't eat at the end. Why am I thinking so much about my sister? Because she was dying. You are not going to die from this.

Just then Donovan entered the room, dressed immaculately in a navy pin-striped suit, a baby blue shirt, and bright tie. Lynn's breath caught when she saw him, acknowledging yet again that he was the most gorgeous man she'd ever met.

"You're going to work?"

"Roy Alloy's lawyers are coming to meet with Rue LA LA's," he said. "It's about that stupid lawsuit he's brought against us. I need to be there."

"Understandably."

"Yes," Donovan adjusted the cuffs on his shirt. "Martin – my personal attorney – is also coming. He's concerned that this lawsuit might impact anything that Mandy is considering."

His mouth straightened into a firm line of disgust. From the kitchen, Mandy's daughter yelled out, "That bitch! Let her try!"

Dara wandered out with the wet tea bag. "Don't forget, Dad, that I'll call her if you want me to."

"No," Donovan said. "She isn't doing anything other than making noise right now." He turned his attention to Lynn. "Magic is going to be here today. She can see that you don't overdo it."

Donovan looked at his daughter as he fidgeted with his tie.

"Magic?" Lynn looked from father to daughter, noting Dara giving her father a hard look, one that said, *"Not this again, Dad."*

"I doubt she'll give you much trouble. It's not like she can go anywhere with an eye like that!" He winked at Lynn to let her know he was teasing, then leaned down and kissed her, then her eye.

"I'll be back for dinner tonight," He picked up his laptop, then said, "And Connor is coming to cook. He wouldn't tell me what he was making, but I imagine it's good. Can't imagine that boy does anything half-assed."

They all laughed at Connor's expense as Donovan headed out the door.

"THEY'RE HERE," LEN SAID AS DONOVAN WALKED TOWARD HIS office.

There goes any humor to this day. Entering the sleek conference room, Donovan first noticed Roy Alloy. *One can't help but notice this guy. What the hell?* Roy Alloy's attire directly contradicted the polished, professional world that his two attorneys represented. Kianna Davidson and Miata Holmes worked for one of the biggest law firms in Los Angeles. They had already opened leather brief-cases and set up their laptops while Roy lounged in his chair, tilting it back on its legs.

On the opposite side of the table, Mason Polk and Darin Hemmingdale sat, representing Rue LA LA. Martin Lawson, Donovan's private attorney, rounded out the group.

"Maybe we should begin," Darin suggested. "You've asked for this meet and greet. What is it you'd like to discuss?"

Miata glanced up from her laptop.

"Our client would like to settle this lawsuit."

Darin sat a little straighter in his chair. "Rue LA LA has not done anything wrong."

Following Miata's repetition of Roy Alloy's allegations, Darin said, "The first thing we did when this came down was review Roy Alloy's contract. Nothing is out of line on our end."

"What!" Roy Allow sat up straighter in his chair, almost tipping it over. "They were all over my first album, promoted it, sent me on tour. This time around, nada."

"Roy," Kianna's tone held a cautionary note. "Leave this to us."

As he sent his lawyer a glare, the Rue LA LA attorneys started to grill him.

"Did you tour?"

"Yes … well, I got tired in Asia. Canceled a few."

"Did you get airplay?"

"Well, yeah …"

"And I know we did marketing," Mason threw some brightly colored slicks on the table.

Roy glanced at them, tossed them aside.

"Not enough!" he thundered. "I didn't sell like I did the first time out."

"Because you didn't follow through," Darin said, grabbing a copy of Roy Alloy's contract. "You didn't re-schedule several major city concerts. "You were asked for interviews and didn't do them."

"Don't like that shit."

"Roy …" Miata tried to haul in her client. But Roy was on a roll.

"He spends a lot of time with that blond piece."

"She has a name!" Donovan said.

Mason put a hand on Donovan's arm.

"And he's harassing women!"

"Those are allegations," Martin said calmly yet firmly. "They have not gone forward because there's no evidence."

"Wait 'til they get some!" Roy's eyes shown with hatred towards Donovan. "Bet your pretty little friend will dump you."

"Enough." Darin tried to stop the singer. Donovan was bristling in his chair.

One more thing about Lynn and I'll –

"No, it ain't enough! I want more marketing, more support, and most of all I want this dickhead to pay attention to me when I want to talk."

"There's nothing in your contract that says Donovan Rue has to talk to you whenever you want to complain," Mason said with a slight chuckle. "No one gets that kind of treatment."

"Used to," Roy said as he slumped back in his chair. "Back when

Daddy ran the company. All those old performers talk about how hands-on Paul Rue was."

Yeah, but they don't tell you how demanding he was, do they, Roy?

The angry singer snapped his fingers and suddenly sat upright again. "But Daddy's being called out, too, right? Are all the Rues sleaze-bags?"

Donovan stood up, hands fisted, Martin following him, a hand on his arm. After slightly pushing Donovan back into his chair, Martin said, "We are not here to talk about that allegation. And you, Mr. Alloy, are not part of it."

"Well, I ain't no woman," Roy answered. "Look, all I want is more money, better promotions, and for this asshole to treat me like one of his stars. Because I am! And if Dymettra and that other woman *do* take you to court and win, you will lose at least two big money makers."

Heavy tension filled the room as Roy Alloy's two attorneys looked at one another. One shrugged, the other asked, "Does Rue LA LA want to work toward settling this so we don't go to court?"

Darin Hemmingdale looked at Donovan. Donovan thought he saw a question in those eyes, then saw Mason Polk give a subtle shake to his head. Donovan shook his, too, knowing that he could've given in, paid Roy off, and be done with it all.

No. No way. I'm not letting this asshole win.

Darin stood and the others, except for Roy, followed suit. "We're done here."

Lynn placed the wet tea bag against her eyes.

Feels good. I wonder if it'll work.

Dara brought her breakfast into the family room and turned on morning TV for Lynn. As they settled in to watch, a huge birthday cake was wheeled onto the set for one of the show's anchors. Everyone was singing and celebrating his birthday.

Dara sighed.

"You okay?" Lynn asked.

After a slight smile, Dara answered, "Yeah, I guess … it's just that it was my birthday the day you got out of the hospital. Dad forgot."

Lynn felt a sudden pang of guilt.

"Oh, Dara! I'm sorry. I'm sure it was just an oversight."

"Of course," Dara answered as she wiped her mouth. "He's had a few things on his mind these last few weeks. And he was really, really worried for you."

"That's nice, but birthdays are important!"

Lynn was already planning on sending a text to either Connor or Donovan about bringing home a birthday cake for dinner. She turned attention to the newspaper that Donovan had left on the table closest to her.

You can't do much with one eye.

It was almost impossible to read the newspaper. Lynn threw it aside and continued to watch shows with Dara. During a break, she grabbed her cell phone and texted Connor and Donovan to alert them about the birthday oversight.

"So, you have a sister?" Dara asked as she picked up a picture frame showing Lynn and a woman who looked very much like her.

"Had," Lynn clarified. "She died about three years ago."

"Did she have –"

"Yes. Cancer," Lynn said in a clipped tone. "But she had a very different attitude from mine. She didn't want chemo or radiation and refused any surgery."

Dara's face, alarmed and concerned, was reflected by her quick question.

"Why?"

Lynn took the frame from her and remembered the night she'd told Cathy that she, too, had breast cancer.

"Jesus … God … Damn it all to hell!"

"I'll be okay, Cath."

"How can you say that? You know our family history!"

"Yes –"

"All those women – including our own mother - all died incredibly young. The women in our family are cursed!"

"Cathy. I am going to fight this."

"Like any of those treatments help. Do you want poison in your veins? Do you want someone cutting into sensitive skin? Good luck with that."

Remembering her sister's tirade, Lynn told Dara, "She didn't want it. She did nothing, and by the time I was diagnosed, she was too far gone to have any treatment."

Lynn set the picture frame down just a tad too hard.

"Did it scare you? What happened to her?" Dara asked, her eyes wide as she listened.

Lynn gazed off into the distance, then changed her cucumber slice.

"Maybe not as much as it should have," she admitted. "By the time I was diagnosed, I'd watched Cathy get sicker and sicker. *That* scared me, I guess. So, I told my oncologist that I'd do whatever she wanted me to do."

Grabbing a tissue, Lynn wiped her eyes.

"You loved her," Dara said.

"I was so mad at her for a while after she died," Lynn said, pulling another tissue out of its box. "She came out here once and spent the whole time treating me like I was the one dying! I couldn't make her see that at least I was trying to do something to get better."

Lynn twisted the tissue in her hands. "She died not long after that."

Silence followed until Dara asked, "How did Michael die?"

After hearing an abbreviated version of the story of the car crash that killed Lynn's husband, Dara asked another rapid-fire question.

"Which of your sons is most like Michael?" she asked as she

picked up cereal bowls, coffee cups, and the small dish of used cucumbers.

Lynn smiled, then gave a short laugh.

"Connor, I suppose! He looks like his dad. Owen is more like me."

"One thing's for sure," Dara said, "I am not at all like my mother." She paused, then continued, "I'm guessing at that. I don't really know her. But from what I've seen of her in media these past few weeks, I don't want to know her *at all*."

"You don't see her?" Lynn asked.

Dara shook her head, then shrugged.

"I tried a couple of times during college, but she just wasn't interested. I didn't see her much." Raising her eyes to Lynn, she said, "So, no mother for me."

"I'm sorry, Dara. That must hurt."

Dara's eyes pierced Lynn's with intensity.

"No. How can someone who was never involved in your life hurt you?" Dara plopped down into the green chair, her eyes cold and set with determination. "I don't want to talk about it anymore."

Chapter 28

The third time the doorbell rang Lynn shuffled along behind. Flowers and gifts had already been delivered. This time the traditional birthday song, done in harmony by a quartet of young voices, was a complete surprise to both Dara and Lynn.

Donovan did well. I wish I had my cell to snap this picture.

"Any more surprises at the front door this afternoon, Mrs. Cerami?"

The quartet was the last of the door surprises. Dara decided to play in the flowers for the remainder of the day.

Lynn called out, "I think I'll go up and take a nap."

Dara waved her off, saying, "I'll be in soon for a shower."

As soon as she entered her room, Lynn went to her hidey spot. The habit, begun when the boys were little, worked well. No one entered her closet except for Bea when she'd helped dress Lynn. And even Bea wasn't aware that Lynn had what her sons referred to as "a stash."

The boys would never come in here. Dara has no reason to and doesn't seem the sneaky type. Donovan probably doesn't think beyond my bed ...

Pulling out various shopping bags, Lynn searched for anything that might work as a gift for Dara. Pushing some bags aside, which held treasures for someone else, Lynn found an unexpected perfect present. When her eyes saw the one athletic clothing bag, she was curious looking at the receipt for a timestamp.

When was I ever in this store?

Sadness overtook her as she read the date on the receipt, not remembering that she had ever gone to that store. Or that she'd ever asked Dara her size. Or that she'd hidden the bag in the closet, hoping to give it at some appropriate time.

What did Owen call what happened to me? Oh, yeah. The Timmy Effect. What that damn tumor did to me is awful.

It was almost scary to realize that there were moments of her life before the surgery that she would not be able to remember. Lynn clutched the bag to her chest and tipped her head back.

Don't dwell, don't dwell, don't dwell!

She grabbed some wrapping paper and a huge bow that she also kept in the stash corner and went to her bedroom to finish wrapping the gift. Sighing, she felt as if she was mourning.

I've lost part of my life. I don't remember doing something. I screwed up at work, too. Unintentional, all of it, but still ...

She placed the bow in the center of the box.

Maybe I should focus on being glad that I'm still here, that this gift is here, and that I can give it with true joy and affection.

Pushing the finished present to the side, Lynn crawled in bed and promptly fell asleep.

Chapter 29

When the doorbell rang yet again the next morning, Dara called out, "What the hell! *More* birthday gifts? Too much, Lynn, too much."

Bea breezed inside before Dara could answer it.

"Hello!" Bea bellowed. "I've come here to help out!"

Lynn smiled at her dearest friend's forceful personality, feeling the warmth of familiarity cover her like a warm blanket.

"What is it you want to do?" she teased.

Bea motioned to the room before her.

"We're going to clean up, Miss Lynn," she said determinedly. "This house needs it! Dara? Interested in helping me?"

Lynn watched Dara nod slowly, knowing that Bea's effervescent personality could overwhelm her.

Gently, Bea. Gently.

"Sure," Dara agreed.

Lynn swung her legs from the couch.

"I can help."

"You can supervise if you want," Bea said, beginning to pick things up from the floor.

"How about I strip the other bedrooms? Wash the sheets?" Dara asked.

Bea eyed her.

"You know how to do that? I mean I'm sure that father of yours hired people to do everything for himself and his daughter."

"Bea!" Lynn knew she had to stop Bea. She was waiting for a fight, noticed Dara getting ready for battle, standing a bit taller, holding her head straighter, planting her feet, throwing back her shoulders, and eyeballing Bea. Lynn imagined Dara saying *"Go on, bitch. Taunt me."* But Dara could hold her own.

"I went to college. By myself. No maid, no cook, no chauffeur, no personal secretary. I did everything for myself. And I *can* do beds."

The two women giggled as Dara wandered off to the upstairs bedrooms.

Bea was still grinning as she said, "All righty then. Miss Rue can do!" She looked at Lynn. "Let's get going! You wanna start here or in the living room?"

Lynn was happy to start with her living room, the sight that first greeted anyone.

How could I have left it go? Was I blind?

Completely nonjudgmental, Bea seemed happy to be helping. Soon, the room's clutter was gone, and Bea decided to dust all Lynn's picture frames.

"When are you going to update these pictures?"

When Lynn looked mystified, Bea continued, "Some of these pictures are old. Don't you have more up to date photos of Owen and Connor? Owen and Maribelle? You don't even have one of their wedding pictures out here. And what about the one of you in my beautiful blue dress with Donovan?"

Lynn looked over her pictures, her boys young and active, Michael smiling in many of them, some of them taken while the boys were young.

Why didn't I frame one of Owen's wedding? Can't I keep the older ones out? I like to look ... wait ...

"There's a picture of Donovan and me at that first music event?"

When Bea nodded, Lynn pursued. "Why haven't I seen it?"

Ignoring the question, Bea said. "A lot of magazines printed that one. Showed off the Lynn dress perfectly."

Lynn gave a short laugh before saying, "It was beautiful, Bea. But why don't I remember the picture? Have I been that out of it?"

Bea took Lynn's hands in hers, lowered her voice and said, "Yes, you were. I wondered why you weren't panicking about lack of privacy when all those magazines started printing pictures, talking about Donovan Rue's date."

"Well, I know the photographers were all at the events." Lynn shook her head. "We couldn't avoid them. There are cameras everywhere at those events ... I never realized ... wow."

"Well, turn it into something good," Bea suggested. "Donovan can get you a copy and you can frame it and place it out here."

Lynn became somber while contemplating it all. Finally, she asked, "And what about Michael's pictures?"

Bea will understand.

"Maybe have a couple of the entire family displayed. Like this one."

She held out one taken at a hockey event, when they were all wearing Blackhawks jerseys. Bea eyed Lynn with compassion.

"But if you're with Donovan now, why not have a picture of the two of you? And it can't hurt to update the boys' pictures, can it? Let's start there."

The decision made, they finished cleaning the room. Lynn was glad that she could keep up with Bea, helping her dust and wipe the glass on the frames despite Bea's threatening to call in a nurse to sedate her.

"The doctors said, 'no restrictions,'" Lynn said, though she smiled at Bea's controlling care.

LYNN CURLED UP ON THE COUCH THAT HAD NOW BECOME HER friend and fell asleep, only to wake up to Connor's deep voice.

"I use eggs in the ricotta. And oregano."

Lynn could hear a whisk moving rapidly.

Hear the whisk? How's that possible?

Next, the television blared. Above where she was lying was an air conditioning vent; Lynn was sure she could hear the air rushing through it.

Everything is loud. Too loud!

It seemed as if she'd placed amplifiers in her ears. But the good thing was that her eye wasn't quite as swollen.

Getting up, she grabbed the remote and turned down the sound. Connor, who could not see into the family room, called out, "Mom?"

Lynn wandered in to see a pleasant mess in her kitchen. Leaning over the counter, Dara was reading a cookbook while Connor was putting together a lasagna, a recipe of his grandmother's. She walked to Connor and wrapped her arms around her oldest son.

"Hi, there," she whispered while he leaned down and kissed the top of her head. When they released, Connor said, "Dara is learning to make lasagna. You don't mind if I give away the family recipe, do you?

"No, of course not. The Cerami family recipes are yours, I guess. Do what you'd like."

"Well," Connor said, a bit shy, "she doesn't know how to cook much … I know I promised to make your favorite dish, but I had all the ingredients, so …"

"And, I'm getting hungry!" Dara interrupted, getting louder. "So, get going! What's next?"

With a jerky movement, Lynn placed a hand protectively over one ear.

"Mom?" Connor looked at her with worry.

Lynn touched his arm briefly. "Nothing. I'm fine. It's just that suddenly everything is very loud."

"Oh! That's why you turned down the sound on the TV? Okay," His smile covered his entire face, a rare occurrence. He lowered the volume of his voice to tease. "Should I whisper?"

Dara was looking Lynn over.

"Your eye is almost normal," she declared.

"I thought it was!" Lynn touched her eye again, then moved her hand up to her head. "It felt different when I woke up. But I think my head is still a bit swollen."

"A bit?" Connor shook his head. "More than a bit, Mom. Remember, they sliced into your head. Doesn't surprise me that it would swell."

Dara moved next to Connor to begin putting together the lasagna. Amazed, Lynn watched her son allow a stranger to help him. She was delighted to see both young people comfortable with one another. Neither were people-oriented. Dara kept her distance to protect herself. Connor was bright, but offended people with his intensity and geekiness. Right now, they were working together, getting along, even looking pleasant instead of tense.

"I'll set the table," Lynn announced.

Dara was quicker, moving toward the silverware drawer.

"Let me do it," she said.

"No," Lynn was insistent. "I can do this."

"Do what?"

They all watched Donovan stroll into the kitchen.

Lynn loved the way her heart lurched a little when he came into sight.

I'm like the schoolgirl who sees the quarterback of the football team and wonders if he'll ever notice her on the sidelines.

"Hi. I'm setting the table," Lynn announced. "I promise not to overexert myself."

"Well, if you do that," Donovan said, "we can walk to the park and back tonight."

Chapter 30

aiting nervously in Dr. Urambu's small reception room, both Lynn and Donovan hoped the staples would be removed. The waiting extended when they were ushered into an exam room.

The quiet tension broke as a pretty Asian woman came in with what looked like a big staple remover, plucking out the staples, chatting away about the weather, California, and other topics. Donovan was talking with her, helping relieve some of the worry in the room. Lynn, fascinated by what was happening to her head, remained quiet.

It doesn't hurt!

Lynn sat in wonder, watching the staples ping into the silver receptacle that the woman – *nurse?* – held. When they were all removed, she cleaned up the congealed dried blood on Lynn's scalp.

Dr. Urambu entered, holding a small laptop. Placing it so that all could see, he pulled up the original MRI that took Lynn to the hospital. On the right side of her brain was a huge white dot that Urambu identified as the tumor.

Timmy the tumor, Lynn thought, using Owen's description.

Then Urambu pulled up the last MRI taken – *when?* Lynn couldn't remember – showing a much clearer brain except for one small dot.

"There's just a little left," the doctor said, making a circle with his stylus on the remains of Timmy. "We'll get it with Gamma Knife."

"Why couldn't you get it during surgery?" Donovan asked. Lynn wondered, too, as she had not heard this information.

"Too close to areas of the brain that I could damage," the doctor replied. "Gamma Knife will not cause damage."

My brain. Gamma Knife. Horrible name, Lynn thought. She was uneasy about the idea of this surgery.

Dr. Urambu continued. "We'll schedule this for a couple of weeks from now, give your head a little longer to heal."

He turned off the tiny laptop, made a notation in a paper file, then glanced at other paperwork. Donovan and Lynn were both lost in their own thoughts when Dr. Urambu stated, "The pathology shows that there is no cancer."

Donovan and Lynn's hands shot out, like bullets aimed at each other.

Grabbing Donovan, Lynn held on tightly. Donovan kept squeezing Lynn's hand repeatedly. Releasing a breath that she hadn't realized was caught in her lungs, Lynn tilted her head back in prayer.

Thank God, thank God, thank God!

Glancing at Donovan who was still crunching her hand, Lynn thought he too might be choking back emotion.

Both overcome, they finished the visit, scheduled the Gamma Knife, and left with a video the still-smiling woman recommended that they view.

Exiting the office behind Donovan, Lynn almost tripped as Donovan stopped abruptly, then whirled around to face her. She was caught up by two strong arms that crushed her against his chest. Hungry mouths collided, first with hard kisses, then colliding tongues, then moans escaping with need. Neither thought about the fact that it was a Thursday morning in a busy office building, how others might view their huge public display of affection.

They did not care.

They were oblivious.

"I love you," Donovan said as he came up for air, his eyes huge, glistening brown orbs in a face that was finally free of anxiety.

Lynn didn't fight the tears that flooded her eyes.

"I love you, too."

"Let's go let everyone know!"

As was becoming usual, Lynn woke with a startle the morning following her visit with Dr. Urambu. But this morning she'd been stunned, awoken by a dream. She lay there quietly, rehashing it, considering its meaning.

Sunlight flooded in, a shaft of bright light again coming from her bedroom windows. Since coming home from the hospital, she'd felt a presence of The Other when awakening. She'd felt Cathy's presence strongly, but she also knew that she was in touch with her spiritual side, the side that she'd ignored during her illness, Michael's death, and following brain surgery.

Too sick? Too upset? Or just ignoring one part of my life that could've brought me comfort?

Smiling, she sat up, glancing over to Donovan who was still sleeping soundly.

Maybe Donovan came into my life for comfort. Or strength. Maybe he's my Peace.

She resisted reaching out to touch him, glad that he was sleeping soundly. Once again, he wore an indie band t-shirt and sweats. He slept on his stomach, his head cast to one side on the pillow, a hand tucked beneath it. Impossibly long lashes graced his face.

Closing her eyes, Lynn began to pray.

Thank you, God, for this day ... for my life ... for this wonderful man who has been here for me during this tough time. Who helped me realize that I am still a valuable person even with a bald head and a damaged body. I'm very in love with him.

"Good morning."

The soft yet deep sound of Donovan's calm voice interrupted her prayer.

Lynn smiled at him, saying, "Good morning to you."

"You were praying again," he stated.

"How can you tell when I pray?"

"Because you close your eyes and tilt your head back."

Donovan mimicked her familiar pose.

"I have never prayed much," he admitted. "At least not until these last few weeks."

"Oh? What did you pray for?"

Donovan turned onto his side.

"First, I prayed for you to come back to me," he said. "Then I prayed that you would get through this surgery!" He paused for a moment, bit his lower lip, then said, "And then I prayed that the tumor would not be cancer."

Lynn nodded, going over what she had just prayed for.

"I have to admit that I never prayed for that," she admitted. "But I was saying thank you for these gifts. And I was also thinking about my dream last night."

"Oh? You dreamed again? You told me that you don't dream very much."

"Lately, I do. A lot." Lynn reached up to touch her staple-free head.

Donovan fluffed up his pillow, then laid flat on his back. At the same time, Lynn scooched back to her headboard and placed two pillows behind her.

Lynn cocked her head to the side as if questioning what she'd thought about subconsciously. "Maybe it's half dream/half memory."

She took a deep breath and began, "This part happened. Michael and I were hiking in the Backyard – that's what we call the mountains in this neighborhood. We'd walked past a guy washing his car. Michael figured he was getting a divorce, especially when a woman walked outside, past the guy, without saying a word."

"You got all that from a glance?" Lynn asked.

Michael could spin a story, but it was always a bit dark.

"Well," Lynn said, "that'll never happen to us."

"Our relationship is rock solid," Michael agreed.

Lynn paused, her eyes dry yet dreamy. "Then he wanted to discuss 'what ifs.' What if he died? He was insistent on it. I remember I asked him, 'Before or after I cry?'"

A gulp and shudder betrayed Lynn's emotions about the memory.

"He told me about how he'd structured our finances so that I'd be good ... if ... That he wanted me to know that he was okay if I found someone else to love." She glanced at Donovan, her eyelashes almost grazing her cheek, "That someone would love me; he knew it." Lynn shrugged then said, "I tried to make a joke."

"Me too. Find a cute brunette when I kick off."

"I'm older than you, Lynn. And men die younger than women."

"We're too young to talk about this," Lynn declared.

"Is that the end?" Donovan asked after a pause, pulling her from the memory.

Lynn glanced down at Donovan and said, "That's where the reality – or memory – ends. All that I just told you happened. The rest of my dream ... no."

She finished her story. "Every detail of the dream changed: the atmosphere changed. Michael got more handsome, and I deteriorated to the cancer-ravaged woman I am complete with head staples."

"Lynn ..."

"And there was a rescue helicopter hovering over us. And then ..."

"You'll be glad we talked about this," Michael stated, his voice sounding as if it were far, far away from the mountains. "Someone is going to meet you, fall desperately in love with you, and treat you like the

princess you've always been. You will be happy again. I want *you to be happy again. I know he'll take good care of you."*

Lynn, dry-eyed, whispered, "That's the end." She ran her fingers across Donovan's forehead. "It makes me realize that I am wasting time when I worry about it being too soon for us."

Leaning up, reaching out, Donovan pulled Lynn down to a flat position in the bed, his arms wrapping around her, spooning her. He kissed her on the top of her head.

"There are answers to prayers," he whispered after a few moments, his voice sounding tight.

"Or dreams!" Lynn agreed. "Or memories? I don't know. I do remember that walk – how muddy it was, the guy washing his car, Michael starting that discussion."

Lynn paused, running fingers along the line where staples no longer existed, brooding over her dream.

Donovan continued kissing the top of her head, just listening as Lynn pulled her face into a tight scrunch, trying desperately to remember an event from ten years before, but to no avail.

"I feel like this was a gift I got this morning."

She quickly turned her body, pushing Donovan onto his back so that she could lay flat on top of him. Resting her head on his chest, she sighed with what sounded like relief and happiness. Donovan stiffened a bit, a signal to Lynn that he had something difficult to say.

"Peace, we should talk about that evening with Dymettra."

"No!" Lynn was adamant. "Not yet. I know there are things to work out between us, but today I want to enjoy the fact that I am – I don't know – relieved? The tumor was benign! And I've finally released myself from the worry of going forward with us. Does that make sense?"

Donovan nodded, his eyes bright with happiness, but then deliberately changed the subject.

"Hey! Aren't you excited to be able to wash all of your head?"

Lynn giggled, remembering Dr. Urambu's release of the restriction of getting any water on her head. But she knew that Donovan really wanted to talk.

Hate to be Scarlet O'Hara about this, but it'll have to wait for another day. Not today.

WHEN BEA CAME OVER LATER LYNN HAD RESIGNED HERSELF TO needing a caregiver.

My babysitter for the day. They all keep taking turns. And they all keep setting boundaries for me.

"Want some help with that head?"

"Help?" Lynn looked up, realized that Bea didn't know the restriction had been lifted. "I can wash it myself; got the go-ahead yesterday!"

Bea smiled and said, "No, silly. I mean cutting your hair."

Lynn fingered the hair at the nape of her neck. Because of the heavy steroids given in the hospital, her hair was the longest it had been in several years. She didn't want to lose it.

"I don't know ..."

Bea grew into the fully authoritative, imposing figure that Lynn knew so well.

"You can't leave it like this! Who the hell wanders around with a half-bald head? You know it'll grow back."

This sucks.

"Don't remember ... Who shaved your head when your hair first started falling out?" Bea asked.

Lynn snorted.

"My hairdresser. But she ended up cutting it into a short pixie style but I wasn't upset, I guess because I had this big blob on my brain ..."

"– Timmy!"

"Yeah," Lynn smiled at how everyone was using Owen's nickname for the tumor, "since I was *Timmified* –"

The two friends paused to giggle at Lynn's new word as the shearer was placed against Lynn's head. Lynn sensed Bea's smile even as the electric trimmer rubbed over her head, so she continued.

"Michael did it the next week."

"He did? I guess I don't remember that. Michael wasn't exactly a touchy-feely sort of guy."

"Maybe not to you," Lynn smiled as she recalled the memory of sitting in almost the same place in their bathroom as Michael shaved her head. "He kept saying *'You are always going to hate me for this haircut'* and *'this will be your worst haircut ever.'* He even got a little teary-eyed."

Bea gently rubbed her hands over Lynn's head.

"That feels nice," Lynn murmured. She'd quit reaching for the longer locks during their conversation.

"I remember," she continued, "thinking that I would never have him do that again. But I never thought there would *be* a next time."

She turned around to glance in the mirror, touching her head, running fingers again along the scar.

I must admit that this looks better than whatever style I had going on.

"Thanks, Bea."

She tried smiling at her friend, one lonesome tear making its way down her face. She touched her head once more.

"It'll grow back; I know that! I just didn't want to do this again." She took a deep breath, brushed the tear away and said, "Thanks for making me face the inevitable. I guess I need to buy some chemo caps again."

"Well, you can go buy more after you see the breast surgeon," Bea said. "Why do you need to go to her?"

"Re-check," Lynn answered. "I have to see her every six months; it got canceled because of the surgery. Now I need to get this done."

ANOTHER DAY. ANOTHER DOCTOR. AGAIN.

Lynn's new normal was seeing a doctor at least once a week. First up, the breast surgeon.

"You still have the port in!"

Lynn sighed. "Yes, I do."

Damn thing. I hate it.

"It has to come out. Leaving it in can lead to blood clots, or infections. I'll speak to Dr. Meyer and we'll get this taken care of."

At the end of the week, Dara the assigned caregiver, Lynn looked at the heart-shaped object as her surgeon held it up.

Is that shape deliberate? Weird.

Aloud she said, "There's the troublemaker."

"Sometimes they make Christmas ornaments out of them."

"Christmas ornaments?" Lynn was incredulous.

But as they left the office, Dara asked whether Lynn needed to go home and rest or if she wanted to stop at a local home goods store.

"I hear it's full of Christmas stuff already!" Dara exclaimed. "I love Christmas."

Lynn was so thrilled with Dara's enthusiasm that she agreed at once.

"If you see something you like, you gotta get it now because it'll be gone in a minute," Dara told Lynn. She picked up a water globe that held a facsimile of a black lab with a bone in its mouth.

"This is what our dog looked like," she said. "Dad loved that dog. We both did."

"Can I get this for him?" Lynn asked as she took the item from Dara's hand. "He likes dogs, huh?"

"Black labs especially," Dara said as she shook the globe. "The last one was called Onyx."

Lynn smiled, placed it in their basket and announced, "My first Christmas present purchase!"

Smug with her new purchase – and the idea for a bigger one – Lynn was surprised to find Owen and Maribelle when she and Dara returned home.

"Mom!"

Owen bounced up like the overly energetic kid he still was. Lynn couldn't help but smile back whenever he was around.

He is better than sunshine, this kid.

"What a nice surprise! What are you doing here so soon after the last visit?"

Owen laughed at his mother's shock.

"I got a shooting gig in LA. Something in the mountains involving scantily dressed, pretty women."

"Hey!" Maribelle pretended to hit him, but she was smiling, too, then added,

"I'm tagging along, but I really wanted to see my family, and see for myself how you're doing."

"I'm great!" Lynn replied as Dara entered the room with a plate full of cookies. Lynn introduced Dara to Maribelle. When Donovan called to see if everyone could meet him for dinner, the group was surprised that they had spent over two hours in conversation.

"I need to freshen up," Lynn said.

Owen held out both hands in front of his mother, a familiar gesture to help her stand. But Lynn was already standing, giggling at Owen's surprise.

"Wow, Mom," Owen became serious. "I haven't seen you stand straight up in a while."

Yes! My balance is returning. Maybe I can go on longer walks, maybe at a brisker pace. Wait till Owen sees that!

She smiled as she headed for the stairs, noticing a mischievous gleam in Owen's eyes.

Is something going on?

Opening her door – *why is this closed anyway?* – Lynn gasped. At first, she thought it was just pretty, new linens. But the entire bed suite was new.

Running her hands over the new blue comforter, she thought about the last few weeks of waking each morning with Donovan in her bed.

"What do you think?"

Owen was standing at the doorway.

"Donovan did this?"

While Owen nodded, Lynn went to him, hugging her youngest son hard. Then she walked back to her new present, ran her hands again over the blue coverlet.

"Wow. I am one lucky mamma."

Owen laughed.

"You are! When I texted him that we were coming in, he asked if I could be here to meet the delivery guy. Said he hoped it wasn't too weird for me."

Lynn looked back at Owen. All she saw was a relaxed posture, tousled blond hair, and bright, happy eyes. Owen was his typical, sunshiny self. Still, Lynn had to know.

"*Is* it weird, Owen?"

Owen straightened from the door jamb, his eyes laughing as he looked it all over. Walking to her, he said, "No, it's not." Then he took her by the elbow and said, "But if you don't get going, you will have two very hungry hombres mad at you!"

Chapter 31

*a*t five-thirty the next cool, dark morning, Donovan drove Lynn to her Gamma Knife procedure, listening to Lynn's nervous litany of medical visits to the many campus buildings.

Once checked in, Lynn's two nurses checked each other's work and explained things calmly, thoroughly.

Are they doing this because of the procedure, or do they sense how nervous I am?

Completing their tasks, they left just as Dr. Urambu walked in, announcing, "Time to screw the crown into your head."

Once the heavy, circular device was placed atop her head, fingers of steel-gray extending down her face, four screws secured it in position. Knowing that this was done to assure that she would not move her head during the procedure, Lynn gritted her teeth.

He even uses an electric screwdriver!

"Are the screws from Home Depot?"

Lynn hoped to hear a laugh but was content with Dr. Urambu's slight smile and answer.

"They could come from there."

After waiting a while, Lynn and Donovan noted other doctors rushing by the open door.

Wonder what's up? We've gone from complete, calm quiet to a low hum of worry, it seems.

Lynn tried deep breathing to find calm, then tried unsuccessfully to tilt her head back for a quick prayer. She giggled when the heaviness of the crown prevented her from the movement.

"You eventually manage to find humor in what you're going through," Donovan said. "What's funny this time?"

"Can you take a picture of me, so I can see this thing?"

Finished, he held out the phone for Lynn to look.

My head is trapped inside a steel cage.

But she couldn't come up with an analogy as clever as Robocop for what she saw.

"How would you describe this?" she asked Donovan.

It took him a few seconds before responding, "You look like Mad Max!"

A thin Asian man, Dr. Wu embroidered on his white coat, entered the room while they were chuckling. He wasn't happy.

"The next step was to have an MRI done, but the machine at the hospital is broken." He shook his head and roared, "This is so unacceptable!"

Lynn envisioned having the crown removed, being told to come back another time.

That's not acceptable to me!

"So, instead we are sending you next door for a CT scan."

A few minutes later the two nurses walked in followed by two paramedics and a gurney.

"What's this?" Donovan asked while Lynn looked on, her eyes a bright blue light behind the gray headgear.

"Standard procedure when we move a patient from one building to another," one nurse explained. "Especially with something this heavy on her head."

Paramedics loaded Lynn into the ambulance and drove her to the next building.

The scan took less time than the ride to the building. When she returned, the nurses attached a huge, plastic bubble scoured with tiny openings, as an additional layer to the Mad Max crown. The Gamma Knife rays would be aimed at Timmy the Tumor now that they were certain of his whereabouts.

Once again pushed back into a machine, her head screwed into place and Adele singing into her headset, Lynn was told to relax.

Less than sixty minutes later, she was being pulled out, stripped of her crowns, and assisted with dressing.

"You okay?" a concerned Donovan asked.

Lynn smiled, a first truly large smile in a long time.

"I'm great," she proclaimed. "Timmy is completely gone now."

Riding home, the two were each reflective, Lynn on her good fortune to have had the deadly tumor found before it was too late. She was also thinking of her luck in having such a caring man by her side.

"Donovan, you are so wonderful to me," Lynn blurted out.

He squeezed Lynn's slender left hand.

"I haven't been good at telling you what you mean to me," Lynn continued, chatty with relief after the morning's events. "You have been so thoughtful – even before this Timmy stuff!" She paused before continuing, "You have no idea how you make me feel."

"Try telling me," he said with another squeeze. Lynn paused, took a deep breath, and said, "I feel like the cheerleader when she sees the hunky captain of the football team," she began. "My heart flutters, my eyes tear ... I'm a mess!"

Donovan was grinning ear to ear at her proclamation.

"So," Lynn continued, "if I don't say it enough, know that I love you."

Donovan pulled into Lynn's driveway. Neither made any effort to get out.

"I love you, too," he said, then added, "I'm so glad you lived."

Tingles went up and down Lynn's spine as she looked into those dark brown eyes.

"I am feeling like that schoolgirl again, Mr. Rue."

Chapter 32

A couple of days later Dara arrived at Lynn's home.

Guess it's Dara's day to babysit me.

"What do you do for a living that you can take time in the middle of the week?"

Dara gave Lynn one of her rare smiles, beautiful and soft.

"I do independent copywriting and social media work for different clients," she answered. "It's something that I can do without engaging with lots of stupid people in an office setting."

"Like I do," Lynn countered.

"I prefer working alone. I get enough work that I can afford to take a few days off here and there. I just got a new client the day you went into the hospital."

"That's great!"

"Yeah. So now that I've met with them a few times, there's lots to do that requires research and writing," Dara said as she pulled her laptop out of a padded bag. "And I can do that pretty much anywhere."

Lynn nodded. Leaning back, she relaxed into her green chair, relieved that the tumor was gone, determined to get on with whatever normal was going to be in her life. As she closed her eyes to contemplate this, Dara changed the subject.

"Connor told me that you like to decorate for Christmas."

Lynn giggled, keeping her eyes closed.

"He did, huh? I imagine that he told you his mother goes overboard with Christmas. Am I right?"

Dara paused a second, then answered, "He said something

about a village, ticky tacky, tins, Santas, and other decorations. Those are his words."

I thought they didn't pay any attention. All the boys ever did was tease me about it being too much.

"I could help you start with decorating the house," Dara announced.

"I don't know. It's a little early," Lynn said, then asked, "What were your holidays like when you were growing up? And now?"

Dara's descriptions of Rue Christmases sounded austere. Trips to Grandma and Grandpa Rue's home – always with Asia Barber in attendance, and then a quick meal and present with Donovan on Christmas Day.

"Nothing big." Dara smiled at Lynn. "Dad doesn't decorate."

How can anyone not want to surround themselves with Christmas spirit?

"It's a little early …" Lynn began to say, weakening with the idea of decorating for her favorite holiday.

"Yeah! But I can help. I'm here now. Let me help you," Dara demanded.

Lynn hesitated, knowing the amount of work involved.

"Okay … you'll see though. It isn't easy."

Although she did groan about the physicality of the work, Dara labored hard to get all the big boxes out of a closet hidden by coats.

"What are these?" Dara asked as she began handing Lynn square white boxes.

"My village!"

Lynn began creating piles.

"Chicago houses," Lynn said while pointing the largest group. "European buildings. And then others; no rhyme or reason to them."

"I don't see a California house," Dara said looking through the "other" pile.

"Well, by the time we moved to California, these porcelain houses weren't as popular," Lynn told her.

When Lynn announced that they needed to remove all the stuff currently filling her entertainment unit's shelves, Dara jumped right in.

"What's next?"

"Snow."

"Snow?"

Lynn pulled old, worn batting out of a box marked *Village Accessories*. Dara shook her head.

"We can do better than this."

Agreeing, Lynn went to grab her purse. Her cell phone rang, Donovan's picture appearing, which put a smile on her face.

"Hi, handsome," she greeted him.

Donovan's sexy, calm voice answered her. "Peace. I'm wondering how you're doing today. You fell asleep in that damn green chair before I even had a chance to say goodbye this morning."

"I feel great! Glad that Gamma Knife is over and done."

"Is that Dad?" Dara asked, holding out her hand. After Lynn handed over her phone, Dara said, "Dad? We're going out to get some Christmas stuff." She paused while Donovan answered her. "Oh, are you nearby? Yeah, we can meet you. See you there in twenty."

Dara drives like a mad woman.

Lynn grabbed the seat bottom as they rounded another corner too quickly. Dara shot her car into a space. As the two women approached him, Donovan stood at the café's door, looking handsome, calm, but not as relaxed as Lynn had seen him yesterday.

Dara and Donovan devoured their sandwiches and soup while Lynn picked at hers. Donovan pointed to Lynn's basil tomato soup.

"You've got to eat more, Peace. You'll waste away."

Lynn nodded, knowing that she needed more. Food still tasted off. Hoping to please Donovan, she took another spoonful.

"How's work?" she asked, hoping to take his mind off her food.

Donovan moved his long legs off to the side of the table, taking a deep breath as he did so.

"Always interesting," he said. Lynn turned a concerned face his way, knowing that there were things she could only offer support for, not help improve.

"We met with Roy's attorneys. He's determined to make life miserable for Rue LA LA."

Dara paused from biting her pickle spear. "What do our lawyers say?"

Lynn asked, "Does he have a case?"

"No, I don't think so," Donovan said. "Our attorneys looked over the contract. They say we've met all the contract's stipulations. Unfortunately, he's trying to go public with this, which of course makes it much more dramatic than it really is. Media loves it. That's never good."

They were all silent for a minute until Dara asked, "Can he wreck the business, Dad?"

Donovan shook his head.

"I don't think so. But he can scare off new talent. And try to convince our existing clients to jump ship."

Lynn asked, "If he thinks he's that great, why doesn't he just find another company to work with?"

"No one would want that scum," Dara chimed in. "He's hard to talk to, so I can only imagine how difficult he'd be work worth with."

"I know you met him, but I didn't know you knew him that well," Donovan said. "But you've got it right. He's difficult; letting the idea of being a celebrity get in the way of becoming a talented artist."

Donovan sighed again, then sat up straighter in his chair.

"And on top of that, we have the Mandy thing going on –"

"That bitch!"

"Dara." Donovan's words were sharp. "She's still your mother."

Dara flung her hair over her shoulder.

"She ain't nothing to me, Dad. Except trouble."

Donovan glanced one more time at his phone, then said, "Much as I'd like to stay with you lovely ladies, I can't. Work calls."

Lynn felt a pang of guilt.

"I've taken a lot of your time away from work."

Donovan kissed her again.

"My pleasure. You take priority over work anytime. You and Dara," he said, glancing at his daughter. Then changing the subject, said, "So, Christmas shopping? Isn't it a little early?'

"Well, sort of," Lynn admitted. "But your daughter seems excited about it and is helping me set up some items that take a while. When we pulled stuff out of one box, we discovered that things were damaged. So, we can't put the snow down yet, and the village really needs snow to look right and –"

Donovan put his fingers gently over Lynn's mouth and laughed.

"Okay, I get it. You need stuff. Have fun!"

Chapter 33

*L*unch with Lynn and Dara lightened Donovan's mood somewhat. He had more lawyers to face in a few hours but found strength at lunch. Plopping down into a chair in front of his desk, Donovan sighed. He could lose Roy, knew that was almost guaranteed. More than one major client leaving his company could make life difficult.

What the hell would my father have done? Things were so much less complicated then.

Donovan could not recall one celebrity of that time who had not respected his father. No one would have threatened him with a lawsuit.

And just the thought of Dymettra going to Mandy ...

Donovan's ex-wife had yet to come forth with any legal accusations; all her allegations were just fodder for a press that loved all the vitriol surrounding men being accused by women of being too aggressive.

Wait. What am I thinking? I have not done anything wrong.

He stood and grabbed the unreviewed paperwork that was on his desk.

Dymettra started a war. She damn well needs to stand back.

Donovan knocked sharply on Len's office door. When he heard Len's greeting, he turned the knob and entered the room like the man who owned the company.

"Donovan!"

Donovan walked confidently toward his second.

"How's Lynn doing?"

"She's great. Better than ever." Donovan's answer was quick, terse indicating that he had his mind on something else. "I want all this out-of-line behavior to end. Now."

"You're talking about Roy? Dymettra?"

"I'm talking about Roy and Dymettra and whoever else we help promote and produce!"

The sudden strength in Donovan's tone had Len sitting up straight, paying attention.

"I'm tired of the disrespect within our business from the people we promote." He raked his hair again. "My father demanded and got total respect from artists. I want that, not only for me but for everyone who works here."

"It's a different time, Dono—"

"Maybe. But maybe it's me? Maybe I've been trying too hard to be friendly with these assholes instead of being their boss like my father was."

Len swiveled out of his chair. Standing quietly by his desk, he looked at his boss fondly.

"I wish it were that easy," he began, "but you know that we just can't make nice and end the Roy Alloy lawsuit. It is going to go forward."

"We could let him go ..."

"What purpose would that serve?" Len asked. "It still wouldn't end the lawsuit and it might add fuel to the fire."

"Like Dymettra."

"Dymettra?"

"She threatened to join forces with Roy *and* Mandy."

"God ..."

"I want others to see that this company is not taking blatant disrespect any longer. Rude behavior should not be tolerated – by us or anyone! I want respect, and I do not want interference in my personal life from anyone."

Len nodded, sympathy on his face.

"You've got to face both these things," he said. "Mandy has been laying low. I'd like to think that your statement scared her off."

"What I said was the truth!"

"And Dymettra has nothing to add to Mandy's allegations, I assume?"

"Nothing." Donovan strode over to the windows in Len's office. "Mandy was a mistake I made before I came to Rue," he said, then looked at his friend. "Did Dad ever say anything?"

"Yes."

Len was tight-lipped, loyal to his friend Paul. Donovan honored it.

"And Dymettra was a mistake once Dad was gone," he shook his head from side to side, then added, "I can imagine what he'd have said."

"But he would have loved your Lynn," Len added, bringing Donovan back to a positive place. "She is probably exactly what your father wished for you, someone with backbone, courage, and who is pleasant and respectful of others."

Donovan's look of respect toward Len was sincere.

Thank God Len is here. What would I do if I didn't have him to make me see through some of this bullshit?

"Okay, the Roy thing goes forward."

Donovan stood and shuffled the paperwork still clutched in his hand on Len's desk.

"But from now on a clause goes into everyone's contract about behavior and respect. Look at some old contracts for wordage, run it by legal."

"Yes, sir!" Len's smile was bright. "I don't know if we'll ever get respect out of some of these kids, but we can try."

Chapter 34

When he got home from work...
Home?

... Donovan found the entire house a complete mess, the women in it blissful. Items that usually graced the entertainment center's shelves were gone. Instead, porcelain houses...

Houses?

... were displayed. He recognized Westminster Abbey and Buckingham Palace right away, thought he saw some iconic Chicago landmark buildings represented and wondered about others.

A bike shop was set up next to a post office. Another shelf had an old English harness shop complete with horses jumping over hay bales or running toward a small fox. Alongside it was a tea shop and an old European-looking church. Six deep shelves provided space for these buildings, although they were unadorned, dark, and to Donovan, just looked ugly.

"Hey, Dad!"

Donovan finished his hello kiss for Lynn, then turned to view his very happy daughter. Dara's eyes were bright, her body relaxed as she came forward to hug her father.

"Hello, Magic! You look happy."

"I am!"

"She's probably exhausted," Lynn said. "We've been at it all day long."

"And there's still stuff to do!" Dara stretched, her arms held way above her head as she pirouetted in position, reminding Donovan of her many classic dance classes that Asia Barber had insisted he take her to. As she finished twirling, Dara picked up her purse.

"Gotta go. I have a date."

Donovan saw a sparkle in Dara's eyes.

"Oh, yeah? Who?"

"Dad," Dara's tone was reprimanding, "I am not a kid. I don't need to tell you about all my dates."

With that, she leaned down and surprised Lynn by giving her a soft kiss. As the door closed, Lynn leaned back in her chair and sighed.

"I had such a good time today!"

Donovan glanced around the messy room with its half-emptied brown and white boxes, and scraps of glittery felt that lay everywhere, and grimaced.

Not the right time to discuss Dymettra. Or anything. Let her stay this happy.

"Looks like you two had fun playing together," he said. "You made a mess."

"Oh, we've only started," Lynn said, wandering into the kitchen to find something for their dinner. "Your daughter was go-go-*go* until it was time to put lights in the houses. Then she decided to stop."

Lynn turned to Donovan.

"I'll have to get the step stool out of the garage to get up to the top shelf and string lights."

Donovan followed Lynn toward the pantry.

My Peace is getting stronger and stronger. More daring, too. I hardly recognize the woman from Music Extravaganza. Or that stupid cancer walk.

He knew the essence of Lynn had never left her, but he was seeing the true beauty and fortitude which Lynn had.

She's resilient! That's what I'm seeing.

Lynn turned on the oven and began preparing chicken for baking. Donovan wondered how she would take his request.

271

"I have a holiday party to attend in a couple of weeks," he began. He waited for an explosive reaction. Lynn kept whisking together eggs, pausing to pour breadcrumbs into another bowl.

"Oh? In LA?"

He named a new hotel with a revolving rooftop restaurant.

"Sounds fancy," Lynn said as she coated the chicken.

Donovan leaned against the counter, "Would you please come with me?"

As Lynn took a deep breath, Donovan felt his resolve starting to wane.

What will I do if she says no?

"Does it mean a fancy dress and jewelry?"

The question sparked hope in Donovan.

"Yes. Bea will have to come up with another Lynn design."

"As long as it's not red."

"Okay," he nodded, knowing how much she hated the last dress. "I'm not into that stuff – jewelry, shoes, whatever. Bea is terrific at that. She figures the entire thing out for you."

Lynn placed the chicken in the oven and set the timer. Opening the pantry again, she asked, "Want some brown rice?"

"My favorite. Sure," he answered as he reached up to loosen his tie. "Trying to avoid answering my request for a date?"

C'mon, Lynn. This is my life; you'll figure out how to fit into it.

"Lynn," Donovan's tone made her look up. "I can't promise that people like Dymettra or Roy won't try to spoil our evenings. But I can promise to be there for you, to defend you from them, and promise always to be honest with you about what's going on in my company that might affect our relationship, or our evenings at these events."

Honest blue eyes looked back at him, focused on his answer.

"That's all I can do," Donovan said, a note of pleading in his voice. "Will you come with me?"

Lynn walked over and wrapped her arms around him. Gently, she placed her lips on his, marveling at the startled yet wonderful feeling that came over her every time she kissed him.

"Yes," she said. "I'll call Bea tomorrow."

As Donovan let out a breath, she added, "But I'm not wearing red to your Christmas party. No matter what."

Laughing, Donovan walked into the family room and turned on music.

"You need practice!" he called out. "Come here and dance with me!"

Lynn wiped her hands on a dishtowel, then made her way to Donovan. The music was upbeat, but slow enough for her to begin her venture back into being his dance partner. She motioned at her yoga pants and t-shirt, then at his elegant suit.

"Clearly, I am not dressed for the occasion."

"Damn right," Donovan teased, then grabbed her waist. "But I'll take you just the way you are right now."

Lynn's eyes were joyful. They leaned toward each other for another soft kiss. Slowly breaking away, not wanting to push her too quickly, Donovan asked, "Do you dance?"

"I love to dance, Mr. Rue," Lynn answered. "Wait until you see me *really* dance."

Laughing, giggling, sometimes whooping from stepping on scattered Christmas items, the two were happy in the moment. All worries about lawsuits and health, completely forgotten during the dance. When it ended, Donovan looked adoringly at his Peace.

"Tired?"

Lynn's smile had remained constant during the dance and did not abandon her now.

"I'm tired of dancing, but I'm ready for something else."

"Oh?"

She took Donovan by the hand and led him upstairs to the new bed. Lynn acknowledged the thrill that went through her body as she closed the bedroom door, pausing for a moment, then glancing at Donovan shyly.

"I want this. I'm just … I don't know … Are you sure you want to make love with a woman nicknamed Robocop or Mad Max? Someone with a less than perfect body and no hair?"

Donovan approached her, taking off his coat.

"Are you serious?" Wrapping his arms around her, he said, "I want this, too. And I want it with you when you are ready. If you're not ready, then I can wait."

He leaned down to kiss her neck.

God, the way he talks. The way he looks at me as if I'm the sexiest thing he's ever seen when I know I'm not.

Lynn's desire grew with his kisses. She pushed away from him and began to reach for the bedside lamp.

"No," Donovan's firm, yet soft voice continued. "Let's leave it off."

She moved her hand to his arm as he said, "Remember the first time we made love? There was only the glow from the living room lamps."

Lynn moved her hand again toward the lamp, adamant in what she wanted. She turned the light on, then pulled off her top.

"I want the light on."

They both removed all their clothes, then eyed one another. Donovan took her slight hand, then pulled her into bed. He felt the silkiness of her skin. Hungry mouths claimed one another as soon as they began kissing. Lynn's mouth opened, and Donovan intruded, their tongues reintroducing each other. Who knew how long they kissed? With no need to keep track of time, they allowed their passion to consume them. Donovan's mouth began to kiss the curve of Lynn's neck, inhaling the slightly floral scent that was Lynn, spending time beneath her ear while his hand moved down to her thigh, brushing softly there until he found her folds and tentatively reached between them. Despite the ardor and passion, Donovan sensed that this was almost like a first time for Lynn. Although visibly aroused, Lynn was dry. Donovan wondered if it was out of fear, or because of medication.

Lynn continued kissing his mouth, gasping for small intakes of air when he pulled slightly away. Her hand reached his stomach, touching his belly, a place that she knew turned him on.

Her kisses expressed want beyond what he'd ever seen. Lynn gently pushed him back flat onto the bed and reached into a bedside table's drawer. Pulling out a tube of lubricant, she moved back to him and gently squeezed some onto her fingers.

"The medications have dried me out," she admitted, but showed no embarrassment at rubbing some of the gel onto Donovan. He took the excess of it off her fingertips and began to coat her, teasing her with his fingers. As her moans of pleasure became louder, Donovan continued exploring Lynn's body. He noted that she placed her hand back on him, this time stroking him. When he thought he could no longer wait, he repositioned them so that she was on her back, then mantled over her body and started gently nudging into her.

Lynn arched her back as she felt him enter, whispering, "God, you feel so good."

Encouraged, he entered a little more, still feeling like this was another beginning for them. He did not want to rush, yet he could not wait to be where he considered home.

"I have missed you so much," he whispered as he filled her, the root of his cock now at the base of her entrance.

They both took a moment to relish the exquisite feeling of finding joy in the other's body. Then Donovan began to move, simultaneously kissing that long lovely neck, her mouth, her neck again. Lynn threw her head back in sexual thrall, one hand cupping his balls while the other slid up and down his back.

When she could no longer control herself, Lynn moved both arms to the slats on the new headboard, gripping them as she came long and hard, calling out his name.

Seeing her response freed Donovan from holding back. He pushed harder and finally succumbed to his own pleasure, coming hard and deep within her body. Spent, he flattened himself against her, his head under her chin.

"I love you," he whispered, his voice shaky.

"Mmm … Me, too."

DONOVAN STARTED LYNN'S FIREPLACE AFTER DINNER, THEN CUDDLED next to her on the couch. Usually, she read while he did laptop work, but tonight they just sat, still in the afterglow of their first sexual encounter in weeks, gazing at the fireplace flames that danced before them.

"I've always wondered why California houses have fireplaces," Lynn mused.

Amused by the random comment, Donovan looked at her.

"Oh? We're not allowed?"

Lynn threw one leg over Donovan's longer one.

"Well, it's just that it made sense when we lived in Chicago, or Michigan or New York where they have real winter weather," she said. "Fireplaces do produce some heat. But here, it makes no sense to me. It's warm outside."

"Warm? You think fifty-four degrees is warm?"

Lynn ran lazy hands through Donovan's curls.

"I know people who live here think it's cold, but to a Midwesterner, this is warm." She sighed and then said, "I suppose since I've lived here for over ten years – and I'm cold most of the time now – that I'm a Californian."

Donovan leaned over for a brief kiss, then returned to staring at the fire. His thoughts were anywhere but fireplaces. He was nervous, wondering how to broach a certain topic when his eyes were distracted by Lynn's favorite chair.

"I hate your chair," he said.

"My chair? What did it do to deserve your hatred?" Now it was Lynn's turn to be amused.

"Because it looks terrible."

When Lynn laughed at his outburst, Donovan continued, "The green is faded, there are tears all over it, and the leather cracked. And although you find it comfortable, I can't find one spot that feels good to me."

Sparks of mischief lit up her eyes as Lynn asked, "So why are you worrying about it? You don't live here. It's my favorite chair."

"Well," Donovan took a deep breath, then asked, "What if I *were* to live here?"

Lynn's eyebrows rose with surprise.

"You want us to live together?"

"No, I don't want just to live together." Donovan's hand went to his head, pulling through the thick, curly strands. "I'm not saying this right," he muttered.

Lynn took one of his hands and said, "Then, just spit it out."

He paused, searching for courage.

"I want to be married."

Lynn's eyebrows crept to her hairline. Her breathing stopped momentarily. Her sparkling eyes from moments before were now tear-filled. Donovan, alarmed by her reaction, tried to read her face.

"I am still not asking this correctly."

"What?"

"I'm pushing you, aren't I?"

"Donovan," Lynn appeared bewildered, lost. "It's not that I don't want to be with you all the time, but marriage … after all I've been through? I can't imagine that anyone would want to be tied down to someone who's been as sick as I've been!"

"What? Lynn, I don't think about you in terms of your health." Donovan looked at her, incredulity written all over his face. "I want to be with you because I love and admire you. I admire you for who you are, your resilience, your utter charm, your sense of humor even during hard times, the way you mother your sons, your goodness, your beautiful blue eyes –"

"– and I love you too." Lynn spoke over the last few words, straightening in her chair. "I love you for your intensity, your care and concern, the way you deal with others – including those who treat you rudely at times. I love the loyalty you have to your father's company, the care you give your daughter." She paused. "But I don't want to add to your stress."

Donovan looked at her with sadness.

"No! Don't be sad, please." Lynn placed both hands on his face and kissed him again. "It's not that I don't want to be with you; I'm trying to save you from becoming a constant caregiver."

"You said just the other day that you realized that you needed to let the past go and enjoy what we have together."

"I may not live a long time, either."

"Someone told you that?"

"No … but I've had enough go wrong these past few years that I can guess I'm on the Grim Reaper's list."

Donovan shifted in his seat to face her squarely.

"What about me?" His intense look said he was all business now. "I have lived a lot of years alone, miserable. Since I met you, I'm happy. I've found peace. I call you that because it's what you bring to me. I want that all the time," he continued. "No matter what the length of time!"

Then realizing that he might open a recently healed wound, he added, "You know *I* could die tomorrow."

Donovan was not giving up.

"Please, Peace. Please consider marrying me," he begged, realizing that it was coming across as a plea.

Lynn kissed him gently one more time.

"A little more time, please," she whispered.

Chapter 35

ea was overjoyed when Lynn asked for a new dress.

"Donovan says that it doesn't have to be long, just something holiday-ish," Lynn instructed. "Not red, Bea."

"Never again!" Bea agreed. She opened her fancy design program, ready to begin designing another Lynn dress. She glanced up briefly to ask, "Are you ever going to tell me what happened the night you broke up with Donovan?"

Lynn relayed the entire bathroom scene, telling Bea all the details, ending with,

"It was awful. Then I told him that I never wanted to see him again."

"Hmmm."

Bea was listening while coloring her design. She raised her serious eyes to look at Lynn and say, "You know you'll bump into her again, right?"

Lynn wished at that moment that she could borrow some of Bea's tough hide. Gritting her teeth, she answered, "I am determined to never let that woman hurt me or Donovan again."

"You go, girl!" Bea turned her tablet to face Lynn. "And this dress will help you feel confident, sexy, and ready to take on the bitches of the world."

The design was a forest green, sleek from shoulders to knees, with a soft caplet of lace over the shoulders hosting little bits of glitter. Bea had drawn the model as blond, but bald.

"Oh, man," Lynn frowned as she looked at it. "I love the dress, but I forgot about my head. What'll I do about that?"

Bea's kind smile told Lynn that her head would not be an issue. "Let me think of something."

WHEN SHE GOT HOME FROM BEA'S HOUSE, A LETTER FROM Brandstone University waited for her, summoning her back to work.

Chapter 36

The following Monday Lynn's right leg shook as she neared the big parking lot outside her office. This restless leg was something new, something she again attributed to her body's rebooting following surgery.

Or maybe it's nerves. Who knows?

Sally, the administrative assistant, looked up as Lynn entered. Not smiling, she looked Lynn over as if trying to find fault. Lynn sensed distrust, nervousness, and perhaps resentment.

For what?

"Good morning," came the cold, perfunctory greeting.

"Sally! Hi!"

Lynn was taking Donovan's advice to be super friendly on her first day back. She was damned if she was going to allow Sally to take her down.

"Nice office!" Lynn proclaimed as she looked around the new reception area, noting black, gray, and chrome colors.

"I'm supposed to give you a tour," Sally said, her demeanor saying that she was bored already at the idea. When the girl stood and her super-short, tight skirt was revealed, Lynn could see that once again Sally was dressed inappropriately.

Sally stood up, grabbed a ring of keys, and motioned at the obvious desk.

"This workstation is for students." She indicated a long table with computers, a fax machine, and paper products. "Our workroom is here," she said opening a door behind her desk. Sally closed the door quickly and started walking down the hall.

I'll give it a thorough look later.

"This is Tom's office," Sally said as she motioned to a closed door. "Cassie has the big office in the middle of the hallway. She's not coming in today. Vacation day. She left you a note with instructions."

Sally's tour had been quick and superficial.

I can look later.

"This is your office," Sally said, opening the door.

Lynn walked into this new space, startled by the sudden illumination, thrilled by what she saw. The huge file cabinets that took more than a quarter of her old office were gone, moved to the workroom.

Finally. Thank God.

Her Italian masks, treasures from Venice, adorned spaces around the office. Her two computer monitors were there, hooked up to the ancient computer that was falling apart. There wasn't as much desktop space as she'd anticipated, and there was nothing on the walls.

And that's okay. I am going to take my time decorating this office.

"That's it," Sally declared, then flounced away.

Wandering back to her office, Lynn noted that every inch of common area wall space was covered in some kind of art.

Cassie strikes again.

Entering her own office, Lynn jumped again as the lights automatically came on.

Gotta get used to that.

Next to her keyboard sat a single sheet of white paper. Cassie's huge sprawling signature was the first thing Lynn saw as she lifted it read. After a few office instructions, Lynn read the shattering last paragraph.

Just so you know, it's been quite pleasant this Fall without all the drama concerning your health. On behalf of your office colleagues – and myself – I want you to refrain from discussing your cancer or your brain tumor. We want to focus on students, not on personal drama.

Tears filled Lynn's eyes.

No welcome back. No, "we're glad you've returned."

Lynn sat at her desk, trying to fight back tears that always seemed to be right on the edge since Timmy had been destroyed.

Why am I so emotional?

Lynn wasn't happy with this part of her reboot, but she realized that she had been unfeeling, unconcerned about most things for the last few years.

Just get it done. Get treated. Get over each day at work. That was my mantra for so long ... no emotions with any of it.

Steeling herself, Lynn decided to do as the note instructed. She'd go see the rest of the new building which Sally evidently deemed unimportant, maybe walk the campus.

"How do I get in and out of the back door? Is there a key?"

Sally rose from her chair and walked past Lynn to the back door.

"Here's the keypad. Just swipe your card; it opens."

Lynn took her ID out and asked, "Can you show me how it works?"

Sally rolled her eyes, grabbed Lynn's ID, and said, "It isn't that hard!" Then she swiped the card. Lynn couldn't tell if the stripe was face in or out.

I'll figure it out.

Lynn wandered around, ending up at the Division Head's office. Brad Petrona welcomed her back with a brief hug. But when he asked what had happened, Lynn was reticent about explaining.

Does Cassie's edict of not talking about medical stuff extend throughout the Division? Am I being tested by Brad?

Instead of answering, she said, "Oh, I'm sure Cassie has filled you in."

Leaving a confused-looking Brad, Lynn went back to her new building and tried her entrance card. It didn't work. She tried again and again, finally giving up, going to the front entrance.

"I can't get it to work," Lynn said, trying to brave through it. "Maybe my ID card needs to be reactivated."

Sally jumped up.

"No, it works. Give that to me."

She grabbed Lynn's ID, walked quickly to the back door, and opened it immediately. Again, it was all done so quickly that Lynn could not see. Tom arrived for work, late as usual, while Lynn was trying to figure it out.

Tom showed her how to use the card, but then went into his office and shut the door.

"You're supposed to do these letters," Sally announced, holding out student requests.

Lynn remembered that the templates were on the shared drive. She sat at her desk, pleased that her old password still worked and allowed her in. Noting that all the letters had been changed or updated since she'd left, with Cassie's signature replacing her own, Lynn felt as if her nerves reached into her fingers.

Great. And, of course, all the students who want these letters have difficult names.

It took the rest of the day to get the letters written. When she went to print them, Lynn discovered that her printer was new, not the familiar old one that she at least knew how to turn on.

"Sally?"

She noticed that Sally was playing a video game, something Cassie would not have allowed.

"Could you please show me how to turn on the new printer? I can't find a button."

Sally sighed, minimized her screen, and followed Lynn into her office where she quickly turned it on.

"When you get them printed, put them on my desk," Sally instructed. "I keep a file for students' letters."

After a dirty look at Lynn, Sally again trounced out the door.

If her skirt was full, it would twirl with every flounce.

ON TUESDAY, PURPOSELY, LYNN GOT TO WORK EARLY. SHE TOOK deep breaths, approached the new back door, and after a few attempts, got into the building. Sally was standing on the other side, looking as if she had been waiting.

She didn't even open the door for me.

"Good morning, Sally."

"Morning," came the cold reply.

Later, the heavy pounce of Cassie's feet announced her arrival. After a few minutes of waiting for Cassie to get adjusted in her office, Lynn wandered off to her boss's doorway.

"Good morning, Cassie."

Cassie looked up.

"Oh! Hello."

Cassie looked Lynn over like she was someone she'd never seen before. Both women were uncomfortable in each other's presence. Lynn broke the silence.

"Did you want to see me before the day begins?"

"Not really," Cassie said, cold, a bit loudly.

I forgot about the volume problem.

Cassie took an enormous bite of a doughnut. "Oh. Welcome back, I guess."

"Um ... thanks. I feel much better; my mind is much clearer."

"Hmmm. Sally gave me your letters; I'll look them over."

That set the tone for another awful day. Cassie was too busy to meet with her and took off for lunch without a word.

Chapter 37

ooking up from his desk, Donovan eyed the people talking to Ana, his administrative assistant. He knew that a manager named Dave was bringing in someone who could be Rue LA LA's next "star." Always grateful for the full glass wall that allowed him to preview his appointments, Donovan saw a long-legged, young woman with a short Afro enter with her manager, Dave Creighton.

Her hair is as short as Lynn's, Donovan thought, wondering how Lynn's day was going. Since her return to work, Lynn had been upset and anxious. Donovan reminded himself that he needed to be fully present at this meeting, to use his talent of assessing people so that the team could decide if this girl was a go.

He watched her. The girl was dressed simply, a short, flirty skirt of black and red, short midriff-baring top in black with a black cardigan over it. Chunky black heels completed her outfit.

Donovan smiled. He knew that once she began a career in the industry, someone would take charge of creating her persona, trying to make her look like no one else so that she stood out.

But no one would try to change her voice which, Donovan already knew, was amazing. He had spent weeks listening to her sing – in the car, at home, while hiking. Although he did not personally pick their new artists, he always got the final vote. While Donovan took his time when he sampled new music, he considered himself to be a good judge of new talent – something he'd inherited from his father.

The young woman's name was Brie Jackson. A simple name, although the last name could be problematic, he noted. As if she sensed his mental critique, Brie turned her head and looked directly at Donovan, those eyes fearless. Donovan chuckled, a smile lighting his face at her youth and tenacity. But then moments later he recalled several upstarts who'd presented themselves as decent people and went on to cause thunderstorms.

You never know.

He watched Ana lead the girl and her manager down the hall, then quickly sent Lynn a text.

Hope today is going well!

Standing in the conference room doorway Donovan noted that everyone was happy. The girl was a bit nervous, but politely smiling and talking to everyone who addressed her. Her manager was solicitous, also expected. Rue LA LA's creative and legal teams were relaxed as evidenced by their easy postures and the loud laughter and talk.

They like this girl.

As Donovan entered, Wesley Graham, the newest member of the creative team, stood up, creating a stir in the manager who also jumped up pulling Brie with him when he saw Donovan.

"Donovan!" Wesley exclaimed, causing the room to quiet down. "Meet Dave Creighton and Miss Brie Jackson."

Dave extended his hand to Donovan who shook it, saying, "I know Dave. You're part of Al Bartleman's firm, right? How're you doing?"

Dave nodded in greeting and then introduced his client, saying, "This amazing young person is Brie Jackson."

"Hello, Brie. You do have a beautiful voice!"

A soft but sure voice came back with a "Thank you." Her eyes were respectful.

"Let's begin this meeting," Donovan instructed like the CEO he was.

An hour later everyone was even happier. Expectations of the artist, her manager, and Rue LA LA were ironed out, only needing a final contract to be drawn up. The only hitch was what to call the new artist.

"My name is Brie Jackson."

She was adamant. Adam Lure, head of the creative team, cleared his throat before countering, "I think we should avoid the use of that last name."

"Why? It's my name." Brie's eyes lit with fire.

Better and better. Kid has spunk.

"Because of Michael Jackson and the entire Jackson family," Wesley answered. "You want to stand out on your own."

"What about using her first name only? Brie?" someone suggested.

Ana, who was taking notes on her tablet, asked how to spell that name.

Brie answered, "B.R.I.E. Like the cheese."

Silence descended on the group.

Adam cleared his throat again.

"I'm not sure how that will go over either," he said. "You don't want media people comparing you to 'smelly cheese' if something were to go wrong."

Everyone looked thoughtful at the comment, some nodding.

"Not that it ever would!" Dave interjected.

Wesley picked up on the manager's concern. "Of course not. But why put it out there for some troll to use?"

They were all nodding except the person whose name it was. Donovan noted that Brie seemed a little lost. Finding some resolve, she said, "But I like my name. I can give up the Jackson, I guess. But do I have to make up some weird name like Roy Alloy? Or T Bone?"

She shivered in her chair while the others quietly chuckled. Donovan leaned toward her.

"No," he said firmly. "No T Bone. Or Iced Tea. Or Queen What-ever. Or Princess SomethingOrOther."

The others were listening to their boss. Brie eyed him with adoration.

"What about dropping the E? Just being B.R.I.?" Donovan asked.

He watched as all the wheels turned in legal, creative, and talented minds.

Brie smiled, then said, "I can live with that."

So B.R.I.E. became Bri, a contract was scheduled to be completed in a few days. And Donovan finally had a joyful day in what had been a series of very difficult ones.

Chapter 38

On Wednesday Lynn arrived early to her office, noting that Cassie was already there, unusually early. Without even a greeting, she called out, "Lyyynnnnn! I want to meet with you in the conference room in five minutes."

Cassie bounded in and threw papers down in front of Lynn.

"What is this?" she thundered as she sat herself down.

Each of the letters that Lynn had written several days before had red corrections marks. Horrified, Lynn realized that she had made mistakes.

"I thought you told me that your mind was clearer?"

"It is."

"This is not clearer, Lynn. These letters are horrible. A fifth-grader could do better than this!"

Cassie then went through each letter, line by line.

"I'm sorry; let me re-do them."

"These forms should be old hat to you by now. You've worked for me for a long time. Where is this clearer mind that you say you have?"

Her tenuous leash on her new emotions, always at the forefront lately, was quickly becoming loose as Cassie continued her rant.

"So, I don't get a chance to ease back into things?" Lynn asked as she found a little courage.

"You should know these forms, Lynn. You said you were clearer to me in the email you sent right before you came back. I think you probably came back too soon."

"Not that I had any choice in it!" Lynn responded, her own

volume rising. "I wanted to stay home until the new semester started, but they threatened to take my job away."

Eyeing each other across the conference table, Lynn tried not to cry. Cassie's eyes held something akin to hate.

"Your work and your attitude have not been the same since your sister died." Cassie's tone was imperial, ice cold.

Lynn gasped, managed to get out, "What?"

I shouldn't be surprised that she'd bring this up. She's always digging up the past to support her tirades.

"That's over three years ago," Lynn answered, almost whispering, trying to rein in overwhelming fear and grief. "You want me to stop grieving or be well just because you pick a certain time."

Wait for it ... get ready ... next, she'll mention Michael's death.

"And then there was all the time you had to take off when your husband died!"

Stunned, Lynn waited until her thoughts weren't shrouded in grief, then said, "I took only what I was allowed to take as a widow."

"It was an inconvenient time for us."

"You can't pick when people die."

"Still, you'd already taken all that sick time ..."

When her own mother died, she was out for a month.

"Since he died, you are not the same enthusiastic worker I hired," Cassie continued. "You missed appointments with students, staff, and don't get me started about the agendas that you couldn't put together."

Cassie shuffled the red-marked letters and then looked at Lynn again.

"You can't even seem to do simple things without help."

"Like what?"

"You had to ask Sally for help turning on your printer ..."

I knew that bitch was keeping track of thinks I asked for help with.

"It's brand new!" Lynn glared at Cassie. "All I asked –"

"And you couldn't open the back door with your key card

either. You ask for help with everything! I don't think that shows that you have a clearer mind."

"Will you stop with the clearer mind stuff?"

Lynn fisted her hands in her lap to prevent them from going up to her face in horror and embarrassment that she had yelled at her boss.

Cassie sat there, resolute.

"Cassie," Lynn started after forcing herself to calm down, "while I was on leave, you moved offices. Everything I left in my old office is gone or moved. This office is different, the door key system is different, the printer is different – new – and the forms are different even though you think they are the same. It takes time to learn all these new things."

Cassie sat there like stone, didn't move, didn't change her facial expression as Lynn went on.

"With so much changing at once, and my recovery, it will take time for me to learn." Finishing her monologue, Lynn's emotions escaped her tenuous control. Tears streamed down her face. "I'm sorry," Lynn said, wondering if she was sorry for losing control, or sorry for the clueless woman in front of her.

Cassie shuffled the papers in front of her. "HR is making me give them a day by day report on your work."

"What?" Lynn was startled. "For how long?"

"Sixty days. They want me to keep track of all your work. Since I can't watch you all the time, Sally, Tom, and the student workers will be telling me how they think you're doing."

Sad, Lynn nodded, swiped her tears again. *I've never hated my job before. But I sure hate the people I work with.*

"We'll go over them together on Friday," Cassie said. "Now go fix those letters. I want to see everything you do – all writing, even student emails."

Then she pranced out of the conference room, leaving Lynn to absorb pain that was not physical.

LYNN NOTED THE LETTERS THAT SHE HAD CORRECTED NEATLY PILED on her desk the next morning.

Better, Cassie's handwritten note said. There were other ordinary things to do making for Lynn's first normal day of the week until late in the afternoon when Cassie's sing-song tone filled the office.

"Lyyynnnnn."

Taking a deep breath, Lynn went to Cassie's office doorway and waited for whatever judgment was coming her way. Her heart was pounding, her legs shaking, as she waited to hear what Cassie would say.

"You forgot to register Michael Blanc in SEVIS."

Lynn's heart dropped.

"When?" she whispered. "And his name is Michel."

"Oh. Michel. Michael. Similar," Cassie said as she held out the student's file for Lynn to see. "Anyway, it was last Fall. You noted in the file that you registered him," Cassie said, then pointing to her computer screen that showed his government record, she said, "but he isn't registered. He's terminated."

Termination. The worst thing that can happen to a student.

Lynn felt her stomach start to churn as she looked at the computer screen and then at the file where very clearly her handwriting had noted that he was registered on the third of September.

"That was the day I left," Lynn mused. "I have no memory of this."

Cassie's face showed irritation and anger.

"Well, whatever. He's terminated."

"Cassie, I feel terrible," Lynn said as she fought back tears – again. "Michel is the perfect student."

"I know." For once, Cassie was not screaming, instead shuffling paperwork again. "Just send him an email, and then you'll need to write a letter explaining what happened."

When she returned from an appointment with HR, shutting her door to focus on more letters, Lynn heard a deep French accent coming through the wall she shared with Cassie.

I'm not brave enough to face him yet.

Twenty minutes later, she heard Cassie say, "I'm worried that we're going to find other mistakes like this, Michel."

It was all she could do to survive the rest of the day. Before she left, she told Cassie again how sorry she was.

"Yeah, well he told me that his lawyer wants a copy of your letter."

Sick from the thought of ruining a student's hope for remaining legally in the United States, Lynn got in her car and cried all the way home.

ALONE THAT EVENING, DETERMINED TO HELP FIX MICHEL'S situation, Lynn immediately sat down to write a blunt letter explaining what probably happened to Michel's registration.

I was the one who forgot to register Michel. I have been ill from cancer treatment followed by a brain tumor. My doctors say that it caused cognitive, behavioral, and physical disabilities.

She went on to applaud Michel's perfect immigration record and begged Immigration to make his record active again. Finishing the letter, Lynn heard Donovan come in.

"Hey, Peace!" He called out cheerfully. His face became serious when he saw hers through the open loft area off her bedroom. He could see that she was very far from peaceful.

"What happened? Did The Bitch say something again today?"

Lynn recounted the entire event, pausing only to take a deep breath between sobs. As she sobbed, Donovan pulled Lynn into a tight embrace. He tried to soothe the woman he loved, listening, rubbing small circles of comfort on her quaking back.

"What can I do? How can I help you?"

Still sobbing, Lynn asked, "Will you read this? Tell me if it's okay?"

Donovan took the letter from her as she continued, "I don't want it to appear like I'm defensive, or that I don't want to accept blame, or that I'm just looking for one huge pity party. I just want them to know what I did that screwed this poor kid's record up."

Lynn untangled herself from Donovan's arms, allowing him to read while she walked into her bedroom.

"It's fine, Lynn," he said. "Well written. Even I understand that the person who made these mistakes on this kid's record was not intentionally making them. It's fine."

She was sitting on her bed, propped against the headboard.

"No!" Her voice was sharp, the tears endless. "No, nothing is right! I really fucked up. I may have ruined a young man's future. And Cassie is such a bitch all the time, and Sally, the admin assistant is worse!"

She paused to blow her nose, then added, "I just want to quit! Isn't that terrible? I love working with my students, but I am a physical wreck when I drive on to campus, and a mental nutcase when I get home. I should just quit."

Donovan allowed her to cry it out, then sat down next to her on the bed, facing her. He was at a loss as to how to help her. "Shhh, Lynn, think this through. You don't want The Bitch to win."

"I can't handle it anymore, Donovan. I can't face going into an office every day and wondering what they're going to find wrong. Sally spends her days writing down what I do, Tom spends his days behind a closed door. Cassie even has the student workers giving her daily updates!"

"Even your favorite, Rafa?"

Lynn tried to smile. "He told me that he was 'absolutely, no way in hell' going to tell either Sally or Cassie anything about me."

Donovan made another circle on her back before Lynn asked, "What should I do?"

As calmly as he could, Donovan said, "I think you should prove to Cassie that you can do this work."

Lynn watched as he assumed his CEO persona, confident in his advice, dressed for the role, despite sitting on a bed.

"You don't want to look back – if you quit – and then wish you'd try to stay and work it out. What if this Michel's situation is sorted out because of your letter? Won't that be a victory?" He brushed his finger along her chin while saying, "You can do this, Lynn."

"I can?"

"You can." He kissed her softly on her nose. "It's hard, but you've been through harder things. Hell, you beat cancer!"

For the first time, Lynn realized that she was indeed cancer-free.

"I did, didn't I?"

Donovan, on a roll, continued, "You just had a brain tumor removed and you are amazing! Everything about you is improved: your balance is better; your mind is clearer; you're happier than I've ever seen you be … well, aside from this crying jag you're on right now."

They both chuckled, but when they were finished, he said, "You are facing a tough road right now. It was probably too soon for you to go back. But I know you can beat this, too."

Lynn finally smiled at him. She felt his strength of will, saw his complete confidence in her, his determination to help her make it.

If Donovan could, he'd probably march right into Cassie's brand-new office and eviscerate her.

Instead, Donovan was giving her the encouragement and strength she so desperately needed to get through an awful return to the workplace. A slight nod from a now smiling Donovan gave her the courage she needed to end her crying.

"I can!" she said and kissed him on the lips.

Chapter 39

assie's absence on Friday gave Lynn time to sneak over to Cergan Hall and check out the new sound system. People with Rue LA LA shirts that said SOUND were running around. Someone sang a short song. Another gave a fake speech while others adjusted the new soundboard. Everything appeared to be working well.

Certainly better than the old system. Amazing.

No loud screeches, no echoes, no sudden loss of sound while the speaker talked.

"What a wonderful replacement for the old system," a cheerful voice called from behind her. Lynn whirled around to find President Rawlings grinning from ear to ear. "I'm sure they thought the old system was wonderful when it was installed," he continued as he came toward Lynn. "This room had the best acoustics on campus in the old days."

Chris Rawlings shoved his hands into his pockets, then said, "Thank you, Lynn."

What did I do?

"Thank you?"

"We're certainly appreciative of what Donovan Rue did for this room and the others."

Lynn startled, her eyes growing wide with surprise. "The others?"

Now President Rawlings smiled. Rocking back and forth from heels to toes, he said, "He had his team look at some of our other large meeting spaces and rooms, had those systems updated or replaced – the dance studio, the smaller gym, the Estates Room ..."

"I didn't know," Lynn said softly.

"No, I can see you didn't."

Chris Rawlings looked down at his brown shoes for a moment.

"We needed a benefactor for this; he was it!" His eyes sparkled. "You bringing him to Brandstone is something I won't forget."

A voice boomed over the new system. "That does it!"

The *Sound* team all clapped briefly, then started to clean up their minimal mess of boxes, wires, and tools.

"Did I miss it?"

Lynn recognized a deep and sexy voice which probably sounded authoritative to his employees.

"Yes, sir," someone answered. "But we can always run through things again if you'd like."

"No, no. I'm sure it's perfect. You guys finish up, take the rest of the day off," Donovan instructed. His eyes found Lynn's which were sparkling with delight.

"Do you like it?" Donovan asked her. President Rawlings held out a welcoming hand.

"We love it!" Chris Rawlings declared, shaking Donovan's hand. "We can't thank you enough."

"My thanks will come tonight when I see people staying in this room for the event instead of walking out holding their hands over their ears like the last time I was here."

Donovan leaned down to Lynn and asked, "It is tonight, right?"

LATER, FINDING A CORNER CHAIR, DONOVAN KEPT HIMSELF occupied with his cell phone while waiting for Lynn to finish setting up. He settled in to read and respond, finding it hard to focus when Lynn's voice called out periodically to students, suggesting ways to do displays, or praising them for the efforts they were putting in for the Culture Fair. He marveled at her new energy, remembering another time when he'd come to an event and she could barely lift a box.

My Peace is a miracle. Thank God for gifted doctors and surgeons. Oh, and resilient women, too!

At six that evening, students and staff started filing into Cergan Hall. Students from Brandstone Media Services were discussing how to best use the new sound system. Several young men were on their phones, finding instructions, trying to be careful with Brandstone's newest toy.

This building has good acoustics, Donovan thought, realizing that without any background music he could hear other conversations easily.

No one noticed Donovan Rue sitting in the corner. Although a little nervous without his dark glasses, Donovan decided that he needed to start being visible in Lynn's world. Her colleagues may have read or seen social media insinuations about who Donovan's new plus-one was. Or they may have read the gossip.

They've seen the allegations made by Mandisa.

There was nothing Donovan could do to stop paparazzi speculations, except to be in plain sight.

"Hello!"

Once again, Lynn's voice drew Donovan's attention.

She was walking over to two young people who were standing at a refreshments table, not far from where Donovan was hiding. One younger person wrapped her arms around Lynn, screeching, "You look so good, Lynn."

As the conversation ventured into the work the former student was pursuing, Donovan saw Cassie Manders stroll in. Her long-sleeved embroidered peasant top, broomstick skirt, messy brown hair, and Birkenstock sandals made her stand out in a crowd of otherwise conservatively dressed academics and students.

Hard to miss.

Cassie applied a plastic smile to her face as she approached Lynn and the student. Donovan watched as she moved to stand by them. Lynn paused to politely ask Cassie, "Do you remember Mia? She was our student intern three years ago."

Cassie shrugged, then said, "There are so many students ..."

Mia said, "Hello, Dr. Manders," then asked Lynn, "You must have finished treatment about the time I graduated, right?"

"I did," Lynn acknowledged.

Mia nodded; it appeared to Donovan that the conversation was wrapping up.

"Do you know the rest of the story?" Cassie asked loudly.

With the room's great acoustics, Donovan – and everyone else who wanted to – could hear.

When the former student shrugged and said, "Guess not," Cassie boomed out, "She had a brain tumor!"

"Oh, my God! Lynn!" Mia reached out to touch Lynn's arm. "I had no idea. What happened? Did you know about it during cancer treatment?"

Although she was not facing him, Donovan sensed Lynn's embarrassment by the way her body stiffened beneath her corporate polo shirt.

"No, later on," Lynn answered. "I knew something was wrong, but they kept telling me that I needed time to recover."

Cassie was pushing her big body into Lynn's personal space, leaning her head down to the two shorter women as if conspiring to keep things quiet, her words loud enough for Donovan to hear.

"I saved Lynn's life!" Cassie stated.

Donovan leaned forward in his chair.

What? Did I hear that right?

The student looked from Lynn to Cassie, then back at Lynn. Lynn said nothing. Casting her eyes downward, Donovan could see that she was struggling to maintain a neutral face.

"I kept telling her to find another doctor," Cassie continued as she placed some chips in her mouth, crunching away and talking. "When she went on leave, she found one. I saved her life."

What?! This is the ultimate insult to Lynn. How dare she do this to her?

Donovan was now standing, about ready to approach the group when he heard Lynn say, "Cassie, I think Ross Urbans is over there, looking for you."

"Oh! The vice president of marketing? Maybe I ought to go talk with him."

"Yes, you should," Lynn encouraged her.

Good. Push The Bitch away. Don't let her talk like that, Peace.

Cassie stepped away, but not before telling Mia again, "I saved her life!" as she pointed at Lynn's back.

The Bitch!

Donovan was stunned, frozen by his table, watching Lynn embrace the former student before her startled, angry eyes locked with his own. Mia turned away as Lynn shrugged at Donovan as if to say, *"oh well."* Then she turned to another student, a friendly smile in place.

THAT NIGHT THEY TOOK A QUICK WALK AROUND LYNN'S neighborhood. Agitated by Cassie's presumptuous comment, her walking was brisk, her words fast and furious.

"How the hell does she think she saved me? If anyone saved me, it was Dr. Urambu who cut Timmy out."

"She probably thinks she helped in surgery," Donovan said, trying to turn the incident into humor so Lynn would calm down. "Maybe she even tells people *that* when you're not around."

"Yeah, probably. Even though she *banned* me from discussing my health!" Lynn paused in speaking, increasing her pace again. "Or maybe the doctor at the MRI place, the man who found the tumor … maybe he saved me. Or Dr. Meyers when she ordered the MRI saved me!"

Lynn was pumping her arms back and forth, increasing her speed.

"How can she even *think* that she saved me!"

"Well, remember. She did take your family out to lunch on the day of the surgery. She saved us all from starvation that day."

Lynn stepped on some crunchy leaves, the noise echoing in the night air as she paced. "She did that *only* to meet Donovan Rue."

"And she did bring you flowers."

"Which thankfully, Dara got rid of, from what I've been told," Lynn said. "I hate Stargazer lilies."

The edges of Donovan's eyes crinkled with mirth as he increased his speed to keep up with his fired-up Lynn.

"Doesn't matter what you like, Peace," he said. "She bought those flowers because she saved your life! She's probably convincing people all over your campus that she saved your life – that she did that brain surgery!"

"Oh, yeah! And probably took a Gamma Knife to my head, too!"

By the time they circled back to Lynn's driveway, they were both laughing with the absurdity of Cassie saving anyone. Pausing at her front door, Donovan exaggerated exhaustion, bending over, placing his hands on his thigh.

He took a deep breath. "Wow. That was the quickest walk I've ever taken with you. I think I ought to get you riled up more often. Or let Cassie do it!"

Lynn delivered a stern look, then couldn't help grin.

"It's crazy, isn't it?" she asked as she opened the door.

Inside Donovan replied, "Thank God we don't have to see her at tomorrow's party, or she'd be telling all of Rue LA LA that she saved your life."

"Only if she qualified it by saying, 'I know Donovan Rue!'" Lynn began to act coy, turning her body sideways, batting her eyes. Opening her arms wide, Lynn said, "I can hear her now: 'I saved Donovan Rue's girlfriend's life!'"

Chapter 40

The evening of the Rue LA LA holiday party, Lynn shimmied the beautiful hunter green dress over her trim body, taking note of the glittery, lace caplet sleeves. The dress was a simple A-line style with a slight scoop neckline, the cap sleeves just dusting Lynn's slim shoulders.

Probably not as flashy as some I'll see tonight, but that suits me just fine.

For the crowning touch, Lynn pulled on a beret that covered almost all her head. The basic cap was constructed of the same green fabric, but the beauty of it was the ornamental flower Bea's team had constructed out of lace and small crystals.

Whimsical. Just a touch, but I love it.

Slipping into simple black heels, Lynn began to adjust the gold rope necklace that Donovan had given to her before another event. He entered the room as she finished.

"Wow!"

Even in a simple suit, Donovan was elegant, handsome, a totally beautiful man.

"Wow to you," Donovan said as he came up to kiss her. "But the necklace has to go."

"What? Why?"

He handed her a Tiffany's box. Taking it, Lynn glanced from it to Donovan's dark eyes.

"This is too much," she whispered.

"No. It's just right," he admonished. "Now, open it or we'll be late."

Lynn pulled off the cream-colored ribbon and then opened the robin's egg blue box to find crescent-shaped, diamond earrings. Without thinking, she began to sway in place, move the box side to side, catching the light that caused the earrings to sparkle.

"They're beautiful. Thank you."

Earrings in place, Lynn walked out the front door with Donovan behind her toward the waiting limo. As they got closer to the venue, Lynn sensed Donovan's uneasiness. As she was deciding how to comfort him, he said, "Roy won't be here tonight."

They were pulling up next to the curb.

"But I don't know about Dymettra. Or the others who were with her that other night."

Lynn took his hand, squeezing hard.

"If anything happens, I'm up for it," she said. "I'm stronger than I was a few months ago – even a week ago. I can handle this."

As they exited the car, camera flashes announced that the paparazzi were there in force. No one stopped them for interviews, but one reporter did call out, "Is that another Lynn dress?" Lynn only smiled politely and nodded.

Bea deserves recognition for her work.

But this wasn't a dress to twirl, so she kept walking briskly, trying to keep up with Donovan who was practically running toward the entrance.

"Donovan! Slow down a little," she said, then grabbed his arm for support. "I'm in heels and you're racing." He pulled her into his protective grasp, wrapping an arm around her waist.

"I don't want them to hassle you," he said. "Besides," now his eyes held a tease in their depths, "I know you can keep up."

"Well, they're *not* hassling me!"

Fractionally slowing his pace, Donovan made his way to the elevator which was whisking people to the top floor.

He placed a hand at Lynn's lower back, escorting her out of the elevator and into the massive hallway just outside of the rotating ballroom. Immediately, Lynn's senses were overwhelmed by music, clinking glasses, laughter, loud conversation, and bright holiday colors. People milled around, drinks in hand. Almost all the women were in red, green, or gold dresses which were predominately long and as usual, sleeveless with long slits somewhere in the skirt. Not at all like Lynn's dress. Lynn couldn't decide if the looks she got from other women were admiring or critical. Deciding that confidence could only help her feel glamourous, Lynn squared her shoulders, smiled broadly, and turned around to survey the room.

"Let's get a drink, Peace," Donovan said, continuing to guide his date with a firm hand toward the bar set up at the end of the hallway. As soon as he handed Lynn a glass of tonic water, Donovan was accosted by people all clamoring to talk with him. Lynn knew that this was the part of the job that stressed Donovan out the most. His hand became tighter at her waist.

"Donovan! Can I get a picture of you with Tanya? She needs the publicity, man."

"Just this once," Donovan replied.

As soon as the cameraman said, "Got it," the smiles stopped, and the woman and her manager walked away without even saying thank you. They were replaced by yet another manager who intruded into Donovan's – and Lynn's – personal space. Lynn recoiled from his nearness.

Ever hear about personal space, dude?

"Oh! Donovan! I need five minutes of your time to discuss my problem with Georgia. Remember? New guy we signed a couple of months ago. Well –"

"John," Donovan held up his free hand to stop the conversation. "This is a party. Please call my administrative assistant and get an appointment."

Donovan guided Lynn away from the bar.

Another manager approached the couple, a huge smile on his face, approaching Donovan as if he were a favorite friend.

"Hey, man!" He reached out as if to clasp Donovan's hand. "I've got this group I want you to hear. They're best live. We could go to seem them later tonight, or I can take you to where they're performing. But you need to see them. Really. Live is best."

"I don't go to live gigs. Send a demo to our creatives."

Donovan's increasing hand pressure urged Lynn to head toward the center of the hallway. Leaving the area did not deter yet another manager from approaching Donovan.

"Did you know that my new client, the hip-hop group, *Better Large,* is leaving their company? Yeah, they need a new home and I think Rue LA LA might be right for them. Can we talk about it?"

"Just make an appointment with Len. He handles those things."

Donovan lengthened his steps, making Lynn skip to keep up. She cast a quick glance at his face, noting his deliberately blank look. On and on and on went the litany of needy people or hungry entertainers. Lynn, silent at his side, watched Donovan steer through it, acknowledging some complaints, but not really solving any singular problem. He was polite, firm, and very aware that Lynn was observing it all.

How does he manage to do this time after time after time?

Finally, the ballroom doors opened, and the crowd surged into the beautifully decorated room. Jazzy Christmas music played them to their seats. Someone rushed by, bumping into Lynn who lost her fragile balance and knocked into Donovan, spilling wine all over Lynn's dress.

"Here, let me help," Donovan said, taking a fresh napkin from a nearby cocktail table to wipe gently on Lynn's dress. "Is it bad?"

"No," Lynn said, "I think I'm fine …"

"Well, look who's here!" came the familiar, throaty sound.

In unison, Donovan and Lynn raised their heads to see a very shiny Dymettra.

Diamonds. She's covered in them – even her hair!

"Hello, Dymettra." Lynn's voice was pleasant, firm.

Dymettra ran an assessing eye over Lynn.

"That's certainly a different look," she said, then asked, "Who designed this? Who wears hats anymore?"

Feeling anger beginning to burn, Lynn placed a soft hand on Donovan's arm hoping the control and politeness she'd just witnessed would flow into her.

No one insults Bea. Not even this she-bitch.

"This lovely hat – and dress – were designed by Beatrice Owens."

As if to assure herself, Lynn patted the cap.

"No one wears hats anymore," Dymettra said as she shook her head. Then extending her finger at Lynn's ears, she said, "But I do think the earrings look good with it."

Tucking her fingers beneath her chin, Dymettra continued her assessment, saying "And most people wear gowns to this event, not cocktail dresses."

"Stop."

Donovan's tone was icy. Lynn tightened her hand on his bicep, but she continued to lock eyes with Dymettra.

"I wear hats, Dymettra." Her eyes glittered like the lace on her sleeves when she continued, "I have to. Unless you think I should go bald?"

"White women don't do bald well, so I doubt it. You wouldn't shave your head anyway."

It was all Lynn could do not to pull off her cap and show Dymettra her bald, scarred head.

"No, I wouldn't," Lynn countered. "At least not by choice. And I imagine most white women who are bald, don't choose it. We don't always have a choice."

Dymettra swung the short train of her red dress around and walked closer to Donovan.

"Yeah, I heard you had some troubles," she said to Lynn without one iota of sympathy. "More cancer?"

"Stop!" came the repeated demand. Donovan removed his hand from Lynn's waist, lengthening his arms by his side with closed fists. Lynn grabbed the cloth of his jacket, wishing she could tele-pathically communicate, *It's okay, it's okay, Donovan. I've got this.*

Holding on firmly, Lynn addressed Dymettra, keeping an even tone.

"No, it wasn't cancer." When Dymettra opened her mouth again, Lynn silenced her with, "And I don't have to explain anything to you."

Dymettra stood there, dumbstruck, unable to add anything. Lynn didn't move her eyes away as she hooked her hand further into Donovan's arm.

"Now, if you're through with your greetings, my date and I are going to find our seats. Merry Christmas," Lynn said as she almost forced Donovan's body away from Dymettra. "Or bah humbug. Whatever suits you."

Steering Donovan toward the table, Lynn felt anger, pride, and adrenaline fueling her every step.

"Well done, Peace!" Donovan said. "I'm sorry that had to happen. I'll deal with it later."

"No, leave it alone. I think I handled it," Lynn said as she shrugged her shoulders. She looked up at Donovan with a satisfied smile. "Let's just forget her and enjoy the party."

No other problems popped up once they found their seats. They sat with people who were not artists or managers, but who worked for Donovan's company and simply looked forward to a nice evening. They all enjoyed the scrumptious meal. The dancing was well worth the practice session a few weeks before.

When it was all over, Donovan leaned back in his car and sighed with relief.

"Thank God that's over."

"Hmm ... of all the events you've taken me to, Mr. Rue, this was my favorite," Lynn stated, then she leaned into him. "And the evening, sir has just begun."

Donovan was surprised, his fingers reaching up to touch the blond strands revealed when Lynn removed the beret.

"Are you flirting with me, Peace?"

Lynn kicked off her heels, then swung her legs over Donovan's lap.

"Mr. Rue, do I have to make an appointment with your administrative assistant to see you in my bed?"

Donovan scratched his chin, then reached up to undo his tie.

"Really?" he looked at her longingly. "Are you serious? You're not too tired?"

Lynn tried to stop amusement from spreading across her face, as she ran her hands through the short hair.

"No, sir. Right now, I'm energized."

"In that case, no need for an appointment," Donovan said, giving her a quick kiss. "Should I tell Desmond to speed home?"

As she was throwing back the duvet cover, he came up behind her, wrapping his arms around her. Cupping her breasts, he began to knead the soft mounds with almost religious reverence, feeling the tips harden. She was giggling as well, indicating that she wanted more.

He moved his hands to the back of the green dress. First there was a cape to remove. Finding a hook, he undid it, pulled it off, and then laid it at the end of the bed. Next, he found the dress's zipper, slowly moving it down Lynn's back, his fingers stroking her spine. Again, with reverence, he pulled the sleeves off, then pushed the rest of the garment to the floor. Lynn stepped out as it reached her ankles. He knelt to remove it. Finished, he smoothed his hands along her sides, going from her ankles to her calves, her waist, until he got to where her black bra was secured. A second later, he had that unsnapped; Lynn pulled it off. Then his hands were on her waist again, descending until he had her black lace panties hooked by his fingers, pulling them off, too. One more time he kneaded the now unfettered breasts before Lynn turned and gave him a sweet kiss.

"You, too," she said, unknotting his tie which he'd already loosened. Before removing it, she pushed his jacket off his shoulders, grabbing it before it hit the carpet, placing it with her caplet and dress. Next, she removed the tie, the belt, and unbuttoned the slacks. Eyeing his tied shoes, Lynn instructed, "Toe them off, love." Then she placed fingers on the sides of a sock, pushing it off. Then the other.

Where is she getting this energy? This patience?

Donovan was trying to keep his control during the entire undressing, wondering how she found the calm that he was seeing when they were both so needy for the other after almost two months without much comfort of the other's body.

His hunger continued as Lynn began to unbutton his dress shirt. Once she'd pushed it back and off, Lynn ran her hands along Donovan's chest. He moved his hands to her back, pulling her to him urgently. Their mouths found each other, kissing, sucking, tasting as if it were all new. Each forgot about time; the kisses went on until Lynn paused for air.

"God, Donovan! I love this."

Gently, still kissing her, he walked her one step back so that her legs were firmly against the bed, then pushed her down onto it. Lynn laid back, maneuvering herself to the middle of the bed. Donovan placed himself next to her, started kissing her again, taking the time to lavish kisses on her slender neck, an area he knew Lynn found especially erogenous. While doing so, his left leg parted hers, revealing the center of his body. His hand drew small circles from her breast until he found the sweet spot in her center, where he began rubbing.

Lynn was panting with arousal. One hand was reaching between Donovan's legs, tracing him all over his mid-section, knowing what felt good to him. She ran the other hand up and down his chest.

When Donovan could no longer wait, he stopped his ministrations and gently drew up over her. Their eyes caught hold, his asking for permission, hers granting him access. Gently, as if this was all new for her, Donovan nudged inside. Feeling Lynn's warmth, he pushed himself all the way to the hilt, fighting to hold on to control. Lynn was not holding off. After three thrusts, she came, screaming, "Donovan!" loud enough to wake anyone else if they'd been in the house. Feeling her spasms grip him, Donovan let go, too. He ended up collapsing on top of her as their orgasms ebbed away

Chapter 41

*D*ara showed up mid-morning the next day, determined to help Lynn finish her Christmas decorating. To Lynn's surprise, Connor marched through the door with her.

"Time to get a tree, Mom!" he announced after giving Lynn a big hug. "There are good ones at Fosters this year."

Lynn smiled at the exuberance seldom shown by this son. Connor's enthusiasm, Dara's joy, and the support of the man she was growing more in love with every day, revitalized her.

It will be a good Christmas!

"Before we go get one," Connor continued, "we have to move some furniture around."

Connor began moving the sofa to a side wall, instructing Dara where to put tables and lamps that would otherwise be in the way of the giant tree Lynn knew he was determined to purchase. Even though they said little, they seemed to be in sync with one another. It wasn't long before the room was redesigned so that a tree would fit in the corner, facing the front door.

"What's going on?"

Donovan bounded down the stairs, smiling at the two young adults as Lynn was placing a Christmas-looking cover over the coffee table that now occupied a corner. He went first to Lynn for a quick good morning kiss, then to his daughter, throwing an arm around her.

"Good morning, Magic!"

"Dad!" Dara's expressive eyes held a plea for him to stop calling her that name. Just as quickly, they sparked with the announcement, "We're going to get a Christmas tree. A real one!"

"You like that idea, don't you?" Donovan asked her, then looked at Connor. "I'm not sure how to get one to this house."

Connor shook his car keys. "Easy. We put it on the roof rack of my car. You guys ready to go?"

Before noon a gorgeous eight-foot Noble fir tree was set up on the cornered coffee table, lit up with jewel-tone lights, ready to be decorated with ornaments. Donovan and Dara were amused at the explanation or story that accompanied each trinket that Lynn removed from special boxes. Emotional, Lynn stumbled when she brought out a few of Michael's old childhood ornaments, but quickly regained her spirit.

"God, Mom!" Connor reached to place his father's handmade toy soldier near the top. "I can't believe how much more interest you're showing this year. You are feeling a ton better, aren't you?"

Lynn just laughed, enjoying the start of the season, reveling in feeling so good after such a long period of awfulness.

It's like a second chance. A fresh start.

Standing back, she marveled at the gorgeous tree, adjusting a new ornament she'd purchased on her first shopping trip with Dara, a picture of Owen and Maribelle at their wedding.

"I feel great! This is just what I needed to get into the holiday spirit!"

Lynn pushed an empty box out of the way with her foot, then said, "I need to get that village lit up."

"Oooh! Let me help, Lynn!" Dara called out.

In the family room, Lynn climbed a small step stool to reach into the back of the deep shelves, reaching behind each house to pull wires and lights into correct placement.

"You okay up there?" Donovan asked with a smile. "Any balance issues?"

Lynn turned from her perch to see him.

"I'm okay!"

Donovan, amazed, was observing all the many electric cords hanging in every which way around the entertainment center. Connor handed him a drink, looking on appraisingly.

"Let me guess," Connor said, "You're wondering how in the hell this is ever going to look good."

"Well … yeah, I am."

Connor gifted Donovan with a rare smile. "Oh, ye of little faith. Just wait. You'll see."

Sipping from their drinks, they both watched Lynn climb to the top step of the small ladder. Donovan held his breath while she stretched up on her tiptoes to reach behind the houses. His eyes wandered around the eight shelves, seeing a British village complete with Westminster Abbey and Buckingham Palace, two Chicago shelves with a Marshall Field's store, Water Tower Place, and the old Orpheum Theatre.

Donovan's gaze settled on a building with a familiar logo.

She's even got a Starbucks!

As he finished his review of the entire village, Donovan nodded his head at Connor.

"You're right. Takes a leap of faith, but it is magical."

Connor was helping Dara place white felt over any cords that were showing, simulating snow piles.

Suddenly Lynn came down from her perch, leaned down to a surge protector behind the television set, and switched it on.

"Voila!"

Bright white light filled every house. Connor turned off the overhead lights while Dara clapped her hands with excitement.

"Dad, I wish we had something like this."

Lynn whispered, "You have it now, sweetie."

As Donovan looked the blinking spectacle over, he pulled Lynn in for a hug.

"I started collecting them when Connor was seven or eight.

People have been giving me them for years. I've been buying bits and pieces to make it look like a village."

As she spoke, she spread her arms out toward the entire unit.

"I haven't bought anything during the last few years. I think I might have enough."

Lynn walked to the last box in the room. Pulling out a ceramic train station, she said, "This is the first house I ever got. Connor gave it to me."

Dara and Donovan swung their heads to Connor who shrugged and said, "I think Dad took us Christmas shopping and this is what I picked out for Mom. I think; I don't really remember since I was only four or five."

"Regardless," Lynn held the small house in both hands, "this house has a special place in my heart because it's how it all started. And it has a special place right here."

Dara spun around at that point.

"I have the first present to give!"

As the others chuckled at her good humor, she rushed out of the room returning with a brown box from a mail-order company. Thrusting it into Lynn's hands she said, "Here. Merry Christmas."

"It's not Christmas yet," Lynn protested. "Don't you want to wait?"

"No!" Dara shrieked her opposition. "Open it now!"

Everyone watched as Lynn opened the brown box, revealing a mission-style house, a replica of many Southern California homes. An orange-tiled roof covered the building which had a huge garage at the front. A separate palm tree figurine accompanied the building.

"California!" Connor called out. "Finally represented."

Analyzing the new house, Lynn placed it on top of her television set. She added the electric cord to the others, lighting it up. Lynn whispered, "Thank you" to the girl who had started the decorating a few weeks before. They wrapped their arms around each other as the doorbell rang.

315

"I'll get it," Donovan said with a knowing smile.

"What's he up to?" Lynn asked Dara, then readjusted the palm tree near her new village home.

A few minutes later two men entered the room carrying a hunter green leather reclining chair. Connor swiftly moved Lynn's old chair aside, so they could place the new one down. After Donovan signed for it, he took Lynn's hand to lead her to it.

"I hadn't thought of it as a Christmas gift until this minute," He said. "I know you like your green chair, but it's falling apart."

"I'll say!" Connor agreed.

Lynn sat in the new one, pulling up her legs and curling into her familiar resting pose before smiling widely.

"I love it. Thank you."

Chapter 42

*D*onovan began to take Lynn on more hikes. At first, they walked in 'the Backyard', the mountains surrounding her neighborhood. Muddy after an unexpected, rare rainfall, Lynn slipped around on the trails.

"I should have worn my hiking shoes!" she exclaimed as she pulled her white sneaker from the trail's mud.

"You have hiking boots?"

"Got 'em the first year we lived in California," Lynn said. She stopped at the top of a steep climb to catch her breath. "I don't remember this trail very well. Is there much more uphill climbing?"

Lynn glanced around the valley that they'd approached. She was happy, energized, and teased Donovan about trying to kill her.

Downhill in the mud was a challenge. Even as she slipped, Lynn laughed, unafraid as Donovan reached out to grab her.

Donovan worked to find trails that were challenging for Lynn, but not off-putting. He selected the Wendy Trail in the Sierra Vista mountains for an early Sunday morning hike.

"This is beautiful!" Lynn exclaimed as they came to a meadow. Donovan motioned toward a trail which was an asphalt fire lane, a downhill walk.

"How far down?" Lynn asked. "You always underestimate these mountain climbs."

"Honestly? It's about three miles down this hill. Then back up another three."

Lynn didn't hesitate.

"I can do this," she said and started off. "Let's go!"

Tenacious woman. I love it!

Filled with blind turns, many hikers, and serious bikers, the trail was a chore to navigate but filled with fantastic views of lush mountain valleys. They enjoyed being together, forgetting the hike's difficulty.

Others enjoyed it as well. A father biked alongside two young sons. Lynn watched as one boy zoomed ahead, remembering a blond daredevil racing against his bigger, darker brother.

Following a break at the bottom, the family turned to start the uphill ride back. Both boys briefly groaned, but there was no recourse. Lynn took it to heart.

I can do this!

She began to push herself up the hill, celebrating with up-stretched arms when they reached the summit. Donovan hugged her, whispering, "I knew you could do this, Peace."

The last bit of the trail was mercifully flat. Others joined them from a connecting trail. The couple jumped at hearing a small child's screech. A family of four walked ahead, Dad and son together, the small boy holding a dog's leash.

The mother was holding a little girl who was crying, her little body shaking. The mom ran her hand up and down the child's back, saying, "It's okay. It's okay." In between sobs, the child said, "She … looked … at … me … funny …"

"It's okay," the mom kept saying. "Shhh."

"Why … did … she … look … at me? I … don't want … her … to … look at me!"

Hard crying began again. Placing a hand at the child's nape, the mom held her child's head to her chest, whispering and running her hand in circles over a bright pink shirt, occasionally, caressing the child's dark curls while her eyes searched for help or guidance. The father continued walking with the boy, oblivious to his wife's distress. Other walkers cast judgmental looks as they passed by, increasing the mom's anxiety. Except for Lynn.

"Give me a minute," Lynn whispered.

She wandered over to the mom. Donovan thought he could see her formulating a plan with every step, every crunch on the gravel.

"Hello there!" she called out in what Donovan recognized as a friendly, inviting tone. "I haven't seen you in a long time, stranger."

Lynn, not making eye contact with the child, turned her head to wink at the mom.

"Hello," the mom said, a little bit of a questioning tone in her greeting, but she was playing along. "How are you?"

Donovan continued to watch as Lynn answered, "Oh! I'm great." She still was not looking at the child who, although still hiccupping with tears, seemed to be calming down, her wailing stopping. Lynn motioned toward Donovan.

"Don and I are out this morning," Lynn said. "I didn't think I'd see you and your lovely family out here. How's everyone?"

Donovan smiled at the use of the strange name.

Is she trying to keep me incognito?

Taking a cue, he waved, watching his Lynn in counseling mode.

The mother shifted the girl in her arms to another hip. Her hand kept soothing the child; both looked a little more relaxed.

"We're … we're doing fine," the young woman said, biting her bottom lip, the tears in her eyes betraying just how fragile she was.

"Can I get down?"

"Sure, Elisha," the mom said, and placed her daughter at her feet. Elisha cuddled next to Lynn, grabbing her hand. Lynn smiled down at the little girl, taking her tiny hand and squeezing it a little. That got a child's exaggerated squeeze back, then a "Can you hold me?"

Without hesitation, Lynn lifted Elisha into her arms, giving her a lovely smile.

Her empathy, unconditional love, and acceptance are why Dara likes her so much. She's not just peace to me. She brings peace to everyone.

Donovan marveled at what he was seeing, remembering angry encounters between himself and Mandy while a tiny Dara watched, sucking her fingers.

"I'm stuck here all the time with that brat!"

"Dara is not *a brat."*

Donovan often wondered when Dara's illness began, if it could have been triggered by her mother's hostility or the angry encounters the child witnessed between her parents.

Too late to speculate about all that. It's long over.

With a sudden flood of peaceful knowledge that his daughter had a positive female role model in her life, Donovan turned and walked down the trail.

A culture center greeted walkers at the trail's end. Its large, covered porch invited people to stop and rest in big Adirondack rocking chairs. Donovan was glad that one rocker was open. Waiting for Lynn, he leaned back, crossing his long legs, right ankle on left knee. Although he removed his hat, Donovan kept the sunglasses on.

No sense in risking it. Too many people here.

It felt good to be outside, enjoying nature, getting exercise while being with Lynn. Donovan marveled at the change in the direction his life had taken.

Please God, let this happiness continue. Her positive energy makes my life tolerable. She's necessary for me.

As he finished his brief prayer, he smiled, realizing that he'd tilted his head back, just as Lynn did when she prayed.

Donovan saw the mom, Lynn, and the little girl walking toward him. Everyone held hands, the women swinging Elisha high into the air while she laughed. When the mom took her to the restroom, Lynn wandered over to Donovan.

"Hello, Peacemaker," he said as he stood and motioned to his rocker. Just then a couple sitting in the other rockers got up, leaving room for both Donovan and Lynn to sit. "What was up with that?"

Lynn answered his hello with a quick kiss, then sat in her chair.

"I'm not exactly sure. I just provided a distraction," Lynn said and then took a deep drink of water.

Elisha and her mom wandered out of the facilities. Seeing her dog, Elisha ran to it while the mom came over to Lynn who stood.

"Thank you," she said with tears in her eyes. "It's so hard sometimes ..."

Lynn wrapped her arms around the younger woman, rocking her back and forth as she said, "You're doing a great job. Hang in there."

Chapter 43

*R*eturning to work the following Monday after an enjoyable weekend was hard. Legs shaking, heart racing, Lynn entered her building without any trouble.

I've got this card entrance thing down!

But she was assaulted the minute she entered.

"Lyyyynnnnnnn?"

"Yes?"

"Come in here."

Lynn paused on the way to her own office to look in on her boss.

As soon as Lynn sat before her, Cassie handed her an evaluation form and said, "She's making me do this."

A daily evaluation from the week prior sat on Cassie's desk.

Cassie interrupted Lynn's reading by saying, "She's making me do this. She's just brutal."

Lynn didn't comment, trying to comprehend every part of her evaluation.

I'm not allowing her to intimidate me anymore. I am not.

"You told me that there was only one thing in the cultural trivia contest that I created that you didn't understand," Lynn said, pointing to item number four. "Here it says three."

Cassie looked at her copy.

"I did? Oh, a mistake. I'll fix that."

She fixed her assessment, said again, "I have to do this, you know. She's making me do this."

"And you misspelled 'according'."

Lynn pointed to the word on her sheet.

"Oh! I didn't catch that either! Let me fix it here."

After she fixed the typo, Cassie said, "She's just brutal. I have to do this, you know."

Lynn looked at Cassie directly.

"Who is 'she'?"

Cassie ran her fingers through one long, tangled lock of hair.

"Oh, you know. What's her name? The woman in HR. The head woman."

"Kathy."

"Yeah. Kathy is making me do this," Cassie said. "Now if you sign it at the bottom, I'll turn it in this morning."

Lynn looked over the form that Cassie had reprinted.

"Before I sign, the dates aren't right. It says November first through December fourth. I came back on November 30."

Cassie looked at her computer screen again.

"Oh! You're so good to check that, too!"

She reprinted it a third time and handed it to Lynn.

I wish I'd signed it, then caught it after she sent it to Kathy. Perfection is required for me, but not for herself.

Despite her annoyance, Lynn signed the form.

"Before you go back to your office, I need you to write a letter for this student – what's his name again? The one stuck in Canada. His passport expired, and they won't let him back into the U.S. Write a letter saying he's our student. Be sure to have me review it. And after I approve it, give it to Sally, tell her to overnight mail it to this address in Canada."

"I'll get it done this morning."

"And I need that letter for Michel Blanc's attorney."

"It's done. Did you want to see it before I put it on letterhead?"

Cassie stood up, look down her nose at Lynn.

"Absolutely. Now, I'm very busy, so …" she waved toward the door, banishing Lynn from the room.

Lynn wrote the letter for the student stuck in Vancouver. She reread Michel's letter, printed it out, and put both on Cassie's desk.

After lunch, Cassie returned the stranded student's in-status letter with a post-it note that said "Great!" Lynn then wrote an explicit email to Sally, detailing Cassie's orders on how it was to be sent, and then hand wrote instructions before walking it out to Sally who was watching YouTube videos at her desk.

"Cassie wants this letter to go by overnight mail to Canada," she instructed the sullen woman. "I've circled the address here."

Sally went back to her video as Lynn walked away.

Good. I've covered those instructions three times. She'll get this.

Two days later Sally blew into Lynn's office and threw the student's file on her desk.

"Why are you writing this letter?" she demanded.

Lynn saw the anger in the kohl-rimmed eyes.

Why is this letter still here? Cassie said it was to go overnight!

"I wrote it because my supervisor told me to write it," Lynn said icily.

Sally flipped open the file and showed a similar letter from a few months before.

"There's already a letter for this kid supporting his passport updates. One you wrote last summer," she thundered, "and another one that Cassie wrote before that. Why didn't you send *those* letters?"

"I don't know why those letters are there, but I do know that Cassie wanted the letter I wrote two days ago to go out that same day. Overnight. To Canada."

"You never told me to send it to Canada!"

Sally's voice was getting as loud as Cassie's.

Lynn, now angrier than she'd ever been at Sally, kept her voice level, but firm.

"Yes, I did tell you. I sent you an email with the details. I gave you a copy of that email with the address. I personally told you that it was to go overnight to Canada."

Sally turned around, swearing under her breath about stupid bitches.

Entering her home, Lynn flopped into the green chair and cried. Again.

I'm turning into a crying machine!

She could not remember once crying about cancer or the brain tumor. She'd cried for Michael – she hoped – but couldn't remember anything else wrenching her emotions as much as these first few weeks back at work.

Flat affect: a not-normal reaction to two things in my life that should have sent me into emotional turmoil. I'm making up for it now during this reboot.

Her brain kept circling back to the encounter with Sally, wondering if she'd been at all inappropriate. As she finished writing a note to Cassie about the event, Donovan entered her house. He knew that something else had gone wrong for Lynn.

"What happened?"

Again, Donovan listened attentively to her story while Lynn cried, told him of the day, and then added, "Listen to me; I am so paranoid."

He took off his suitcoat then sat in the old green chair that Lynn had moved to the loft. "What was it like before? Before cancer, before me. Tell me more about working for Cassie Manders."

"Well …" Lynn began after considering where to start. "You know, we plan an event and then, on the morning of it, she decides that she'd rather have egg sandwiches than cereal! Or purple linens rather than red. She plans to attend, then she doesn't show up. Or bows out at the last minute. Stupid stuff like that which can throw the linen providers into a tizzy or require us to cancel one food order and try to get another one going at the last minute."

Lynn detailed a few events.

"A micro-manager," Donovan stated. "Has she always been like this?"

Lynn sighed, adjusted her position at the desk. "Yes."

"Have you ever confronted her?"

"Only once," Lynn answered. "And she turned everything into something that was my fault."

"I don't want to talk about that ... I just want you to know that I do not appreciate it when you yell at me in front of colleagues or students!"

"Good!" Donovan said, interrupting her story. "That put her in her place."

"You wish. I wished! Instead she decided to tell me that she was disappointed in everything I'd done that year."

"This past year? Everything. Everything from last year was embarrassing, Lynn."

"Okay, I've heard enough!" Donovan thundered. He quickly stood, feet flat on the floor, shoulders thrown back, his voice that of the CEO he was. "I don't think I can handle hearing anymore. She's a terrible manager. She *is* a bitch."

Lynn wiped her nose with a nearby tissue and said, "That's why I have to document this thing with Sally. If she's going to evaluate me every day for HR, then I'm going to write down what's happening to me, too."

Donovan kissed the top of Lynn's head.

"I rarely like to think about litigation," he said, "but if she fires you for this stupid thing then I will get a labor lawyer involved."

Lynn placed her arms around him, snuggling into his chest.

"I really don't want to sue," she whispered. "I like my work; I like my students. I hate Cassie. And Sally."

"Well, if this keeps going, we'll find someone. Enough is enough."

Chapter 44

*B*reathing a sigh of relief as she left the Brandstone building to begin Christmas break, Lynn contemplated having fun with her children and the Rues who had decided to join them.

Owen, who'd flown in earlier that day with Maribelle, smiled as Lynn entered the driveway.

"Hello, Owen!"

"Mom! You look great! The house looks amazing! Just like the old days," he said.

He opened her door, saying "They fixed the side mirror. Good."

Lynn looked first at her perfect outside mirror, then at Owen, asking, "Was something wrong with it?"

Owen just laughed, offered his hand out to help her out.

"It's all good, Momster."

Lynn went to bed that Christmas Eve feeling all was well in her world.

WHEN DONOVAN WOKE HER EARLY THE NEXT MORNING, LYNN groaned. Sleeping flat on her stomach, she opened one eye to see her clock.

"Wait! I'm sleeping past five-thirty for the first time since the hospital, and you're waking me up? For what?"

Donovan swatted her lightly.

"Get up, woman. Mass is at 7:30!"

So much to be thankful for.

Sitting toward the front of the beautifully decorated church, Lynn noticed that all the women wore holiday green or red, including Lynn who wore a red, boiled-wool coat over a red silk blouse with black pants and a red chemo cap that had some satin and beading on it thanks to Bea. The only outliers in color were four white-clad nuns.

She closed her eyes and thanked God for her life, her family, and the wonderful man sitting next to here. Opening her eyes at the last bit of prayer, Lynn saw Donovan's observant expression.

"I know," Lynn said. "I'm tilting my head back."

When he smiled, she took his hand lightly in hers.

"I'm glad you brought me here. It's beautiful."

No one was awake when they got home. Lynn placed her homemade coffee-cake in the oven, began frying bacon and swirling together eggs and milk for scrambled eggs. In between coming over to her for hugs and kisses, Donovan set the table, poured juice, and made coffee. It wasn't long before they heard upstairs doors opening and closing. Everyone was awake.

Owen was the first to bounce into the kitchen.

"Smells great, Mom," he said as he reached for a piece of bacon. "Let me help you get this to the table."

After the breakfast tradition ended and the young people cleaned up the feast, the clan gathered in the seldom-used living room to open presents. Instead of a Christmas sock, Lynn had filled Christmassy shirt boxes with small items like seeds for Dara, a cookbook for Maribelle, photography items for Owen, and kitchen things for Connor. Bea, who'd sent her items over earlier, gave them each a beautiful silver picture frame. Lynn's frame held the famous picture of her wearing the Lynn dress, ensconced in Donovan's arms.

As Donovan opened one of his gifts by ripping the bright red paper off in one movement, Owen left the room, missing Donovan's stunned face. A water globe that held a black lab – the first gift that Lynn had purchased when Dara showed it to her.

"It's Onyx," Dara said. "Can you see him?"

Donovan nodded, then leaned over to kiss Lynn. But before he got to her lips, a joyous bark came from the end of a leash that Owen was holding. The puppy bounded into the room, panting with excitement, a big green and red bow secured to his collar. He shook himself, eyed the gathering, then ambled over to where Donovan was sitting. Still astonished, Donovan picked the puppy up.

"Who are you?" he quizzed the small dog.

"This is Rue," Dara announced. "Isn't he cute?"

Donovan continued petting Rue but avoided the licks, sending the message that dog kisses were not something he tolerated.

"He's great," Donovan proclaimed, moving his head in time to avoid getting a big slobbery tongue on his chin. "Who ...?"

"All of us chipped in," Owen said. He plopped down next to his wife, handing the leash to Donovan. "Dara told us about how you grew up with black labs and a lot about Onyx. We decided you needed to have this little one."

Connor reached over to pet the dog, too. "We've had him at a trainer that Dara knew. He's housebroken. Probably more than ready to be in a home."

Donovan looked at the young men, his hands still petting Rue, now trying to avoid little bites. "This is great! But do I have food, a crate, all that stuff? I got rid of it when Onyx died."

Lynn pushed a big box forward while Dara took the leash from Donovan, causing Rue to jump in her lap.

"Open this," she said.

Inside were all the things that Donovan would need for his new pet.

"Wow." Donovan took the puppy away from Dara who was allowing face licking. "This is totally unexpected. I hadn't even thought about getting a new dog." He glanced at Lynn, delight on his face. "I've been preoccupied."

"It seems an appropriate gift for someone who can have anything he wants," Owen said, "And it was Mom's idea."

"But how did you hide him today? Where's he been?"

Donovan asked more questions, and the others answered them, but Rue's appearance ended gift giving. They all sat around, Donovan alternately petting his new dog, then kissing Lynn. Dara, Maribelle, and Connor were looking over recipes in a new cook-book while Owen left the room again.

Lynn could hear the beginning of the Beach Boys song *Kokomo*, begin. She grabbed Owen's hands when he entered the room. Giggling with joy, Lynn danced him around the room. Owen, was lip singing all the verses, hamming it up for his wife's filming. Donovan and Dara Rue looked on in amazement.

"Mom had songs for each of us," Connor explained. "They dance this way whenever they have an opportunity."

Connor was smug.

"I lucked out. No dance for my song."

As he finished saying that, the tune *She Drives Me Crazy* by Fine Young Cannibals started playing. Instead of dancing, Lynn pirou-etted toward Connor feigning anger while he remained smug.

As other songs rolled along, people took turns dancing in the paper-strewn living room. The music phased into Christmas songs which were not danceable. Suddenly, they were cleaning up, deciding what to do with the rest of their day. Donovan, Connor, and Owen decided to take Rue on a short hike in the Backyard. Dara, Maribelle, and Lynn watched old Christmas movies and made the feast for when the men returned.

A Norman Rockwell Christmas, Lynn thought, smiling as she watched the men leave, the small puppy waddling on his leash.

Maribelle lounged on the couch, soon in a deep sleep. Left alone with Lynn, Dara asked, "Do you ever dream?"

"More than ever." Lynn smiled remembering some of the

recent dreams of Cathy, and one full-color dream that she wished would return. "Why?"

"I've been dreaming a lot about my mother." Dara pulled a Christmas afghan over her legs, then looked at Lynn. "They aren't happy dreams, believe me." As Lynn turned a log over in the fireplace, Dara said, "Did Dad tell you that he and Mom divorced when he found out she was cheating on him?"

"Yes, he mentioned it once."

"Did he tell you that she hit him?"

"Hit him?" Lynn turned from the fireplace, shock on her face. "Your mother 'hit' your father? Like a small hit on the arm?" Lynn mimed the action.

Dara's eyes grew wide. "No. It was a hit. With a heavy object." She pulled her legs up under the afghan. "I can't seem to remember the entire thing, but I remember Dad calling out 'Ow!' " As Lynn sat back down in her chair, Dara looked at the mesmerizing fire and said, "Maybe I was too young."

"Well, if it did happen, it would have been pretty traumatic for a … how old were you?"

"Two, maybe three."

"Wow," Lynn couldn't imagine it, but she knew from Donovan's stories that Mandy had not been an easy person. "Have you told your dad? Maybe he can fill in the blanks."

Dara snuggled down under the afghan, eyeing a still sleeping Maribelle with envy. "Not yet. Maybe when it gets a little clearer. He says that she's not pressing the issue, so … mmm … I think I'll close my eyes for a few minutes, too."

AN EXHAUSTED PUPPY WAS ASLEEP IN HIS CRATE NEAR LYNN'S bedroom fireplace. Lynn and Donovan snuggled together, leaving the young people downstairs.

"I hate when Christmas day ends," Lynn declared as she stared into the fire. "It was such a nice Christmas. I'm glad that you and Dara could share it with us."

"Thank you for having us," Donovan answered. He smiled softly and asked, "Are you ready for your present, Peace?"

A small thrill ran through Lynn followed by guilt.

"You've given me so much, Donovan! Fancy clothes, jewelry, a chair ..."

"But today is Christmas!"

Donovan stood up, found new music on his playlist. He motioned for Lynn to join him in another dance. Ben Harper's *Forever* played as they swayed gently in place. Lynn's body grew warm, her heartbeat increased at an idea of what Donovan's present might be.

"Donovan," she whispered as his lips grazed her cheek, their feet barely moving as he swayed her back and forth. His dark eyes sparkled, but he looked intense, needy.

"Just let me talk, please," he pleaded.

He quit dancing. Taking a deep breath, Donovan took both of Lynn's hands into his own.

"Lynn, you totally captivate me."

His hand swiped through that raven hair again.

"I can't imagine being without you. I love you so much."

Donovan looked upward, closing his eyes tightly for a minute.

"Shit! I can't even put this into coherent words."

Lynn's eyes widened in amazement. She was tongue-tied, too. Before she could find words to encourage or comfort him, Donovan was on one knee, still holding her hands. Lynn gasped, breaking her right hand loose from his hold, covering her mouth in surprise.

"Lynn, would you marry me?"

Now Lynn took back her left hand, bringing it up to join the other on her face. Tears sprung into her bright blue eyes; she still could not communicate.

Donovan wasn't sure what to make of a subdued Lynn.

"I know we haven't known each other long, but I know what I want when I see it."

Again, he ran his hand through his hair.

"You see me for who I am, not the celebrity that the media makes up. You bring peace, happiness … shit, Lynn! I don't care if I get sixty years with you or six minutes. I can't live without you! I don't know how to …"

"Yes."

Lynn sucked in a breath after she said the one word. Looking down at the man she loved, she saw a mixture of surprise, then relief, then complete love.

"Yes?" he whispered.

"Yes!" Lynn repeated, then grabbed his hands, intending to help him off the floor. Instead, Donovan pulled her down, wrapped his arms around her, and kissed her as if he was afraid the answer would change.

"I was afraid you would say no, say it's still too soon," he said when he broke the kiss.

"What's too soon?" Lynn asked. "I've been thinking a lot about this since your first proposal. If I've learned anything, it's that time does go quickly, and you'd better grab what you want when the opportunity presents itself. And enjoy every second you have."

Donovan pulled Lynn to him, surrounding her with strong arms.

"Absolutely!" he agreed, then continued. "I mean it when I said the time thing. I need to enjoy every minute with you, whether it's ten minutes or one hundred years."

Lynn leaned over to give Donovan another big kiss.

In the morning Connor baked a frittata while Maribelle created a huge fruit plate. Dara, seated at the table, was answering a social media question from a client. Owen was trying to keep up with a British soccer game. Although tired from the holiday, all were still upbeat.

Donovan and Lynn walked in, hand in hand, smiling. Dara and the two boys looked at their parents with suspicion. Oblivious to the looks being thrown at them and between their children, Donovan pulled out Lynn's chair and held it for her as she sat down. Neither stopped smiling. After beginning to spoon food onto plates, Owen again eyed his mother, then Donovan.

"All right. I'll bite," he said, then took another bite of his toast. The others stopped what they were doing to look at him. Mouth full, he asked, "What's up with you two this morning?"

Lynn blushed, but her smile did not fade.

Dara now eyed her father.

"Yeah, what's going on Dad? You guys look like two high-schoolers at the after-prom breakfast."

Donovan took a sip of tea, then eyed Dara thoughtfully.

"Did you go to prom?

"Dad!"

"I forget. Really?"

Donovan's widened eyes encouraged Dara to walk right into his tease. She pushed her hair off her shoulders.

"Prom doesn't matter," she stated.

"Oh! I look like a high-schooler, huh?" Donovan continued. "And how should I describe the way you've looked the last few mornings here?"

"*Dad!*"

"We aren't curious about how Dara looked the last few days," Connor quickly interjected, wanting to pursue the original question. "We want to know why you and Mom are so … so lovey-dovey this morning."

Lynn started to play, too.

"We haven't looked lovey-dovey at all the past few days?"

"*Mom!*" Owen couldn't wait much longer, his attention span that of an ant. "Just tell us what's going on!"

Lynn took Donovan's hand. Looking into his laughing eyes, she asked, "Want to tell them?"

"Guess we'd better."

Donovan cleared his throat and stood up.

"Connor. Owen. And my darling Dara. I was going to ask you for permission, but it's too late to do that. And I am firm about this."

"Oh, boy … watch out!" Dara said under her breath.

He cleared his throat, then said, "I have asked Lynn to marry me. And she said yes."

The table went quiet with the news. After a few seconds, Dara was bouncing up and down, saying, "Oh, my God, oh my God, oh my God!"

Donovan waited for her to calm down – a little – then continued, "By some good luck, or grace from God, this remarkable woman came into my life. I can't live without her, and it seems, she can't be without me. So, we are getting married."

Dara jumped out of her chair, upsetting the beautiful fruit plate that Maribelle had slaved over.

"Dad!" She wrapped her arms around her father's neck, squeezing him as hard as she could. "Dad, I'm so happy for you!"

Owen was also up, pulling Lynn out of her chair, grabbing her in an enormous hug that took her off the floor.

"This is great!" Placing Lynn on her feet, he reached over to Donovan and shook his hand heartily. "Man, I'm so glad this is happening! Congratulations."

Maribelle was wiping tears from her eyes as she said, "Congratulations." Lynn reached over to squeeze her daughter-in-law's hand.

Without any noise, Connor stood up more slowly than the others, but he couldn't suppress a grin. He leaned over to kiss his mother, whispering, "Congrats, Mom."

Then he eyed Donovan, saying, "I'm happy for you. I can't imagine anyone making Mom happier. And I'm glad that it's happened since her health is better and her confidence is back. I know that's partly because of you."

As he and Donovan shook hands, Connor tried to settle his face into seriousness. "But just be aware that my brother and I were both wrestlers and hockey players. We'll take you down if you hurt our mother."

"Connor!" Lynn scolded. Donovan and Connor were laughing, doing that man-hug thing that men sometimes did.

"That will never happen, I can assure you," Donovan said. "Besides, I'm still in good shape."

Lynn continued her scolding although it was good-natured.

"Wait until you ask a girl to marry you. I hope her father is easier on you than you've been on Donovan."

Owen, who had again disappeared, came back from the dining room with champagne and six flutes.

"Where'd you get that?" Dara asked. "Give me that!"

Expertly, Dara twisted the cork out of the champagne, getting some of it on the disrupted fruit tray. They all laughed as it spilled, Owen declaring, "That'll make Maribelle's fruit tray even more impressive."

Joy swirled through the air. Lynn could feel Dara and Owen's exuberance; Maribelle's quiet happiness, and even thought Connor was on her side. As she watched Owen starting to pour, she reached for the orange juice already on the table.

"Let's take the orange juice and make mimosas," she suggested. "Something a little different for an engagement toast. Okay?"

Rescuing some strawberries from the platter, Maribelle decorated the lip of each glass with one, then handed each person a flute.

"I guess the toast is on me," Connor said as he took his glass.

Dara immediately grabbed hers and said, "No! I think it's my right!"

Without waiting for Connor to argue, she jumped to her feet, glass held high. "To Dad and Lynn! Congratulations!"

The glasses clinked loudly as they reached toward the middle of the table. Sipping the cocktails, the others settled back, all except Donovan who twirled his glass around and eyed the happy group.

"One thing," he said. When they all trained their eyes on him, he said, "This has to remain a family secret. I don't want the media jumping on us with questions, or putting out false stories, or bugging us on every corner with their damn cameras."

The smile left Lynn's face.

"I hadn't thought about that."

Placing his glass down, Donovan picked up a fork to spear some eggs.

Dara whispered, "Roy Alloy."

"Not just him."

Dara put her own glass down, then said, "Mandy."

Donovan raised his eyes to look at his daughter. Seeing her distressed face, he tried to smile reassuringly, but there was no getting away from the fact that Mandisa Phillips Rue was making horrible allegations.

"There are haters out there," he said.

Owen tried to change to atmosphere back to joy.

"When are you getting married?"

Donovan looked at Lynn for an answer.

"I haven't gotten over his proposal yet!" Lynn turned to face her fiancé. "Have you thought about that?"

Donovan shrugged, then said, "It can't happen fast enough for me."

As they all sat in a dreamy disposition, all wondering about an upcoming wedding. Lynn interrupted with, "You know, I think you ought to plan it, Donovan."

"Me?"

"Yeah, you." Her eyes sparkled with the same mischief that Owen's usually held. "Just let me know the details and I'll show up."

When she saw the others' questioning looks, she continued.

"It's not that I don't care about *our* wedding. I just think he should be the planner."

Dara laughed. "Not that Dad couldn't plan his wedding, but I think he'll probably get someone for all the details, Lynn."

"Okay." Lynn continued to act nonchalant about it. "Get a wedding planner."

"Well, they ask you some questions," Maribelle said slowly. Since she was the most recent bride at the table, her own event planning was still fresh in her mind. "Like, do you want a church wedding?"

Donovan and Lynn looked at one another.

"Yes," Donovan said as Lynn nodded her agreement.

"Small or large?" Maribelle continued.

"Small. Ish." Donovan said, again looking at Lynn. She was nodding, then said, "Please! Let's not invite all of LA, okay?"

"Okay. Just all of Rue LA LA," he answered with a grin. Lynn took her napkin and pretended to hit him.

Maribelle continued with, "Formal or informal?"

Donovan paused a few minutes and said, "In the middle? I mean I'd like it to be nice, but not over the top. After all, this isn't the first time we've been to this rodeo."

Lynn was nodding, went to get more coffee. As she poured it from the pot, she said to Donovan, "See! You've answered all the questions. Now you can plan the details. Or get someone to execute the plan for a church wedding that is small and formal, but not overdone."

Chapter 45

I'm first here again, she realized as she started down the hallway toward her office.

"Good morning."

"Ahhh!"

"Is your power out?"

"What?" Cassie's look was lazy, her eyes barely focused, her voice quiet. Then, "I turned them off. I don't want any lights."

With only the dim hallway light, Lynn could barely see Cassie sitting at her desk.

"I didn't mean to frighten you. I came in early."

Cassie pointed to a chair across from her desk, an invitation for Lynn to sit.

"It's okay …" Lynn didn't know how to take a quiet, inviting Cassie. She unbuttoned her coat, then took the proffered chair.

"You are here early," Lynn acknowledged. "Lots to do?"

She probably has a lot to do that I'm not aware of.

Cassie shuffled some paperwork, then eyed Lynn as if planning her approach to the question.

"There's always stuff to do."

"Oh! Well, maybe I should leave you alone …"

"Tom has cancer."

Lynn gulped. She didn't know much about Cassie, but she knew that Tom had been retired for a while now, but Cassie claimed that she was not ready to stay home, that there was too much to do at Brandstone.

If Michael had retired, I would have quit the next day. If Donovan retires, I am out of here.

But aloud, she said, "Oh, Cassie. I'm so sorry to hear this."

Cassie reached for her papers again, shuffling, then stacking them on another part of her desk.

"You know, he's twelve years older than me," Cassie said.

"No, I didn't know that."

Another reason to retire. He's a lot older. Don't judge, Lynn.

Cassie looked up at an old picture as if to force back accumulating tears.

"Yeah, he is. I never thought that I'd be taking care of him. I thought I'd retire in eight years and then we'd travel."

That's what I thought ...

Clearing her thickening throat, Lynn said, "The commonly held belief is that men die first." Then reaching deep down Lynn resurrected more resilience. "Cancer is not always a death sentence, Cassie."

Cassie's look was disdainful, almost hateful.

"For some people. Maybe people who also survive brain tumors are that lucky."

"Lucky?" Lynn fought to keep her voice low and even, her tears at bay. "I'd hardly call the last few years of my life *lucky.*"

Cassie snorted, becoming the hard boss Lynn knew so well.

"I do. You've beaten cancer. You survived a brain tumor. You've –"

"– lost a husband." Lynn's strength returned. "And it *is* hard! But I think part of it is the attitude you have while you're sick."

Cassie did not respond, her silhouetted face hard. Lynn continued, "And it's also about the support you get from others."

Cassie looked down at her lap, wringing her hands while Lynn added, "I would not be here with the help of my sons, my friends, and Michael ... while he was here."

"And Donovan Rue." Cassie flashed a look of intense jealousy mixed with anger. "I'm sure he's helped, too."

Lynn barely reined in a gasp.

This woman is such a bitch!

Aloud, she said, "Yes. He's very supportive."

"In more ways than one, I bet," Cassie sneered.

Lynn stood at that, losing her cool.

"Sometimes I can't believe what you say!"

She gathered her things and went to the doorway, pausing for a moment to say, "I'm sorry Tom is ill, Cassie. Let me know if you need me to take anything on for you. Believe me, I know what he'll be going through in the next year."

"It's not breast cancer!"

"Whatever it is, it's cancer. Cancer treatment is hideous. He'll need you or your children or his friends to be there for him."

I am not going to let this woman turn me *into a bitch.*

"And Cassie?" Lynn started out of the office, as she ended her visit saying, "You'll need some support, too."

In downtown Los Angeles at the Rue LA LA office, Len watched the workman take down the office holiday Christmas decorations. Although the company did minimal decorations, the removal created lots of commotion. Ladders clanged together, lights hit boxes, and the eventual thud of the real tree that Donovan had requested made quite a racket on the first day back after the holiday. As Len stood eyeing the mess, Donovan entered.

"They're quick to get it all down."

"Glad to see it go?" Len asked.

"No, not really." Donovan was thoughtful, quiet, as he led the short walk to his office, motioning Len to follow. "Did you have a good Christmas?"

"Yeah! The kids were home. Good to get away from here for a few days," Len said as he followed Donovan to his desk. "You?"

"Wonderful!" Donovan placed his bag on the desk. "I haven't had this nice a Christmas in years."

"You went to Lynn's home? Celebrated with her family?"

"Yes. Dara and I went. It was all good."

He waited until Len settled in a chair, then sat himself down, pushing back from the desk so he could cross his long legs.

"Can you arrange security for Lynn?"

Len did not seem surprised.

Probably already looking into hiring a personal security officer just for Lynn.

"Sure. Close protection detail?"

Donovan nodded, running his hand through his slightly over-long hair.

"I think it's time."

"Something change?"

"Just concerned for her. She's with me a lot, has been identified as my girlfriend. Then that thing with Dymettra –"

"Whatever that was!"

Donovan smiled. "I just want her covered."

It was said simply, slowly, and without any indication of a change in Donovan's relationship with Lynn. But Len, he knew, was not easily fooled.

"I'll get right on it, boss."

LYNN GLANCED AROUND THE DANCE STUDIO. NO, CASSIE, SO FAR. She'd said something about coming but had done her usual last-minute backout of the event. President Rawlings had also declined her invitation to attend so she was off the hook as far as entertaining powerful guests. Except for Donovan Rue.

"I thought you were really busy tonight?" she asked as Donovan kissed her on the cheek in greeting.

Donovan took off his suit jacket and threw it to the side.

"I've been hearing about this for weeks," he said. "I want to see how it all comes together."

The students seemed enthusiastic about this program – a

ballroom dancing event. Mary Anderson, the professor who taught World Dances was arranging partners around the dance studio.

"Okay! Ladies and gentlemen, we're going to begin with a waltz," she said. As the melody began, students began to dance, some giggling with nervousness.

Donovan placed his hand on Lynn's back, asking, "Do you dance?"

Lynn smiled, loving the question which he always came back to.

"A little," she admitted, placing her hand in his and wrapping the other arm around his strong back. "But it's been a long time."

"Let's show them how to dance, Peace."

At first, Lynn laughed at the idea of them instructing others to dance. But it soon became apparent that she and Donovan were out-dancing the students.

Oh no! I don't want them to not enjoy themselves.

While Donovan led Lynn around the dance floor, Lynn noticed that the professor was watching them, only occasionally glancing at the other couples.

This is not what I planned.

The waltz ended; the dance instructor approached them.

"You didn't tell me that you danced so well, Lynn!"

"I really would rather focus on the students learning to dance, not us."

The teacher was unimpressed.

"Of course," she said, ice in her reply. "But they will learn more from watching a couple who knows what they're doing!"

She turned toward the students, her voice rising into teacher tone, the volume carrying across the room.

"Ladies and gentlemen! Get into your partnerships again. This couple," her motion indicated Donovan and Lynn, "will be the ones to emulate … er … watch. I will replay the music, and we will all watch them do the steps. Pay attention to the way he holds her, the way he leads her around the room, the grace of her movement, the beauty of their partnership."

As the music started and Donovan began the steps, Lynn stumbled, her mind still trying to figure out how to rescue her student program before it became an adult evening class.

Sensing her tension, Donovan whispered, "It's okay, Peace."

Lynn shook her head.

"It's really not! I wanted the students to have an opportunity to learn these dances. I didn't want to be the exhibiting dancer!"

"Enjoy this," Donovan commanded, his voice was a soft croon, meant to relax his partner. Lynn realized that they had been gliding around the room effortlessly. They were so in tune with each other as dance partners that they went through the motions even while arguing.

Too late now. Might as well enjoy this!

The grinning teacher quit watching them as she pulled a cell phone out of a back pocket. Everyone saw the change in her attitude. As she held the phone, a worried crease sprouted in between her brows; she was no longer focusing on anyone dancing. As the music wound down, she again approached Lynn.

"I'm sorry, Lynn, but I just got a phone call that my son is in the hospital." As she tried to fight off tears, she sobbed, "I have to go. I'm sorry."

Lynn placed a hand on the woman's arms. "Don't be. I'm sorry to hear about it. Go, be with your son."

I'll figure this out ... I hope.

Lynn wondered what to do with the ten couples who were looking thoroughly confused.

This is really not going to plan ...

"Okay, everyone!" boomed a familiar deep voice. "Let's split the guys from the girls; I'll try to teach you a few things."

Donovan wandered over to the brand-new music control center, courtesy of Rue LA LA, selected a few tunes, then started to instruct the men on how to hold their dance partners. The girls, looking on, were chatting in their own languages, giggling, but Lynn could tell that they appreciated Donovan's instructions.

She took a deep breath and called them.

"Ladies, just come over here and I'll show you what *you* should be doing."

Excited, the girls surrounded Lynn as she Lynn demonstrated what she could. Giggling, smiles, and bobbing heads told Lynn that she was making headway with her impromptu dance clinic. Almost done with her explanations, she heard Donovan call out, "Whenever you're ready, ladies, we're ready to pair up again."

Eager to try it out, the couples re-formed. Donovan turned on his more modern selections.

"Lynn and I will wander around you, telling you individually what to do to be a better pair."

The couples started gliding again, some of them with more confidence. A few partners worked well together, telling one another what to do and making significant strides as dancers. Some were stopping, laughing at their inability, but obviously enjoying the activity anyway. Donovan and Lynn made their way among the group, instructing where they could, making sure that everyone understood that it was meant to be fun.

As the song ended, Donovan took control again. He taught the group a cha-cha, a jitterbug, basic swing, and a few dances Lynn had never heard of.

Oh, hell, I'm glad I lost Dr. Anderson. Donovan is making this so much fun.

"Now let's see if we can do a bunch of different dances to one song!"

Remembering their evening at the Rue LA LA dance studio, Lynn wondered what he would choose for music. Donovan began leading the students while he partnered Lynn. They started with a sedate two-step.

"Okay! Now the cha-cha!" he called out, releasing Lynn from

the waltz's hold. Some students attempted to follow their lead. Most were laughing.

"And now swing! Remember to bounce back and forth," he demonstrated, now holding Lynn close.

"And now the waltz right ... *here!*"

Donovan took a huge waltz step, gliding Lynn around the room. Twenty students laughed, snorted, giggled to a tune that really was not made for a waltz.

The evening ended with a student asking if they could do their own dances. Donovan and Lynn leaned against the dance studio wall, enjoying bottles of cold water as they watched the students dance.

"Where did you learn all these dances? Or get the ability to teach? You saved my program."

Donovan smiled the widest grin Lynn had yet seen, his eyes sparkling with delight.

"I love, love, love dancing." He leaned down to nuzzle Lynn's nose with his own. "Almost as much as I love you, Peace."

Leaning back against the wall again, he looked out at the students and said, "I wanted to dance for a living, but my dad had other ideas."

He looked at the one talented student, watched him trying to teach another a certain move, and remembered his father's consternation at his young son's laid-back attitude to life.

"I came home from a camping trip, filthy. First thing he did was scold me for laying my pack on Mom's kitchen floor, then he got mad – again – about my lack of ambition to take over his business. And Mandisa. He really hated her. He'd always say, *'You can do better, son',* or *'She's just a tramp.'* "

Lynn nudged his arm with hers.

"So, he knew all along?"

"She's out for the money!" Paul Rue's voice boomed across the kitchen. Donovan wondered why the glass in the windows stayed intact when his father got this angry.

346

"Yeah." Donovan's eyes were glassy as he continued to watch Hui try to dance Jing around the room. "He would probably say 'I told you so' about the shit she's trying to pull with those allegations. But he was also right about getting me to own up."

"Can we talk later, Dad? I've got a class –"

"Another dancing class? That's pointless! You won't make a living dancing or teaching people to dance. I already told you that when you wanted to major in dance at college."

"Dad."

"No! Sit down. Listen to me. Tomorrow night you'll come with me to the Alumni Banquet."

"Aw, Dad. A bunch of old has-beens."

Donovan could see the anger flare in Paul Rue's face, worried that his father would one day have a major heart attack in front of him. Then he watched as Paul calmed down, drawing on his expertise as a man who could manage anyone successfully.

"Those 'has-beens' put meals on our table, bought your cars, financed your education, and even paid for all those trips you took all over the world during your gap year. Show some respect!" Paul's voice was at full volume on the last sentence, then settled again. "It's time for you to come work at Rue. Learn the ropes."

Paul Rue ran his hand over his tight, short hair, then scratched his face before saying, "I started this company hoping that I'd turn it over to my child one day. You are that child, Donovan."

"Not my choice."

Paul's hand slapped Donovan before he saw it coming, echoing throughout the kitchen. Donovan knew his mother probably heard at least the slaps, if not the yelling.

"I will not support you any longer," his father stated, standing up, heading out of the room. "You will come to Rue on Monday. Dressed decently. And from now on you can pay for your camping trips and dancing lessons."

He paused at the door.

"And lose the girl. She's nothing but trouble. You'll only have heartache with a girl like that."

Donovan sighed as he ended his story.

"So, I went to Rue the following Monday. But I couldn't give up the girlfriend because she was pregnant."

His eyes went dark as he cast them down at the much shorter Lynn.

"That did not go over well."

Lynn's mouth set in a serious line. "But Dara is a great gift. At least, I think so."

Without a pause, Donovan answered, "Definitely."

They watched the students gather up their belongings, some heading out of the room.

"And I gave up dance lessons."

As they were turning off the room's lights, Lynn's cell phone rang, making her cringe. Tom was getting ready for another event in the campus chapel.

"Tom," Lynn forced herself to sound upbeat. "How's it going?"

A few minutes later, she was clicking off her phone, half smiling at Donovan.

"Sorry, but Tom needs some backup. I shouldn't be long."

"I'll go with you. Where? It's raining out, so maybe I'll bring my car closer."

ENTERING THE CHAPEL, DONOVAN FOUND LYNN STANDING IN THE center aisle, clipboard in hand. Pausing at the entrance, he watched her direct another group of students.

She's beautiful. Peaceful. I can't live without her anymore.

Donovan tilted his head back to a moment's thankful prayer.

"May I help you, Mr. Rue?"

Donovan broke his trance, turning to a portly, aging gentleman who looked apologetic at intruding on a quiet moment. The man's gentle smile encouraged Donovan to grin back in welcome as he extended his hand and said, "Good evening."

"Hello! I'm Scott Larson, campus pastor."

"Lynn has told me so much about you," Donovan said, pumping Scott's hand with more warmth. "Thank you for all the care – and prayers – for her. I know it meant a lot."

Pastor Scott never stopped smiling.

"She's pretty amazing. Fights through anything, that one. She was at the top of the prayer list for a long time. I guess I shouldn't tell you that."

Bursting into a loud laugh that caught the attention of everyone in the room, including Lynn, Scott's whole body shook with his elation.

"I'll be right there!" Lynn called, then turned back to the dance troupe.

"Pastor Scott," Donovan spoke quickly now, seriously, "I'd like to talk to you."

Out of the corner of his eyes, Donovan noted Lynn walking toward them. "Can I give you a call? Some time when I'm alone."

"Certainly." Scott was equally serious in his answer, then ebullient when he turned toward Lynn. "Lynn! It's so good to see you utilizing the chapel for more than just International Chapel."

"Hey, I use it for more than that," Lynn said, wrapping her arms tightly around the pastor, her eyes closed, but still smiling. "Actually, it's nice to come here for something more than a bitch session."

After Scott let out another loud guffaw, Lynn said, "I'm happy we can do this program here, too."

As they watched, the band began a softer song, the dancers swaying with the music.

"Well, I need to get home," Scott said, then acknowledging Lynn, continued, "Good luck with your practice and tomorrow's event." Eyeing Donovan, his eyes communicated more than the words, "Donovan, it was nice to meet you."

Donovan took Lynn's hand as she led them back into the chapel. They stood listening to more music, admiring the graceful young bodies who were flowing in a contemporary dance.

"This is a cultural event?"

"Yes. We only get ninety minutes, so we have to move quickly."

Her eyes sparkled at him.

What does she see in me?

"By the way, thank you for re-doing the sound system in here, too!" Lynn stood on tiptoes to kiss her thanks. Donovan's left arm wrapped around her waist. "Did you fix *all* the sound systems at Brandstone?"

The band began playing a light jazz piece as Donovan grabbed Lynn's right hand and began to sway.

"Maybe," came his non-answer.

He paused to twirl Lynn around, watching as she completed the move effortlessly. Finishing her circle, Lynn glanced around the room.

"What?" Donovan asked as he began to sway again, Lynn instinctively following his lead. "Do you dance?"

As Donovan's original words tumbled out, Lynn's giggle covered an answer he did not really hear. This time he moved his feet to the tune, leading Lynn in several dance moves down the aisle, toward the performers. At first, she was tense and slow. Then her body complied with the mastery of Donovan's familiar lead, following him back down the aisle to the chapel doors.

"Relax into it," he commanded.

"It's not that."

Lynn's eyes were darting everywhere.

"I'm just not sure we should dance in a church," she whispered.

"Why not?"

She looked up at Donovan but could see that he was serious in his question. After another big circle, she asked, "Did you dance in church?"

"All the time. It's another way to praise God, at least in my community."

They continued dancing out into the gathering area where Donovan was able to move her through wider steps, encouraging Lynn to relax, extend her graceful arms, and add a few mildly sexy moves. The young band members missed a few notes – it was practice after all – and Donovan continued despite the mistakes while Lynn giggled. They continued dancing around the empty narthex, interrupted when the large chapel door squeaked open.

"Oh! I'm sorry to disturb you," Pastor Scott said. "It's starting to rain, and I need my umbrella."

Lynn yanked herself out of Donovan's arms.

"Sorry! Sorry!"

"For what?"

Lynn was blushing, her face turning a light shade of pink.

"For dancing in church."

Scott smiled, answering, "There's nothing wrong with dancing in church. At least in this church! This space especially should be open to all sorts of different ways of praising the Lord."

The band had finished; several of the musicians were clapping while one called out, "You go, Lynn! Hi, Pastor Larson!"

Pastor Scott waved at the group, then chuckled.

"Take advantage of this space, I say!"

He wandered off to his office. Taking her position back in Donovan's arms, hearing the group being another song, Lynn looked up and said to him, "It's been a long time."

Chapter 46

a s Donovan entered Len's office, he gauged the newcomer waiting before him. Alek Grambler was a six-and-a-half-foot tall bruiser, his blond hair cut in short, military precision, his sharp green eyes roaming the office, assessing the windows, the doorway, and finally Donovan. The newcomer's physical presence, stern countenance, and critical glances cast a domineering presence.

No one is getting away with anything while this guy is around.

Although Donovan had already read Alek Grambler's resume and knew that he was thoroughly trained to be a security officer, he now witnessed the tremendous strength radiating from this man. Dressed in a pristine black suit, white shirt, and conservative tie, Alek continued scrutinizing Donovan as the two men faced one another in front of the desk, even as introductions were made.

"Sir." Donovan acknowledged a firm handshake. Alek did not appear to be talkative, not reacting or participating in the greetings Len and Donovan gave each other. Donovan never let his eyes off Alek, even as he and Len participated in a small joke.

"Mr. Grambler, Len tells me that you are the man to be close protection for Lynn Cerami."

Alek nodded, still looking Donovan over. When he appeared done with his assessment, Alek's deep, gravel-filled voice said, "Yes, sir."

"You've done this for a while?"

"I've been doing this work since I finished with the Marines, about five years now."

"And why would this assignment interest you?"

Donovan's eyes looked deeply into Alek's, never wavering in intensity. Neither did Alek's.

"I was personal protection for two Saudi princesses for over four years. Both married recently; their husbands secured other people to protect them. I wanted to come back to the United States."

"He knows Desmond," Len added, reminding Donovan that Alek had been referred by Donovan's bodyguard.

"Oh?" Donovan played along. "How?"

"Desmond and I were in it together," Alek clarified. "I contacted all my service buddies about openings here. Desmond told me you wanted someone to watch over your girlfriend, sir."

Donovan continued his uncomfortable stare for a few minutes before stating, "She's very important to me."

"Yes, sir," Alek fired back, his eyes brightening with sudden intensity. "The princesses were important to their parents, too; their father told me something similar before giving me that job." He paused a few seconds, then stated with even more conviction, "I take this work very seriously."

Breaking his eye lock, Donovan motioned for everyone to sit down.

Maybe this guy would work.

He was beginning to relax, accepting of another man spending lots of time with Lynn.

"Okay," Donovan said as he crossed his legs. "What are your concerns or questions?"

Alek rubbed his large hands over muscular thighs.

"Does Mrs. Cerami know that you're looking for protection for her?"

This guy does not *mess around.*

"Not yet," Donovan admitted, feeling a little guilt at keeping this hire a secret until it was completed. "I wanted to tell her once we found the right person."

"How will she take it?"

Donovan saw Len's knowing smile, how he covered his mouth to prevent a laugh from intruding in the delicate conversation.

"Oh, she'll be stubborn about it. She likes her independence," Donovan admitted. "But she's gotten a lot of attention from paparazzi, and others ... and I can't be with her all the time."

Len interrupted with, "We can't stretch Desmond that thin anymore."

Alek was nodding, then asked, "What are your expectations for the man who gets this job?"

Donovan reached up to touch his chin, then stated, "I want Lynn to be accompanied wherever she goes by her officer, especially when she's not with me. That could mean accompanying her around the college where she works, at her home, or even at the mall."

Did I just see a tic in his jaw?

But as Donovan wondered which of those venues were causing Alek to twitch, the candidate said, "Yes, sir. Larger spaces present problems, but I'm very good at scoping things out."

"Good. I'm sure you are if you've worked with Desmond."

At that, Donovan looked at Len who had been eyeing Alek critically, but with a slight smile. Len met Donovan's eyes and nodded his approval.

Len likes this guy. Me, too. I think this'll work.

"When we both attend an especially big event you and Desmond would work together."

"Yes, sir. Understood."

"And I'd like you to be ... how do I say this? Not obvious, I guess. I don't want you or Desmond to be hanging on our tails."

"You want us to be discrete," Alek restated. "A huge part of the job; I understand."

Donovan took a pen, began tapping it against the desk's edge, deciding how to phrase the rest.

"As for Lynn ... she's a sweetheart, cares for just about everyone and everything." He paused for a second, stilling his pen before continuing. "She's already been through hell – more than once – and I want to do everything in my power to prevent anything more from causing her distress. At least, what I can prevent."

"Prevent, sir?" Alek's green eyes flashed with multiple questions. "May I ask details ... or do those come once I'm hired?"

Donovan stood, the other two men quickly following him.

I can feel it. This guy will be a good addition, a good man for Lynn. Gotta go with my gut here.

He stretched his hand out to Alek and said, "I'd like you to start as soon as you can."

Alek allowed a smile.

"You won't regret it, sir. Thank you."

"Now let's go to lunch and I'll give you more details."

Chapter 47

*R*unning late for his lunch meeting, Donovan signaled Desmond to get the car. Alek was shadowing Desmond today, onboarding as a new Rue LA LA employee.

Although you could hardly say that he's a shadow, Donovan thought as he trailed the big man to the front door.

Donovan met Al Bartleman, Asia Barber's long-time agent, in an old, established restaurant in downtown LA. Walking into the Bridgemont, Donovan felt like he was time-warping back to his father's era. The restaurant was aged; it had not changed its décor much since opening its doors during Paul Rue's years of running the company.

Thank God there's no longer any smoking in here. I remember coming here with Dad and the air was thick!

Al stood to greet him.

"Donovan, thank you for meeting me," he said and then indicated the chairs.

"Something to drink?" The waiter barely let Donovan's seat hit the chair.

"Water, please," Donovan said, then noted that Al had something amber-colored in a cut-glass tumbler, "And can we order? I have a packed afternoon."

"So, it's been a while," Donovan said as soon as the waiter left, hoping that whatever Al was going to tell him wasn't bad news.

I've had enough of it. But still ...

Al picked up his glass again, took a swig, and laughed.

"No, nothing horrible." Al placed his glass down. "I'm retiring."

Congratulations!" Donovan smiled. "About time! You're older than my dad, right?"

"A good five years or so," Al said. "But Paul Rue would never have retired. That's why he dropped dead at his desk."

A sharp emotion hit Donovan, but he just nodded.

Al continued, "Sometimes I miss the old ways. Paul was a good man, just very direct." Then, as if he realized who he was talking with, Al tipped his glass toward Donovan and said, "I stayed for Asia. She's really my only client." He took another swig of his drink, then said, "But she's going to live forever."

Both men laughed at his comment. Al continued. "I wanted you to know that Sam Meyers is buying my company. Do you know him?" At Donovan's headshake, Al continued, "Sam's a good man. Pleasant to work with; artists like him. He's already taken on some work." As their lunches were set down, he said, "I know he can handle the Dymettra types. I'm tired of them."

Donovan sat through a lunch riddled with Al's memories of by-gone artists, most of them discovered by his father and Len.

"Say, Al," Donovan began the awkward conversation, "did my father... you know he was married to my mom over fifty years and he traveled a lot ... did he ever ..."

"You're asking me if your dad fooled around?" Al pushed his empty plate away. "Your father was the most decent man I knew."

Relief flooded Donovan at the older man's declaration.

Al leaned back. "All these damn allegations." Al threw his napkin on the dirty plate. "Retirement is making me blunt, I guess." He paused to take yet another drink. "Is what your ex-wife saying true, Donovan?"

"All you are hearing is noise," Donovan assured the older man. Then, he grabbed the bill, finished the meal with good wishes for Al, and headed towards the restaurant doors, unaware of his two large security officers until Desmond suddenly veered in front of him. Hearing a growing hum of outside noise as they neared the door, Desmond held up a hand to stop.

"Let me check this out." His eyes voiced concern to both Donovan and Alek who was now backing up the boss.

"This? What's *this*?" As Donovan tried to move around Desmond, Alek snaked around him. The two security men made a formidable blockade. As Desmond opened the soundproof door, Donovan heard a female voice yelling into a bullhorn.

"Send a message that harassment must end!"

Her cry was almost covered by the shouts of at least a hundred other women who had gathered outside the Bridgemont, most of their heads covered in bright pink stocking hats.

Desmond closed the door, asking, "Is there a back way out of here?"

"There is, but we'd still have to get to the car, there." Alek pointed to the waiting vehicle at the curb.

"You know this?" Donovan asked, surprised at the new guy's initiative.

Alek's look was hard, his green eyes sharp and ready. "I checked it out."

"Okay," Donovan shrugged his shoulders as if resettling his suit coat. "We go through the front. No way around it."

"Sir," Desmond's voice was firm as he glanced first at Alek and then Donovan. "Could we wait a bit?"

"Why?" Donovan tried again to get past the men, was prevented from doing so, again. "I need to get back. What will they do to me, anyway?"

Both security men cringed a bit, but then found their fortitude.

"Alek, I've got the front. You?"

"The back is covered, Desmond. Mr. Rue, stay close."

Desmond opened the restaurant door to a pulsing sound wave. Donovan felt the pressure of Alek against his back. While moving toward the car, a swarm of women covered the body of the car like cicadas. The two security officers continued their protective press, Desmond's domineering pressure forcing women away from the back door of the car which he threw open. Alek followed Donovan's body into the car, saying, "All the way over, sir." Donovan skid across the bench seat.

"Go! Go! Go!" Alek screamed as he slammed the passenger door shut.

Desmond couldn't pull away quickly. Women leaned on the trunk top, yelling, *"No more! No more!"* The front of the car was covered by other women who were slamming their hands atop it, screaming, *"Me Too! Me Too!"* Around them, other women were chanting, holding homemade signs that proclaimed their anger.

Donovan was grateful for darkened windows and the cops who were trying to corral the demonstrators away. None of the men said a word until Desmond cleared the throng, pushing the accelerator to the floor as soon as the car cleared the last woman, and Alek said, "You're clear, Des."

"Jesus!"

The relief in Desmond's voice was evident.

Donovan relaxed, asking, "Did we know that they were planning that rally?"

"No," Desmond replied, adjusting his speed to what was normal now that they were clear of the scene. "A group of women decided to hold the rally where entertainment types eat lunch. You weren't the only exec eating there today."

"Yeah?"

"Larry Knightly. Peter Freiler. A couple of television people," Desmond responded.

Donovan reached into his suit pocket, pulled out his vibrating phone.

"Lynn."

"Are you okay?"

"How'd you find out?"

"It's all over the news; I saw it when I was walking through the Student Union on the big screen in there. Are you okay?"

"Yeah, yeah." Donovan shot his hand through his hair. "Shook up, okay otherwise."

"I know you," Lynn said. "Those women do not. And Dara and I are the only ones you need to worry about."

Donovan felt the tension leave his body. He couldn't resist adding, "And Asia Barber, too."

ALEK PULLED THE CAR INTO THE FRONT CIRCLE DRIVE OF DONOVAN'S Malibu home. Lynn entered the foyer, straining to listen for any sign that Donovan was home. The house was quiet; even the security wing was silent although she knew that was where Alek would head after he parked the car.

I'll just wander on the beach until he's home.

TOSSING A FRISBEE TO RUE, DONOVAN FELT HAPPINESS SURGE through him. A beautiful California day complete with perfect temperatures had lured him to take the afternoon off. Rolling waves against a sandy beach, the smell of sweet azaleas wafting in the air, and an orangey-pink sunset made his time on the beach beneath his home priceless.

His new dog was quickly becoming a cherished pet. Rue ran to get the squirrel-shaped cylinder, pawing through the beach sand with ease. Petting his black head, Donovan prepared to throw again. He stopped when he saw the slight, blonde woman walking toward them.

"Peace!"

A perfect day! I am so lucky.

She'd already ditched her flat shoes to navigate the sand. Pulling up the hem of her light pink maxi dress revealed long lithe dancer's legs. Her hair, still growing back from the surgery, was beginning to curl on top of her head. Big square sunglasses covered the bright eyes that Donovan knew matched the ocean color at its brightest.

Flicking his wrist, Donovan shot the frisbee past Rue and then jogged to meet Lynn. After a quick kiss, he asked, "What are you doing out here?"

Lynn smiled at the question, her eyes taking in a bare-chested athlete, an Adonis, wearing only khaki-colored shorts, playing with an overly excited puppy as if he himself were one.

"You don't want me out here?" she teased. "Mad at me?"

"Never."

Donovan took the disc from Rue's mouth, then shot it back out toward the water.

"Are you still upset with me for hiring Alek?" he asked.

Dropping her shoes, Lynn wiggled her toes in the sand, letting the smoothness soothe her tired feet.

"Not anymore," she said. "After all, I've had a couple of weeks to get used to the idea." When Donovan grinned at her answer, she drew a long line with her foot, then added, "But I still think you could've let me know before you hired the guy."

"My bad. I guess I could've done that better," Donovan admitted. Rue had circled back to stand in front of them. Donovan threw the frisbee again. Rue ran to the ocean, getting in front of the disc, jumping nearly two feet in the air to catch the bright orange ring, making a huge running arc as he jogged back to Lynn and Donovan before dropping it at Donovan's feet. Donovan threw the frisbee again, then asked, "Have you thought about where we'll live once we're married?"

Lynn shook her head.

"No, not really." Mulling it over a few minutes, she asked, "Where would you like to live?"

"Here."

The answer came without pause. Then a bit slower, Donovan added, "I have never lived here as a married man. I built this house thinking it would keep me safe and isolated. But I love it more when you are here with me." He cocked his head to the side, then said, "It's like I didn't know when I built it, that you were coming."

"Aw. That's so romantic."

"Once in a while!"

Lynn gazed up at the home above the beach, then back at the ocean, her gaze scanning it. "I think I could live here."

Donovan's face revealed shock, joy, surprise – and love.

"Really?" A plea more than an answer.

Lynn stood, moved her arms in a big half-circle indicating the water, the beach, the short trek back up to the mansion Donovan called home. Almost the entirety of the back of the building was windows overlooking the now calming ocean. Lights were beginning to glow from selected spots on an outdoor patio.

"What more could a girl want?" she asked.

Donovan grabbed her with ferocity, smashing his lips to hers.

"Thank you," he gasped as they paused for air.

Lynn's hands wove into his soft, dark curls.

"Yeah, but you still have to plan the wedding."

Donovan laughed. "I can. I will! But I still can't believe that you don't want to plan it yourself. Isn't that a girl thing?"

Lynn bent down to pick up her shoes.

"I suppose it is," she answered. "But remember that I'm not a young bride-to-be anymore."

She whooped with glee when Donovan scooped her up, sending sand through the air. Marveling at the ease with which he held her as he walked back toward the house, Lynn said, "Although you do make me feel like a girl sometimes. Like a hopelessly, head-over-heels-in-love teenager."

"Let's do what teenagers do when no one is around," Donovan growled as he lengthened his steps up the path. "Because tomorrow you have your Brandstone gig and Dara and I are going to the MLK celebration. We won't have any time together."

Security in tow, Donovan and Dara wandered around the Oxnard Performing Arts Center, barely glancing at the Martin Luther King Junior displays or the vendors' booths.

Dara stopped to look at a head-scarf but placed it back on the table.

"Not my style," she said.

"What is your style then?"

Surprised, the Rues looked up at a voice not heard for over twenty years.

"Mandisa." Donovan's greeting was polite, not friendly.

Dara's eyes widened at her father's acknowledgment. She grabbed his hand just as Mandisa said, "I'm surprised to see you, too."

"Maybe we shouldn't talk to her," Dara whispered as she started to tug her father toward the room where she knew there would be food.

"Don't dismiss me like that!" Mandisa came a little closer to her daughter, scrutinizing her from top to bottom.

"You look like him," she stated, motioning at Donovan.

"Well, he is my father," Dara answered, then sneering at her mother, said, "I'm glad I don't look like you."

"Dara!" Donovan shook his hand free. "You know better than that."

"Dad, I'm an adult."

"Then, act like one," he said. "She is your mother. Act respectfully."

Dara pulled the strap of her bag up her shoulder as she eyed the mother she hadn't seen in years.

"Think I'll go see if they have peach cobbler," she said as she motioned toward the room where a sign indicated a fundraiser that one of the sororities was hosting. She turned hard eyes toward Mandisa and said, "Mother."

When Dara was no longer in sight, Donovan turned toward his ex-wife.

"She doesn't know you at all."

"Whose fault is that?" Mandisa roared at him. Loud voices filled the room; Mandisa's blended in. She looked Donovan over a few times, then said, "Not that I wanted her at the time. Such a brat –"

"Dara is not a brat!" Donovan could feel his temper flaring. He rolled his shoulders, hoping it would halt his rising anger. "You don't have other children?"

Mandisa snorted. "One was enough to tell me that I really don't like kids."

They stood there, awkward, uncomfortable, nothing except Dara in common. Finally, Mandisa cleared her throat and asked, "You?"

"No," Donovan admitted.

Should I even be talking with her?

"Well, your business is probably your life," Mandisa said. "You're what? A Gazillionaire?"

"People talk a lot, Mandy," Donovan said. "Look, I'd better catch up with Dara. Get myself some peach cobbler."

Mandisa looked down at her shoes then mumbled, "Does she remember?"

"What?" Donovan couldn't help but stare hard at her. "The beatings? I hope not. Fortunately, there weren't any physical scars. Plenty of psychological ones, though."

"What?" Mandisa seemed surprised. "No way. She was barely three. No way she could remember all that shit."

"Dara fights demons every day," Donovan said. "I sometimes wonder if they started because of all that went down between us when she was little."

"Demons?" Mandisa looked perplexed. "What do you mean?"

She's clueless.

"She's bipolar."

"Pft!" Mandisa brushed her hands toward Donovan as if she could push that information aside. "Kids today have no resilience."

"Dara has *plenty* of resilience. She's amazing."

"So maybe she remembers?"

"She may, may not," Donovan said, "but I sure as hell do."

"Do you?" Mandisa's eyes hardened. "then you remember when you hit me?"

Oh, no way in hell am I talking to you about this shit.

"I'm done, Mandy," he said. As he turned toward the *Men Can Cook* sign, Dara approached, avoiding looking at her mother.

"They won't let people take food out of that room or I would've brought you some," she told Donovan. "Reminds me of grandma's and Miss Asia's cooking!"

"No peach cobbler?" Donovan asked as he ran his fingers through Dara's long hair, pushing it gently off her shoulder.

"Plenty! Men can cook, but they all follow mama's recipes!" She handed him a ticket. "Better hurry, Dad. With all the people here, they'll run out quickly."

"Okay." He grabbed Dara's elbow and began steering her toward the room.

"Aren't you going to follow your own advice?" Mandisa asked.

Identical eyes – father's and daughter's – looked at her quizzically.

"You told our daughter to be polite," Mandisa said. "You can at least say goodbye to me."

It won't end if I say goodbye and I sure as hell don't want to say 'Later.'

As Donovan glared at Mandisa, Dara pulled the arm he cradled. "Let's go, Dad." Sensing his turmoil, Dara let loose with "Fuck off, Mother!" and left a stunned Mandisa Phillips standing alone in the crowd.

Chapter 48

isappointment flared when Lynn opened her home's door and found Alek, not Donovan, standing in her doorway.

"Ma'am."

"Alek."

Turning away for a second, Lynn grabbed a soft shawl to cover her shoulders.

If Donovan were here, he'd place this on my shoulders. And probably give me some outrageously expensive jewelry to go with this dress.

Donovan had called earlier to say that he was running late.

I hope it isn't something with Roy Alloy.

Walking out her door, she handed Alek her keys.

Silently, they approached the Lexus. Lynn waited until Alek was backing out of the driveway before she began to talk.

"Did Donovan tell you how much later he'd be?"

"No, ma'am. He just said he would be late."

Lynn sighed and settled into her seat.

"You can call me Lynn, you know."

"No, ma'am." Alek looked briefly into the rear-view mirror. "I am not comfortable with that."

As the car wove through her neighborhood, toward the freeway, Lynn considered ways to get Alek to open up about himself. He'd only been her security for a few weeks, but she knew precious little about him.

"Mr. Grambler?"

His head tilted a little toward the back seat.

"Yes, ma'am?"

"Mr. Grambler, are you from California?"

"You may call me Alek, ma'am," he responded, paused, and then answered, "No. I'm from Chicago, Illinois."

"Oh!" Delighted with the news, the first bit of personal information he'd shared, Lynn said, "I'm from Chicago! Which suburb?"

"I grew up on the North Shore, ma'am."

Nothing further. No suburb's name. No street names. Not one to play Twenty Questions. I guess I talk all the way there.

"I grew up in Crystal Lake," Lynn stated, fingering her soft pink shawl.

"Crystal Lake is *not* a suburb," Alek said, then added, "Ma'am."

Lynn scooted forward in her seat, her seatbelt pulling against the pink gown. Placing her hands on the back of the chair in front of her, she said, "I beg your pardon, Mr. Grambler, but Crystal Lake is one of the most northern suburbs of Chicago."

"Call me Alek!"

He let out a big sigh. Lynn thought she heard a quiet *"damn it."* Then Alek was lecturing her.

"Anyone who's from Chicago knows that Crystal Lake is a quiet town with a train link which people take to their weekend homes."

Lynn sat there, a little astonished that Alek could hold a conversation about more than security locks on doors and windows.

"It's not a suburb to a true Chicagoan," he continued.

"A true Chicagoan?" Lynn was affronted. "I grew up there, went to DePaul, shopped at Marshall Field's, ate at Gino's East! I got married in Chicago! To a man born and raised in the city proper!"

The car slowed to a crawl on the 101 freeway, red taillights guiding the way into the city.

"We will be late, ma'am," Alek said, modulating his tone back to respectful civility.

"Figures," Lynn mumbled and sat back in her seat. But she wasn't quite ready to give up with her questioning. "So, do you still have family there?"

"Yes."

No other information. This is going to be one long-assed ride if he doesn't start sharing.

"Are you a sports fan?"

Alek gave in to a half-smile.

"I am a diehard Cubs fan, ma'am."

"Of course, you are! You're from the North side!"

"And you, ma'am?"

Aha! Finally, something he'll bite on.

"I had to be both a Sox and a Cubs fan. My dad liked the Sox; my mom, the Cubs. When I was young, the Cubs still played afternoon games and the only show we watched after school was a Cubs' game … if they were on."

Alek chuckled.

My God, he has a sense of humor! Who'd have thought?

"And when the Cubs weren't playing?"

Lynn laughed a little, too, remembering times when she and Cathy would come home from school to see her mother cheering on *her* team.

"Then we got to watch whatever cartoons were on Channel Nine."

"So, you hoped for the Cubs to be out of town? Or on a rain delay?"

"No, Mr. Grambler," Lynn answered as she ran another hand over her shawl. "I liked watching the Cubs."

Traffic seemed to be easing up as Alek threaded the Lexus around slower vehicles.

"And the Bulls? The Bears?" he asked. "Ma'am?"

"I'm a Blackhawks fan, Mr. Grambler. Hockey."

Did his shoulders just stiffen? Maybe he's not much of a hockey fan.

"And will you *please* call me Lynn?"

Alek sighed. The smile left his face, the icy façade returning as he said, "I can't do that. It would be inappropriate for me to call you by your first name."

Silence shrouded the car for a few slow blocks.

"You work for me, right?" Lynn asked.

"I work for Mr. Rue."

"But I'm the one you follow around all day."

"I am the man hired to be close protection for you, ma'am."

"Well, Mr. Close Protection –"

"*You* may call me Alek, ma'am."

"No!" Lynn had had enough. "If you're going to call me 'ma'am', then I'm calling you Mr. Close Protection. Or Mr. Grambler."

Lynn's tone was dangerously stubborn.

"My name is Lynn," she added, then as if to throw a dog a small bone, "Maybe you could call me Mrs. Rue after we're married."

"Instead of Lynn, how about Mrs. Cerami? Would that be better?" Alek asked.

A gasp from the back seat made Alek glance quickly in the rear-view mirror.

"No. Absolutely not!"

Alek was quiet again, his stern mouth telling Lynn that he was not sure why she'd reacted to her married name.

"I'm sorry, Alek," Lynn said, her own voice apologetic. "That subject is still difficult for me. Have you been told my story?" She reached into her small clutch for a tissue.

"Some of it," Alek said. "I know you've been very ill. Hospitalized."

Lynn saw his face suddenly flinch and she knew that some memory had returned to him, making him understand why she'd become upset.

Alek glanced toward the back seat as he said, "And that your husband died. I'm sorry; that wasn't very kind of me."

Lynn blew her nose, then took out a compact to check her eye makeup. The rest of the ride was silent until they reached the venue. Alek pulled behind a line of cars waiting to drop off their passengers.

"Ma'am, I need to let you off here, but I will be in the ballroom tonight if you need anything. You have your cell phone on you, right?"

"Yes, I do," Lynn said, the strain of the drive finally over, her battle to be called just one small name, lost. She watched a popular singer get out of the silver car in front of them. Smiling, the woman turned and waved to the cameras, uncaring about the meat market waiting for her.

"Where do you hang out?" Lynn asked. "I never see you."

"I'm in the crowd. Part of the job is to be discrete."

Lynn nodded, wondering why she had been blind to all the bodyguards who filled the events' rooms. Another car stopped in front of them. This time a family got out, the father of the group hurrying his teenage daughters toward the red carpet. As they straightened from the limo, two burly men, dressed in black suits, surrounded the family of four, obscured the sight of them.

I need to pay more attention to these guys. Are there girls, too?

"Ma'am?" Alek interrupted her thoughts, waited for Lynn to look at him. "What if I call you Lynn when it's just the two of us?"

A genuine Lynn smile lit up the car.

"I would love that," she answered. "Thank you."

Alek cocked his head to the side, made a small unpleasant sound, and said, "I can't call you that when we're in public, especially when we're around Mr. Rue, Desmond, or anyone from Rue LA LA."

"But Donovan would be okay with it!"

"No!" Alek held up a hand, motioning her to stop. "I'm breaking the rules here, Lynn. Please bend a bit for me. In public, I'll call you 'ma'am' until you are officially Mrs. Rue. How's that?"

A valet opened Lynn's door, causing both to look him. As she made to move out of the car, Lynn turned her head toward Alek with one last thought.

"Okay, for now we'll play it your way."

Standing outside the car, she bent to address him before the valet closed the door.

"But I'm still from Chicago!"

AFTER ALEK DROVE AWAY, LYNN FOLLOWED THE CROWD TOWARD THE
event's ballroom.

A year ago, I was by myself, sick, and I did okay.

Lynn smiled as she remembered meeting Donovan, those dark
eyes, those gentle hands leading her around the dance floor.

Now I'm better than okay. I can do this.

Squaring her slim shoulders, Lynn focused on looking confident. It was not hard this year. She felt the now-familiar surge of
energy, a part of her rebooting, course through her body. Lynn was
fifty, but her body felt like that of a thirty-year-old, her body more
refined from all the hiking.

Bea had designed another stunner, this time a light pink gown
with a softly pleated chiffon skirt flowing down from an empire
waistline. A thin, sparkly belt sat at the raised waistline. Small
crystals were sewn into the cap-sleeved bodice, catching the
light.

Bea was sure that this dress would be another great success,
thundering *"Another Lynn dress!"* when Lynn twirled in pleasure at a
fitting. Lynn had to admit that she felt glamorous walking toward
the check-in table. But halfway there she saw the one person who
could ruin the night.

Dymettra twisted, turned, preened, and smiled at photographers, ignoring anyone around her. Lynn was hoping to skate
around her. The young woman at the check-in table didn't help
matters when she called out, "Hello! May I help you?"

"Um, hi," Lynn pushed her hands toward the floor, hoping that
the girl would understand the request for being quiet. She did not.

"You're Donovan Rue's girlfriend, right? Lynn?"

Cringing at the volume with which the girl spoke, Lynn looked
around to see if Donovan had made it. She found Alek standing

across the room, eyes still shaded by his glasses, but no Donovan or Desmond.

"Um, yes," Lynn said, trying to be polite. "May I get my seating assignment?"

"And is that a new Bea Owens dress? I love Bea Owens!"

"She's definitely lost some," came the nasty voice that Lynn recognized immediately. "Who wears pink to something like this?"

Turning from the table, Lynn flashed angry eyes at the star.

"I do," she said. "And probably tomorrow morning, other women will call Bea and ask for copies. By the end of the week, dozens of women will own this dress."

Dymettra swung the long train of her gown around and posed for another round of pictures. One of the photographers recognized Lynn and began yelling, "Hello! Lynn Cerami? Donovan Rue's date? Is that a Bea Owens dress?"

Lynn had no choice but to look up and answer. "Y-yes, it is."

Determined to do Bea's dress justice, she did a quick twirl, sending sparkles around the brightly lit room. Strategically placed small crystals glittered when the skirt's movement was quick. As she swung around, more photographers joined the first, causing Dymettra to bristle with anger.

"Everyone knows that Beatrice Owens' designs are old news," she called to the group gathering around Lynn. She started twisting, turning, adjusting her train by herself, patting the large baubles at her ears. No one paid any attention.

"Now, *my* line?" Dymettra called again. "That's what's good now."

"*Your* line?"

Another familiar voice came from behind Lynn who twirled yet again to find Bea. Dressed in her signature column gown, Bea was unobtrusive, the role she chose to play in a room full of trendy designer fashions. Her polished silver jewelry caught the faintest silver sparkle of the rich fabric.

"Since when is copying *my* dresses from years ago, your own line?"

"They aren't yours," Dymettra snorted. "I've updated dresses from the early 2000s."

Elegant as always, Bea walked toward Dymettra. Her eyes were midnight thunder as was her voice as she directed her words toward the celebrity.

"You stole my designs, Dymettra."

"This dress is one of *my* designs!"

"Yes, I know that," Beatrice looked the dress over from top to bottom. "I would never design anything that ugly for anyone."

Dymettra dropped her pose as she lost her temper.

"You bitch!"

Beatrice did not back down. "I may be a bitch, but I'm honest about what I design." She turned toward Lynn. "Ready to go inside?"

Not needing another invitation Lynn hooked her arm through Bea's and strode toward the center table, photographers following, cameras clicking away. Adrenaline and anger were feeding every long stride Bea took. As they neared Lynn's assigned table, Bea let loose.

"That woman is such a mean, overly curvy, gaudy-dressed, ferret-faced, royal bitch!"

Lynn felt a soft hand on her back.

"You aren't talking about my date, are you, Bea?" asked Donovan.

Lynn tossed her clutch onto a chair, freeing both hands to clasp Donovan's face for a quick kiss.

"She's talking about another royal bitch."

"Let me guess," Donovan said, then stated, "Dymettra is here?"

"In all her goddamn glory!" Bea huffed. "Look, I gotta go adjust a Hungry's dress."

Donovan chuckled. "Is it Bri?"

Bea nodded.

"You should know," she said, then ordered, "Now enjoy tonight. Dance! And show off that dress, Lynn."

Bea had barely left them when other guests appeared and began forming a line to talk with Donovan.

"Donovan!" the first woman said. "I have someone I want you to meet!"

Donovan gave the woman a cordial smile, then said, "Not tonight, Donna."

"But, Donovan?"

Donovan raised his eyebrows, then said, "I said, not tonight."

The woman darted away.

Impressive moves on six-inch stilettoes. I could never do that.

Donovan pulled out a chair for Lynn, but before she could sit down, another popular artist came up to them.

"Mr. Rue! I have a great idea for you!"

Gazing at the crowd. Lynn saw a familiar, sullen face close to them. Dressed casually again, it was his demeanor that caught Lynn's attention.

What's he trying to do to upset Donovan tonight?

Donovan's deep voice pulled Lynn back to the artist at the table.

"Not tonight, Joe."

Joe! Big Little Joe. Hip-Hop guy. I remember!

"But ..."

"Did you get the addendum to your contract?"

"I don't know." The young man looked puzzled, pulled out his cell phone and began scrolling through it.

"This isn't the place to catch up on emails," Donovan said. "But it says you are to show respect for the officers of my company as well as any family members or friends. Now, give me my space. Call your manager; tell him your idea."

As the young man started slinking away, Lynn noticed that Roy stood with his head cocked their way, listening, considering his next step. But he came no closer.

Joe was still apologizing.

"Sorry, man. Guess I forgot about the whole 'dendum' thing."

All the exchanges were loud enough that everyone in the line to see Donovan heard. They faded away, going back to their tables. Including Roy Alloy. Finally, Lynn sat in the chair that Donovan motioned to, before taking his own seat.

"Wow!" Lynn glanced around the room, then up at Donovan who was smirking with satisfaction. "Your idea is working."

"Yeah, for now." Donovan reached for some bread. "Let's see how the night goes."

When the awards began shortly after dinner, the lights went down. Everyone adjusted their chairs to better see the stage. Donovan, seated on Lynn's left side, reached for her left hand, his fingers searching, noting the absence of the engagement ring that they had agreed would not be worn in public just yet. He chuckled, then pulled out a beautiful pear-shaped aquamarine ring, placing it on her finger. Donovan lean forward, moving his lips to her ear, whispering, "It's beautiful. Like you're beautiful, Peace."

Lynn gave him a quick kiss. Their first agreement had been to keep the engagement a secret; the second was to limit PDAs.

But this ring ... this moment calls for a kiss.

They both settled in for the long presentations, Lynn moving her hand around, trying to catch some light, Donovan chuckling. When Bri was announced as the year's best Young New Artist, Donovan shot to his feet, his smile huge, his hands clapping hard. Bri walked gracefully up to the microphone and began reciting her thank you speech. Her nerves were apparent, the trophy shaking despite her tight grip.

"And I want to thank Donovan Rue, 'cause without him, I'd never have gotten this far. Thank you, Mr. Rue."

Applause started again but was interrupted by a loud, angry voice coming from the furthest corner of the room.

"Thank you, my ass!"

As if a cloak smothered the entire room, all noise ended. People

375

turned their heads as if they were watching a tennis match, from smiling with glee at Bri, to looking in horror at Roy Alloy who was shaking a finger, now walking toward the young woman, stealing her moment.

"Girl, you've got no idea what's in store for you! Wait until your first flop. He won't support you! He won't care!"

Lynn glanced at Donovan noticing that he was glued in horror to the scene, the happy smile for Bri gone. Another commotion caught her eye as two black-suited men strolled toward Roy, attempting to calm him down.

There they are. Alek was right; the black suits are everywhere!

"I think we should leave, Mr. Rue," said an increasingly familiar deep voice. Lynn swiveled in her chair to find that Alek had snuck up on them during the outburst. She felt Alek's strong hand wrap around her bicep, noticed the other held Donovan's upper arm.

"No." Donovan's voice was unyielding, in charge. "Let him get it out. I'm not going anywhere."

Alek looked away from Donovan at Lynn, asking, "Should I take the lady away, sir?"

Lynn gave Alek a dirty look before answering for herself.

"No way in hell. I'm a big girl. He hasn't threatened me and I'm here with Donovan."

Dropping their arms, Alek moved into the shadows with the other security personnel who'd entered the ballroom, all their eyes trained on those they were hired to protect.

As if cued by Lynn's words of solidarity, Roy's next statement zeroed in on the couple.

"Yeah, got him some. Yeah, a skinny blonde woman takes Donovan Rue's attention from everything. His father wouldn't have let that happen. Rue LA LA is dead!"

Two more dark suits were now on either side of Roy, urging him to shut up, sit down, or leave.

"No! I'm going to get my say!"

Lashing out an arm in anger, Roy punched the arm of the man

on his right. Seen as an attack, the men knew they could forcibly remove Roy Alloy. One grabbed his right arm, the other his left. Both dragged him toward the exit. But Roy would not go quietly.

"These thugs were probably hired by Donovan Rue to get rid of me! Well, they ain't!"

Roy twisted and turned to release himself from the stronghold without success. Roy's shouts muffled as they dragged him into the hallway, the band playing music over it all.

The audience, tired of Roy's attack, whispered among themselves. Someone led a shaken Bri off the stage toward her chair. As she passed by Donovan and Lynn, Donovan stopped her with a soft hand signal. The girl couldn't even look him in the eyes.

"It's okay, Bri," Donovan said soothingly. "Congratulations! You've worked hard; you deserve this award."

When they were back in their chairs, Donovan looked at Lynn. She was smoothing her skirt, spinning the new ring around her finger, this time as a nervous reaction.

"You okay?"

"I'm fine," Lynn assured him. "But do you think we'll ever come to this event and not have our evening disrupted by that idiot?"

Donovan grimaced, then grabbed the hand where he'd placed the new ring.

Lynn found another topic. "Are you ever going to ask me to dance?"

Chapter 49

*G*osh, it's quiet in here.

"Hey, Lynn!" a student called from a booth where his laptop lay open. Everyone at his table and the others facing the school's park had a drink. Lynn waved, then looked around. It wasn't hard to locate Connor, sitting on a soft sofa near the fireplace.

"Hey."

Connor stood as his mother approached. He smiled briefly then kissed her before going back to the intense person he was.

My handsome son ... looks so much like his father.

"I'll go get something to drink."

Connor held up a deep purple cup.

"The usual? A double mocha?" he asked.

"God, if they ever tell me I can't drink coffee or eat chocolate, I'm in trouble."

Sitting down, they both took a sip of their drinks. Lynn noted that Connor was dressed impeccably in a suit and tie which meant that he'd come from work.

"This is such a rare treat, Connor! When was the last time you came to Brandstone for coffee with me?"

Connor fidgeted. "Don't remember," he admitted. "But if it's all the same to you, I'll stay away from your office. I hate The Bitch."

"Connor!" Lynn's tone was mildly sharp. "Be careful. She's my boss, you know." Lynn glanced around the area they were sitting in; no one was looking their way. "Others know her, and it can be pretty gossipy here."

Connor shrugged. "Just sayin'. You weren't there for the show

378

she put on when you were in surgery. She insisted on feeding us, but we knew two minutes into lunch that she only wanted to meet *the* Donovan Rue."

The sarcasm in his voice spilled as if he'd turned a coffee upside down.

"You're not still angry with him?"

Connor ignored her question. "And to give you Stargazer lilies."

Lynn paused, considering the subject change.

"Thoughtless," Lynn muttered, then took another sip of her drink.

Connor straightened in his chair.

"I'm here to tell you about Dara and me," he started. When Lynn didn't show any surprise, he continued. "She and I are – have been – seeing each other for a while."

"I knew something was up."

When Connor cocked his head in surprise, Lynn continued.

"Well, you two seem to show up at the house at the same time, conveniently. And I knew there was some sneaking around at Christmas."

Connor was startled. "How did you know about Christmas?"

Lynn smiled at her son.

"Moms know this stuff, Connor. You two thought you were evasive, but …"

"Are you mad?"

Connor appeared horrified that his mother knew.

"Absolutely not! You mean because I know you were together at Christmas? No!"

When Connor turned his darkening face down to his lap, Lynn reached over and took his hand.

"No, Connor, I'm not mad in the least," she told him. "I like Dara. I love you!"

Connor turned his long-lashed eyes up to his mother, finally starting to smile.

Always so intense.

"Mom," he started, then crossed a long leg over a knee, took a drink, and shifted again in his chair. "Dara and I are thinking long term."

"Oh." Now Lynn was surprised. "Do you mean marriage?"

Lynn was almost giddy with the thought of her oldest son finding happiness. Connor trained his eyes on her.

"Yes. Eventually."

Lynn squeezed his hand.

"That's great, Connor! If she's the one that you want to be with forever, I'm thrilled for you."

"No concerns?"

"You know about her bi-polar," Lynn said evenly. "And I'm guessing all those times you asked me about dating someone with mental illness were about Dara, right? You've seen some of her ... um ... moments? If not, you should take a class about it. Donovan's taken some in the past. I could ask –"

"I'm taking them now," Connor admitted. "Dara's pretty open about her problems. She's done some things that have scared me, made me really think about what it'll be like to live with this forever. But it's not enough to chase me away. I just have to learn how to be there for her."

Lynn nodded, encouraging his discussion.

"It's not easy for her, Mom. I've seen some of the impulsivity, the mood swings, and even a manic episode. But she's a great person in so many ways: she loves her dad, she's always there for you, and I know that she loves me." He scoffed at the last words. "Which isn't always easy!"

"Connor!"

"Hey, I'm no prize. I know that." Connor didn't even grin. "But Dara seems to think I am. Anyway, we were thinking about letting you guys know about us before Timmy."

Lynn did the mental math.

Some time ago.

"Why did you wait?"

"Well, first there was Timmy and all of that nightmare. Then recovery time. And my new job –"

"How's that going by the way?"

"It's great," Connor said, picking some lint off his pant leg. "Busy, but good. Sometimes I wish I could bounce ideas off Dad."

When he paused, Lynn gave his hand two more squeezes.

I wonder if we'll ever get beyond losing Michael.

Connor took a sharp breath, then said, "And then I was going to say something the day after Christmas!" He fingered the rim of his cup and smiled at his mother. "But you guys went and ruined that chance when you gave us your big news."

Lynn smiled back, releasing Connor's hand.

"Sorry 'bout that … Not really though."

"I didn't think so," Connor said. "Are you good with all this, Mom?"

"Connor, she's your choice, not mine. I'm happy for you. Dara is a wonderful girl and I think you make a great couple."

Connor tilted his head back, his relief evident in his first relaxed pose of the afternoon.

"Is Dara telling Donovan?"

"As we speak," Connor answered.

"Are you planning to marry soon?"

Connor looked thoughtful for a moment, then said, "We haven't discussed an actual date, I think because I haven't officially proposed. Dara is a traditional woman in some ways. But we did discuss things about what it means to be married. You know, like fidelity, religion, children."

"All the things we talked about when we were in that new Italian restaurant?"

Connor looked at his mother again. "You got me."

"Well, I'm not stupid …"

"No," Connor placed his cup down, uncrossed his legs. "That you are not, Mother mine."

"Well, I'm glad you're discussing that stuff," Lynn said. "So many young people don't, and it only leads to heartache."

"Mom," if possible, Connor's voice got more serious. "Did you and Dad ever have any bad times?"

Seeing the smile leave his mother's face, Connor said, "I'm sorry if that makes you sad. I just wondered."

Lynn shrugged. "It's okay." She fingered the hem of her jacket. "Of course, we had disagreements, usually about money. We could never buy a single car without one of those car reports –"

"Except for the Fun Car!"

"Okay. One time. *One time!*" Lynn's voice spewed happiness with the memory. "Michael Cerami let loose and spent a lot of money on something he really wanted. *One time!*"

An odd mixture of warm memories, grief, and amusement settled in Lynn's soul.

"And we couldn't buy an appliance without checking Consumer Reports!" She shook her head. "And you know what? I probably miss that part about him the most."

Her voice faltered on the last word, biting her bottom lip. When Lynn looked at Connor, she saw glassy dark brown eyes. She knew that Michael had been special to her oldest son, that his death had changed Connor fundamentally.

"So, you and Dad discussed fidelity? You kinda mentioned that at dinner the other night."

"Oh, yeah." Lynn became thoughtful, then amused with her memory. "All the major topics – Dad brought them up. But I always knew we were rock solid in our relationship."

"Do you and Donovan talk about this stuff?" Connor glanced down at his hands, rubbed them together, said, "Sorry. That's probably personal."

"Yes, it is, but it's okay and yes, we discuss these things." She paused again, gazing at the swooshing sliding doors. "I guess our biggest discussions – and arguments – have been about being in the public eye, what that means and how it affects me. It's the reason I got angry and broke it off with him right before Timmy."

"I wondered what caused it!"

"Yeah, it was a hellish night; I lost it."

Lynn grabbed her jacket bottom again.

"But we talked it through, and I've adjusted. We're good."

"And the allegations?" Connor was almost afraid to bring them up. "I mean, Dara tells me that her mother is a jerk. And everyone knows that Dymettra is a fading star trying to get back in the public eye. But how has that affected you and Donovan?"

Lynn settled back into her chair, watching a group of her international students go up to the ordering counter, their Mandarin phrases sounding fast, tough.

"When you really love someone, and you've committed to marrying him, you know – just *know* – that this person is not who the media makes him out to be. And that Mandy person – and God knows, Dymettra – are just evil creatures trying to ruin a good man."

"And his woman."

"Yeah, me too, I guess." She laughed. "Me Too!"

Lynn reached over to Connor, ran her fingers through the thick locks just as she'd done when he was little.

"Have you and Dara discussed all this?"

"More like argued about it!" he chuckled. He then went on to say that they'd discussed their differences in attitudes toward religion and money. "Although we do reach decisions on issues. We're on the same page about kids; we share a similar work ethic. But she could spend money like water if she didn't try hard to rein it in."

"Could be part of her illness."

"Yeah, it is. She admitted that."

When Connor paused, Lynn wondered how that had gone down.

"And we've talked about fidelity. She has struggled with it. In the past."

Lynn knew by the way Connor finished that thought that she would not go there. It didn't seem to be causing him alarm.

His voice had grown stronger, louder as he made more passionate statements. As she'd listened to Connor's profession of love, Lynn had finished her coffee.

"It all sounds good," she said. "I have to go back to work. Before you leave, can I ask, are you good with Donovan now?"

Connor took the coffee cups to the trash receptacle, Lynn following. They walked out the sliding doors together, then hugged once again.

"We're cool, Mom," Connor said, then paused. "At least I hope so, after Dara talks with him."

Chapter 50

Walking away from Connor, Lynn made her way through the busy campus toward her office. Her steps were bouncy, reflecting the good news she'd just received. She couldn't help but smile at the thought of Connor and Dara together, something she'd had an inkling was happening. She thought of them as kind people, each tormented in different ways.

Students began nodding at her, infected by her smile and happy bearing.

Rafa called out, "Lynn! How are you today? You look amazing!"

Lynn shouted back, "I am *amazing*! I feel great!"

Seeing a throng of students in the lounge, Lynn realized that the coffee date had taken more time than normal. An annoyed Sally, anger permeating like waves of perfume toward Lynn, stood as the advisor entered, glaring at Lynn in anger.

"Brad wants to see you," she said.

"Now?"

"He said to tell you 'immediately,' so I guess that means now."

Lynn turned to retrace her steps but caught sight of students who'd been waiting for her.

"See if you can help these students." She motioned toward the student lounge. "I'll be back as soon as I can."

"Lynn."

Brad Petrona, head of Student Affairs, stood as Lynn entered, but seemed especially serious. He was shifting through paperwork as he motioned for Lynn to sit on a side sofa.

Is one of my students sick? Did someone die? Did I do something wrong again?

Finally, Brad put his paperwork down and crossed over to the area where Lynn was sitting. A large man, he plopped down into a leather chair and crossed his legs before removing reading glasses. Sticking one of the temple pieces into his mouth, he stared off into space, quiet, pensive.

"Bad day?" Lynn wanted the conversation to begin.

Brad grimaced. "You could say that."

He sat up straighter in the soft couch, taking a more formal posture before he said, "Lynn, I'd like you to be Director of International Student Services."

Worry turned into wonder as Lynn stared at Brad's light brown eyes. She wasn't sure she'd heard him correctly.

"What?"

As she replayed his words, Lynn refrained from screeching.

What? Is he crazy? What happened? Oh. My. God!

Brad scowled again.

"Cassie Manders is resigning as of today."

Lynn startled at the announcement.

"Resigning?"

Brad looked at the paperwork, then cocked his head questioningly.

Need to know. I get it.

Lynn offered, "Cassie told me that her husband is sick – with cancer. She told me that she'd be taking lots of time off to be with him."

"So you know," he said. "She called this morning to find out about the protocol for resigning her position. She needs to be home, immediately."

Brad stood and went to the paper piles stacked on his desk.

386

"I'm looking at your personnel file. I always look them over for promotions."

Lynn mulled over his statement then finally asked, "Promoted?"

"Let me ask you a few things," Brad countered, although his smile was pleasant, his tone light.

"Are you fully certified in all areas of visa advising?"

"Totally. I've gone to all the required workshops."

Brad finished looking over the folder.

"Your student programs have always been exceptional," Brad said, looking over yet another paper. "And the President and cabinet are still raving about you getting Donovan Rue to redo all the sound systems."

"I didn't do that! Donovan did it."

"Still, it was impressive. You've had stellar reviews until right before your leave. And I've never had any student give you anything other than a five-star review, Lynn. They love you."

Lynn watched Brad lightly toss the folder back on his desk.

"I want you to be Director," he said. "You deserve this appointment." He added, "People respect you both as a work colleague and for what you've been through personally. Your students write glowing reviews about you. Hell, students stop by to tell me how much they love you!"

"Really?"

"Yes, really," Brad chuckled.

I almost quit this job. I would've lost this opportunity. Donovan was right to push me to keep trying even when it was so awful to show up.

"If you agree to this, I want you to start immediately," Brad said, strength in his voice. "HR will have the paperwork." Pausing, he smiled and then asked, "Do you need to think about it? Talk with someone?"

Lynn came out of her fog.

"I want this promotion, Brad. I know I can do it. Thank you for appointing me."

After an instruction to not tell anyone the appointment was announced, Lynn headed back to her office. Unlike her earlier brisk clip, Lynn strolled back slowly to the International Student office, her head full of Connor's news and the unexpected promotion.

Never saw that coming.

More students were waiting in the lounge, waiting with their quick questions which hardly ever got fast answers. All of them turned to smile at her, expectant that she would right their world.

Oh, my God ... I'm like Donovan at all those events: everyone needs a minute.

"Give me just a minute, please," she begged the students, walking to Sally's desk.

"Where've you been?" Sally thundered. "It's crazy here! Everyone is asking to speak to you – Cassie, HR, Donovan Rue, some chick named Dara. Your crazy son Owen. And all those kids out there!" Sally shook her hand at the mob in the lounge. Her hands sat on her hips as she ranted, "Cassie has to come back. Soon!" She thrust a file at Lynn. "You obviously can't handle it all, Lynn."

"Enough!" Lynn exploded at Sally's attitude. Then centering herself, she said, "Give me a second. Then find these students' files, and then bring them to me one at a time."

Lynn dialed Donovan when she entered her office. He answered on the first ring.

"Peace!"

"Ohhhhh, I am anything but peaceful right now."

Instead of hearing the happiness, Donovan became concerned.

"What's the matter?"

"Do you have a second?"

"Anytime for you. But please tell me that everything is good; you're breathless."

Lynn took a deep breath.

"I am fine, Mr. Rue. More than fine! I just got promoted to Director." As she told him, a small laugh gurgled up and she began to stomp her feet like a small child. "Cassie quit today. I don't have many details."

As Donovan congratulated her, Lynn noticed through the door's window that students were waiting.

"Look, I've got a ton of kids to talk to and it's three-thirty. Yikes! Can we talk tonight?"

"I'm so happy for you," he said.

Lynn imagined his grin.

"Let's eat somewhere special tonight to celebrate," he suggested. "You can tell me all about it then."

Ninety minutes later, Lynn had handled the quick questions of eight students, signed papers for two, and set up additional sessions with three more. Glancing at her watch, she decided the time was right to call Cassie. When a subdued voice answered the call, Lynn wondered if she had the wrong number.

"Cassie?"

No reply. Lynn could not even hear breathing at the other end.

"Cassie, it's Lynn."

"Oh."

No emotion. Then, Cassie took a breath and said, "Lynn. I suppose Brad's already cleaned out my office and had it repainted for you."

Lynn took off her reading glasses closed, then rubbed her eyes. After a few details concerning Cassie getting her personal things, Cassie said, "Well, you'll have a lot to deal with. You're a compassionate person, and you're good at event planning. But you aren't a perfectionist and some of what I do – did – requires that."

"Yes, Cassie."

"And another thing," Cassie began a litany of her perception of Lynn's unsuitability to manage. Lynn sat with the phone near her ear, suddenly wishing she could stop all the constant life changes.

She wanted the call with Cassie to end. The promotion to have never been offered. She wished life could go back to what it was almost four years: before cancer; before Michael getting hit by a car; before Timmy. She would keep her old job, her current office. But then she thought of all the battles with Cassie.

I don't want those back. Never again.

She realized the good in her life, too. Donovan was the biggest blessing. But her children, Dara, and Bea all made her life bearable and she did not want to lose any of them. Lynn realized that without all those things happening, her life would not be what it was at that moment.

Still, she wanted the phone call to end.

When Cassie took a breath, Lynn barged into her rantings, asking, "Anything else I can do for you, Cassie?"

Please don't ask me for food, or to pick up something. I'm not that kind.

"No."

"Okay. Bye, Cassie, take care," Lynn said, "I wish Tom the best."

Several hours later Lynn quit her gabbing long enough to look down at her untouched plate of lasagna.

"Sorry!" she placed her hand over his. "I'm just babbling on and on tonight."

"I like your babbling. I enjoy hearing about your days," Donovan said as Lynn scooped up a forkful of ravioli. "They're so different from mine."

"Tell me about your day," Lynn said while adding another forkful in her mouth.

Donovan sighed and looked over the small, casual restaurant.

"We start depositions with the Roy thing on Monday."

"Oh."

Now Lynn put her fork down, her appetite gone.

"Yeah, the lawyers want to talk with Len and me on Monday."

Lynn took a drink of her water, then said, "It seems like this and that other allegation thing are going on and on."

"Well Mandy, I think, is giving up. But Roy is not. So, we must give these depositions, a common procedure I'm told in these kinds of cases."

"I know you're worried," Lynn asked.

Donovan smirked, picked his wineglass up for a quick sip.

"I'm worried about the company. Dad grew it from nothing, and I was taking good care of it. I think I was, anyway." He shrugged his shoulders before adding, "Roy could ruin the whole damn thing. I'm worried about Mandy and Dymettra destroying our reputations. The public likes hearing about all these bad boys being caught. And I'm really worried that this could hurt you. Make me look like a cad."

"You're not!"

Donovan's eyes twinkled at his fiancée's unconditional support.

He drained his wine glass, placed it back on the table before saying, "I can handle the 'cad' description –"

"You *have* handled it!"

"I just can't stand the idea that Roy could ruin an innocent woman's reputation just to get at me!" His eyes blazed, his tone indignant. "I'm so sorry, Peace."

Lynn squeezed his hand, giving him a confident smile. "I'm a big girl. I can handle it as long as we're together."

"Part of loving someone is standing up for them when things get hard. You were there for me during Timmy, and especially during that awful first month back at work." Lynn shivered at the memory. "I'm good now; it's my turn to be there for you."

"I'm so damn lucky. How did this happen?"

They paused as the server cleared their dishes away, avoiding the entwined hands that lingered on the tabletop. When they were alone again, Donovan said, "But I have to warn you; you might get asked to come in for a deposition."

Lynn shrugged. "Okay."

"Okay?" Donovan thundered. "No, Lynn, it's not okay!" Struggling to keep his voice at a quiet, private level. "The good news is that you weren't on the list for first depositions. Maybe what they want or need to hear will come from everyone else before they haul you in."

Lynn considered what 'hauling in' might mean, but only continued to gently squeeze Donovan's hand.

"Let's worry about it if it happens," she said, then remembered another wonderful part of the day.

"How was your meeting with Dara?"

Donovan smiled, seemed pleased with the subject change.

"Good!" he said, running his hand through his hair. "You prepared me for it, though – at Christmas. And they're always together."

Lynn giggled. "I pretty much told Connor the same thing. You should've seen his face! I guess children – no matter what age they are – think parents are ignorant."

Both grinning, Lynn continued to squeeze Donovan's hand before asking, "But you're good with my son wanting to marry your daughter?"

Donovan reached up to rub his chin as if making a big decision.

"I asked her if she knew what she was getting into –"

"Into? What *she's* getting into? What do you mean?"

"Well, yeah," Donovan said, casting his eyes around the room. "Connor's not exactly my biggest fan." He paused as some exiting patrons curved around their table. "Things seem to be getting better, I think. I just wonder what kind of 'in-law' fights they'll have whenever Connor gets upset over something I do."

"I hadn't thought about that," Lynn said as her eye wandered away in thought. "It's important to me that we all get along," she said.

"Agreed."

Chapter 51

*T*wo weeks later, accompanied by Rue LA LA attorney Mason Polk and the ever-present Alek, Lynn entered a Santa Monica law office to be deposed.

"What do they want to know from you?" Donovan asked. "He's contending that we didn't pay him enough, that we violated his contract, used Rue LA LA's money for purposes other than business-related concerns, but what has that got to do with you?"

Watching Donovan almost pull out his gorgeous, curly locks with worry, Lynn was glad to get the deposition over with.

It isn't like I have something to hide.

During the two prep hours spent with attorney Mason Polk, Lynn also wondered why they wanted her. Dressed in a deep purple business suit with a pale pink blouse beneath it and a conservative strand of pearls, Lynn felt confident, professional.

When she saw how Roy Alloy's attorneys were attired, she was glad that she'd pulled out what she called her interview suit. Both were stunning black women, extremely distinguished-looking in their silk blouses and pencil skirts, their demeanors serious.

I wonder if these are their corporate uniforms.

"Would you like water, Mrs. Cerami?' One attorney asked as she placed a folder on the table.

Is using that name deliberate?

"Coffee or tea?" the other woman asked.

"Water is fine, thank you."

They all sat at one end of the long table. After introductions and basic information – and acknowledgment that the deposition was bring recorded – Miata Holmes looked at her partner and nodded to begin.

Kianna Davidson caught Lynn's gaze, held it with a penetrating stare.

"Please tell us how you met Donovan Rue."

"I met Donovan Rue at the Music Extravaganza."

"Did he approach you?"

"He came up to my table."

"And you had never met him before that event?"

"No, I had not." Lynn returned the stare, then got over it, remembering Mason's warning that they would be intimidating, that she should answer clearly, succinctly, and try to maintain a poker face.

"I don't keep up with celebrity things. I knew of Donovan Rue, but I didn't realize that was who stopped by my table until later in the evening."

Miata's face may have cracked a little.

She thinks I'm lying. Well ...

The attorney asked, "Had you ever met Roy Alloy prior to that evening?"

"No. And I didn't meet him that night. No one introduced us."

"But you knew who he was?"

Sure, everyone knows him because of his temper and his persona. Wish I could say that to this woman.

Lynn pushed away slightly from the table, crossed one leg over the other before she said, "I have heard his music before, yes."

On and on went the questions asking which artists she knew, which Rue LA LA staff members. Lynn answered truthfully, wondering what all this had to do with Roy's lawsuit. Just as she was beginning to think that the questions would never ask anything other than who she knew, Miata shifted in her seat and trained a hard look at Lynn.

"Has Donovan Rue ever purchased anything for you?"

"Purchased anything?" Lynn ran through the mental list of

things he'd given her, reliving the moments when he'd placed a gilded rope around her neck, handed her a robin's egg blue box, and slipped a ring on her finger in a dimly lit ballroom. All were cherished gifts. As she mused, Mason asked, "Where's this going?"

"We are entitled to this information," Miata said without taking her eyes off Lynn. "Mrs. Cerami?"

Lynn inhaled, dragged herself out of the warm memories, and said, "Yes, he has bought me gifts."

"What are they? Can you list them?" Kianna shifted through her paperwork, withdrawing what was possibly a list. Lynn wished she could read it from her side of the table, but all she saw were black marks on white paper.

"Well, he has given me some jewelry. Over time. And a new chair for my home. And a bedroom set."

"Can you list the jewelry?"

Lynn paused, tilting her head to the side to mentally list those items.

"There was a gold rope necklace, a beautiful cuff, some earrings."

"That's all?"

Lynn could see that there were two lines on the paper without red check marks. Suddenly, she knew what this game was about.

"An aquamarine ring."

With a flourish in her marking, Kianna finished her check-off list. Miata didn't need to look at anything before she asked, "Did Rue LA LA pay for these items?"

"What?" Appalled, Lynn completely forgot Mason's instructions to not let the proceedings get to her. The idea of these treasured gifts being a business expense could crush their worth if Lynn allowed it.

But I know Donovan better than they do.

Drawing on infinite resilience, Lynn took a deep breath, and answered, "I would not know how Donovan purchased them – with what account or credit card."

And I would give them all to you if you would make this lawsuit go away.

Ignoring Lynn's outburst, Miata took another list from her papers.

"Now, we'd like to ask you about the time you've spent with Donovan Rue." She paused to take the paper into both hands. "Tell me where Donovan Rue took you socially."

"Again, is this really necessary?" Mason's voice deepened as he looked at the two female attorneys. "Do you really need to know the specifics of each time my client spent with her fiancé?"

Miata looked up from her list and answered, "All of this bears on the lawsuit, Mr. Polk." Her eyes swerved from his to Lynn's. "Mrs. Cerami?"

Lynn was flabbergasted.

"I don't know if I can remember every place we've been to." Releasing a gasp of air, Lynn searched through her memories, a furrow showing in the middle of her forehead.

"Let's see ... we go to The Grind a lot – a coffee shop near where I live. We've done lots of hikes and walks all over Ventura County. We've hiked up to the Ronald Reagan Library from my home ..."

Lynn looked upward as if that would unlock memories of where she and Donovan had gone.

"Out to dinner, a few random coffee shops, about a dozen events as his plus-one ... I can't possibly remember all the places we've been in the last year!"

"Other than social events, Mrs. Cerami, what other time has Donovan Rue spent with you?" Miata's voice was cold, distant, uncaring.

"Maybe you should ask me about specific times since I do not understand you," Lynn's tone became icy. "What is it you want to know?"

Both attorneys looked at one another before Kianna asked, "Was Donovan Rue with you during your recent hospitalization?"

"Yes."

What's wrong with that, you bitch?

"How long were you hospitalized?"

Yeah, you can't find out those things, bitch. Not with HPPA laws.

"Four days. And, yes, Donovan was there most of the time."

"Did he spend time with you following your hospitalization?"

Lynn allowed the warm memory of Donovan making her oatmeal that first morning home, coaching her to eat, to walk as much as she could, shadowing her up and down the stairs, falling asleep with her especially that first night home when she was overwhelmed.

"Yes," she answered softly. "Yes, he did."

"Can you give us an idea of how much total time he was with you?"

Losing patience, Lynn shifted in her chair, briefly glancing at Mason who interpreted it as a request for help.

"Mrs. Cerami was recovering from brain surgery. Mr. Rue is her fiancé. He was there frequently. Again, what are you getting at?"

Before they answered his question, Lynn completed shifting through the days following her surgery.

"I can't remember how much time he was there, but I do remember that when he could not be there it was because of Rue LA LA's business. His company is very important to him."

"Did he also accompany you to doctor's appointments? Procedures?"

"Yes." Lynn could see the next question coming. "He went with me to a Gamma Knife procedure and several doctors' visits."

Next, they're going to want my complete medical history ... who's on trial here?

The two women shuffled papers and remained poker-faced Lowering her voice, Miata said to Kianna, "I think we can leave this unasked."

Maybe she thinks my hearing is bad. Wrong!

"Were you going to ask me if Donovan harasses me?" Lynn called out.

Mason's voice was as low as Miata's when he said, "Lynn …" as a warning. "no need …"

"The answer is," Lynn said as she straightened in her chair, her feet flat on the floor, "Donovan Rue has never been anything other than kind and understanding to me. He has never threatened me or touched me in any way that could construed as harassment."

"And Mandisa Phillips and Dymettra's allegations have not been brought forward," Mason stated.

"Agreed." Kianna nodded.

A few minutes later, the deposition ended. Alek was right outside the conference room door, cell phone in hand. The three walked outside of the building, Lynn taking in a gulp of fresh air.

"If I could," she said as she adjusted her sunglasses, "I'd have a strong drink right now."

"No kidding," Mason answered. "I'm sorry you had to go through that, Lynn, but you did really well. I guess we know what they're thinking now."

"That Donovan is spending company money on me? Taking time away from work? Causing the company to not pay enough attention to people like Roy Alloy? That he might be harassing *me*?"

"That's my guess," Mason responded.

"So, can't they just ask Donovan for his personal receipts? I mean, they already had that damn list; they didn't need me to tell them! What the hell was that about?" Lynn was on a roll. "And doesn't the company credit card get justified by someone – Ana maybe? I'm sure your human resource department keeps track of employees' vacation and sick time, right? Even the president of the company?"

Mason Polk angled his head to the side and let out a breath. "Well, it's time for me to find all this out." He held out a hand to shake Lynn's. "Mrs. Cerami, you were great in there! Can you get home from here?"

"I'll see to it, Mr. Holmes," Alek responded.

Lynn looked out at the impending sunset. The office building faced the beach. Orange and pink colors slipped through the thin clouds, touching the water.

Nothing as pretty as a sunset on the ocean.

Beginning to de-stress from her horrible afternoon, Lynn was jarred by the sound of Alek's phone.

"Grambler."

There was a long pause as Alek listened to the person on the other end.

"Yes. Yes, I'll tell her." He listened intently as he was given more information. "Got it. Yeah. Later, Desmond."

Turning off his phone, Alek shoved it into an inside suit coat pocket, then extended his hand out to Lynn, offering to help her. She ignored the hand, walking on her own.

"Bad news," he stated as they walked toward the car. Since he didn't seem too alarmed, Lynn waited for him to speak.

"Asia Barber died."

Chapter 52

As Desmond drove the limo to the church where Asia Barber's Going Home ceremony was to be held, Donovan sat subdued. Her sudden death, along with the pressure of Roy Alloy's continuing lawsuit and Mandisa's pending charges, made him pensive.

"Donovan?"

He inclined his head toward Lynn.

"Hmm?"

"I'm nervous about going to this service."

Donovan became alert. Instantly, he sat up straighter, giving Lynn his full attention.

"Because you've never been to a service like this?" He asked. "It's long, but it's just time sitting on your butt, listening to people give eulogies, or sing. You'll be fine."

When Lynn let out a long sigh, Donovan saw that it was more than just the service she was worried about. Her face was pale, sad.

"Are you not feeling well, Peace? I could have Desmond take you home after he drops me off," he offered, "Or Alek once he gets here with Dara and Connor. Would that help?"

"It's not the service per se." Lynn looked up at him, her bright blue eyes covered in tears. "It's a *funeral* service." When Donovan still looked confused, she took his hand. "This is the first funeral I've been to since Michael's."

"Oh…"

Lynn squeezed his hand, then turned her eyes out on the awful Los Angeles traffic.

"Yeah ... oh." She said it so softly that Donovan could barely hear her. "I just want you to know in case I lose it."

Donovan kissed the top of her head.

"No worries," he said, realizing that this was the first time he was not jealous of a dead man. They settled into silence as the limo inched its way to the church. To try to get her mind off her grief, Donovan told her what might happen.

"It'll seem like a gauntlet, a bit. No red carpet, obviously, but lots of celebrities, their managers, dignitaries. And her family."

Desmond guided the car into line with others. Lynn saw other people exiting their limos, walking up the stairs to the large church.

"So ... Dymettra and Roy?"

"Yes, they should both be here. Truth be told, Dymettra idolized Asia and Asia took her under wing until Dymettra got too full of herself."

He shook his head, disgusted with the memory. "And Asia called Roy out repeatedly when he misbehaved. Even at that event where Dymettra was so cruel to you, Asia was there to tell them off."

"Really?"

"Oh, yeah! I don't think we'll have any confrontations here," he said, "but I can't promise because who knows with those two? Also, anyone can come up to me just like they do at other events. But it would be very disrespectful to the family and to Asia. I've never seen anyone – including those two bad-mannered snobs – act out at a service."

The limo halted in front of the church entry. Desmond jumped out, surveyed the scene, then opened the back door for the couple. As she exited the car, Lynn noticed Alek pulling up in Donovan's Lexus. Standing at the door of the car, seeing Lynn, Alek called out, "I'll be right here. You've got your cell, right?"

Lynn nodded back, smiling at the new bond between them, then felt Donovan take her elbow. As they walked into the massive church, Lynn was amazed at the people there. As they entered the vestibule, Lynn saw Dymettra walking down the aisle, dressed sedately for a change.

"Dad!"

Lynn turned to see Dara walking toward them from across the church's large gathering space, Connor holding her hand. Dara was also dressed conservatively wearing a large black hat with a white flower that had fronds coming out of it. She wandered over to her father, surprising him with a kiss.

"I'm sorry, Dad."

"Yeah, she meant a lot to me," Donovan acknowledged. "And I know you loved her, too. She always thought you were magical!"

Donovan and Dara handed cream-colored invitations to the ushers who then escorted the foursome to reserved seats. Both women inhaled deeply, the smell of roses perfuming the sanctuary. Asia's deep oak casket was up on the chancel, closed, covered with white roses. White roses lined the center aisle, adorned the altar, and decorated the wall behind the altar. Most of the women wore black, their hats or shoulders adorned with Asia's signature white flower.

As they walked down the long aisle, Lynn saw Roy Alloy enter from a side door. Even he was respectful, dressed in a dark gray suit, red shirt, matching tie, and even conservative shoes and socks. Lynn noted that he appeared upset, not the usual angry, young man that he pretended to be. She turned to look at Donovan who had also caught sight of Roy.

"Maybe we'll be okay," he murmured, ushering Lynn into the pew. Connor and Dara were already ahead of her.

The service was long, with much music, readings, and eulogies. A tremendous gospel choir sang Asia's favorites, many of which she had recorded. There was a short film about her rise to celebrity, and then the start of many eulogies.

At first the speakers were family members, most of them trying hard and losing their battle with control. One woman kept referring to Asia's 'long illness' until Lynn leaned over to ask Dara, "What kind of illness did she have?"

Dara paused only a moment before responding, "Cancer."

Lynn didn't have time to react as Doc Brandon, another music legend, older than Asia, made his way to the pulpit. A tall man who'd been seated with the family supported Doc as he made his slow way to deliver his remarks.

Exeter! That's Exeter!

Lynn recognized the tall, handsome crooner.

Exeter stood back as Doc grabbed the sides of the pulpit. Buoyed by the solid wood, Doc stretched to his full height, straight as an arrow before eulogizing Asia.

"Asia Barber was a good person," he stated in a deep, booming voice. "Some will say that she had immense talent," Pausing for effect, he glanced out at the crowd, then declared, "And she did."

One member of the congregation called out, "Yes, she did!"

The eulogy was the longest, the congregation calling out when Doc paused. Finally, after speaking of her early history and her success as a singer, Doc launched into her legacy.

"... if she had advice, she'd share it. If someone needed money, she'd help them out! If she could help in *any* way, she did. Because she was that kind of good woman."

An organ started playing a few notes, the time-honored way of telling a celebrity to exit the stage, but Doc appeared oblivious.

"Asia Barber did not suffer fools. She expected – got – respect. But she also earned it! She was kind to others and expected it back in return. When she saw new, young, upcoming artists misbehaving, she told them in no uncertain terms that they were going to ultimately fail!"

Roy, calling out with the others, was antsy in his seat, running his fingers beneath an eye to swipe what Lynn guessed were tears.

Does he know that this speaks about him? Does Doc know?

Before Lynn could analyze any more, Doc caught her attention again.

"... do we hurt one another – try to destroy a good person's name – instead of trying to lift up and care for people like Asia did? I pray that all of us look to her as an example of how to be a good person, not just a celebrity. 'Cause Asia Barber was a good person. I will miss you, Miss Asia."

As he walked by, holding on to Exeter's arm, Doc Brandon kissed his fingers and gently touched Asia Barber's casket. Lynn felt the lump growing in her throat as she witnessed the quiet gesture of love and respect. Her stomach no longer hurt. Asia's funeral was not at all like Michael's.

"She sounds wonderful. I wish I could've known her," Lynn whispered to Donovan. He squeezed his hand in response; Lynn knew that he didn't trust his voice.

As the gospel choir got ready for their last hymn, Roy Alloy stood up. Donovan's hand tensed in Lynn's, worrying as she did that Roy would do something completely inappropriate. But the young man seemed blind as he darted out the same door he'd entered earlier.

"Guess he's not interested in us today."

"Give him a minute," Donovan answered which told Lynn that his anxiety had not abated.

THE RIDE BACK TO DONOVAN'S HOME WAS QUIET. HE SAID NOTHING, placing his chin into his palm, his arm leaning against the door, lost in thought. Sunglasses covered his eyes. Lynn felt anger and sorrow shrouding the car as if the service had deepened his anger and anxiety.

She took his hand, hoping the small gesture would indicate her sympathy. Although he looked down at their two enjoined hands, Donovan didn't squeeze back and quickly resumed looking out the window.

Mercifully, the early afternoon traffic was light. They were pulling up to the Malibu mansion just as the atmosphere in the car was becoming oppressive. Desmond opened Lynn's door. She barely had her legs out when Donovan was in front of her, hand extended. She took it, felt the thrill of love race up her hand and arm.

I so love this man.

Donovan led her through the front door which Mariel, his housekeeper held open. He sprinted through the foyer, through the sunlit great room, Lynn skipping to keep up with Donovan's longer strides. Closing his bedroom door, Donovan uttered his first words since leaving the church.

"I love you. I need you."

Without hesitation, Lynn threw her clutch on a chair and began to strip. There was nothing sexy about it. Carefully, she removed the black and white hat that Bea had said was necessary to wear. Off came her black jacket, her black and white silk blouse, her black pants. As she undressed, so did Donovan, throwing off his suit coat as he toed off his black shoes. His dress shirt, tie and socks followed. Lynn, finished with undressing, watched as he was undoing his belt buckle. Pants and briefs hit the ground while Lynn threw back the bedcovers.

Donovan grabbed her shoulders, forcing her back flat on the bed, following quickly. And although he kissed her, there was no foreplay before he entered her body. He pounded away while Lynn, mildly aroused anyway, went along for the rough ride. She imagined him thinking *I hate Roy Alloy, I hate Roy Alloy, I hate Roy Alloy* with each thrust.

It ended almost as quickly as it started with Donovan exploding, yelling out, then collapsing on her. Seconds later, he was moving to his back, his arm swung across his eyes. Lynn took the time to pull up the sheet and cover them. She snuggled into him, relieved when Donovan's other arm cradled her.

"I'm sorry," he whispered.

"Why?"

"I didn't think about you. Sorry."

His voice broke on the last word, tears escaping from beneath the strong arm placed over his eyes.

"It's okay, Donovan. It was rough to see him after last week's depositions. I get it," she whispered.

The arm flew off his eyes, revealing the moisture collecting on his face. Lynn turned to her side of the bed, grabbed a tissue, gave it to him, then snuggled back into him.

Donovan wiped his face and said, "He's not the only thing getting to me." He threw the used tissue to the ground. "Although it does worry me."

"You gave those horrid lawyers copies of all your receipts for the gifts you gave me," Lynn said, starting to stroke his arm with tenderness. "You had HR show them that you'd earned the time you took off, just like any other company employee."

Donovan let breath hiss out between his teeth.

"It's not just that shit," he said, his hand reaching up to his hair. "I worry that they'll find something else! Assholes like Roy can ruin everything in a moment."

"We both know that the public is not exactly happy with Roy right now, especially after his antics with Bri."

Donovan nodded, sniffling back the last of his tears.

Something is bothering him ... something more.

"You said that Roy's not the only thing that's bother you," Lynn started as her hand made one soft circle on his best. "What else is it, love?"

One tear slid down Donovan's cheek, but he didn't cry as hard as Lynn thought he had earlier.

"I will miss Asia so much."

He looked at Lynn, then up at the ceiling. "She was like a mother to me. Do you know about Other Mothers in black culture?"

When Lynn nodded, he said, "I loved my own mother, of course. But Asia was always around, always there for me when I was little, when I was a wild teenager, when Dad was so rough on me, when I first took over the business, when Dad died. She was supportive during this stupid lawsuit. Never ever questioned me about the harassment thing. And she was completely supportive and encouraging about my relationship with you."

"I didn't know that!" Lynn continued her soft circles but felt a twinge of regret for not getting to know the gracious woman so many had mourned that day.

"I didn't tell you about it. Miss Asia called me, told me it was time to take her to lunch!" Donovan laughed as he continued the story. "That's how things were between us. She asked me a lot of questions about you and I think once she heard how crazy I am about you, she encouraged me to marry you."

Donovan's eyes were gleaming, finally rid of the gloominess that had been in them most of the day. Lynn smiled back at him, adjusting her body so it was closer to his.

"I wish I'd known her," she whispered.

Donovan's phone chirped.

"I should've turned the damn thing off," he groused, but got up to remove it from his suitcoat pocket. Without glancing at Caller ID, he said, "Donovan Rue."

Lynn couldn't see his face from where she was lying, but she could see Donovan's shoulders tense.

"Why?" he asked. His shoulder grew impossibly tighter. Lynn swung out of bed, placing her feet on the floor.

"When?" A hand raked through his hair, then Donovan was asking, "Should I bring my lawyer with me?" His tone grew cautious then asked another question, "Are you bringing your lawyers with you?"

Roy! Roy Alloy called Donovan?

"Later."

Donovan clicked off his phone, barely had it on the table before Lynn asked, "What does he want?"

Donovan reached down for his clothes, beginning to redress.

407

"He wants to talk … says he needs to talk to me immediately." As he finished zipping up his pants, he admitted, "I'm a little concerned that he doesn't want lawyers involved. What do you think?"

"I'm not sure … but isn't it usual to have lawyers around when there's a lawsuit happening? What if you say something, or don't say something, and he turns it on you?"

Donovan paused in buttoning his shirt, retrieved the phone and pressed a preset number.

"Len? Yeah, it was nice as far as those things go. Well-attended. Listen," Donovan was speaking too fast, wanted to get past the pleasantries, get right to his issue. "Roy Alloy just called. He wants to meet with me."

Donovan sat on the bed next to Lynn.

"Yes, I want to be careful, Len." Again, he listened, then said, "Okay. Great. I'll let you take it from here. Thanks, man."

Lynn could barely wait for Donovan to click off.

"Well?"

"Well, Peace, turns out Len agrees with you. He doesn't want me anywhere near that asshole. So, he's calling Mason Polk, having him deal with Roy."

Donovan stood, gathering the rest of his clothing and placing it on the bed.

"Good." Lynn sat at the edge of the bed, aware that she had nothing on. Tucking the sheet under her chin, she relaxed.

Donovan started stripping again.

"Again? We really are not twenty-somethings."

Donovan grinned.

"Definitely not. I need a shower, then we need to eat."

Chapter 53

*a*s he sat in his office, Donovan's thoughts were crowded with Lynn, Asia, and Roy.

Lynn was always on his mind. Pulling out a manila file from his desk drawer, Donovan looked over all the things he'd planned for their wedding, noting that all it needed was a firm date. Donovan put it back again. It would have to wait until the lawsuit was settled.

Who knows how long that will be?

He felt tears again as he thought of Asia Barber's passing. Asia had been present in both his personal life and his work world.

"How do you know she's good for me?" he'd teased her when they dined at Musso's. He already knew that Lynn was perfect.

"I can see the peace she brings to you," her melodic voice replied, that voice as sweet as her soprano singing voice.

"That's what I call her! Peace."

Asia turned her worldly eyes on him, serious and yet still loving, just like a mother's should be.

"Don't wait too long to make her your wife, Donovan. Everyone can use peace, and it's elusive." Again, the last syllables drawn out long, softly. "Grab it, son."

Although there had been numerous flower arrangements at the church, this morning there were more at Rue LA LA's offices, along with hundreds of condolence messages. Donovan readied to acknowledge each note and flower arrangement with a personalized thank you.

And then Donovan kept thinking of Roy Alloy.

No peace can come from this.

Donovan ran his hands through his hair yet again. His stomach knotted with the thought that this one man could completely ruin the company his father had created. He could bring unwarranted media attention to Lynn, someone who had never imagined or wanted such scrutiny. Donovan was still embarrassed that all his worries had erupted in bed of all places, taken out on the one person he loved and cherished most.

"Mr. Rue?"

Donovan jumped at the interruption, then caught his breath when he saw Mason Polk in the doorway.

"I'm sorry. I knocked a couple of times, but ..." Mason made his way to the corner television set, turning it on. "You need to see this."

Donovan waited while Mason turned it to a Los Angeles station that was streaming a news conference.

Wait. Is that my lobby? Are they having a news conference in the Rue LA LA lobby?

A door opened and in walked Martin Lawson with Dara. Martin approached the podium, introduced himself, then went over the allegations that had been made by Mandy and Dymettra against Donovan. He declared that Dara Rue would make a statement concerning her father, that there would be no questions following it.

No, no, no ... I don't want her to do this.

"My name is Dara Elizabeth Rue. I am the only child of Donovan and Mandisa Rue. During the time that they were married ..."

LYNN HAD TAKEN THE DAY OFF FOR DOCTORS' VISITS. SHE WAS JUST about ready to turn the television off when the local station cut in with a special report.

She thought the lobby looked vaguely familiar, then was

surprised when Dara came on screen, a thick-set man introducing her, saying she was going to make a statement concerning her father. It didn't last long, Dara looked directly at the camera and ending her statement by saying, "My father is a good man, a credit to society, and would never harm anyone."

Lynn was crying yet beaming, feeling triumphant as she watched.

May this end this stupid thing!

She watched Dara being led out of the room by the lawyer and sandwiched from behind by Desmond. Connor followed them. The news anchors were going over parts of the statement, commenting on the fact that the tables seemed to have turned in Donovan's favor.

God, I just hope they leave Dara alone. I don't want this setting her back because they get all in her face.

Lynn wasn't surprised when her cell phone rang.

"Peace! I think I'm cleared!" came the gleeful deep tones.

"How will we know for sure?"

Background noise told Lynn that people had entered Donovan's office, one of them saying something that she couldn't quite hear. Donovan paused, then said, "Wait. Hang on."

Lynn could only hear mumbling until Donovan came back on the line. "Lynn! Alison Berg – Mandy's attorney – just called to say they are dropping the entire thing. We are done!"

Lynn succeeded in suppressing shrieks of joy but could not stop her tears of joy.

"Donovan, I'm so glad –"

"She's magic! I'm telling you, magic."

Lynn was confused. "Who's magic?"

"My daughter!" A long laugh came through the phone lines, causing Lynn to pull her phone away.

"Sorry," she said. "I don't get it."

"I'll tell you later! But, believe me, Dara is magic! Again!"

As soon as the others left the room, Mason Polk cleared his throat and said, "I have some other good news."

"More?" Donovan ran a now relaxed hand through his hair, pausing as something occurred to him. "Wait! If it has anything to do with the Roy Alloy case and its good news, I'm looking forward to hearing it."

"Yes, sir." Mason looked at the paper in his hands, cleared his throat. "Roy is dropping the case."

"What?"

Donovan was standing instantly, his voice reaching the highest octave it could.

Settle down. Get a grip.

"You're kidding me! Why? Where did this come from?"

Could I possibly be so lucky to get two horrible things to end in one day?

Mason placed the official notification on Donovan's desk.

"I met with him here last night, privately. Simply put, he just wants the lawsuit to go away. He met with Asia Barber several times during the last few months and she was advising him to give it up. Sounds like she gave him quite a talking to."

Mason rolled his eyes as he smiled.

"I can imagine," Donovan said. "Did you know her at all, Mason?"

"Not really. Only from seeing her in the office which wasn't often," Mason replied. "Roy was considering dropping parts of the lawsuits after Lynn's deposition. Asia Barber, turns out, talked him into it."

"Wow." Donovan was grinning. "So, is it over? That easily?"

Mason took the paper in hand again. "His lawyers had this document couriered over. This ends it."

"Rue LA LA is out of danger?"

"Yes, sir."

Donovan raked his hand through his hair, then looked up and laughed. "What a day this has been! First Dara with her statement. And now this Roy thing is gone!"

"Actually, the Alloy lawsuit ended earlier this morning, before your daughter's conference, but, yes, they are both done."

Donovan looked down at the famous picture of Lynn in her first Lynn dress dancing with him at Music Extravaganza.

Could we really be free of all of this? Can we get married and start fresh from here?

"Thanks, Mason." Donovan stood to shake his hand. "I think this may be one of the best days ever!" As Mason got to the door, Donovan remembered to ask, "Do you know who gave Roy my personal cell number?"

Mason stood in the doorway, hesitating to answer. Finally, he muttered, "Dara." When he saw Donovan's surprise, Mason said, "At least that's what Roy told me."

Donovan sat back in his chair, mulling over the sudden change in his life, thinking about the magic that happened concerning Dara. It was all quite involved – *when isn't it involved with Dara?* – but ultimately it ended up good.

Realizing that there were no obstacles in the way of his wedding, he opened the desk drawer and again pulled out the wedding file. But first, he needed to let Lynn know that this huge worry had ended. She answered on the first ring.

"Peace! Guess what? Roy's dropped the lawsuit."

Hearing Lynn's delighted shriek, Donovan found himself laughing, unable to tell her that shrieking was inappropriate.

Because today, damn it, it's okay to shout out loud!

*T*he air that morning was light with wisps of cool wind blowing through Lynn's hair.

Hair! How long has it been since I could feel the wind in my hair? When was the last time I complained about it getting messed up?

A bright blue, cloudless, ocean-colored day greeted Lynn as she walked to her building.

This makes me happy. I could care less if my hair is a mess. I'm here and I'm happy.

Mornings were always quiet, especially after commencement when students were home and summer classes had not yet started. Usually, Lynn could get a lot of planning done in the few months of summer.

Lord knows I need it with this new job.

As she entered the office suite, Lynn wondered where the others were. Trevor, the new administrative assistant, was charged with getting there early to open everything up. His attitude was cheery, his manner cordial. After the fiasco of Sally, who quit once Lynn's promotion was announced, Trevor was a very welcome addition to the team. Tom was blossoming. With a new supervisor he was doing twice as much work, happy, better with students. Life in International Student Services was good, getting better each day.

Walking into her repainted and redecorated office, Lynn reached down to start her computer.

Where is everyone?

"Hi," came a familiar voice. Lynn looked up, startled to find

Dara standing in the doorway. The spook vanished; she was happy to have Dara in her life.

"Hi, sweetie! What are you doing here?"

"Don't you want me to be here?"

Lynn knew that Dara's automatic replies were always hedging, her self-esteem never as secure as it should be.

"Of course, I want you here. It's just that you don't come often. What is this? The third time, maybe? And it is kinda early in the morning."

Dara giggled a little.

Does she seem nervous?

"So, what's the reason for the honor of your visit?"

"Just coming to see you," Dara said, her eyes suddenly radiant with happiness. "Will you walk with me?"

After leaving a note on Tom's door – *where is he?* – they walked out of the building, back into the beautiful sunshine.

"Where do you want to walk?"

Dara was still smiling, her eyes sparkling with mischief. "Remember you told me that the chapel has a pretty rose garden? Prove it."

Situated directly in front of the building, the chapel roses were currently in bloom, a multitude of buds indicating that there would be flowers for a long time.

Lynn thought Dara might want to linger in the garden, but instead the young woman veered away from it. Walking to a side of the nondenominational chapel, Dara aimed for the classroom entrance.

Okay. I'll play along. No looking at the roses. Doesn't surprise me that she doesn't want to enter the Chapel's main doors, but why are we going here?

Lynn wondered how Dara even knew about these doors which were heavily shaded to prevent people from looking in. Pulling the door open, Dara bowed, indicating that Lynn should enter first.

Lynn's eyes went first to the left side of the room where desks and chairs were pushed up against a wall.

Maybe they're getting ready to clean carpets?

Her feet stopped when she glanced at the right side. Bea and her team of beauticians hovered near a temporary makeup station, like the ones brought to her home before big events with Donovan.

"Okay ..."

Not comprehending, Lynn continued staring at the strange setup. A couple of large tarps covered the carpeting. A makeup table was set near a large standing mirror, its top covered with beauty items, three small bouquets, and a vase of larger roses. Several spotlight lamps focused on an empty chair. A dress rack stood off to one side, Bea Owens holding onto the handle.

"Lynn!"

What's going on? Bea is wearing my favorite color for a change!

"Let's get going, girl. We don't have that much time," Bea instructed, moving toward the cosmetics chair.

"Time for what? What are you up to, Beatrice?"

Bea took Lynn by the elbow and directed her toward that chair.

"Fixing you up for a wedding," she answered. "Only have an hour."

"A wedding? Wait a minute ..." Lynn started to protest then smiled, a huge ridiculous grin that made her entire face light up. "Donovan planned a surprise wedding?"

"You told him to plan it, right?" Bea asked as the makeup artist covered Lynn with a black drape. "You didn't ask him to tell you the date?"

"No, she didn't," Dara said as she pulled a dress from a garment bag which was the same brilliant blue as Bea's.

"C'mon, Lynn! You don't want to keep Donovan waiting any longer," Bea said.

Dazed, Lynn sat in her chair while technicians went to work on her makeup, her hair, even her hands. Several technicians who'd helped Lynn before commented on her color improving, her bright eyes, and her hair finally growing longer as well as shinier.

"You're making their job easy!" Bea declared.

Lynn grimaced, then really looked at herself in the well-lit mirror, fearing what she might find.

I'm not a twenty-something bride, but this is pretty damn good for a fifty-year-old.

Lynn did recognize the life spark now in her eyes, the message she hoped said she was resilient, able to get through the tough times in life and carry on. She saw what she knew Donovan first recognized in her when he'd asked for a dance.

"C'mon, now!" Bea was not allowing any downtime. "Major step."

Following Bea, Lynn walked into the chapel lounge area which was also covered in protective sheets. Another big garment bag hung from a taller rack. As Bea unzipped it, the white equivalent to the first Lynn dress – the one she'd worn the night she'd met Donovan – escaped from the bag. This dress also sparkled, but it was pure white, a shimmering fabric overlaying another sleeker white material. Overwhelmed, Lynn reached out to touch it.

"I know you liked that dress. Knew that Donovan *loved* that dress," Bea said as she ran her hand along the fabric. "I even considered having you re-wear the original blue one. But it's supposedly bad luck for the groom to see the bride before the wedding."

Lynn's hand skimmed the glimmering dress which seemed to sparkle more as she moved it with her gentle touch.

"But it wasn't a wedding dress," Lynn murmured, awed. "And we had just met."

"Yeah, you're probably right, but I'm sticky about superstitions. Don't want to mess this up, because I like you and Donovan together," Bea said in her usual forthright manner. "So I found this white fabric and had it re-made. You will be a stunning bride."

There was no time for Lynn to react any further. Bea and Dara helped her into the dress and matching shoes. Someone handed Lynn a bouquet of white roses.

"Wait."

As the team of technicians, Dara, and Bea waited, Lynn admired herself in the mirror, then reached toward the large vase for one big white rose. Pulling it gently from the vase, she held it out.

"Can I wear this in my hair? Somehow?"

A few seconds of consideration passed before Bea took the flower, handing it to the hair technician.

"Okay, okay. That'll work," Bea was rushing her words. "But absolutely no veil." The hairdresser placed the flower behind Lynn's ear. Lynn reached up to touch it, realizing that it was in the same place that Asia Barber always wore her symbolic rose.

"Now, let's get going," Bea said as she handed a smaller bouquet to Dara and took one herself.

In a fog, Lynn followed her two supportive bridesmaids to the church's narthex. Connor stood, waiting, dressed in an elegant black tux with a satin stripe running down the outside of each pant leg. Before he greeted his mother, he bent down to kiss Dara, telling her, "Babe, you are gorgeous." After the kiss and a few minutes of appreciating Dara's stunning look, Connor turned to his mother, becoming the intense man everyone knew and loved.

"Ready, Mom?"

Lynn looked into Connor's deep brown eyes, so much like Michael's – serious, intense, not missing a thing. Today they were calm.

Perhaps because he's near Dara.

She desperately wanted Connor to approve of her marriage to Donovan.

Dressed in wedding finery, bringing up a topic that they'd already covered, Lynn knew it was a ridiculous question, yet she asked it.

"Are you good with this?"

"Mom, it doesn't matter what I think," he said, crooking his arm toward her. As Lynn slipped her hand around it, Connor said, "I couldn't be happier for you."

Organ music signaled a beginning. Bea walked down the aisle, a sassy bounce to her walk. When she stopped at the altar, Dara started her turn, her serious look one of total concentration. Next, it was Lynn's turn. She started slowly, smiling widely as Connor led her to Owen who walked from the chancel to the center of the aisle. Stopping when they reached Owen, Connor gave Lynn a sweet kiss on her cheek. Owen took his mother's other hand and looped it through his, then kissed her other cheek. Lynn was amazed at how cleaned up her shaggy, blond-haired son was. No jeans or ratty t-shirts today; his hair was clean and neat; his tux matched his older brother's.

"Owen! You look …" Lynn lost her ability to form words.

"Nah, I'm just a puppet in this play, Momster," Owen said. "This is all about you and Donovan."

"And you're good with that?" She repeated the question.

"I couldn't be goodier!"

As he ended his quiet chuckle, Owen and Connor began a slow, formal walk, guiding their mother to the base of the altar steps. Lynn focused, finding Donovan standing off to the right, wearing the same tux as her sons, a big smile that mirrored Lynn's on his face.

This is like a dream. How did I ever get this incredibly lucky?

Donovan walked to the step, held out his hand, palm up. Owen placed Lynn's tiny hand in Donovan's. As Donovan and Lynn locked eyes, Connor said, "Donovan, I've witnessed your concern and love for our mother. I've seen her love for you. She has taught us what it is to love someone completely, unconditionally. On behalf of my brother and myself, I ask that you take good care of our mother."

"Absolutely," Donovan stated, his eyes never leaving Lynn's.

"All the best to you," Owen said, the words sounding a little choked. Both sons stepped back from the couple, moving slightly to the right of where Donovan had been standing. Donovan helped Lynn walk up the two steps to the polished oak floor of the chancel. They stopped in front of Pastor Larson, the Cerami boys on Donovan's right, Dara and Bea to Lynn's left. Dara took Lynn's flowers. The pastor patiently waited for Donovan who stroked Lynn's cheek and said, "You are the most beautiful bride ever, Peace." Lynn looked down at her glittery shoes for a second, then back up to Donovan. She couldn't resist teasing him, asking, "A surprise wedding? Really?"

"Really." Donovan's eyes were reflecting the lights from above, his smile nearly creasing his cheeks permanently.

After giving them those first humorous minutes, Pastor Larson asked them to face one another. "Are you ready for this?"

"I do. I mean, I am," Lynn whispered back.

"More than ready," Donovan agreed.

The pastor then addressed the crowd.

"Welcome to the wedding of Lynn and Donovan. We celebrate the joining of two people finding peace and love in each other's company. So, let us begin."

Lynn heard Donovan say "I do" several times; then said those same words to the questions the pastor asked. But when the pastor told the witnesses that they would say personal words as part of their vows, she had a moment of panic and was grateful that Donovan took the lead. Donovan tilted his head back, eyes closed for a moment. Lynn caught herself in a silent gasp, aware that he was praying for something.

His head righted, his eyes found Lynn's as he said, "Peace." He let that sit for a moment, then said, "Lynn." Donovan seemed to find his stronger voice, his eyes now dancing with humor and intensity. "I want to be with you always because I love and admire you. I thank God for you every day. I admire you for your resilience, your charm, your humor, your goodness, your beautiful blue eyes. I will honor and love you for as long as we are given to live. I will respect you always. And I pray that God will watch over both of us."

"Amen!" came a call from somewhere in the chapel. The white folk who were not accustomed to the call and response common in black churches, giggled a bit, but then it was Lynn's turn when Pastor Larson looked her way and said, "Lynn."

Lynn took a deep breath, realizing that although edited, the words were ones that Donovan had spoken to her when he'd proposed. A moment passed while she collected herself, trying to remember what she'd said all those months back. When her memory kicked in, and she started to speak, Lynn realized that she had tilted her head back, too. Donovan must have caught her realization because he let out a quiet chuckle which she returned before she went on.

"And I love you, too. A day doesn't go by when I don't thank God for sending you into my life. I love your intensity, your care and concern for others, your loyalty to your father's memory and his company, the care you give your daughter. I promise always to respect you, love you, and take care of you for as long as God gives us. And I also pray that God watches over us."

Both participants understood the meaning behind the words, better than their younger selves would have years before. They spoke fervently while looking into the other's eyes.

"Amen!"

"Jesus loves you both!"

They didn't hear the sniffles of the audience, didn't look to check on their children, or Bea, Len, Tom, Maribelle, or any of the few celebrities that had been invited. The moment belonged to them.

As Pastor Larson pronounced them man and wife, music started that was distinctly non-traditional.

"Jazz?" Lynn asked, listening intensely to the upbeat sounds of bass, guitar, piano, and drums. As realization occurred, Lynn looked at her new husband. "Swing?"

"It's written just for us," Donovan said, pointing at the small band up in the balcony of the church. He led her down the stairs to the aisle. Taking her in his arms, Donovan declared, "We're dancin' our way out of here!"

If you enjoyed this Tale of Resilience, you may like **Making Magic**, the story of Dara and Connor. Here's a chapter from the second book in the **Tales of Resilience** series.

Crisis Averted

*D*ara looked forward to sleeping well after a good workout. Following her evening at the Fitness Center with Connor – *where he even took off his shirt!* - she thought it would be easy.

Can't sleep. Another night. Another night without sleep.

All the exercise in the world could not exhaust her mind.

Too much to think about.

No relief.

Ever.

Dara swung her legs out of bed.

I'm hungry.

She switched on her lights.

Not really but fuck it.

I eat too much.

She prowled into the kitchen.

Who cares? I want to eat! What do I want to eat?

She pulled an ice cream sandwich out of the freezer. Quickly eating one, she didn't notice that she'd left the empty box behind. It was her third sandwich that day.

Still hungry. How can I be hungry? Fuck it. Who cares what I look like? Maybe I should cook something? I still have that frozen pizza, right?

When she couldn't find the pizza, she remembered that she'd eaten it earlier that evening.

Cookies! I want cookies!

There were a few left in a box.

Now what do I do? No work. I refuse to do any work tonight.

After a day of sitting at her computer working on clients' social media, Dara was tired of the computer.

I know ... I'll shop! Retail therapy, that's what I need!

She quickly pulled up her favorite website and began looking for new shoes. It didn't take long to find cute, red, strappy sandals. And chunky black heels. And new tennis shoes. Dara plugged in her credit card number. The screen announced that her card was declined.

What'll I do? Love these shoes ... oh, I know! Dad's card. Where did I put that number? Where ... where ...

Rifling through her desk, Dara pulled out scraps of paper with all types of numbers written on them. Her credit cards. Old cards. Cards she'd opened, but never used. Scribbled information on passwords for other accounts.

I should organize this, but – here it is! I knew I'd find it.

As she began to type in her father's credit card number, she remembered his concern for her overspending.

"Really, Dara? Really? You needed to buy six pairs of shoes at 2am?" he'd asked one time. *"And why do you need all these?"*

"For work! For clubbing! And cause I just like them!" She got angry with him then. *"Do you monitor everything I do?"*

"When you're out of control, I sure do." She could hear his mounting rage. *"I feel so angry when you do this shit."*

She got to the last four digits of his visa card and stopped, taking deep breaths, trying to remember what Crystal Allerbee had suggested she'd do when she was impulsive.

Deep breaths. I hate making Dad angry. Deeper breaths ... Do I really need these? ... More deep breathing ... Shit! I can't do this alone!

Shaking, the website message flashing *Almost Done*, she abandoned her purchase and grabbed her cell.

Donovan's phone rang and rang and rang.

Probably left it in the kitchen. Probably sound asleep. Grrrr ...

Next, Dara dialed Lynn's number. She had not yet confided in Lynn about this issue, but Lynn seemed to be understanding of anything and everything.

Again, the phone rang and rang and rang.

Should've guessed. Lynn isn't exactly in love with technology. What does she call it? Her ball and chain ... whatever that means ... who to call, who to call... who...

Dara's eyes wandered back to the payment page.

Those shoes are so cool. Yeah, they're expensive, but I deserve it, right? I work hard. And I got that Winneman account! Yeah, I deserve a reward for that one.

She entered two more numbers from Donovan's card. Then stopped as if a wall of sanity was building itself around her fingers.

Dad will be so angry. Why can't I just say no? Who should I call for help?

Dara scrolled through her phone, finally stopping at Connor's number.

Don't really know him that well, yet. But Connor ... he's so confident, so strong.

She pressed the call button.

"Hello?" A sleepy voice answered.

How do I bring this up? And why doesn't he have Caller ID?

"Hello?" The deep voice grew in strength. "Prank phone calls went out before cell phones, dickwad."

Dara opened her mouth, trying to say anything, stuck in her hell. She heard Connor suck in a huge amount of air.

"Mom? *Mom?!* Are you okay? Should I come out there? Should I call the paramedics?"

This time the voice was panicky, finally breaking Dara's muteness.

"It's Dara."

God; he's had enough worry with his parents. Don't want to add to that!

The rapid breathing on the other end slowed down but his voice still held panic.

"Dara! You okay? It's two thirty in the fucking morning."

"No. No, I'm not." Dara fought off tears, felt her throat thickening with emotion. "No, I'm not okay."

How do I explain this?

"Okay. Okay," came Connor's deep staccato voice. She heard the rustle of linen, imagined him pushing back the brown sheets, crawling out of his king-sized bed.

"Let me come to you. Should I call an ambulance? Will you be okay until I get there?"

Dara took a deep breath.

"Yeah. Yeah, I think so. But can you hurry?"

She heard keys tinkling and then a door opening and closing.

"I'm – what? Ten minutes from you?"

"Yeah, but your idea of hurry and mine are different."

She couldn't help getting in a dig at Connor's strict adherence to all vehicular laws. She managed a little laugh and thought maybe he might grin. "If I had to get to a hospital to give birth – an emergency – you'd be the last person I'd ask to drive me." She snorted back more tears and said, "Like I'd ever get pregnant!"

She heard the roar of a car motor and knew he was on the way.

"I'm coming. Tell your doorman." After she did that, Connor demanded, "So, talk to me. I've got the phone in the hands-free thingy you gave me."

"Of course, you do."

Dara smiled as she wiped the tears from her eyes, took another deep breath and said, "You know that I'm crazy, right?"

"I know that you have a mental illness, yes," came a normal voice. "You've been hinting at it for so long that I finally asked Mom."

Thank you, Lynn!

Connor continued. "I didn't mention you by name," Connor

told her, then paused before asking, "Is something happening tonight?"

"Well, sort of... I have impulse issues."

"What does that mean?"

Dara broke a rule and ran a hand through her hair.

"It means that I occasionally can't sleep, can't control my thoughts, can't stop myself from doing impulsive things like hurting myself or buying things I don't need, or -."

"You are *not* fucking hurting yourself, are you?"

This time Connor's voice hurt her ears.

"No, no, *no*! I did hurt myself once, but that was a long time ago," she answered.

Dara rocked back and forth in her chair, not waiting for Connor's comment which didn't come.

"No. I just want to buy three hundred dollars' worth of shoes. I've done that before. Actually, one time I bought way over a thousand dollars and Dad lost it because I used his credit card – without telling him." Dara took a shaky, sobbing breath. "I just tried calling him, and he isn't answering. I tried calling your mom, too, but we both know how she feels about phones."

"Yeah, she doesn't like technology much. I can't get her to take the damn phone up to her bedroom at night," Connor admitted.

When the silence became too much for him, Connor said, "I'm almost there. About a mile away."

"Okay ... hurry ..." Dara's voice was soft now.

"So, you called me." Connor knew he had to keep her talking.

"I'm sorry. It was another impulsive thing to do, I guess."

"No! I want you to call me! I want to be there for you!"

Dara heard the car engine again and knew that Connor had turned, hopefully onto her street. A few minutes later the car engine died altogether, and she heard the door opening and then slamming shut.

A quick rap told Dara that Connor had made it, exactly ten minutes after she'd called him. The door had barely closed when she wrapped her arms around his lean waist, leaned her head against his chest, and began to sob.

"Shhh. It's okay," Connor whispered as he kissed the top of her head. Dara felt warmth at the familiar words, spoken by her father whenever he comforted her. Her crying simmered, but she continued to hold on to Connor who did not seem to mind her outburst of emotions. Then, abruptly, she pulled away.

"Sorry about that."

Connor took off his coat and flung it onto a nearby chair. He threw his keys on her kitchen counter.

"Don't be," he said.

Dara went to her living room couch. She turned to see a conflicted man hanging back a little.

He's being careful, trying not to patronize me. Whatever Lynn told him, he's a quick study.

Connor sat next to her and waited. And waited. And waited. Dara dried her eyes, blew her nose, and then started. "It sucks," she admitted. "I do okay and then completely lose it. I wish I could figure out the triggers. Not sure where this came from."

Connor simply nodded and reached for her hand. She laid hers in his outstretched palm. He folded his fingers tightly around hers.

"You probably won't want to be with me anymore, huh?"

Connor's eyes flashed with a touch of anger. "Who said that?"

"You don't have to say it; I know. Who'd want to be with a crazy woman?"

"I don't think of you as a 'crazy woman,' Connor said carefully. Then chuckled, "at least not any crazier than any other person I know."

"Well, I am. I was going to buy three hundred dollars' worth of needless shoes."

"But you didn't."

"Only because you rescued me."

"How is it a rescue? You recognized that you were on shaky ground, you called, and I came over. Isn't that what friends are for?" Connor toed his shoes off and placed his feet on her battered coffee table. "Aren't you a friend for Mom when you go over and help her out with all the gardening?"

"Your mom isn't crazy, Connor."

"No, she's not," he agreed. "But she is sick. And extremely tired. She needs some help with things, and it sounds to me like you've been very helpful."

Suddenly, Dara slumped back into the couch's thick back cushion and placed her arm over her eyes.

"God, I hate this! I hate it!" She was trying to hold off more tears. "I just want to be like everyone else."

"We all have our issues, Dara."

"Like what? What are your issues? You seem very together to me! An educated ... ok, maybe a little intense – "

"Well, there you go: one of my issues is intensity," Connor sighed. "I'm so intense that I scare people away. Or insult them, like my work buddy Nick. I piss him off all the time. I make other office people angry. So, take your pick."

She leaned into his side, pulled her legs up on the couch. A big yawn from Connor spurred one from Dara.

"I'm tired, but I can't sleep," she said.

"What do you do for that?" he asked. "When you have trouble falling asleep?"

"Oh, I've had sleeping pills before, but they make me a zombie the next day," she said. "And I've tried all sorts of natural remedies. Nothing works."

"Hot milk?" Connor asked.

Dara shook her head slightly. "I've never tried that one."

"How about Hershey's syrup? Got that?"

"I have both," Dara shot back.

She hoisted herself up from the couch and Connor followed.

"Then, I'll make you my mom's home remedy for sleeplessness."

They walked into the kitchen where Dara went to a shelf for chocolate syrup while Connor pulled a milk carton out of the fridge. Reflexively, he checked the date on the carton. Finding a clean saucepan, he poured the milk into it and then turned on the stove. Dara handed him two coffee mugs and watched while he squeezed a bit of syrup into each one.

"Won't the chocolate keep me up? The caffeine?"

"I didn't put in that much," Connor said. Smiling, he added, "It never kept Owen and I awake. Mom made this a lot when we were little."

As soon as he finished stirring both mugs, Connor motioned back to the sofa. Dara drank hers and then settled back into the comfortable position against Connor who wrapped his arm around her, holding his mug in the other hand.

"So, did you buy the shoes?"

She motioned towards her computer.

"I was in the process of adding Dad's visa number when I freaked out and started calling for help."

Connor gently removed his arm from Dara, who, in her sleepy state, slouched onto her side. Standing, Connor went to the laptop. He read the order, deleted it, and then turned the computer completely off. Glancing once at Dara to see if she was upset with his interference with her retail therapy, Connor noted she seemed fine and closed the laptop lid.

"Crisis averted," he said softly

Also by Adelyn

Coming Soon:

Tales of Resilience:

Making Magic

Overcoming Obstacles

Caring for You

Fine, Just Fine

Snippet of Making Magic

About Adelyn

Adelyn Zara knew she wanted to be a writer after creating a paragraph about a snowman in 4th grade.

She taught herself to type when her grandfather brought home an old typewriter from his job in Chicago.

She loved working with international students but hated the pressure cooker of work. So, she retired! But she continues to belong to NAFSA, National Association of International Educators.

She has compassion for the mentally ill, joined NAMI (National Alliance of Mental Illness), taught Family to Family classes for them, and keeps learning more about it.

She faces an ongoing battle with breast cancer and considers herself earning a Ph.D. in it, something she never wanted to do.

She's been told she's RESILIENT, and by God, those are the woman she admires most! Her stories feature men and women who are encountering problems in life and figuring out how to overcome them.

Keep in Touch!
www.adelynzara.com
Facebook: authoradelyn.zara
Instagram: adelynzaraauthor
Twitter: ZaraAdelyn

Made in the USA
Monee, IL
24 March 2023

30451746R00240